LOVECRAFT'S
LEGACY

LOVECRAFT'S LEGACY

EDITED BY
Robert E. Weinberg
Martin H. Greenberg

TOR®

A TOM DOHERTY ASSOCIATES BOOK
NEW YORK

LOVECRAFT'S LEGACY

This book is printed on acid-free paper.

A Tor Book
Published by Tom Doherty Associates, Inc.
175 Fifth Avenue
New York, N.Y. 10010

Tor® is a registered trademark of Tom Doherty Associates, Inc.

Library of Congress Cataloging-in-Publication Data

Lovecraft's legacy / edited by Robert E. Weinberg, Martin H. Greenberg.
        p.   cm.
    "A Tom Doherty Associates book."
    ISBN 0-312-86140-0
    1. Horror tales, American.   2. Lovecraft, H. P. (Howard Phillips),
1890–1937—Parodies, imitations, etc.   I. Weinberg, Robert E.
II. Greenberg, Martin Harry.
PS648.H6L68   1996
813'.0873808—dc20   95-41932
                                                     CIP

First hardcover edition: November 1990
First trade paperback edition: April 1996

Printed in the United States of America

0   9   8   7   6   5   4   3   2   1

PERMISSIONS

CONTENTS

viii

INTRODUCTION:
An Open Letter to H. P. Lovecraft
Robert Bloch

Dear HPL:

Are you surprised to hear from me?

It's been quite a while since I've written to you—well over fifty years, in fact, since I posted my last letter around the beginning of March 1937.

I knew you were having health problems, but you didn't tell me how serious they were. Whether my reply reached you at home is uncertain, because on March 10 you entered the hospital. And it was there that you died, just five days later, on the morning of March 15.

I don't know where to send this letter.

You left no forwarding address. And I doubt that with your beliefs—or disbeliefs—you'd expect to take up permanent residence in either a celestial condominium in heaven or a hothouse in hell.

For that matter, you used to indicate quite firmly that after death there would be no *you* residing anywhere at all. But I'd like very much to think something of yourself still remains; to believe that somewhere the essence of H. P. Lovecraft survives.

In life you were always a voracious reader, devouring everything in print. So on the off chance such an appetite remains, I'm writing this letter for publication, trusting that sooner or later you may run across it in these pages.

And perhaps you might, because you were always seeking out things that had to do with writers and writing.

You yourself were that most accursed of all creative creatures—a "writer's writer." You analyzed and edited the work of others as a generous gesture of friendship, and earned a pittance rewriting or ghost-writing the work of lesser talents. Your own efforts were admired by fellow professionals in the so-called "Lovecraft Circle" of correspondents, most of whom followed your example by contributing stories to *Weird Tales.* And there were fans, readers of this magazine, who found your work superior. Their comments must have pleased you, just as you seemed pleased that other writers tried to emulate your style and borrowed some of your concepts. I certainly did just that, and since you encouraged such efforts, it leads me to believe you enjoyed the positive aspects of being considered a "writer's writer."

But I can't help wondering about the negative side. How did you feel about that?

For years *Weird Tales* was just about the only magazine in the world which published fantastic fiction on a regular basis, including most of your work that saw print. And while the majority of its readership granted you grudging respect, the bulk of them reserved their most lavish praise for other authors. Your enthusiastic admirers were outnumbered and outvoted by the rank and file, and there were times when the realization must have hurt.

It harmed you financially as well. At a time when you were in desperate need of income, your byline on a story was never sufficient to guarantee a sale, and quite a few of your submissions got bounced. Only three landed elsewhere; the rest didn't see print until after your death. So much for the lot of a "writer's writer"—respected but rejected.

I don't mean to pry, but how did you react to the fact that in all those years not one of your stories ever merited a *Weird Tales* cover illustration? Luminaries like Speer and Davidson made it, but not HPL.

It must have been particularly rough for you during that six-month period back in 1931 when the magazine serialized *Tam, Son of the Tiger,* a hackneyed hack job by the immortal Otis Adelbert Kline. Nobody ever accused this prolific pulpster of being a "writer's writer" but his six-part epic got four cover illustrations in a row.

Over that same period you yourself were represented in three issues. A reprint of "The Outsider," one of your most famous tales, didn't even rate an interior artwork heading, nor do I recall anything of note for a new title, "The Strange High House in the Mist." And at the height of the *Tam* tumult, in August 1931, the magazine published a novelette, "The Whisperer in Darkness," which ranks as one of your very best stories. It *did* have an interior illustration, but only to add insult to injury—for the piece of alleged artwork completely gave away the climactic revelation which your entire tale was based and built upon.

What did you think about that, Mr. Lovecraft? What did you think about cover art devoted to detective Craig Kennedy or to a dubious medical specimen called "Dr. Satan?" How did you rate the luscious nudes of artist Margaret Brundage, whose weird attributes consisted only of their excessive mammary development?

Where were you, Richard Upton Pickman, when we really needed you?

Did you ever ask yourself that question? If so, we'll never know. Because in spite of biographies, memoirs, reminiscences and the wealth of attention devoted to your private correspondence and published work, we still have a lot to learn about the man behind the writer.

I'm not talking about psychological profiles now, or scholarly analyses of source material; these are all well and good, but they don't tell enough. There's more to a writer's existence than just his literary life.

Take your aunts, for example. During most of your adult years you shared a home with one or both of these genteel New England ladies. One gathers that they were "poor but proud," as the old phrase would have it, that they still were conscious of status even when forced to seek gainful employment, and that they regarded you fondly.

But both your parents had been subject to the stigma then attached to mental illness. How did they feel about *that*? Did they suspect a certain degree of social ostracism arose from your presence in the household? Were they upset by your pattern of daily—and nocturnal—living? Your choice of occupation might have justifiably excused you from ordinary domestic chores in their eyes, during a time when writing was still regarded in some circles as a gentlemanly profession. And yet *what* you wrote might have upset them. Did they ever take you to task for your choice of subject matter?

After all, it's one thing to tell your cultured lady friends that you have a nephew who's a published author—and quite another to reveal he writes stories about rat-chewed corpses, human brains transported by winged creatures flying to distant stars, or a man who mated with a gorilla.

Did they read these stories, Mr. Lovecraft, or even know their subject matter? Where did you stash away those issues of *Weird Tales,* and what about those Brundage covers?

Apparently they had no problem accepting your middle-years' marriage to a Jewish divorcée, particularly since your brief residence with this apparently quite charming lady was in New York, and thus not a matter of constant local scrutiny. But she must have had her own adjustments to make with your life style, old-fashioned attitudes, and oddities of diet. According to information she volunteered long after your leaving and subsequent demise, you two were sexually compatible, yet this wouldn't necessarily mean a change of habit in a man who suffered from chronic insomnia. Did you still spend your nights in letter-writing or solitary wandering instead of remaining in the connubial bed? Forgive me for asking, but the answer might well afford a clue as to your adaptability under unusual circumstances. All we know is that when you returned to Providence you spent your final decade in nocturnal wanderings.

It wasn't until the middle of that decade, you may recall, that we became acquainted through correspondence. As a teen-age fan, the generation gap prevented my asking you these questions, so they remained unanswered.

Upon request you sent me snapshots of yourself, and while one picture may be worth a thousand words, your photos told me little. These shots taken in the twenties and early thirties revealed nothing except changes in clothing styles, a temporary gain in weight during your New York sojourn, and a subsequent loss thereafter, plus a consistent tendency to face the camera with a sober stare.

You were never much of a smiler, were you? In a way, that expression you maintained was almost Keatonesque, the look which Buster affected onscreen. Years later, when he and I met, I soon learned his look masked a man far removed from the impassive image he projected professionally. But was this the case with you? No matter, I suppose, for unlike Buster, your face was never your fortune.

Fortune was in your hand, and I'm not referring to the findings of palmistry. What I'm talking about was something almost unique in our society, an appendage that set you apart from the majority of your fellow men.

Yours was a hand that never molded snowballs, tossed footballs, clutched a cigarette, cut a poker deck, gripped a tumbler of whiskey or turned an automobile's steering wheel. But one day that oddly inexperienced hand held a pen to write a single word. And when that hand of yours inscribed the word *Cthulhu* on paper, it set you on the road to fame.

Your journey was a long and difficult one, filled with obstacles and detours; a journey which led you to recognition only posthumously, as was the case with Poe.

And like Poe, you were not without detractors, even after death. For some years certain colleagues, editors, and a portion of the academic establishment took potshots at both your personal and professional idiosyncrasies. Their main target seemed to be your stylistic excesses, hyperbole, purple prose. But I suspect that wasn't the real reason for such attacks, which were often phrased in stylistic excesses, hyperbole, and purple prose of their own.

It seems to me that perhaps what they actually resented, consciously or unconsciously, was the cosmogony you created—what's come to be called the "Cthulhu Mythos."

The real problem with you, Mr. Lovecraft, is that you were a *religious* writer.

Your Mythos repudiated Biblical texts and substituted a new theology, with its own gods, its own explanation of creation and mankind's insignificance in a universe devoid of moral law or values. Abandoning anthropocentrism, dismissing concepts of good and evil, right and wrong—that's what agitated devout believers. Eliminating scientifically based explanations caused equal indignation amongst orthodox atheists.

And the way you went about it touched a nerve; you made your stories the narrations of scholarly, intelligent men whose skepticism was relentlessly overcome by proof that "nameless horrors" existed. You invested your weird world with plausibility by interweaving it with the one we knew, strengthened your tales with internal logic and a chilling consistency.

In some of the stories not based on the Mythos your imagination soared beyond that of your contemporaries. Today much of supernatural fantasy has gained its greatest popularity in films, but even now comparisons show your own work still excells in the daring of its scope.

Rosemary's Baby was a child of the Devil, one of many found in folklore and fable. But her Satanic spawn with the strange eyes is hardly in a class with the terrifying twin offspring of Lavinia Whateley and Yog-Sothoth, her significant other, in "The Dunwich Horror."

Responding to *The Call of Cthulhu*, men go mad and dreams haunt the sleep of certain artists and intellectuals all over the world, heralding the resurgence of the monster-god entombed in deathless slumber beneath distant seas as it stirs to arise and ravage the earth. But all the Roman-numeralled nightmares of the pimpled adolescents on Elm Street can produce nothing more awesome than old frizzled-face Freddie.

Poltergeist offers a tract house built on the site of an Indian burial ground, which menaces innocent toddlers and sucks them into limbo beyond a bedroom closet. The special effects are elaborate, and the soundtrack extremely loud, but the premise is hardly convincing.

That's where you had them licked, my friend. You knew that cold logic made for cold chills. There's a reason for the rats in your walls, the dreams in your witch house, the whisperings in your darkness.

In the beginning it was your style which attracted imitators. Many young writers—myself included—tried writing "Lovecraft stories," often using Mythos concepts with your full and generous permission. But as time passed, most of us came to realize, each in our own way, that your true skills lay not in adjectivitis, references to weird deities mentioned in weird reference works, or a reliance on italicized emphasis. The real secret of a good Lovecraft story was its ability to create a temporary suspension of disbelief. Making the incredible seem credible lent those tales a literary life which endures to this day.

"This day" now marks the centenary of your birth. Over half that period has passed since you penned your final efforts, but your influence has waxed, not waned. New writers are discovered every day, but it's constant rediscovery that keeps their names and their creations alive.

Some of the authors represented in this volume were

not even born until after your passing. But all of them launched their own careers after finding their way to the realm of fantasy in which you remain enthroned. All of them, in one way or another, were influenced by what you wrote. Their contributions to these pages constitute a *homage* to your memory.

So now you begin your second century, Mr. Lovecraft, as an acknowledged master of fantastic fiction—and that, perhaps, is in itself a fantasy you never imagined.

But it's a reality you richly deserve.

LOVECRAFT'S LEGACY

A SECRET OF THE HEART

Mort Castle

What is it that
troubles you?
Death?
Who lives forever?
—Schemuel Ha-Nagid

Whosoever ponders on four things, it were
better for him if he had never been born—
what is above, what is below, what is be-
fore time, and what will be hereafter.
—The Sages

Prologue: Of Age and Appearance

I have been known by various appellations, but, for the present, let me call myself William Roderick. If you have descried me going about this town of Kingsbay Port in my commercial, social, or philanthropic errands—and mine is a righteous and a charitable reputation, with many accounting me the most compassionate Christian (I permit myself a discreet smile at the irony!)—or if perhaps you have observed me in the undertaking of my daily constitutional in all weather, fair or foul, it is by no means unlikely that you have remarked upon the aura of vigor and liveliness by which I am distinguished. True, there is my slight deformity (the more seemingly negligible, I might add, when compared to the horrendous scars and *tragic* loss of limb borne by so vast a number of veterans of the recent conflicts), but this minor *singularity* serves only to draw your attention to my *otherwise* overall wellbeing. Indeed, beholding me, you might be passingly envious, dependent upon your own years and circumstance, thinking, *Would that mine is that honorable gentleman's soundness of health when I reach his laudable age.*

Worthy Citizen! Do you wish to have an . . . extended, even an *infinite,* time upon this Earth?

Fair Youth, at sporting play with jolly companions, your cheeks aglow with the vivacity of your effort, your blood singing the song of life in your veins, would you turn from such sunlit endeavors to walk in shadow and mystery—so that you might not die?

Kindly mother, were I to whisper to you a secret that might enable your sweet babe now asuckle at your breast to live beyond the niggardly three score and ten to which the Book says we are entitled (there is *the* Book—and there are *other* Books!), would you thank me for this and deem it a gift?

Would you forswear the God Jehovah to kneel in obsequious fealty to other deities?

Would you sacrifice a part of yourself?

Would you do all this and more, *so that your flesh might remain uncorrupted,* might never suffer the encompassing, unending *horror* of the tomb, so that you might live and *live* and *LIVE?*

Good fellow, cast your discerning eye upon me. (And should you think present the slightest tinge of *mockery* as I return your gaze with my no less keen orb, it strikes me I have the right!) Pray, do not seek to flatter me, nor need

you fear tending insult: Do you ajudge my age as sixty-
two years? Sixty-five? Seventy?

Seventy, you say, *why, yes, this Mr. William Roderick
could well be seventy, a venerable age, and one which
suits him like a carefully tailored suit of clothing!*

Permit me to state the truth, and to do so in a simple and
unostentatious manner that of itself might impress you
with my veracity: I am one hundred and ninety years old.

Ah, you doubt. You scoff. How can you do otherwise?

But I hereby attest, through knowledge neither known
by nor intended for the public, the common man, the rab-
ble, I am Immortal!

Nay, suffer me to qualify such declaration, even as you
deride it or brand me lunatic. If you are picayune, you
might demand, in the cause of exactness, I say only that I
am *virtually immortal.* Should there transpire a cosmic
cataclysm beyond our ken, resulting in an ending to this
spheroid upon which we dwell, it *might* mean my conclusion as well, although such demise is not inevitable. If
God (*your* God, the Not So Old One), in His Alleged
Wisdom, elects to sound the Call to Judgment in this century, or the next (or the next!), then it is *possible* I shall
not, let us say, "fare well."

Yet I ridicule the likelihood of such an otherworldly
summons to justice. Can you, speaking plainly and forth-
rightly, truly claim at the very least *to sense,* if not *see,* the
movements of a Just and Righteous Supernatural Fatherly
Hand in the affairs of Man?

Your God, I fear, has absented Himself from our firma-
ment and that matters not a whit.

There are other gods.

They have granted my wish, my heart's desire: TO LIVE
FOREVER!

Now it is that you shrink from me, your very flesh
acrawl with the fear of a mind so riotously disordered, an
intellect so crazed and debased as might not be possessed
even by one addicted to the strongest of spirits and the
most pernicious of drugs.

Regard me! Madmen sweat and shake; they mutter to

themselves and shout at delusional wraiths only they can apprehend. The iris of the madman's eye is grossly dilated, the lip atremble, the hands aflutter. Madmen rage, they fume, one moment seeking to slyly cajole the listener to belief, then threatening him the next.

Look into my eye to find therein not a glimmer of inner turmoil. See my folded hands, my casually reclining posture. Listen to my tale—rather, attend with your ear to *my true and honest history,* which I will relate calmly and rationally. Neither hysteria nor passion shall modulate the timbre of my voice, and events shall be presented in simple guileless chronology, without employment of any fictive artistic devices by which unduly to gain your credulity.

You will note how *exceedingly* I am at ease *whenever my discourse touches on the subject of Death,* as frequently it must. Surely you have seen how the vast majority of people are *reluctant* to discuss Death, nay, even to mention it; there are many otherwise candid, thoughtful, intellectual persons who become utterly incapable of even pronouncing the word, and who thus are forced to utilize dreary, foolish, specious euphemism when conversing about "the demise," the "passing away," the "ascending to glory," of even a casual acquaintance!

To me, Death is as Nothing.

I have naught to fear.

And thus, I commence:

I. Lynella

Of my country and family I will say no more than is demanded for the establishment of the truthfulness of this narrative: be apprised that I was born in the year 1650, in London, some sixteen years before the Great Fire, which claimed thirteen thousand and destroyed two-thirds of the old city, my ancestral home on Seething Lane happily not accounted for in the conflagration. (The house stands to this day.)

My father was Dr. John M——, a *medical* physician, duly respected and with an eminent clientele; although not of noble blood, he was regarded as a man of noble intellect and purpose. Before calamitous events which I shall soon relate, Father was a man for whom altruism and rational Christianity were *synonymous.* My father's neighbor, no matter his rank in society, was entitled to regard and respect, concern and compassion, for were we not *all* Children under the Fatherhood of a merciful God? At Christ's Hospital, Father generously gave of his time and skills in caring for the indigent, and in those situations in which neither his nor any doctor's skill and art might effect cure, still he spoke words of sincere consolation and sympathy.

My mother was a gentlewoman, a goodly mistress of the domestic arts as befit her station, capable of directing our servants without threat or even a raised eyebrow. Moreover, she possessed a refined intelligence and an artistic aptitude and sensibility. She was graceful in both English and French, played well upon lute and Spanish guitar, and sang in a lovely, if untrained, voice.

There are times yet, so many years later, when a pensive melancholia makes me long to hear the gently rhythmic strum of Mother's fingers upon the strings and the sweet trills and dulcet cooing as she sings a simple lyric of her own creation.

This is one I remember from my youth:

> The happiest day—the happiest hour—
> That e'er I might once have known,
> Is from my childhood's innocent yearning
> For the moon, all silver,
> And the sun, bright gold!

I digress, I realize, yet is it not peculiar that here am I, a man approaching my *third century,* and in my eye now resides a bittersweet stinging tear as I recollect my mother's song?

Away and be gone, O Sentimentality! Your refined feelings have not been incentive and inducement for my achieving a Life Eternal.

I continue.

There was yet one other who dwelled in my paternal halls, she whose early years illuminated my own and those of all around her with an angelic radiance of joy; she it was who inadvertently introduced me to Despair and its crony, Terror, just as she it was who led me to my inevitable Quest. Lynella and I were distant cousins of the same age exactly; it is a matter of not simple coincidence, I think, that we both emerged from our (respective) maternal wombs at the corresponding moment. Lynella's progenitors, burdened with twelve previous offspring, could but ill provide for still another, and so my family was entreated to undertake the care and guardianship of the infant Lynella.

Together, then, we grew, surrounded and comforted with the constant love of doting, indulgent parents. Lynella was a child of rarest beauty, and not more lovely than full of glee. Innocent and happy were we! Lynella and I engaged in those frolicsome entertainments of children throughout the ages: on holiday, ours the berry-picking and the ramble upon the hillside, the wildflower gathering and the clamorously yelling chase which muddied her frock and tore the knee of my trousers, earning a reproof from Mother, who could not help soften her words with a smile and a kiss upon our dirty cheeks!

Lynella! Vivid now her image before me, as in those halcyon, treasured days of our light-hearted, exuberant delight! Oh, Lynella! Gorgeous, yet fantastic beauty! Your lovely eyes, of the azure of stained glass, and the delicate rosebud of your lips. . . . Lynella, with no effort at all can I summon from memory's vaults the jingling silvery bells of your childish laughter: *ding-ting, ding-ting, ting-ding.*

Ah! Sweet and golden child! I state with no jealousy that Lynella was the favorite of my parents, for no less was she *my* favorite, my dearest heart's companion!

Forgone it was that, upon our attaining majority, Lynella and I would wed.

But then, in my eleventh year—in *our* eleventh year—there came an autumnal day in which the sky seemed to vanish utterly, so that all of the city were roofed over by a leaden gray thickness which one might touch were he to stand upon his housetop and stretch forth his hand. Then, more ominous, more *eerie,* came evening, a night of strange and, I might conjecture, *portentous* darkness, and with it, mighty winds, winds which shrieked most unnaturally up and down the streets of London, winds which bore upon them a stench, a stench which might have been of the grave—or of the *promise* of the grave! Our sturdy house shuddered as the incessant ferocious blasts encircled it about, tormenting the windows and rattling at the shutters and gates.

Lynella was afraid. I chided her for cowardly foolishness, playing the manly part, but mine was a *poseur's* rôle, one enacted poorly at that, for inside me was a heavy, albeit *incomprehensible,* dread.

"Come, darling children," Mother said, "I shall play on my guitar; I shall sing for you. We will be gay and of good spirit. After our fun, we will be off to bed, and, in the morning, the sun will give us its warm and familiar greeting, and the winds will be no more than the gentle puffs of a butterfly's wings as it rises from the comely flower."

"No," Lynella contended. It is not the vagueness of remembrance over many, many years, nor a spuriously claimed, youthful prescience, but my compulsion to tell the absolute truth that now makes me state I *heard* a pronounced, weighty, *sorrowful* gravity in the utterance of that sole word, a doleful distress that *never before had colored the speech of my dearest companion.*

Mother led the way to the small parlor, asking the maid of lower chambers to fetch biscuits, nuts, and watered wine for us. Mother sat upon a cushioned ottoman, her guitar of fine mahogany and sprucewood upon her lap, Lynella and I at her feet. She inquired what we wished to have her perform; my teasing request was "Cora o' the Willow," a coarse ballad taught me by our groom, which never failed to bring my mother's scolding admonishment, but before such chiding resulted, Lynella interrupted.

"Sing 'The Palace Beneath the Seas.'"

Mother's countenance grew pallid; I saw her artistic fingers become cataleptically rigid upon the strings.

"That song," said she, a tremor to her speech, "is hardly suited to this evening."

Lynella arose as though one somnambulistically entranced. Though always the most remarkably obedient child, Lynella commenced to sing—a song of Death!

> Here Lord Pluto has raised himself a throne.
> Here is He Sovereign, One and Alone.

Mother looked stricken. "No more," she decreed. "Young miss, leave off this appalling singing at once. It is too awful to be endured."

As though she heard not a word, *as though her hearing were not receptive to the Sounds of this Mortal Plain but were instead conscious of the Echoes of Realms the more grotesque because they are at most* dimly Imagined *by the majority of Mankind,* Lynella paid no heed. In a ululating voice, that of Harpy or the Mythic Ban-a-shee oft mentioned in Gaelic-Celtic folkloredom, Lynella crooned:

> Far down within the dim West,
> where the good and the bad and the worst
> and the best
> Have gone to their unhappy rest. . . .

And at this did Lynella hasten to the parlor's lone casement and throw it freely open. "No!!!" came Mother's anguished shout as the fierce gust, a dreadfully cold miasma, impetuously entered. I made to dash to close the window, but froze as though metamorphosed into a statue, for it *seemed* to me that a murky cloud were in the room, a cloud laden with an odoriferous dampness, a phantasmal vapor which settled about my beloved cousin, Lynella, like a ghastly shroud.

For the merest instant, *I could not see Lynella's face.* Then as though peeping from a mist, her features appeared before me, but devoid of color and so horribly,

horribly gaunt that it looked as though the cheekbones might protrude through her flesh.

"I am ill," Lynella said. She staggered, and I would have made to steady and support her, but I was seized by a nameless terror at her awful, still continuing transformation: *Lynella's temples grew hollow and bruised; her eyes, lusterless; her lips, thin and shrunken, lips which parted in gross caricature of a smile.*

I remained for some time breathless and motionless, my gaze riveted upon her person. As though from a great distance, my mother's whispered "Oh, my poor dear!" faintly impinged upon my consciousness.

"This is a night of nights," Lynella said, weakly but with a distressing composure, "for it shall be my last night among the living."

"No!" I managed at last to free myself from the abnormal paralysis which had gripped me. "Lynella, do not speak so!" I implored her. I held out my hand. Our palms met, our fingers intertwined.

"Farewell, my dearest mother," said Lynella, and from the corners of that pitiful child's eyes descended tears, not ordinary tears of salt and water and sorrow, but tears of *impossible* scarlet, thickly viscous. Lynella was weeping tears of blood! Then brightly gruesome beads of *gore* blossomed upon her brow and upon her cheeks and upon the slim fleshy column of her throat.

"Farewell, my heart's own companion," said Lynella to me, and, as she withdrew her hand from mine, I realized with shocked revulsion that my fingers were sticky with her life's elixir. Blood gushed from Lynella's mouth, seeped through her frock beneath her arms, at bosom and waist; and then, she crumpled into a bloody, *malodorous* heap of bone, flesh, and cloth.

I do not know if it was my scream or Mother's which brought Father. He carried Lynella to bed in his strong arms.

He will rescue her, then, was my desperate thought. *She is sick, she is gravely ill, but Father is the most learned*

*of physicians. He has studied in Scotland and in Venice!
He will not let Lynella perish!*

As my parents attended my poor cousin, I lay unsleeping in my bed, the awful winds still marauding without, while for a lengthy time, I focused my attentions on the sound of the clock at the far end of the hall, its metronomic *click-clack, click-clack, click-clack* implying permanence and steadfastness, a metaphysical hint that all might yet be well.

I did eventually drift off into sleep, to be awakened by the doleful chiming of the clock as it tolled the midnight hour. Before the last echo of the final stroke had echoed into silence, came Mother's despairing wail—and I heard more, heard—*somehow*—a sound akin to that of seeds being shaken within a dry gourd, a sound which was at the same time a bubbling, gurgling *liquid* sound. It was the death rattle of Lynella, as thus she perished.

II. A Dream of Death

The boundaries which divide Life from Death are at best shadowy and vague. Were this an account of fancy or imagination and not of fact, I might now declare that, one night, a fortnight after the death of Lynella, I *traversed* those boundaries. But my rational intellect tells me that what transpired was only a dream, yet a dream of such intense realism and detail, that it infused the totality of my life—rather, the earlier years of my life.

This is that dream:

"Willie! Willie!" It is Lynella's voice as she beckons me. "I am alone. I am lonely. Can you not come to abide with me?"

"No," I reply, "we must remain apart until we meet in Paradise."

"Then we must be parted *forever,* dear Willie."

"What is it?" I ask. "What do you mean? Is there not a

better world to which our souls are uplifed upon our leaving *this* one?"

"Willie, beloved cousin, permit me to instruct you, to show you what follows Death."

Then I hear the *click-clack* of gigantic Deathwatch beetles, and smell black earth smells and the rot of flesh, and I see the repulsive wriggling maggots of luminous white. And then, it is I—*not fair Lynella!*—who has died, and *mine* is the experience of the horror of burial—the unendurable oppression of the motionless lungs—the damp clinging of the death garments—the blackness of the absolute Night—the unseen but palpable presence of the conqueror worm!

Nothing upon the Earth is so agonizing as this! I try to move. *I cannot.*

I say to myself, "I am dreaming," but this is said with *motionless* lips. "I will rouse myself. I will know the chill of sudden wakefulness, but not this unendurable chill of the grave. I will be in the dark of an unlit room—and not the smothering eternal dark of Death."

But I cannot move, nor can I force my mind to a conscious state wherein I might banish this dream.

So for Time that seemed unending, I lay not in the safety of my bed *but in the grave*—for this is what I believed, no matter the actuality!

But eventually morning came, and with it, *Life*—however, I could not throw off the multitudinous awful sensations of this dream. This fantasy, then, extended its terrific influence into every conscious hour of my days. I was prey to perpetual, deep-rooted, unending fright. It was the gripping apprehension which might be known by the condemned man as he mounts the gallows, or by the soldier as he is ordered to charge the vastly superior force of the enemy encampment—but *my* fear of dying was with me—ALWAYS!

Thus resulted my determination *never to die*!

III. Of God and Gods

Mother grieved for our lost Lynella, until social custom
forbade her the sorry comfort of formal mourning; then
she lamented within her breast. From that time on, no
more did she smile. Ne'er again did she sing or play upon
the guitar. Deeply etched at the corners of her once soft
mouth were harsh wrinkles, her posture became stooped
and her gait unsteady, causing her to appear of more advanced age than was the case.

I? As I have remarked, my dream of death—*and its
boding illumination of the Nature of Death*—led me to
meditations and broodings most somber. It is no exag-
geration to say that a church bell's tolling for the dead
prompted in me the most awful vexation, that seeing a
dead dog in the gutter brought to me premonitious images of my own death, that even reciting the line of the
simple child's prayer—*if I should die before the morn!*—
made me shudder and quake as though I'd been smitten
by the St. Vitus Dance.

But the most profound alterations of character were
those in Father. Previously a temperate man, he took to
bouts of expansive imbibing. He drank French brandy and
colonial whiskeys. He drank Reisling with a cost of a
dozen shillings a bottle and drank ports that could not
have cost a dozen shillings the hogshead. Frequently,
Mother pleaded with him. Father's invariable reply was an
oath of outstanding vulgarity and venom, at such volume
that all the neighborhood might hear.

Father abandoned his medical practice entirely, the income of previous wise investments permitting us to continue in material circumstance as comfortable as before,
despite the gloom of our household. Frequently, Father
went ajourneying (said he, "to the country") for a fortnight or longer, nor would he brook any questions.
Though Mother and I were not privy to his exact where-
abouts or undertakings, disconcerting rumors reached us
of aberrant and bizarre behavior: Hearsay had it that Fa-

ther undertook travels with horse-trading Gipsies, that he aided and abetted smugglers and thieves, that he robbed graves with the so-called "Resurrection Men," who were also called, in those times, the "Gang of Ghouls." Nor were these the most distasteful reports which reached our ears. Of these crimes that were not legally felonies was he *alleged* to be guilty: He found lodgings in the Jewish quarter at York to study with one of that ill-fated race's rebbes, notorious for talents in the Black Arts. He became an acquaintance of the infamous Radical and Satanist, Sir Francis Malcolm, a founding member of the Harrow Hell Club. On a desolate isle off the Scottish coast, he plaited vines in his hair and danced naked beneath a full moon, participating in a rite more heathen than any practiced by even the most savage American Indians.

So passed three anguished years, and, at those times when Father was home, Mother and I comported ourselves most gingerly and inoffensively about him, fearing to provoke him. Father had become like a stranger unto to us—and an insane stranger at that.

Then upon a morning when the sun shone brightly and a gentle and steady breeze brought promise of approaching summertime, Father returned from one of his covert excursions. His left hand was heavily bandaged, and under his right arm, he bore a tattered saddle bag. He made no response to Mother's timid questions, but chortling a demonic laugh—*heh-heh-heh-heh*—he closeted himself (along with several bottles) in his library, from whence we might hear him muttering or—twice—*shouting* phrases that were unknown to us.

It was well after sunset that Father summoned me. In better days, ever had I been *thrilled* to be granted entry to Father's study, for there, amidst the pungent aroma of leather-bound books and the heady atmosphere of such a vast repository of knowledge, I felt myself a privileged, even a secret, sharer in intelligence and lore to which few were given privy; but now, I knew not what to think.

Upon Father's desk lay the saddle bag (to which previously I have alluded), as well as his pen and ink pot, and a small lamp that burned low, casting taunting, flickering shadows. Father, slouched in his grand Heathcote chair, his shoeless feet up on its rest, held a bottle by the neck in his unbandaged hand. His face was bloated and blotched, the whites of his eyes shot through with red. Even as I gazed at him with the filial respect a son owes his forebear, I experienced a moment's sharp fright at an unwarranted passing thought: *I do not know this man.*

Then he spoke:

"Since the . . . *death* of our little Lynella," said Father, "I have been insane, with intervals of sanity. Whether it is proper to refer my insanity to the drink"—and here Father raised the bottle to his lips and had a great bubbling swallow—"or the drink to my insanity is of little consequence. Of more momentous significance is that, through mental cogitation and variety of experience, I have reached *certain conclusions.*" Father leaned forward, his eyes narrowed. "I, who prided myself on being a rationalist, an empiricist, I—*heh-heh-heh!*"—(his jocular exclamations were hardly those of a man in control of his senses!)—"I have had . . . REVELATIONS!"

Father fell into a fit of laughter of the most shocking kind; he attempted to steady himself with a drink, but the brownish-purple liquor spewed from his lips, spattering his shirt-front and me.

"Revelations!" Father said once more.

He pointed to a shelf of handsome volumes. "What do we have there?"

"Books," I replied.

"Books! Knowledge! The *conventional* wisdom! The *accepted* theories of medical science! Yes, we have Hooke's *Micrographia* and Harvey's most commendable scientific proof of the circulation of the blood. Next, we find McKinnon's insightful dissertations on the treatment of lung inelasticity, and my own rather too highly esteemed monograph on the necessity of dietary restrictions for the cure of gout. *Heh-heh-heh! Heh-heh-heh! Heh-heh-heh!*"

The bottle dropped from Father's grasp, rolling across

the carpet, the contents spilling; I did not dare pick it up, for, just then, with the most heart-rending sob, Father cried out: "*Lynella*! That sweet and innocent lamb! More dear to me was she than my *own* life. . . ."

Behind glittering tears, accusation burned in Father's eyes, though later would I realize *it was he himself he condemned and not me.* "A *good* doctor! That is what I am reckoned by society—and that is how I, a d——fool, thought of myself! *Hubris*! The horrid, unique pestilence . . . blood its *avatar*, blood its *seal*. . . . The blood pouring from her, it came rushing and pulsing, and I could not help her! Not a clew did I have to what infected her, not a clew to treatment that she might be rescued. Oh!!!"

Father reeled back as though dealt a heavy blow. "Since our darling's *passing*, I've continued to search, to *re*-search," he said, with a weary gesture indicating his bookshelves, "seeking, for grim satisfaction's sake, to know what claimed her. I found no disease in the least similar in the standard Latin or Greek texts, nothing in German or English." Father shook his head, again laughing in that terrible, humorless manner. "Perhaps I might find a new measure of medical fame by the publication of a treatise on 'The Red Death,' but I think not."

Father affixed me with mournful eyes. "Lynella is *departed*," he said, his voice becoming that of temperate reason. "She is lost to us."

Now Father smiled in a taunting and interrogative fashion. "Where is Lynella now, my son?"

I answered by rote, as would any properly educated Christian:

"Lynella is at peace. She is with our Lord in Heaven."

And then my mind was overcome with the burdensome memory of my dream of Lynella, and of being *dead*! and with this recollection, came the icy intrusion of Doubt!

"Is she?" said Father, his features twisted into an expression of cruel mockery. "Is a graceful, glowing angel even now bringing our baby Lynella a delicious *bonbon* while Israfel strums his lyre? Is our Merciful and Compassionate

God Himself chucking Lynella's chin and calling her His pet?"

An onslaught of tears filled my eyes. "Why do you torment me so?" I implored.

"So that you might *know*!" roared Father as he leaped from the chair to loom over me. "So that you might not be deceived! So that . . ."

There, with mournful sigh, he broke off. He strode to the window, gazing down at London's darkened streets. His voice a laconic monotone, as though he were testifying in court on a matter of no great issue, he said, "When, there beside her bed, it came to me that I might do *nothing* to save her, nor even to *succor* her—when I realized that I was *ignorant* in all the essential matters, those of Life and of Death, no more sagacious or capable than an African savage with a bone adorning his nose, I do now confess, I fell to my knees. I *prayed.* I humbled myself. Mine was no pretense of piety; there was naught of the cynic or agnostic in it. Believe me, the fervor of my prayer was as heartfelt and genuine as that of the most illiterate pig farmer. I forswore all my esteemed power of ratiocination and deduction and cast my lot—and *her* lot—with those who abide on Faith. I entreated God's Mercy. I called upon God to spare this lovely child who had given offense to no one, who was as pure as the golden sunlight which wafts down from His Own Ethereal Paradise!"

Father turned to me. In the chamber's dim gloom, the dark of night seeming to gather behind him as though a shadow wanting only a moment to take on fearful shape, he said, "Then that little girl died and her death was *abominable.* Her body spasmed in frightful pain. Her features contorted. Ha! There are those fools who speak of the mild, placid, *accepting* mien worn by one who is given over unto Death, but, my son, let me put you awares, our Lynella, to judge by the agony on her face, had hardly reconciled herself to this fate."

"But," said I, meaning no disrespect, "it was God's will. We cannot argue. We can only accept."

"God's will?" Father said, wonderingly. "God's will!
GOD'S WILL!" He upraised his right hand, brandishing it
in a most threatening way. He said:

"I, who have never struck you, my son . . . I, who have
never *punished* you with a blow or even overly harsh
word . . . Son, what might you think of me if *now* I were
to beat you?"

"For what reason, sir?" I inquired; I meant no imperti-
nence, but I was astoundingly baffled by his actions.

"For *no* reason! Ha! Or perhaps a whim. Ha! Caprice! I
beat you because it strikes me as something I might do!"
roared Father.

Suppressing my fear, I heartily replied, "Then I would
deem you unjust, Father, unjust and unreasonably cruel."

Now I steeled myself for the blow—but, to my surprise,
it was not forthcoming. Rather was there the loving touch
of Father's fingers on my cheek and words as gentle as his
hand:

"Truly, were I arbitrarily to hit you, to cause you pain
when you had done *nothing* to deserve such hard treatment, *you would be fully in the right to think me unjust
and cruel.* What, then, am I to think of a God, a God Who
is perceived as a God of Love, Compassion, and Mercy,
yet Who is a God who—*without cause*—killed the fair
Lynella, a God Who heeded not my prayers—what, then,
am I to think of God's rôle in the Universe, when, in a
Cosmos the true foundation of which was Logic, the abiding Love of our family for Lynella *of itself ought to have
sustained and protected her, delivered her from Death*?

"Would I be justified in HATING such a God?"

For the longest of moments, I regarded Father and his
words, then, with a reflective sob, I was forced to ac-
knowledge the irrefutability of his reasoning. In my bosom was a sharp rending, a tearing, as though something
were being ripped loose—and within me, I knew the sudden frozen vacuum of one who has lost his faith.

"No, I do not hate. I merely abandon empty ritual and
gesture, because this is what I have come to believe, my
son; this is what I have come *to know,*" Father stated.

"God is *not* cruel. God is *not* unjust. The God called Yahweh by the Hebrew and Jehovah by the Christian, the God Whose deeds and commandments are recorded in the Bible, and to Whom off-key hymns are sung on Sunday, and Whose name is invoked by an Honorable Judge every time a poor wretch is condemned to hang for stealing a shilling, this God has either grown powerless or He has vanished. We cannot call upon Him with hope of being heard."

"Then we are . . . forever lost! All is . . . Chaos!" I exclaimed with a despairing cry.

"No!" responded Father. "We do not have *God* to rely upon—but we can call on . . . *Gods!*"

I gasped at this audacious blasphemy.

"Ha!" Father laughed. "There are *Other Gods,* my son, and *older.* In a number of *those* books"—here Father made a casually deprecating gesture toward his bookselves—"those petty, ill-informed, short-sighted volumes of Orthodoxy, the Other Ones are disparagingly alluded to, even as we mortals are sternly cautioned *ever* to seek them not. A believing Christian might speak of gigantic devils or demons or tiny imps, a reverent Mosilman, *of djinn* and dark seraphim, a Gipsy of *beng* or *diakka,* but our mundane society would not have us know the reality of these Older Gods—lest we have intercourse with them and thus gain in power and knowledge. Oh, the world does not suffer its geniuses gladly. Far better, the popular philosophy has it, to be ordinary, plain, and undeveloped, to be properly modest about modest abilities, to be dim of wit and dull of eye; but if your mind can conjure up Great Thoughts, and your eye can pierce the veil of illusion to remark reality's essence, the world does not want you. In fact, you are *Superman*—but derided as *Madman.*"

My head was aswim with abstract conceptions I could but vaguely comprehend. Yet I strived to give full attention to Father's words as he proceeded:

"If we may glean but little of the Other Gods (and much of that inaccurate) from the *traditional* sources of learning, then we must seek out other venues of knowledge—books of *forbidden* ritual, and teachers and practitioners of the Prohibited Occult Arts and Proscribed Metaphysical Sciences. And that"—and here Father drew a long, weary breath—"is *precisely* what I have been doing. I have delved into ancient, arcane texts, those books the world calls profane, unholy—and wicked! From a Hindu *fakir,* I have learned to stop and start my heartbeat by my will; from a Gipsy *ababina,* learned to *dukker* the future from the lines of the palm; from the Hidden Acolytes of the Golden Pentangle, learned to perform the Shadow Ritual."

"But, Father," I said, "to what *purpose?* What is it that you seek to accomplish?"

"What is it that the poet seeks to achieve with the sonnet or the painter the portrait? What is it that the minister, in honest if erroneous belief, promises his congregation? What is it that *all* men wish?"

I grew dizzy and weak, as if through long inanition, but in actuality because of the grandiosity of the thought which burst into my now frenzied intellect. So awesome was it that I could but whisper: *"Immortality!"*

Father clapped my shoulder. "The Other Gods are harsh, my son. They make no pretense of Goodness or abiding concern for Humankind; we are less to them than is a crawling louse to Man; dare we anger, disappoint, or even irk Them, by intent or carelessness, They think *naught* of destroying us. If the dark ceremonies They have decreed in Honor of Themselves are not performed *correctly* in all ways, They do not hesitate to *annihilate* Their servants and petitioners. Likewise are the Other Gods the most canny of bargainers. If They are to *give much,* then likewise do They *demand* much. From me"— Father commenced unwinding the bandage about his left hand—"*this* is what was demanded!"

Father cackled with each freed circumference of rather unclean cloth. Proudly, Father held his left hand before my horror-stricken eyes—and I saw four fingers—and *no thumb*! Severed at the very root, apparently cauterized with fire (for the puckered, angry, ridged flesh looked but recently subjected to the searing of intense flame), the thumb of my father's left hand had been . . . amputated!

A haze of pure befuddlement clouding my brain, I was gently guided around the desk by my father's unmutilated hand upon my elbow. "Now, look. Look! *But do not dare to touch!*" Father instructed, as he unfastened the two clasps of the saddlebag (somewhat clumsily with his lacking an oppositive digit) and drew forth a thick and weighty book of obvious antique origin, with a binding of a material akin to leather—*but which was not leather.*

"The Book of Might!" Father proclaimed, his tone reverent and crazed. "The Book of Power! The Book of Life!"

"It is . . . it is very old," said I, knowing not what else I might say.

"The eighth century," Father explained, "though the knowledge compiled and explicated herein far pre-dates the Pentateuch. Its author is Yusif-bin-Yusif Al-Sofi: Yusif, the son of Yusif, Yusif *the Wise,* physician, philosopher, astronomer, and poet—and devoted servant and Chronicler of the Other Gods. Official histories, when they deign to mention Yusif at all, dub him 'Mad Yusif.' Ha! Thus the world does mistake wisdom for lunacy!"

Again cautioning me that I dare not lay hand upon the text, Father, with his thumbless extremity, traced the ornate, flowing, arabesque lettering on the cover, pronouncing the title in a whispery, hissing, Semitic-sounding language, which I then did not understand—a title which *I am now forbidden to speak.*

But of the book, I may state that upon its pages is contained a totality of knowledge by which anything and everything Man wishes may be vouchsafed him. Wisdom as is only hinted at in such metaphysical works as *Kabala, Sefer Yissrah, Zo-Har* and *Summa Perfectis* is elaborated upon (one must become proficient in ancient Hebrew, Arabic, Aramaic, and Chaldean to study Yusif's work!); the work *proves* there need be no chasm between metaphorical statement and literal reality!

Of course, all this I did not know until far later in my life.

Pray, allow me to continue my narrative of this initial encounter with the writings of Yusif-bin-Yusif, as Father, with an attitude of most enthusiastic reverence, muttering under his breath of "signs and wonders, wonders and signs," turned the pages until he came to a parchment leaf upon which was written this and this only:

The scholar of Semitic languages will recognize this symbol as an amalgam of the Hebrew letters *Haih* and *Yude.*

But it is more—ever so much more!

As Father, in tones of the most solemn awe, declared:

"It is the *Chai,* not merely the Symbol, but the true Mystic Source of Life." Father's voice grew quieter, became a whisper, but a whisper of such intensity that it had stronger effect upon me than would have the most thunderous shout. "And if the *Chai* be inscribed upon the heart, one may live . . . forever!"

"But," I said, dumbfounded, "how can that—"

"Heh-heh! Heh-heh-heh! Heh-heh-heh!" interjected Father, "I do not know—not yet! but I shall read—and I shall study—and I shall know! I SHALL NOT BE DENIED!"

Father bade me depart. He seated himself at the desk. He turned up the lamp, and in the improved light I could see his eyes glimmering with obsession as he cautioned me to tell Mother *nothing,* for she would not understand.

For the greater part of a week, Father remained shut up in the confines of his library, a servant bringing what little nourishment he demanded at irregular intervals. Then, one night, I found that sleep, inexplicably, would not approach my bed. From time to time, irrepressible tremors pervaded my frame, and, at length, there invaded my consciousness a feeling of anticipatory alarm. With each tolling of the clock, the sensation grew magnified and the more horrid, so that it was *almost* as though I were experiencing the immeasurable agonies of the grave—as I had in my loathsome Nightmare!

At the chiming of the midnight hour, I sat up in bed, being forced to place my hand over my mouth to stifle the shriek which threatened to burst from the very depths of my being.

But my cry was not destined to be heard at the curious, haunted instant that divides Night from Morn; rather it was the tortured, afflicted shout of Father, a scream which still must be drifting in its volume and misery upon the Ether—and accompanying it was one other cry—*louder, far louder!*—a cascading, reverberating peal of *laughter* as could not have been produced by the vocal mechanism of *anything like unto a human being*!

All of the household, Mother, I, and the servants, in fearful dismay and disarray, gathered in the hall at the portal to Father's library. Below, seemingly leagues distant, came a beating at our front gate and the inquisitive demand of the Night Watch.

Then, seizing the initiative, the butler opened the library door. Upon the desk, enveloped by a flickering, bluish-white flame, which in just seconds reduced it to fine ash, was the book of Yusif-bin-Yusif Al-Sofi.

And there, in the center of the study, suspended above the floor as if hanging from an invisible noose, was Father, his feet performing the most frantic gyrations, his body convulsing brutally, as though he were a field mouse being savaged by a spirited terrier! "Help me! Oh, help!" he managed to peep, before his tongue protruded from his bleeding lips, blocking off further entreaties.

Then he fell to the carpet—say, rather, he was *dropped* thereupon—and his whole frame at once—within the

space of a single minute or even less, shrank—
crumbled—absolutely *rotted* away. Before our entire
company, there lay a nearly liquid mass of detestable pu-
tridity, which, in its sheer *awfulness,* attracted even as it
repulsed me, drawing me nigh so that I alone might hear
the nearly inaudible ultimate words of that which had
been my father:

"I . . . made . . . a . . . mistake."

IV. Dr. Valentine of Paris

"I am convinced he dared to meddle into dark affairs Man
was not meant to know." Some short time after Father's
funeral (a discreet, if not actually clandestine business, conducted by a clergyman so given to drink that he might not
have known if he were performing wedding, baptism, funeral, or Satanic rite!), thus did Mother pronounce her
opinion, and, as you may understand, while such words
were not chiseled into stone, Mother considered her statement fitting epitaph for Father—and a warning for Mankind.

Not I.

I had seen briefly an exercise of supreme power and
majesty, and, while I rightly feared its possessors, as one
might fear the fury of the maelstrom at sea, likewise did I
long *to avail myself* of such magnificent energy, to meld
my will with it—with the Incontestable Prowess of the
Other Gods—so that I might never perish, so that I must
never endure the Infinite cold and gloom and darkness
that was Death.

"If it can be conceived in the mind of Man, it can be
accomplished." That is a statement of what we term
"common sense wisdom" (which has been over-praised, I
think, by such egalitarian populists as Mr. Benjamin Frank-
lin!), and, as do *all* such simplistic philosophies, it has
other statements of "common sense" by which it is re-
futed: "Easier it is said—than done," for one example.

Thus did Father's shocking end serve to engender

within me a fierce determination to accomplish what he had tried to achieve.

The Chai *would be inscribed upon* my *heart, and* I *would live forever!*

But how? How would I effect this remarkable transmutation whereby I, a Mortal, might ascend to the ranks of Immortals?

Cautiously would I act—and all the more so having seen Father transformed into a stinking puddle of slop— and *methodically,* so that proper protocols were observed—and *surreptitiously,* so that neither my character nor my deeds might lead society to hinder me.

Not until I reached my majority might I undertake my quest of the *Chai,* my search for Immortality, but shortly after that occasion, Mother suffered a burst blood vessel and, eyes rolling wildly, pinkish foam upon her lips, she died in *seizure apoplexia.* With no one then to hold me by any means accountable, with no one for whom I bore responsibility, and enjoying a luxurious income, I set off to explore worlds known and worlds unknown.

Of moments so tantalizing that my teeth were set on edge in expectation of gaining my heart's desire, of incidents which frustrated me, bringing me near to the point where I might pound my head on the wall, cursing the little knowledge I possessed that had set me seeking more, of experiences in which so completely did I play the fool that I was compelled to laugh at my own folly, and of dire times whereby my life was saved only through the means of a hair's-breadth escape, I might fill ten volumes.

In the South of England, I fell in with a riotous crew of blood-drinkers who claimed to be under the dominion of Satan, but who more often served that more approachable devil, *Spiritus Fermenti*! In Prague, I studied with a hook-nosed man who claimed kinship to the mystic Rebbe Yehudah Lowe, whose mastery of the Esoteric Sciences (as recorded in the *Nifloet Mihrl*) first brought into being the man of clay called the Golem. In such abysmal poverty did this unfortunate Jew live, with his shaven-headed, cross-eyed wife and thirteen puling offspring, that he would have revealed any or all secrets for a few coins. He told me, plainly enough, how fasting, prayer, and the inscription of *certain sacred Hebraic letters* upon the forehead of a clay figure might vivify such a being, but, when I appealed to the Jew to tell me how yet other *Hebrew letters* might be etched upon the living, beating heart of man, he became agitated near to incomprehensibility. In arrogant fashion (hardly suited to his social station), he ordered me from his hovel.

In a long house of the American Indian, I smoked strong tobacco and had a vision. In far-off Arabia, disguised as a Mosilman so that I might be granted entrance to places otherwise forbidden to "Infidels," I kissed the black Kaaba stone which had fallen from the sky—and felt *its distinct and most unnatural emanations flow into me, dynamic and extraordinary!* Far off, in the most barren desert, in the ancient ruins of a nameless city, I sat by a feeble fire all the long night, protected only by sign and symbol I had scratched into the sand, while encompassing me were whisperers in the darkness.

But it is not my intention to present the chronicles of my travels and learnings; this is not an Oriental Romance, nor am I a mythic Sinbad whose adventures are meant simply to provide a few evenings' imaginative entertainment.

In as factual and objective a fashion as possible, I will merely say that after significant hardship, travail, and disappointment, but stubbornly refusing to abandon my *Life*'s undertaking, at long last, *in my seventieth year,* I found, in Paris, the redoubtable Dr. Valentine—and Immortality!

By no means is it unlikely that you have heard of Dr. Valentine. He began as a disciple of the noted magnetist, Dr. Robert Fludd, and later studied with the Swabbian priest, Gassner, but his doings and renown soon surpassed those of his mentors. That Dr. Valentine could heal such diseases as king's evil, eczema, epilepsy, the goiter, etc., etc., there can be no doubt, for many in medical literature are the verifiable accounts of his cures.

But not to be found in *medical literature,* either of that

time *or of the present,* are those hushed reports of his accomplishments being duly attributable to—*other*—than the rational and logical sciences. Indeed, in the provinces of France Dr. Valentine did not dare to venture, for fear that the superstitious peasants might do him grievous harm because of his purported affiliations with devils—and *worse* than devils!

And so, to the opulent, splendidly appointed apartments of Dr. Valentine did I go, and from the first did the man *intrigue* me. He certainly seemed to be *still* a young man—and he made a point of speaking about his youth—yet there was an air about him that permitted me easily to think him *a hundred years of age.* He was singularly tall and thin. He stooped much. His limbs were exceedingly long and emaciated. His complexion was absolutely bloodless. His mouth was large and flexible, and his teeth were more wildly uneven, although sound, than ever I had seen in a human head. The expression of his smile, however, was by no means unpleasing, as might be supposed; rather, it assured and projected a marked tranquility and confidence. His right eye was abnormally large, and round; upon any accession or diminution of light, the pupil underwent remarkable contraction or dilation. Surprising was it that Dr. Valentine's *left* eye was hidden by a black patch. Though his raiment was otherwise unremarkable, Dr. Valentine had a blue, red-flowered cloak—like that of a theatrical conjurer—hanging from his slender shoulders.

As was polite, Dr. Valentine and I sat and conversed for a time, our talk mere prattle and courtesy. Then, with a keenly interrogative note, Dr. Valentine asked: "What is the affliction that has brought you to my humble abode?"

Speaking in a veiled manner, I said, "I am afflicted by that tragic condition which we are all of us heir to: the *human* condition."

"Sir," said Dr. Valentine, "I do not take your meaning. Could you expound upon the subject?"

"Indeed," I said, "the subject is Death. It is a concern to me. I will die, and, because of my advanced age, it is reasonable to assume my death will occur in the none too distant future, *unless it is given to you to prevent my dying.*"

With a wave of his hand which struck me as fully disingenuous, Dr. Valentine said, "I regret, sir, that I do not comprehend."

"Perhaps *you* might wish to consult others—*Older Others*," said I, as though I were the most callow fellow. "Perhaps you might discuss the questions of Life and Death with someone—oh, let me suggest—Yes! His name is on the very tip of my tongue now. . . . Who is it that I am thinking of? Oh, I am an old man, and so my mind is muddled; certainly you can aid me with this. He is a physician, a philosopher, and an astronomer, and, furthermore, a poet! He is a Man of Antiquity, of ages-old learning. His name is—help me now, Dr. Valentine—his name strikes me as being . . . *Yusif* . . ."

"Yusif-bin-Yusif Al-Sofi," said Dr. Valentine in an unmodulated tone. "You know him. You know his book."

"No," I said, by way of correction. "I know *of* him and *of* his book."

"I see," Dr. Valentine said.

There fell a lengthy silence between us, and, when again we spoke, we were confederates, nay, more than that—we were *partners!*

I might be granted the Immortality I so fervently craved; its cost was a *part* of myself.

I was . . . agreeable. Dr. Valentine assented to—*treat*—me upon the morrow; and his personal, professional fee: half of all my earthly possessions, a price I found by no means excessive.

The following evening, I returned to the lodgings of Dr. Valentine, bearing with me a signed letter of credit from the Bank of England. "So," said Dr. Valentine, accepting my offering with a satisfied expression, "let us commence."

He conducted me to a chamber pentagonal in shape and of capacious size. Within the confines of an apartment building though we were, the gloomy-looking oak ceiling of this room was excessively lofty, vaulted, and elaborately fretted with the wildest specimens of a semi-Gothic, semi-Druidical device. Despite the vastness of this chamber, within was but a single three-legged low stool as might be found in the chilly cell of the most ascetic monk.

Dr. Valentine told me to strip to the waist. I did so. Dr. Valentine told me to sit upon the small stool. I did so.

Then it was that Dr. Valentine's slender, expressive hands began to move about in so graceful a manner that they might have been sprites performing an aerial ballet before my eyes, and as my gaze was riveted to the curling and flowing of his fingers, so, too, did his rhythmic speech and euphonious tone arrest my auditory sense, as the doctor said:

"Animal Magnetism! Its existence is but grudgingly acknowledged by commonplace physicians, and it is a term greatly abused by charlatans, who know not what they do—but it is the dynamic *foundation* of Life itself, as revealed by that Ancient Master, Yusif-bin-Yusif . . . Yusif *the Wise,* Yusif, whose Teachers were the Other Gods Themselves who Spoke to Him in Shadow."

Now it was that I grew faint and dizzy, as I focused upon Dr. Valentine's remarkable hands, the left passing in front of the right, the right before the left, the two hands blending, so that ten fingers came together—and then doubled, so that twenty fingers waved and writhed. And from those hands came subtle but distinct, invisible but forceful, *discharges,* probing the flesh of my face.

And all the while, Dr. Valentine continued his lulling yet *compelling* monologue:

"At the instant the foetus *quickens* within the mother's womb, each organ develops magnetic impulses and vibrations. The most vital organ within us, of course, is *the heart.* As long as the heart beats, one has life. At the cessation of the beating of the heart, Death results."

By now, I was experiencing something akin to a stupor. A lethargy gripped me, bringing me near to a cataleptic state; yet, at the same time, I felt within so violent an agitation of mind that I would have screamed—had I possessed the strength—or the will!

Dr. Valentine's mouth, with its markedly uneven teeth, with its wetness of lip and tongue and its crisp articulations, became the focal point of my attention, as he said:

"The problem then is, how do we maintain the beating of the heart—for *all* time? How is it that the sacred *Chai* is written upon the heart so that Life might be eternally preserved?"

Now Dr. Valentine's smile, though unchanged upon his face, impressed me as haughty and horrid, the smile of a Monstrosity and not a Man!

"Ha!" continued he, "it is a simple enough matter for one such as I! First, we seize an *expendable* organ"—and here, the hand of Dr. Valentine darted at me, obscuring the vision of my left eye—no, *more* than impairing sight—*blinding me*—and then Dr. Valentine exclaimed: "And thus we redistribute the magnetic energies, BRANDING the *Chai* upon the heart . . . THUSLY!!!"

And with that, his hand, fingers gathered together like a crane's beak, painlessly and bloodlessly *passed through my bosom*! Though this Occult Medicine, this which might be condemned as "Sorceric surgery," caused me no physical discomfort, I cannot fully relate the furious anxiety, the psychic unrest, elicited by Dr. Valentine's nimble fingers within me as they traced the pattern of the *Chai* upon my now frantically leaping, furiously palpitating heart, transferring the dynamic energy which had been that of my EYE into my HEART!

Less than an hour later, I departed Dr. Valentine's quarters, blind in one eye—AND IMMORTAL!

Epilogue: Of Life Without End

As you have probably surmised, in the years since my "treatment" by Dr. Valentine, I have dwelled (comfortably and well) in a myriad of far-flung locales, as I do not wish to attract attention by my unusual longevity; the world will not abide what it cannot understand, and we are not yet many years past the time when those thought to "traffic with the Devil" (or some such rubbish!) were hanged or burned. My goal reached, I count myself fortunate, and have not again called upon the Other Gods or their acolytes in any matter—well I know the power of the Other Gods and I fear to vex Them. I can but guess at what They might do to an Immortal who failed to please Them; is not Death the most severe Punishment, one might say—but I have no wish to learn if They can invent that Which is Worse than Death!

Of *close* companions I have had few, for I have reasoned that true intimacy with others becomes an impossibility if one knows he will have no end of living, while his friend must perish.

Yet *casual* companions have been numerous throughout my lengthly life, for it is often pleasing to engage in intellectual discourse.

Currently boarding in my abode is a young man with a philosophical turn of mind, one who likes to argue the *fundamental* questions. Nervous he is, very, very dreadfully nervous—and he starts easily; that is, I think, because he seems to possess the pronounced acuity of hearing that is often found in those of a brooding, overly meditative humor.

My conversations with him amuse me. His company, despite his sometimes near-frenzied manner, is entertaining. For my part, I have, on occasions, aided him financially, and have shown him many kindnesses.

It is apparent that he likes me, yet there are times when (I believe) my disfigured eye disconcerts him in a peculiar way; moments when he thinks I am not aware, I sometimes catch him gaping, then lowering his head, a blush of embarrassment upon his cheeks.

When Dr. Valentine requisitioned the vital energies from my eye, he did not *remove* the orb. *Sans* its magnetic force, my pale blue, dysfunctional eye quickly developed a protective membrane covering it, a translucent film, so that it is very like the eye of a foul, carrion-eating buzzard.

But if I possess the eye of a vulture, I count it small sacrifice for a heart that will beat and beat and beat—*forever!*

Afterword

It's simple.

Ask Miles Davis about Louis Armstrong. Wynton Marsalis. The late—bless him—Chet Baker. If you are a jazz trumpet player, then you are either playing *like* Louis Armstrong—or working *not* to play like Louis Armstrong. And eventually, if you've *got it,* you find your own coppery-round sound somewhere in between "like Armstrong/not like Armstrong."

Ask the saxophone players, Eddie Harris, Branford Marsalis, the late—bless him—John Coltrane, about Coleman Hawkins, and they'll tell you: You either play like Coleman Hawkins—or you're working not to play like Coleman Hawkins. And eventually, if you've *got it,* you find your own humming warm sound somewhere in between "like Hawkins/not like Hawkins."

Ask the horror writers . . .

No, let's make that ask the horror writers who read, those who have a sense of the past, those who realize Stephen King did not by himself create the genre, those who are striving to write stories that will speak to us now—and to those who are around 150 years from now—and they'll tell you about H. P. Lovecraft: If you are writing good horror fiction, then you are writing like Lovecraft—or you're striving not to write like Lovecraft.

And you discover there is space between "like Lovecraft/not like Lovecraft"—and in that space is the particular sound of your own voice.

Because, as Lord Buckley phrased it, "when that cat laid it down, he *laid* it *down.*"

It's that simple.

About "A Secret of the Heart"

"There is a ghost haunting . . . Providence . . ." I came across that line in the "Introduction" to *The Portable Poe,* edited by Philip Van Doren Stern.

More likely, there are ghosts haunting Providence, those of Edgar Allan Poe and Howard Phillips Lovecraft, and equally likely, they spend considerable time (if such an abstraction exists in the afterlife) discussing this and that: Literature. Women. Literature. Politics. Literature. Etiquette. And literature. Of course, literature.

Mr. Lovecraft, a gracious ghost, acknowledges the debt his work owes to Mr. Poe.

Mr. Poe says had he known he would have such an influence on Mr. Lovecraft, why, he'd have tried to be more . . . influential!

It is the sort of dry remark both ghosts enjoy.

It is good to think of them this way, with their place in Literature and in Providence.

They laugh quietly, and go on about their hauntings.

THE OTHER MAN
Ray Garton

My wife's body was empty again.

She lay beside me in bed, eyes closed, breathing so shallowly that when I placed a mirror beneath her nose only the faintest vapor appeared on the glass. Even the small twitches and tics her body usually went through during sleep were absent. The muscles of her face were so flaccid that her cheeks seemed to sag, as if about to run fluidly off her skull.

I lifted her arm, then let go; it dropped heavily to the mattress like the arm of a corpse and she did not stir.

I pinched the back of her hand hard. No response.

I clutched her shoulders, shook her violently and shouted her name. Nothing.

Sharon was not there.

I sat on the edge of the bed for a while, holding my head in my hands, thinking thoughts that made me doubt my sanity, absurd thoughts that had haunted me for weeks, seeming less and less absurd as time passed.

Putting on my bathrobe, I left the bedroom, made myself a drink and started a fire in the den's fireplace. With only the light of the small lamp beside my chair and the flickering glow of the flames, the den became a ballroom where shadows danced with light all around me, mocking me, making light of the cold fear that grew in my gut.

There were three books stacked on the lamp table. They were *her* books. There were others like them scattered all over the house. I reached for one, stopped, then jerked my hand back as if burned. I stared at the book warily, as I might have stared at a poisonous snake coiled to strike. To open one of those books and begin reading would be to admit that my idea might not be absurd at all. I wasn't sure I was ready to admit that yet.

The room grew cool as the fire waned and I finished three drinks, all the while sitting in my chair staring at the top book on the stack. The liquor made me tired, but I knew I wouldn't be able to sleep.

Finally, I opened the book and began to read. . . .

The first change I noticed in my wife was her silence in the evenings. After twelve years of marriage, I had grown fond of our conversations at the end of the day, our dinner table banter and discussions of the day's events. But eight months ago, I ate dinner alone for the first time I could remember. When I asked Sharon why there was only one place set at the table, she said she'd already eaten and left the dining room. After dinner, I found her in the den curled up with a book before the fire. I asked her what she was reading, but had to repeat my question again before she was even aware of my presence.

"Oh, I'm sorry, Jim," she said, distracted. "Just a book I picked up." She continued reading.

She picked up a lot of books over the next few weeks, some of them dusty and dog-eared used copies, others brand new and all of them about the same thing: astral projection.

I had always known Sharon to be an extraordinarily rational, level-headed person who was so uninterested in sensationalism that she didn't even glance at the tabloids at the supermarket check-out stands. Even more odd than her new interest was the growing distance between us. There was less and less conversation between us; we never made love anymore; and when she was reading one of her books—which she seemed to be doing all the time—I felt completely alone in the house.

When I tried to get her to talk about whatever was wrong, she would only smile, maybe laugh and swipe a hand through the air gently, and assure me that *nothing* was wrong, she was just *reading,* that was all.

"But why are you reading *that?*" I asked one evening.

"This? Because it's interesting."

"But you've never been interested in that sort of thing before. People floating around outside of their bodies? Come *on,* Sharon."

"So I'm interested now. What's wrong with that? I had no idea there was so much written about the subject, that there was such a large pool of knowledge. It really is fascinating, Jim. You oughtta give it a chance."

She went back to her book and I walked away frowning.

I finally decided it was nothing more than a passing preoccupation and tried to bury myself in my work . . . until she started talking in her sleep.

I began to wake up in the early hours of the morning to the sound of Sharon's voice. I couldn't understand her words the first time, but she spoke urgently. Then, after a few moments, she sighed, rolled over and was still.

It happened again the next night. And several nights after that. And it was always at about the same time—shortly before four a.m.—and only for a few moments. Then she would roll over and fall silent. Sometimes I was able to make out a few words—"It's coming . . . I'll help you . . . I promise . . . it's coming . . . hurry, hurry . . . it's coming. . . ." But nothing that made any sense to me. And always, even in the grogginess of sleep, her voice sounded so urgent and passionate and . . . so very *secret. . . .*

On one of those dark early mornings as I listened to Sharon's unconscious ramblings, it struck me: she was talking to another man in her sleep . . . a man she'd no doubt been seeing for some time . . . the man who had put such a chill in my once warm life. . . .

I was unable to face her the next day and was grateful, for once, that she was somewhere in the house reading when I got home. The day had been long and painful; unable to work, I'd agonized over my suspicion, wondering what I might have done—or might *not* have done—that would turn Sharon's eyes to another man. Was I boring? Had I grown stagnant? Did she even *love* me any more? I even found myself wondering if I loved *her* any more. I was unable to eat dinner and, instead, vegetated in front of the television. I waited until long after I knew she was asleep before I went to bed—in fact, it was about three-thirty in the morning, maybe a little later—knowing that I wouldn't sleep but willing to try. I slid carefully into bed, not wanting to wake her and reached for the light when I noticed something . . . *different.*

The room was completely, utterly silent.

My hand froze half way to the lamp and I listened. Nothing.

Sharon had never been a silent sleeper—who is?—and I had spent twelve years falling asleep to the rhythmic sounds of her slumber: the throaty breathing, the occasional snore, the sniff or cough that was usually followed by a change of position under the covers. I heard none of those sounds as I sat up beside her, arm outstretched toward the bedside lamp.

I turned, leaned toward her.

She lay on her back, arms outside the covers, hands resting one atop the other on her abdomen. Her lips were parted slightly, her hair pooled about her head. But her breasts did not rise and fall as she breathed; there were no facial tics, no sleepy stirrings. Even her eyes did not move beneath her eyelids, subtly shifting the thin flaps of skin as they usually do during deep sleep.

I felt a jolt of panic and touched her hand.

Her skin was cool. *Too* cool.

"Oh, God," I hissed, leaning down and pulling the covers back so I could put my ear to her breast. I heard nothing. And when I pressed two fingers to her throat, I felt no pulse. "Oh, my God, Sharon? *Sharon!*" I clutched her shoulders and began to shake her vigorously; I lifted her into a sitting position and shook her some more, making her head loll back and forth like that of a rag doll.

I dropped her back onto the mattress and stared at her stupidly; I found myself unable to breathe, to move for a moment. Then I bounded for the telephone to dial 911. My fingers suddenly had no feeling and punched the wrong buttons repeatedly. I don't know how many times I hung up and tried again before I finally made the connection. The *burrrr* of the phone ringing at the other end seemed eternal and I felt myself beginning to hyperventilate, suddenly having forgotten the possibility of Sharon's infidelity, and—

—I heard a sound and stiffened, spun around.

Sharon's head was rolling back and forth slowly on the pillow. Her mouth was moving. She began to speak very softly.

". . . Coming . . . it's coming . . . I'll . . . be back . . . promise . . . I'll help you. . . ."

I dropped the receiver back in its cradle as I stared at her, dumbfounded.

After a few moments, she smacked her lips a few times, then rolled over and began to snore softly.

I plopped onto the bed, jaw slack, my body weak with sudden exhaustion. "Sharon?" I asked, my voice hoarse. I touched her shoulder. "Sharon? Are . . . are you all right? Sharon?"

She stirred, muttered, "Fum? Shebble carf?"

"Are you all right, Sharon?"

Her eyes opened slightly. "Corsham. Gosuhleep."

I did not sleep, though. As I sat there, I found myself staring at the book on Sharon's nightstand. It was a new one. The title was written in shimmering gold letters on the cover: *Going Solo: Adventures Out of the Body.* For the rest of the night, I couldn't get that title out of my mind.

It happened again the following night, but I was waiting for it. When all signs of life left her at about one-thirty a.m., I began trying to wake her. I shook her, I shouted at her, I pinched her—*hard*—and even, much to my shame, gave her a solid slap in the face. Nothing worked. I finally gave up and just watched her until, shortly before four o'clock, she began to stir, mumble and then snore.

The next day, I noticed her books around the house more than ever before. They were on the coffee table, in the kitchen, in the dining room, the bedroom, the sewing room . . . there was even one in the bathroom. The titles caught my attention, held it, and wouldn't let go: *Astral Travel . . . Leaving the Body: A Personal Memoir . . . Outside the Earthbound Carriage . . .* and more . . . so many more. . . .

With each book I saw, I remembered Sharon lying in bed, still, lifeless, cold, *empty,* and I began to think thoughts . . . consider possibilities . . . that made me ashamed of myself, that even made me doubt the state of my mind.

That night it happened again, at the same time, in the same way. Except on this night, I got out of bed, went to the living room, opened the closest book and, against my better judgment, began to read.

I was still reading when it came time to go to work and found it difficult to put the book down. Not because it was such a great book, but because I was finally getting a glimpse of what had been holding Sharon's attention in such an iron grip, and it read like a long, elaborate gag. And yet, after my initial reaction, I began to realize that there was a certain kind of logic to it all—a bizarre kind of logic, granted, the kind of logic one might find between the covers of a complex, well-thought-out fantasy novel, but logic nonetheless—and I began to play a sort of connect-the-dots game with it all, connecting the bits of information I found in that book and the others on the lamp table with the strange things I'd witnessed over the past several nights.

I put two of the books I hadn't opened yet into my briefcase and took them to work with me, leaving shortly before I knew Sharon would be waking up.

With the help of a lot of coffee and a couple No-Doz, I managed to stay awake that day, but I got little work done. I worked in a small tax consulting firm but did not hold a terribly important position, so I was able to postpone my one appointment, lock myself in my little office and read.

I read until my eyes watered. I read until I'd finished both books, then went back and read over sections that were particularly interesting.

According to the books, the best time for a beginner to try leaving his or her body was during sleep. In fact, the author claimed that many dreams were not dreams at all but memories of out-of-the-body journeys experienced during sleep; the sensation of "falling awake," as the author called it—the sudden feeling that one is falling, and then waking abruptly, startlingly—was actually caused by the spirit "falling" back into the body of the sleeping traveler. Both of the books I'd taken from the house included long chapters giving explicit instructions for preparing oneself, before going to sleep, to leave one's body during the night. It read like self-hypnosis to me, but neither book used that term.

The most disturbing thing I found was a single paragraph under the heading, *Soulmates:*

> It is almost unheard of for one to find one's
> true soulmate in the physical plane, but not
> so on the non-physical planes, although it is
> rare. There have been passionate romances
> between out-of-the-body travelers who have

never met physically, in the physical plane, both parties have been involved with other people. According to those who have experienced them, out-of-the-body soulmate romances eclipse anything they've experienced in the flesh, but, in the end, they remain unconsummated and, therefore, they remain unfulfilling.

That single paragraph gave me a flesh-crawling chill and made me want to read more on that particular aspect of out-of-the-body travel. Unfortunately, that was all I could find in the two books I had. So . . .

When I went home that night, I avoided Sharon—which, of course, was easy—and gathered a few more books together, took them to the den, locked myself in and began poring over them like an adolescent hunched over his father's girlie magazines.

I found little more information on soulmates meeting outside their bodies . . . just enough to feed my suspicions that perhaps I'd found the man to whom Sharon had been speaking in her sleep for a few minutes each morning.

I was shocked by my own thoughts, shocked to learn that I was even capable of taking such a fanciful idea seriously. But somehow, it felt right. The idea that Sharon had been seeing another man—actually having an *affair*—simply did not ring true to me; but the idea that she was meeting with someone *outside* her body. . . .

I was growing so tired that I was unable to continue reading. Sharon was fast asleep in bed. Before joining her, I read once again the instructions for preparing for out-of-the-body travel during sleep and, once I'd committed them to memory, went to bed.

As I lay in the dark staring at the ceiling, unable to sleep at first despite my weariness, I felt a bit nervous, like a schoolboy about to give an oral report in front of the whole class, a report for which he was not prepared.

Part of my unrest was due to the stillness of what I was

about to try. But when my hesitation went on too long, I turned to my right and watched Sharon for a moment as she slept, her head tilted toward me, lips almost but not quite smiling. I wondered if that look was caused by some whimsical dream she was having or the knowledge that she would soon be with her ethereal lover . . . if in fact he existed. As I watched her, I felt a jealous ache in my chest and found myself unable to doubt the existence of the other man.

I looked up at the ceiling again, closed my eyes and began taking the slow deep breaths that the book said were necessary to start my journey. I relaxed each and every part of my body, felt myself sink into the mattress as if it were shifting sand.

Following the book's next instruction, I visualized a gentle blue light glowing softly inside my body from head to foot. When the image was clear in my mind, I began to concentrate on the very center of my body, pulling that blue light into a single throbbing globe in the pit of my abdomen.

As I continued breathing deeply, slowly, eyes closed, body limp, I began to drift off.

The last image I remember before falling asleep was that of the blue globe rising slowly out of my body.

I awoke suddenly with my body stiff, hands clutching the mattress.

I'd been startled from my sleep by a falling sensation, as if I'd been thrown from the bed.

Almost ninety minutes had passed, barely enough time for me to dream. But I *had* dreamed. I remembered a vague but unsettling image from my sleep; I'd seen *myself* from above—my body lying beneath the covers, lifeless— as if a part of me were hovering over the bed. . . .

The next morning I awoke with unexpected enthusiasm. I left the house as if to go to work but called in sick and rented a cheap motel room.

Not wanting to raise Sharon's suspicions, I didn't take

any of her books from the house. Instead, I went to a local bookstore and bought half a dozen books on astral projection.

In my motel room, with the DO NOT DISTURB sign on the door, I spread the books out on the bed, opened them and went from book to book, reading them urgently, like a knowledge-hungry student. In fact I was exactly that.

I read and meditated, as the book directed; I underlined and took notes, memorized and recited. I hadn't worked so hard since my last college final exams.

As the shadows lengthened in the late afternoon, I grew tired and hungry, but couldn't bring myself to stop yet. I hadn't really done anything; so far, I'd just studied the books, inhaling information like fresh air.

Finally, I stacked the books on the floor, took off my shoes and lay down on the bed. It felt good; my neck was stiff and my shoulders ached. It would have been so easy simply to go to sleep, but I couldn't.

I closed my eyes and breathed deeply.

I visualized the cool blue light inside me and willed it to merge into a fist-sized sphere in my center.

As the sphere began to rise from my body, I allowed myself to drift off. . . .

Soon I began to dream of floating. I was floating above my body, watching it lie motionless in bed. I moved around the motel room, inspected the dirty corners where the walls met the ceiling, saw the dead insects that lay inside the opaque cover on the overhead light.

When I woke later, rather suddenly, I tried to tell myself that it had not been a dream, but I couldn't. It had possessed the vague soft-focus of images that came during sleep and had looked no different from any other dream I'd ever had.

I'd slept for less than an hour and decided to take advantage of the fact that I was awake. I got up, opened the books again and continued reading.

It was getting late and I knew I would be getting home much later than usual, but couldn't stop yet. I continued

studying . . . underlining . . . reading aloud to myself . . .
memorizing.

I skipped the sections of the books that seemed irrele-
vant or silly, but absorbed everything else.

Soon I was nodding off even as I read.

I put the books aside once again.

I went through the steps once again.

And, once again, I slept. . . .

In the dream that wasn't really a dream, I opened my
eyes and saw the motel room's stained ceiling. The ceiling
began to lower and the stains grew larger as the room
seemed to tilt back and forth. But the room wasn't moving at all and the ceiling was where it had always been.

I was rising.

I could feel nothing; I was weightless and no longer felt
my own body. Slowly, unsure of myself, I turned over.
Normally, what I saw would have made me gasp, but I no
longer had breath.

About four feet below, I saw my body lying on the bed.
It was exactly like the dream I'd had the night before, but
much more vivid.

I continued to rise; my body grew smaller and smaller
until—

—I felt an odd feathery tingling sensation and—

—I was outside, rising above the motel. I saw my car in
the parking lot, the 7-11 across the street, the mini-mall
on the corner, all of them shrinking until they looked like
toys.

My first reaction was one of amazement and wonder
but it was quickly replaced by fear as I passed up through
vaporous clouds, higher and higher until the evening light
began to fade and I was moving through a vast, utterly
empty blackness. When I began to shoot through the
darkness at lightning speeds, I tried to control my direction, hoping to turn back, but failed. I wanted to scream,
but had no voice.

Specks of light began to rip silently past me like tracer

bullets trailing iridescent streaks that lingered for a few seconds before fading. More and more passed by me—or was *I* passing by *them?*—and the blackness around me began to dissolve slowly. I sensed that I was approaching something and, for no reason I could see, I began to slow down.

There was light ahead . . . no, *below* . . . the light was *below* me. Was I . . . *landing?* Once again, I passed through clouds, but they were unlike any clouds I'd seen before; there were layers and layers of them, each layer a different color from the last, and tiny pinpricks of blue light—like small jolts of electricity—shimmered through them this way and that, crisscrossing and zigzagging.

I knew, although I'm not sure how, that I was suddenly no longer alone. Somehow, I sensed the presence of others. A moment later, I sensed the *communication* of others. And shortly after that, I sensed an end to it as something else approached. Whatever it was, it was not yet in sight, but there was a new feeling in the atmosphere . . . a throbbing feeling . . . a distant pulse that was growing rapidly . . . growing more intense and closer . . . closer. . . .

The sparkling pinpricks of energy in the multicolored clouds around me stopped, remained still a moment, and I felt a final communication. It was not in the form of words, it was literally a *feeling,* but unmistakable in its urgency. Had words been spoken, they would have been, *it's coming . . . it's COMING!*

I remembered what I'd heard Sharon say in her sleep: *It's coming . . . I'll help you . . . I promise . . . hurry, hurry . . . it's coming. . . .*

What's coming? I thought as the shimmering clouds around me began to disperse as if blown away on a strong wind.

The throbbing grew louder. I could somehow *feel* it now. And it felt . . . bad. Wrong. *Malignant.*

Without having seen the source of the sound, I sensed its strength and enormity, and suddenly I feared that an arm—perhaps a long, tentacle-like arm ending in a hideous claw—might shoot from the surrounding darkness, perhaps *several* arms, all of them attached to the same black, throbbing mass of a body. I willed myself away from the approaching entity and found myself moving suddenly back the way I had come. In a blurred rush, I passed back through the darkness, down through the clouds and toward the small buildings below, which grew larger and larger as I fell toward my motel, down . . . down . . . until—

—I sat up in bed with a startled yelp.

I sat there for a long time, staring at the opposite wall, holding my breath and listening to my heart. It throbbed loudly in my ears, making a sound not unlike the one from which I'd just fled in my—

"No," I said to myself, getting off the bed. "That was no dream."

I searched through the stack of books until I found one in which I'd skipped over a section titled, *Dangers of the Non-Physical Planes.* I'd skipped it because it seemed un-important; I did not yet believe in a non-physical plane, so how could I possibly feel threatened by the dangers to be found there?

Now I felt differently. Whatever it was I had fled in that strange cloudy place, it had been dangerous . . . malicious.

I flipped through the pages until I found the section I wanted.

> Just as it is in our physical existence, the astral planes hold their share of evil. How-ever, there are two differences. First of all, the evil is far more powerful, infinitely more consuming than any evil *we* know. Sec-ondly, it cannot be hidden; if an evil entity is near by, it will not—it *cannot*—hide its intentions, and you will *know* that you are in danger. In such a case, it is essential that you flee, and the only safe place to which you can flee is the physical plane—your own body. Waste no time in doing this, be-

cause if you are taken by such an entity, *you
will NOT return to your body.*

There was more, but I read no further. What else did I
need to know? My body chilled for a moment at the
thought of what I'd just done, at the realization of how
much danger I'd been in, however briefly. But more than
that, I realized that Sharon was exposing herself to that
same danger every night.

I thought of her sleepy words once again: *It's coming
. . . I'll help you . . . I promise . . . hurry, hurry . . . it's
coming. . . .*

What was coming? And who had she promised to help
again and again every night?

Whatever it was that had been rushing toward me in
that dark place, it was something so evil, so unimaginably
deadly, that its malevolence had preceded it. I shuddered
at the thought of it, and I groaned at the thought of
Sharon being taken by it.

I couldn't let that happen. To prevent it, I might have
to face that thing again, but even so . . .

. . . I could *not* let that happen.

It was dark outside. Dusk had come and gone long ago.
I gathered up the books, checked out of the room and
hurried home.

When I got home, Sharon was busy writing letters—or
so she said as she sat at the desk in the kitchen—and did
not even ask why I was nearly four hours late from work.

I made a sandwich in the kitchen and ate it quickly as I
continued reading in the den. I learned nothing new, but
reviewed everything I had learned.

I did not look forward to repeating the experience I'd
gone through earlier; my skin crawled at the very thought
of coming within range of whatever hideous, filthy thing
had been pulsing its way through the darkness.

It's coming . . .

But I knew it was necessary.

. . . I'll help you . . . I promise . . .

I was willing, if necessary, to meet it face to face in order to keep it from Sharon.

. . . hurry, hurry . . . it's coming . . .

I read late into the night.

Sharon went to bed without saying goodnight.

I joined her later, hoping I would be able to leave my body at, or close to, the same time she left hers.

I slid under the covers and visualized, once again, the soft blue light. . . .

When I left my body for the third time that day, I felt no amazement or wonder as before; instead, I focused my attention on Sharon to see if she was still there. Her body did not move; there was no sign of life; I knew she had gone before me.

I rose from the room, out of the house, above my darkened neighborhood and into the black sky. I passed quickly through the darkness that had so frightened me before, until pencil-thin streaks of light were shooting by me, until I found the shimmering clouds I'd seen earlier.

I moved among them, sensing the wordless conversations that passed between them, listening without ears, eavesdropping not on conversations but on feelings, until I picked up something that made me stop. There were no words as such, but I recognized the emotion, the sensations that passed through my non-physical body.

I'll help you, I promise. It's only a matter of time. Just a matter of time.

It was Sharon. But there was someone else, someone whose emotion was just as strong. . . .

But how can you be sure it will work?

Because I know. Trust *me!*

Trust you? I love *you!*

When that sensation reached me, I ached. Although I had no blood, I bled.

The sensations were strong and I searched for the closest entities. I found them: Two nebulous clouds shimmering with energy, both of them a soft yellowish-green.

The unfamiliar entity continued:

And even if I didn't love you, I have to trust you. I have no other choice. I've been here so long. I've been running for so long! I can't run any longer.

I love you, too. And don't worry. I'll help you.

I was devastated. But I had no fists to clench, no teeth to grind, and no voice with which to protest.

How did they communicate? There had been nothing in the books about communicating on the astral planes. I was mute, a helpless observer. I waited for more, bracing myself for something even more painful.

Then it happened.

The throbbing.

It was distant at first, even more distant than before, but coming closer. I sensed Sharon then; had she been speaking, she would have recited the words I'd heard her speak in her sleep so many times.

It's coming. It's coming!

Yes, coming again, I know. But we've had so little time.

You have to go. I'll help you. I promise! *It won't be long now.*

The two yellowish-green clouds began to move along with all the others. They were whisked away from me as if blown on a breeze.

I followed.

The throbbing grew louder, closer.

Hurry, hurry, please . . . it's coming closer. . . .

I followed them into the darkness, deep into the black nothingness that lay between me and my body. I waited for the familiar sight of clouds, of my neighborhood far below. . . .

But it did not come.

Instead, a vast, unfamiliar landscape appeared below. I followed them downward. The ground below began to take on shape. It was clay-red, the flat ground webbed with great jagged cracks from which rose tall peaks of all heights—some short and stubby, others tall and needle-like.

The two clouds before me moved low to the ground

and headed for a dense group of peaks and hills. I tried to follow them closely—all the while trying to ignore the horrendous pulsing behind us—but they increased their speed and began to zigzag between the hills and mountains, moving so quickly that, in a short while, they were nothing more than green streaks ahead of me that appeared in flashes as they shot out from behind the mountains ahead of me, moving back and forth, back and forth, until . . . until—

—they were gone.

I stopped, positioned between two towering mountains that rose high above the others on the alien landscape. Below, I no longer saw the dry, cracked ground I'd seen before; there was only darkness, as if the mountains rose up from endless nothingness.

And somewhere behind me, the throbbing continued. It grew closer, louder. . . .

If my voice had been with me, my scream would have echoed through the darkness, bouncing off the dry clay walls of the peaks and hills, continuing endlessly downward in the depths that fell below me.

I fled.

Behind me the evil drew closer.

I tried to move faster through the blackness, but wasn't sure if I was successful. In the darkness, it was impossible to tell.

For a short time, I passed through familiar surroundings; once again, the specks of light shot past me, leaving behind their colorful tails.

Then they were gone and I was once again blind.

Until I found the clouds.

Although the throbbing continued behind me, I felt relieved. It wasn't long before I saw the familiar sight of lights below.

Streets.

Houses.

My house.

I moved faster.

The throbbing grew more and more distant. The feeling

of danger—the sensation of being pursued by a black, cancerous mass—subsided.

I was in my bedroom.

I saw my bed. I saw my body, lying peacefully beside Sharon, who was equally motionless.

I fell as fast as I could, unable to re-enter my body fast enough. But something made me freeze.

Sharon moved. She jerked, stiffened beneath the covers, then sat up, her eyes wide. Her head turned and she stared at my body with an odd expression on her face.

I dropped lower and lower until I was mere inches from my body and—

—I froze once again.

My heart would have stopped if I'd had one.

I saw my eyes open. I watched my shoulders jerk. I saw my body sit up. Its head turned to face Sharon.

She seemed tense for a moment, squinting as she asked, in a breathy voice, "Is . . . is it *you?*"

My face smiled. My head nodded. My voice said, "Yes. It's me. I'm here."

Sharon's face split into a grin and she shrieked like a happy child. "It worked! It worked, just like I thought! Just like I promised!"

My arms lifted slowly and my hands touched her shoulders.

Sharon's arms embraced my body and she laughed, "My God, we're finally together!"

My own laugh filled the room, deep and heartfelt.

They kissed passionately, hands moving intimately over one another's bodies.

"I told you," Sharon said, kissing her way down my neck, "I *told* you it would work." Kissing . . . kissing . . . like she hadn't kissed me since the early years of our marriage. "I knew if I left the books around the house . . . he'd read them sooner or later." They disappeared beneath the covers, their bodies nothing more than jostling lumps. "I knew he'd get suspicious," she went on, her words interrupted by loud wet kisses. "I *knew* he'd try it after a while . . . I *knew* he'd follow me . . . you're safe, my love . . . *safe* . . . it can't find you here . . . it can't chase you any more."

It . . .

There were no more voices for a while. Only labored breathing and squeaking bedsprings . . . moans of pleasure and wet smacking sounds. . . .

The movement of their bodies became very familiar; they were moving in ways that Sharon and I had not moved for a long time.

They were making love.

Her moans and sighs stabbed me like hot knives.

I watched helplessly, hovering above them, as Sharon began to speak, her voice growing louder and louder.

"Yes . . . oh, God, *yes* . . . don't stop . . . more . . . *more.* . . ."

The sounds that came from beneath those covers were wet and rhythmic. I wanted to be sick . . . but, of course, I couldn't.

Then I heard it.

The throbbing.

It was far above me at first, nothing more than a *feeling.* But it was growing closer, growing louder, more intense.

"Oh my *Gaawwd,*" Sharon hissed.

It came closer, that malignant thing that had pursued me through places known only to the disembodied spirits of the living and the lost souls of the dead. The throbbing became louder and louder, as if it might surround the entire house and swallow it whole.

"I'm coming," Sharon whispered, "my God, I'm *coming*! I'm—"

—*coming, it's coming, it's—*

"—*coming,* I'm, I'm, oh God, I'm—"

—*coming, it's coming, hurry, hurry, it's—*

"—*coming,* I'm *coming!*"

There was nothing to do but go. I rose from the bedroom, up and up until I could see the entire house below me. And yet I could still hear her.

"I'm *coming,* my *God,* I'm—"

—*coming, it's coming, it's—*

"*—coming, I'm coming!*"

It was close, so close that I could sense its form, the lumpy, pustulous surface of its massive flesh, and I fled. I shot upward into the darkness as the throbbing grew louder behind me. I envisioned its limbs—numerous and writhing, reaching outward for the nearest life force, the closest source of energy to feed its insatiable hunger—and I continued upward.

My cry, if I'd had voice, would have been endless. My fear was beyond description.

I fled, screaming silently, into the vast and endless blackness. . . .

Afterword

I think H. P. Lovecraft was the first writer of horror fiction—and one of the very few—to give me a wide-eyed sense of wonder and make my skin crawl at the same time.

I first read him in high school, but find myself returning to his work now and then in later years because, even today, he instills in me that same awe and fear; but now I read him with a new admiration. He did what he did better than anyone then or since and I think writers in the field today—whether they think so or not—can learn a lot by enjoying his work over and over again.

WILL
Graham Masterton

Holman sounded uncharacteristically excited on the phone, almost hysterical. "Dan, get down here," he said. "We've dug up something terrible."

"Terrible?" Dan queried. He was trying to sort his way through four hundred black-and-white photographs, and his desk was so heaped up with them that he had lost his mug of coffee. Dan didn't work well without coffee. Instant, espresso, mocha, arabica, it didn't matter. All he needed was that sharp jolt of caffeine to get him started.

Holman said, "Rita came across it this morning, about twenty yards away from the east wall. I can't tell you anything else; not over the blower."

"Holman," Dan told him, "I'm far too busy to come over now. I have to have these goddamned preliminary site photographs ready for the goddamned Department of the Environment by nine o'clock tomorrow morning. So far they all look like mud, mud and more mud."

"Dan, you'll have to come over," Holman urged him.

"You mean it's so terrible that it can't wait until tomorrow afternoon."

"Dan, believe me, it's terrible. It could hold us up for months, especially if the police want to investigate. And you know what the hell *they're* like, trampling all over the shop in their size twelves."

Dan found his coffee, in a red mug with the slogan *I Dig Archeology* printed on it. The corner of one of the photographs had fallen into it, and it was scummy and cold. He drank it all the same.

"Holman," he said, wiping his mouth with the back of his hand, "I simply can't make it."

"It's a body," said Holman.

The rain had eased off less than an hour before, and the greasy blue-gray clay was slick and shining under the soles of his green Harrods wellies. A watery sun floated over Southwark, glancing occasionally off gray-slated Victorian rooftops or distant sash windows; or the wide green curve of the Thames. There was a smell of impending winter in the air, a sore-throaty rawness that Dan had forgotten from his last excavation in England. In San Antonio, it was easy to forget that something called cold had ever existed.

Holman was standing on the far side of the low east wall, next to a makeshift screen made of canvas and old front doors. He was very tall and stooped in his mud-spattered duffle coat, with loose horn-rimmed glasses which he constantly pushed back onto his fleshy nose. He was trying to grow a beard, not very successfully. It wouldn't have been hard to mistake him for one of those ferret-eyed men who spend their nights in cardboard boxes, rather than Manchester University's most admired excavator of difficult historical sites. By comparison, Dan was shorter, but much more athletically built, with the kind of wavy-haired leonine looks that reminded women of Richard Burton. He was always dressed casually but expensively. Holman called him Dapper Dan the Sartorial Archeologist.

He reached out a long arm as Dan approached, and shook his hand. "There he is," he announced, without any further preliminaries. "The man who never left the theater."

Dan drew aside the canvas, and saw a mud-gray figure lying on its left side in the mud; a small bald monkey of a man with his legs drawn up into the fetal position. He appeared to have been wearing doublet and hose when he died, although his clothes were less well preserved than his skin, and they were so stained with mud that it was impossible to tell what color they might have been.

Watched closely by Holman, Dan leaned over the body and examined it with care. A thin-faced man, with a few wisps remaining of a pointed goatee, and lips drawn back in a hideously tight grimace, exposing broken and rotted teeth. His eyes were as milky as a boiled cod's.

"How long ago did he die?" asked Dan.

Holman shrugged. "Difficult to say. He's like the bog people they found in Jutland and Schleswig-Holstein, perfectly preserved by the clay. The bog people were carbon-dated as being anywhere between sixteen hundred and two thousand years old. But obviously *this* fellow isn't anything like as old as that."

Dan hunkered down beside the shining gray body and stared into the face. "He looks as if he could've died yesterday, doesn't he? Did you call the police, just in case?"

Holman shook his head.

"Well, you have to," Dan insisted. He stood up. "This is probably exactly what it looks like, which is a mummified Jacobean. But you never know. Somebody might have been devious enough to murder his wife's lover, dress him up in a rented costume, and bury him right here, on the site of the Globe Theatre, where everybody would *think* he was Jacobean."

"That, Dan, with all due respect, is about the most far-fetched theory I have ever heard in my life," Holman replied. "Apart from which, the clay around the body was compacted hard, exactly like the clay around the remains of the theater walls. If it had been buried recently, the disturbance in the clay would have been quite obvious."

He held up a small age-darkened piece of wood. "Look what we found tied around his neck. An actor's gag. The piece of wood they put in their mouth to exercise their tongues. That's where we got the phrase 'telling gags' from. Definitely Jacobean."

"We still have to call the police. It's the law."

"Very well," Holman agreed, impatiently, flapping his arms. "But can we delay it please for forty-eight hours? In fact, can we not tell *anyone* about it for forty-eight hours? I just want to carry out some preliminary tests without hundreds of sight-seers. I want to be alone with him."

Holman stood up straight and looked around the muddy sun-glistening trenches, and then back down at the body. "Do you realize, Dan, this man probably witnessed a live performance of a play by William Shakespeare? One morning in the early 1600s he dressed in these clothes and left his house and went to the Globe, and died there. Maybe he was caught in the fire in 1613, when the Globe burned down."

"Well, let's hope so," Dan remarked. "The last thing we want right now is a full-scale murder inquiry, right in the middle of the dig. It's going to be bad enough when the Press get to hear about this anyway."

They were still talking when a girl of about twenty came walking towards them across the site. She wore a yellow safety helmet and a ballooning green anorak. A long wisp of blonde hair curled down one side of her face. She was hardly more than five-foot-three, and exceptionally pretty in a dolly-eyed snub-nosed way. But apart from the fact that she was an excellent archeologist, which both men respected, she was seriously engaged to a broad-shouldered professional tennis-player called Roger, and Roger combined a short temper with a ferociously jealous nature, so most of her fellow archeologists kept well away.

"Hallo, Dr. Essex," she said, as she approached. "What do you think of him? I've decided to call him Timon. Just like *Timon of Athens,* you see, Shakespeare's worst play— he died a death."

"How're you doing, Rita?" Dan asked her. "Congratulations. This is quite some find, if he's the genuine article."

"Well, of *course* he's the genuine article," said Rita, kneeling in the mud beside him. "He must have been trapped in some kind of cellar, poor man. I found him underneath all of that solid oak boarding. We had to use the JCB to lift it off."

She meticulously brushed more clay away from Timon's chest. "I want to get him out of here as quickly as possible, and into a controlled environment. There's no telling what might happen to him once he's exposed to the air. We could lose him in two or three days, maybe sooner. Look at these buttons he's wearing! Beautiful, mother-of-pearl, all hand-carved."

"This is really something, you know, Dan," said Holman. "This is history, right before your very eyes."

Dan lifted his hands in surrender. "All right. You've got your extra time. I'll have a word with Dunstan & Malling, too, to see if they can beef up their security. Of course I won't tell them why." Dunstan & Malling were the property developers who had first revealed the ruins of Shakespeare's seventeenth-century Globe Theatre, three days after they had begun to excavate the foundations for a twenty-two-story headquarters, Globe House. Publicly, their directors had talked about "protecting England's cultural heritage." Privately, they had been infuriated by the delay while Dan and his team had been called in by the Department of the Environment to excavate the site, and to suggest feasible ways of preserving it as a tourist attraction.

Buttoning up his coat against the wind, Dan turned to go. As he did so, however, Rita called out, "Wait, Dan! Look!"

Dan found dead bodies particularly unappealing, even three-hundred-year-old dead bodies whom he didn't know. But he turned and came back to the canvas screen where Rita was working.

"Look," said Rita. "He wasn't killed in a fire, or anything like that. Look at his chest."

She had turned him over slightly so he was staring sightlessly but accusingly over her right shoulder. Then she stepped away, and stood up, so that Dan could see the enormity of what had happened to Timon for himself. From his groin to his breastbone, the left side of his body had been torn right open, as if a huge and maddened beast had attacked him. His body cavity was filled with wet clay, but it was still possible to see that most of his internal organs must have been ripped out of him.

"Jesus," said Dan, and approached Timon with awe. "What the hell could have happened to him?"

"I don't know. Maybe he was impaled by a piece of falling timber, when the theatre burned down," Holman suggested.

"It looks more like he was attacked by a wild animal," Dan remarked.

"Maybe he was attacked by a bear," said Rita. "They used to bring in bears sometimes, to entertain the audience. If there was a fire, the bear could have gone berserk."

"That's a bit over-inventive," said Holman.

"I don't know," said Dan. "I don't care for this at all. It definitely looks to me like something *bit* him, something very big and something very mean. Look at the way his shirt's been ripped. A bear didn't do that. A bear plays with you, claws at you. Whatever did this, it took one long look and then it went *nyyunngg!*"

"*Nyyunngg?*" queried Holman. "What on earth did they have in Jacobean London that could have gone *nyyunngg!*"

"Well . . . maybe that's a little too fanciful," Dan agreed. "But maybe I could check up on the day the Globe burned down, and see if there's any contemporary mention of casualties, and how they died."

Holman clapped him on the back. "Good luck, then,"

he said. "And . . . well, thanks for the extra time. I know it isn't all that easy, with the Government and the developers and the Press all climbing all over you. Not to mention Rita and me."

Dan wiped his nose. "Deal with our friend here as quick as you can, okay?"

Holman took a long look at the greasy gray remains of the man called Timon. "If all goes well, Dan, this chappie's going to make us famous. The Essex-Holman Man. But before anybody else gets their sticky fingers on him, I want to do my best to find out who he was, and how he died."

"I wish I could give you longer," said Dan.

"That's okay. I'll stay here all night; and all tomorrow night, too, if I need to."

"Christ, you'll get cold."

"I'm used to the cold. I was brought up in Yorkshire, remember."

Dan checked his watch. He had a lunch date with Fiona Blessing, the triangular-shaped power-dressed lady executive from British Fuels, who were interested in financing something cultural with a capital "C" and tax-deductible with a capital "T." Then he had to take the bus to Chiswick to pick up his Renault, which was being repaired for the third time this year. He would have liked to have stayed and watched Rita painstakingly excavating Timon from the mud. But he had to keep this dig going in any way he could, especially with funds so low and the developers hovering over his head like a giant black anvil out of "Roadrunner." He shook Holman's hand, waved to Rita, and returned to the taxi that was waiting for him.

The cab driver said, "What's that, then? Looks like a bleeding graveyard."

"A dig," Dan replied, patiently. "An archeological dig. By the time we're finished, we should have a pretty clear idea of what the Globe Theatre looked like."

"Oh, yeah?" asked the cab driver, as they jostled through the lunchtime traffic. "What you want to know that for, then?"

For the first time, Dan couldn't think what to say. Maybe there was no reason. Maybe he was searching for nothing more than the living proof that the past really existed; and that men knew things then which they will never know again, not unless they seek them out.

He couldn't sleep. He kept dreaming that he was lying on his side in gray shining mud. He was cold, but he couldn't think how to get warm again, and somebody kept calling his name.

He sat up and switched on the bedside light. As usual, the other side of the bed was empty. Margaret hadn't wanted to join him in London, she hated London. He didn't really blame her. At this time of the year it was damp and expensive and derelict, the dark capital of a grim, worn-out culture. Everywhere he walked, there were black bronze statues of stern, eccentric and long-dead men.

He read for a while, from some of the books that he had been able to find in the Kensington Library. *Shakespeare's Life And Art* by P. Alexander; *Shakespeare at the Globe* by Nigel Frost; and a fascinating monograph called *The Sharer* by Dudley Manfield. By 1598, when the new Globe Theatre had been built, Shakespeare had already become one of the most prosperous actor-playwrights in the country, and he was one of the theatre's "sharers" or shareholders.

There was something about Manfield's account that Dan found strange and intriguing. It referred again and again to Shakespeare's twin children, Hamnet and Judith, and how Hamnet had died in 1596 at the age of 11, a tragedy which Shakespeare had called "my Payment." At the same time, Manfield frequently referred to "Shakespeare's Debt," as if Shakespeare had somehow made a promise to somebody, or borrowed money from them. One passage from the diary of a fellow actor at the Globe Theatre, Ben Fielding, made repeated mention of it.

In this ye sommer of 1611 we perform'd for the firste time The Tempeste which drama

Will declar'd to me was the nearest he dar'd
to speak of the Great Olde One to whom he
had made his Pledge. He said it was a Debt
which No Man could honour & that he
woulde have given all his wealthe never to
have made it. For the time cometh alwayes
when a Debt must be redemed.

So it appeared that for some reason, Shakespeare had
entered into a binding commitment with "the Great Olde
One," whoever that was. Dan got out of bed and went
through to his living room to find his paperback collection of Shakespeare's plays. He leafed through to *The Tem-
pest,* and read passages from it at random, but he could
find no indication of what Shakespeare might have been
trying to say about his Debt.

One phrase did catch his eyes, however. *"He that dies
pays all debts."*

He returned to Manfield's book. By 1613, the year that
the Globe burned down, Shakespeare had retired almost
permanently to his house in Stratford. But Ben Fielding
had written,

Will confided in me then that his Debt had
given him no peace; and that it must at last
be settl'd by Hee himselfe, whate'er the
coste. He must needs return to Southwarke
there to face his Tormentor & to make his
peace. All of which he spake he also writ,
and lodged with John Heminge.

That was the last entry in Ben Fielding's diary. According to Manfield, Fielding had disappeared on the night that
the Globe caught fire, and had been presumed burned.

Dan read and reread Fielding's words, and then
switched the light off again and tried to sleep. But all the
time he had the strangest feeling that something was

badly wrong; as if the world had silently decided to start turning backwards.

He arrived at the Globe site a few minutes after seven the next morning. It was cold and foggy but the rain had stayed away. He unlocked the gates and plodded across the clay to Holman's site hut, his hands thrust into his coat pockets.

Unusually, there was no smoke pouring from the hut's tin chimney. At this time of the morning, Holman was usually brewing up tea and cooking his breakfast. Even more unusually, the site hut door was ajar. Dan climbed the gritty wooden steps and put his head around it.

"Holman?" he called. "Holman? Are you there?"

The inside of the hut was chilly and dark. Holman's untidy cot was empty; site drawings and blueprints rustled on the notice board like the whispering of mourners in a shadowy chapel. The stove was cold, the kettle lidless and unfilled.

"Holman?" Dan repeated.

He left the hut and made his way across the muddy site toward the screen of canvas and old doors where the body had been found. Maybe Holman had decided to make an especially early start, and have his breakfast later. A fine drizzle was falling across Southwark, and a barge hooted dolefully on the river.

He shifted aside one of the old front doors. "Holman?" he called; and then he saw why Holman hadn't replied; and he stopped where he was, breathing in quick, shallow gasps, as if he had been running. At first, he could scarcely understand what he was looking at, but gradually the intricate loops and tangles of scarlet and gray became clear. His throat tightened, and his mouth suddenly filled with bile and tepid coffee.

Holman had somehow been torn apart; ripped to pieces and dragged around the site in long strings of entrails and glistening muscle. His ribcage lay on the far side of the excavation like the parts of an abandoned car. Part of his flattened face stared up from the mud close to Dan's right foot. One eye, half a blood-clotted beard, no jaw. His spectacles lay nearby, both lenses blinded with sticky blood.

Shaking with cold and fear, Dan crossed to the center of the site where Rita had discovered the mummified body. It was still there, but it had been thrown to one side, and one of its legs was sticking out from underneath it at an impossible angle. Next to it, the clay looked as if it had been churned up by their mechanical digger. God knows what had happened here. Holman would never have done anything like this, not to such an important archeological find. And what had happened to Holman?

Dan sniffed the morning air. Sharp and cold as glass paper. And there was a smell to it, too, which wasn't just the smell of a ripped-apart human body. It was a musty, fetid smell; like a roomful of hymnbooks which has been closed for too long. A closed smell. An airless smell. An *old* smell.

Dan circled the muddy site with legs that felt like lead and didn't know what to do. He stood still for a while, with his hand pressed over his mouth, trying to decide if he needed to vomit. But it was then that he heard a whimpering noise, like a run-over cat. He frowned, turned; and for the first time saw Rita crouched behind one of the doors. She was smothered in clay from head to foot, and her eyes were bloodshot and staring.

He knelt down beside her and took hold of her clay-slimy hand.

"Rita? Rita, it's Dan."

She stared at him wildly. She was shuddering all over, and she kept jerking and nodding her head like a mad-woman.

"Rita, for God's sake what happened?"

"It came out," she whispered, through mud-gray lips. "We turned him over; and the ground looked as if it was boiling. *And it came out!*"

"What came out? Rita, what was it?"

She shook her head furiously from side to side. "There was a wind . . . a wind that came *downwards.* And then the ground was boiling. And then Holman was screaming because it was black with tentacles and it kept changing shape and it tore him to pieces."

Dan held her close while she shuddered and rocked and shook her head. At last he wiped the grit from her forehead and said, "It's all right. It's all right now. I'll call for an ambulance."

He went to visit her two weeks later. She was staying at Ettington Park, a huge Gothic hotel of cream and gray stone, set deep in the Warwickshire countryside just south of Stratford-on-Avon, amongst rook-clotted elms, beside a slow-moving river.

They walked through the grounds and the cold afternoon was quite silent except for the occasional cawing of rooks. She said, "What are they going to do about the dig?"

Dan lit a cigarette and blew out smoke. "The plan so far is to fill it with sharp sand, to preserve what we've excavated already, then build the office block's foundations on top of it. Nobody will get to see it again till they knock their damned office block down."

Rita said, "It's nice here. Really quiet. They've got a library and lots of open fires and an indoor swimming pool."

"Have you managed to remember what happened?" Dan asked her; watching her closely.

She looked away, her eyes stony. "Only what I told you. The wind came down and the ground boiled and out it came. The police said it was probably an explosion of marsh-gas; some freaky accident like that. Will-o'-the-wisp to the nth power."

Dan took hold of her hand, and squeezed it. "Be lucky," he told her, and left.

Under a dour sky he drove to Stratford-on-Avon and visited the Shakespeare Library next to the Memorial Theatre. For the rest of the afternoon he sat at a small desk in the corner, under a window, not reading the works of Shakespeare, but of Shakespeare's fellow player at the

Globe Theatre, John Heminge, who had helped to compile the First Folio of Shakespeare's works.

It was almost dark when he found the letter, and the library's fluorescent lights were flickering on. He found it almost as if it had been waiting for him, bound into a volume of John Heminge's diaries. Part of it was illegible; and nobody who hadn't seen Holman's body would have understood what it really meant, or have realized that Shakespeare himself had written it. It was dated 1613, three years before Shakespeare's death, and ten years before Heminge had put together the first collection of Shakespeare's works.

&, John, this is an errand from which I shall never return. I offered him my life in return for my success; but never did I think that he would demand my poor child's life. I realize now that such an arrangement was not mine to make, nor any man's. Only God can decide one's fortune, not this creature from times when God was not, & places where God had no dominion. I have enjoyed my good fortune, but I have grieved much, and now the price must be paid. Poor Hamnet, please forgive me.

Be warned, John, of the Great Old Ones, who came from Outside. They have the power to give all that a man could desire; and the power to exact a punishment beyond all reason. Be warned most of all of Y'g Southothe, who came from beyond the very bounds of space and time, but who dwells now beneath the cellars of the Globe.

The Globe was built in such a shape in order to give him a Hiding-Place; so now must the Globe be razed; and the cellars fill'd & boarded; and I with them; in order that Hamnet may live again.

Later that evening, Dan went for a long walk beside the Avon; finally arriving beside the memorial statue of the Bard. The sodium streetlights were strident and orange; they made the statue look as if it had been cast out of some strangely unearthly metal. Dan was beginning to form an idea about what had happened, although he couldn't completely understand it. From his letter to John Heminge, it seemed as if Shakespeare had achieved his huge success as a playwright by striking a bargain with "Y'g Southothe," which was some kind of primeval life-force *"from a time when God was not."* Dan could only guess that this life-force had for some reason demanded Hamnet's life. Perhaps as insurance? Perhaps to force Shakespeare to build him a "Hiding-Place" on earth, by demolishing the old theatre and building the Globe on the same site?

Nobody would ever know what had really happened. But from the letter he had written to John Heminge, it appeared that in 1613 Shakespeare had been able to bear the guilt of Hamnet's death no longer, and had traveled to London to burn down the Globe, and to destroy this "Y'g Southothe" for ever.

There had been one clue which had survived down all these centuries. In Shakespeare's letter, he had concluded,

> I shall carry with me the gag that Hamnet
> gave me when he was just ten years old—
> the gag which he had whittled himself, and
> which I could never use because of its dis-
> comfort. It shall be the token of my craft
> and the token of my love for the son which
> I have loste.

Dan returned to London early the following morning. The archeological dig was foggy and abandoned. Strings of red warning pennants hung in the airless chill, and there were Metropolitan Police signs everywhere, warning Danger: Inflammable Gas.

He climbed awkwardly across the muddy ruts and

jumped over the half-finished trenches. The body had been covered by an aluminum-framed tent of heavy-duty builder's polythene, and a full-time security guard now occupied Holman's hut. He waved to Dan from the front steps as he emptied a potful of used teabags on to the clay. "Morning, Mr. Essex! Brass monkeys this morning, ain't it?"

Dan lifted aside the fog-moistened polythene. The gray mummified body was lying where it had been flung on the night that Holman had died: untouched, but much more sunken-looking now. Nobody had been able to decided who it belonged to; or who it was; or whether it should be touched at all.

Dan stood looking at the body for a long time, smoking. Then he knelt closer, and said, "Will Shakespeare. In the flesh. So who's that buried in the chancel of the Holy Trinity, at Stratford, next to Anne Hathaway?"

The mummified face grinned sightlessly back at him. Now that he was sure who he was, Dan could see the strong resemblance to Martin Droeshout's portrait in the First Folio. He reached out and touched the bald domed forehead, beneath which there had once been the brain which had created Macbeth and Hamlet and Othello.

"He that dies pays all debts."

Dan felt the ground shudder and churn. There was a slow sucking noise, like thick cement being drawn down a metal chute. He hesitated; but then he smelled that decayed-hymnbook smell, that *old* smell; and he backed out of the tent and across the site, to the corner where the bright yellow mechanical digger was parked.

He managed to start the JCB after three tries. The engine bellowed, black diesel smoke blurted into the morning air. Then, steering with jerky, awkward movements, he maneuvered it over to the polythene-covered tent.

The security guard, his hands in his pockets, came out to watch. Dan gave him a salute and he saluted back. *Poor sucker,* thought Dan. *Wait till he sees what I'm going to do.*

Dan lowered the vehicle's shovel-blade, and began to

drive it slowly forward, scraping up huge carpet-like lumps of solid gray clay as well as timber shoring and tools and old doors and debris. He forced the whole shovelful into the tent, which immediately collapsed. Then he backed up and dug up even more mud.

He thought for a moment that he might have gotten away with it—that he might have reburied Y'g Southothe without any more trouble. But as he was backing up the JCB for a third time, the mud suddenly erupted and splattered the vehicle's windshield like black blood.

Dan wrestled with the digger's gears. But then the engine stalled, and there was nothing he could do but to watch the ground boil up in front of him a huge thrashing mountain of liquefied clay.

Timber and tools were hurtled in all directions. A blizzard of debris clattered against the digger's cab.

Then the mud itself opened up like a grisly maw, turning faster and deeper. Dan smelled a sickening cold slaughterhouse smell, a smell which came from somewhere *outside* of the world, rather than within it. And out of the mud, brighter than the sun, rose globe after globe of shuddering light—globes which broke apart and disgorged a glistening black tentacled protoplasm. *Y'g Southothe, the Elder God, from a time so far back that it was unimaginable; the lord of the primal slime.*

He didn't hear himself screaming. All he heard was the bellowing of the JCB's restarted diesel, and the protesting whinny of its transmission. Then he was forcing heaps of raw clay into the open maw, and backing up, and pushing in more clay, while the site glittered and shuddered with the awful power of Y'g Southothe.

A devastating explosion split the morning air. A crack that was felt as far away as Croydon, seventeen miles away. A feeling that the very substance of the world had broken; which it had.

The security guard saw the JCB dissolve into dazzling white light; and then the site was empty; and there was nobody there. No light, no shuddering globes. Only the fog and the flags and the mournful unseen barges on the early-morning Thames.

It was almost a month before Rita received the scribbled notes that Dan had sent her. She had left Ettington Park and gone to stay with her parents in Wiltshire. Most of the notes she couldn't understand. But the very last note, torn from a springback reporter's notebook, had a terrible logic that almost turned her senses.

> I am sure now that Y'g Southothe forced Shakespeare to build the Globe Theatre by taking his son Hamnet; and that it hid there and dominated life in Jacobean London for years. I am also convinced that Shakespeare burned down the Globe himself; losing his own life but releasing Hamnet at last from Y'g Southothe. The man who tried to write Shakespeare's last play, *The Two Noble Kinsmen,* was not Shakespeare himself but his son Hamnet, reincarnated, or released, whichever you can believe most easily. According to contemporary records, Hamnet 'had the looke of his Parente,' and after fifteen years in the guardianship of this Y'g Southothe he probably looked almost as old. I am convinced that this is the truth of what happened to Shakespeare. Remember that "Will Shakespeare" couldn't finish *The Two Noble Kinsmen* and that it was necessary for John Fletcher to write Acts II, III and IV.
>
> I don't yet understand what this Y'g Southothe actually is; but what it did to Holman shows that it is infinitely dangerous. It was I who initiated the project which led to its being dug up. It is up to me to bury it again. I am sending you these notes in the unlikely event of something going wrong.

Three days later, Rita drove to Stratford-on-Avon in her father's car, and laid a small old-fashioned posy on the tomb in the Holy Trinity which was supposed to contain the remains of Will Shakespeare. The message on the posy read, "For Hamnet; At Long Last; From the Father Who Loved You More Than Life."

Afterword

I first borrowed from the demonology of H.P. Lovecraft in 1975, when I wrote *The Manitou*. I was writing an exclusively American horror novel, based on the conflict of America's past culture with its present technology. Therefore Satan and Baal and all the rest of the European demons were really no good to me. I wanted to refer to an ancient evil with which readers would already be familiar, yet which was exclusively American.

Cthulthu and Yog-Sothoth came to the rescue. They came from primal times, reconjured in that "strange, lonely Dunwich country" north of Arkham. Most importantly, the great majority of horror enthusiasts had already heard about them, and were prepared to shudder just at the mention of their names. On and off I have been weaving occasional references to H.P. Lovecraft's Elder Gods into my horror novels ever since.

For me, H.P. Lovecraft's achievement was to create a genuinely frightening atmosphere of ancient dread—a dread that was reinforced by the documentary way in which his protagonists gradually learned of the Elder Gods' terrifying existence. This tale—*Will*—my personal tribute to H.P. Lovecraft, was inspired by the recent unearthing in London of the Rose and Globe theatres.

Almost all of the facts in *Will* are true. Only H.P. Lovecraft will be able to tell you which of the references have been invented . . . and by then, of course, it will be too late.

BIG "C"
Brian Lumley

Two thousand thirteen and the exploration of space—
by men, not robot spaceships—was well underway. Men
had built Moonbase, landed on Mars, were now looking
towards Titan, though that was still some way ahead. But
then, from a Darkside observatory, Luna II was discovered
half a million miles out: a black rock two hundred yards
long and eighty through, tumbling dizzily end over end
around the Earth, too small to occlude stars for more than
a blip, too dark to have been (previously) anything but
the tiniest sunspot on the surface of Sol. But interesting
anyway "because it was there," and also and especially
because on those rare occasions when it lined itself up
with the full moon, that would be when Earth's lunatics
gave full vent. Lunatics of all persuasions, whether they
were in madhouses or White Houses, asylums or the
army, refuges or radiation shelters, surgeries or silos.

Men had known for a long time that the moon controlled the tides—and possibly the fluids in men's brains?—and it was interesting now to note that Luna II appeared to compound the offence. It seemed reasonable to suppose that we had finally discovered the reason for Man's homicidal tendencies, his immemorial hostility to Man.

Two thousand fifteen and a joint mission—American, Russian, British—went to take a look; they circled Luna II at a "safe" distance for twelve hours, took pictures, made recordings, measured radiation levels. When they came back, within a month of their return, one of the two Americans (the most outspoken one) went mad, one of the two Russians (the introverted one) set fire to himself, and the two British members remained phlegmatic, naturally.

One year later in August 2016, an Anglo-French expedition set out to double-check the findings of the first mission: i.e., to see if there were indeed "peculiar radiations" being emitted by Luna II. It was a four-man team; they were all volunteers and wore lead baffles of various thicknesses in their helmets. And afterwards, the ones with the least lead were discovered to be more prone to mental fluctuations. But . . . the "radiations," or whatever, couldn't be measured by any of Man's instruments. What was required was a special sort of volunteer, someone actually to land on Luna II and dig around a little, and do some work right there on top of—whatever it was.

Where to land wasn't a problem: With a rotation period of one minute, Luna II's equatorial tips were moving about as fast as a man could run, but at its "poles" the planetoid was turning in a very gentle circle. And that's where Benjamin "Smiler" Williams set down. He had wanted to do the job and was the obvious choice. He was a Brit riding an American rocket paid for by the French and Russians. (Everybody had wanted to be in on it.) And of course he was a hero. And he was dying of cancer.

Smiler drilled holes in Luna II, set off small explosions in the holes, collected dust and debris and exhaust gasses

from the explosions, slid his baffles aside and exposed his
brain to whatever, walked around quite a bit and sat
down and thought things, and sometimes just sat. And all
in all he was there long enough to see the Earth turn one
complete circle on her axis—following which he went
home. First to Moonbase, finally to Earth. Went home to
die—after they'd checked him out, of course.

But that was six years ago and he still hadn't died
(though God knows we'd tried the best we could to kill
him) and now I was on my way to pay him a visit. On my
way through him, travelling into him, journeying to his
very heart. The heart and mind—the living, thinking or-
ganism, the control center, as it were—deep within the
body of what the world now called Big "C."

July 2024, and Smiler Williams had asked for a visitor. I
was it, and as I drove in I went over everything that had
led up to this moment. It was as good a way as any to
keep from looking at the "landscape" outside the car. This
was Florida and it was the middle of the month, but I
wasn't using the air-conditioning and in fact I'd even
turned up the heater a little—because it was cool out
there. As cool as driving down a country lane in Devon,
with the trees arching their green canopy overhead. Except it wasn't Devon and they weren't green. And in fact
they weren't even trees. . . .

Those were thoughts I should try to avoid, however,
just as I avoided looking at anything except the road unwinding under the wheels of my car; and so I went back
again to 2016, when Ben Williams came back from space.

The specialists in London checked Smiler out—his
brain, mostly, for they weren't really interested in his cancer. That was right through him, (with the possible exception of his grey matter), and there was no hope. Try to
cut or laser *that* out of him and there'd be precious little
of the man himself left! But after ten days of tests they'd
found nothing, and Smiler was getting restless.

"Peter," he said to me, "I'm short on time and these
monkeys are wasting what little I've got left! Can't you get
me out of here? There are places I want to go, friends I

want to say goodbye to." But if I make that sound sad or melodramatic, forget it. Smiler wasn't like that. He'd really *earned* his nickname, that good old boy, because right through everything he'd kept on smiling like it was painted on his face. Maybe it was his way to keep from crying. Twenty-seven years old just a month ago, and he'd never make twenty-eight. So we'd all reckoned.

Myself, I'd never made it through training, but Smiler had and we'd kept in touch. But just because I couldn't go into space didn't mean I couldn't help others to do it. I'd worked at NASA, and on the European Space Programme (ESP), even for a while for the Soviets at Baikonur, when *détente* had been peaking a periodic upsurge back in 2009 and 2010. So I knew my stuff. And I knew the men who were doing it, landing on Mars and what have you, and the heroes like Smiler Williams. So while Smiler was moderately cool toward the others on the space medicine team—the Frogs, Sovs and even the other Americans—to me he was the same as always. We'd been friends and Smiler had never let down a friend in his life.

And when he'd asked for my help in getting him out of that place, I'd had to go along with him. "Sure, why not?" I'd told him. "Maybe I can speed it up. Have you seen the new Space Center at the Lake? There are a lot of people you used to know there. NASA people. They'd love to see you again, Smiler."

What I didn't say was that the Space Center at Lake Okeechobee also housed the finest space medicine team in the world, and that they were longing to get their hands on him. But he was dying and a Brit, and so the British had first claim, so to speak. No one was going to argue the pros and cons about a man on his last legs. And if that makes me sound bad—like maybe I'd gone over to London to snatch him for the home team—I'd better add that there was something else I hadn't mentioned to him: the Center Research Foundation at Lakeport, right next door. I wanted to wheel him in there so they could take a look at him. Oh, he was a no-hoper, like I've said, but . . .

And maybe he hadn't quite given up hope himself, either, because when they were finally through with him a few days later he'd agreed to come back here with me. "What the hell," he'd shrugged. "They have their rocks, dust, gasses, don't they? Also, they have lots of time. Me, I have to use mine pretty sparingly." It was starting to get to him.

In the States Smiler got a hero's welcome, met everybody who was anybody from the President down. But that was time-consuming stuff, so after a few days we moved on down to Florida. First things first: I told him about the Foundation at Lakeport. "So what's new?" he laughed. "Why'd you think I came with you, Yank?"

They checked him over, smiled and joked with him (which was the only way to play it with Smiler) but right up front shook their heads and told him no, there was nothing they could do. And time was narrowing down.

But it was running out for me, too; and that's where I had to switch my memories off and come back to the present a while, for I'd reached the first checkpoint. I was driving up from Immokalee, Big "C" Control ("control," that's a laugh!) Point Seven, to see Smiler at Lakeport. The barrier was at the La Belle–Clewiston crossroads, and Smiler came up on the air just as I saw it up ahead and started to slow her down a little.

"You're two minutes early, Peter," his voice crackled out of the radio at me. "Try to get it right from here on in, OK? Big 'C' said ten-thirty A.M. at the La Belle–Clewiston crossroads, and he didn't mean ten-twenty-eight. You don't gain anything by being early: he'll only hold you up down there two minutes longer to put you back on schedule. Do you read me, old friend?"

"I read you, buddy," I answered, slowing to a halt at the barrier's massive red-and-white-striped pole where it cut the road in half. "Sorry, I'm early; I guess it's nerves; must have put my foot down a little. Anyway, what's a couple minutes between friends, eh?"

"Between you and me? Nothing!" Smiler's voice came back—and with a chuckle in it! I thought: *God, that's courage for you!* "But Big 'C' likes accuracy, dead reckoning," he continued. "And come to think of it, so do I! Hell, you wouldn't try to find me a re-entry window a couple of minutes ahead of time, would you? No you wouldn't." And then, more quietly: "And remember, Peter, a man can get burned just as easily in here. . . ." But this time there was no chuckle.

"What now?" I sat still, staring straight ahead, aware that the—tunnel?—was closing overhead, that the light was going as Big "C" enclosed me.

"Out," he answered at once, "so he can take a good look at the car. You know he's not much for trusting people, Peter."

I froze, and remained sitting there as rigid as . . . as the great steel barrier pole right there in front of me. Get out? Big "C" wanted me to get out? But the car was my womb and I wasn't programmed to be born yet, not until I got to Smiler. And—

"Out!" Smiler's voice crackled on the air. "He says you're not moving and it bothers him. So get out now—or would you rather sit tight and have him come in there with you? How do you think you'd like that, Peter: having Big 'C' groping around in there with you?"

I unfroze, opened the car door. But where was I supposed to—?

"The checkpoint shack," Smiler told me, as if reading my mind. "There's nothing of him in there."

Thank God for that!

I left the car door open—to appease Big "C"? To facilitate his search? To make up for earlier inadequacies? Don't ask me—and hurried in the deepening gloom to the wooden, chalet-style building at the side of the road. It had been built there maybe four years ago when Big "C" wasn't so big, but no one had used it in a long time and the door was stuck; I could get the bottom of the door to give a little by leaning my thigh against it, but the top was jammed tight. And somehow I didn't like to make too much noise.

Standing there with the doorknob clenched tight in my hand, I steeled myself, glanced up at the ceiling being

formed of Big "C"'s substance—the moth-eaten holes
being bridged by doughy flaps, then sealed as the mass
thickened up, shutting out the light—and I thought of
myself as becoming a tiny shrivelled kernel in his gigantic,
leprous walnut. Christ . . . what a mercy I never suffered
from claustrophobia! But then I also thought: *to hell with
the noise,* and put my shoulder to the door to burst it
right in.

I left the door vibrating in its frame behind me and
went unsteadily, breathlessly, to the big windows. There
was a desk there, chairs, a few well-thumbed paperbacks,
a Daily Occurrence Book, telephone and scribble pad: everything a quarter-inch thick in dust. But I blew the dust
off one of the chairs and sat (which wasn't a bad idea, my
legs were shaking so bad), for now that I'd started in on
this thing I knew there'd be no stopping it, and what was
going on out there was all part of it. Smiler's knowledge
of cars hadn't been much to mention; I had to hope that
Big "C" was equally ignorant.

And so I sat there trembling by the big windows, looking out at the road and the barrier and the car, and I
suppose the idea was that I was going to watch Big "C"'s
inspection. I did actually watch the start of it—the tendrils of frothy slop elongating themselves downwards
from above and inwards from both sides, closing on the
car, entering it; a pseudopod of slime hardening into rubber, pulling loose the weather strip from the boot cover
and flattening itself to squeeze inside; another member
like a long, flat tapeworm sliding through the gap between
the hood and the radiator grille . . . but that was as much
as I could take and I turned my face away.

It's not so much how Big "C" looks but what he *is* that
does it. It's knowing, and yet not really knowing, what he
is. . . .

So I sweated it there and waited for it to get done, and
hoped and prayed that Big "C" *would* get done and not
find anything. And while I waited my mind went back
again to that time six years earlier.

The months went by and Smiler weakened a little. He

got to spending a lot of his time at Lakeport, which was fine by the space medics at the Lake because they could go and see him any time they wanted and carry on examining and testing him. And at the time I thought they'd actually found something they could do for him, because after a while he really did seem to be improving again. Meanwhile I had my own life to live; I hadn't seen as much of him as I might like; I'd been busy on the Saturn's Moons Project.

When I did get to see him almost a year had gone by and he should have been dead. But he wasn't anything like dead and the boys from Med. were excited about something—had been for months—and Smiler had asked to see me. I was briefed and they told me not to excite him a lot, just treat him like . . . normal? Now how the hell else would I treat him? I wondered.

It was summer and we met at Clewiston on the Lake, a beach where the sun sparkled on the water and leisure craft came and went, many of them towing their golden, waving water-skiers. Smiler arrived from Lakeport in an ambulance and the boys in white walked him slowly down to the table under a sun umbrella where I was waiting for him. And I saw how big he was under his robe.

I ordered a Coke for myself, and—"Four vodkas and a small tomato juice," Smiler told me! "An Anaemic Mary— in one big glass."

"Do you have a problem, buddy?" the words escaped me before I could check them.

"Are you kidding?" he said, frowning. But then he saw me ogling his huge drink and grinned. "Eh? The booze? Jesus, no! It's like rocket fuel to me—keeps me aloft and propels me around and around—but doesn't make me dizzy!" And then he was serious again. "A pity, really, 'cos there are times when I'd like to get blasted out of my mind."

"What?" I stared hard at him, wondered what was going on in his head. "Smiler, I—"

"Peter," he cut me short, "I'm not going to die—not just yet, anyway."

For a moment I couldn't take it in, couldn't believe it. I was *that* delighted. I knew my bottom jaw must have fallen open, so closed it again. "They've come up with something?" I finally blurted it out. "Smiler, you've done it—you've beaten the Big 'C'!"

But he wasn't laughing or even smiling, just sitting there looking at me.

He had been all dark and lean and muscular, Smiler, but was now pale and puffy. Puffy cheeks, puffy bags under his eyes, pale and puffy double chins. And bald (all that shining, jet-black hair gone) and minus his eyebrows: the effect of one treatment or another. His natural teeth were gone, too: calcium deficiency brought on by low grav during too many missions in the space stations, probably aggravated by his complaint. In fact his eyes were really the only things I'd know him by: film-star blue eyes, which had somehow retained their old twinkle.

Though right now, as I've said, he wasn't laughing or even smiling but just sitting there staring at me.

"Big 'C,'" he finally answered me. "Beaten the Big 'C' . . ."

And eventually the smile fell from my face, too. "But . . . isn't that what you meant?"

"Listen," he said, suddenly shifting to a higher gear, "I'm short of time. They're checking me over every couple of hours now, because they're expecting it to break loose . . . well, soon. And so they'll not be too long coming for me, wanting to take me back into that good old 'controlled environment,' you know? So now I want to tell you about it—the way I see it, anyway."

"Tell me about. . . ?"

"About Luna II. Peter, it was Luna II. It wasn't anything the people at Lakeport have done or the space medicine buffs from the Lake, it was just Luna II. There's something in Luna II that changes things. That's its nature: to change things. Sometimes the changes may be radical: it takes a sane man and makes him mad, or turns a peaceful race into a mindless gang of mass murderers, or changes a small planet into a chunk of shiny black slag that we've named Luna II. And sometimes it's sleeping or inert, and then there's no effect whatever."

I tried to take all of this in but it was coming too thick and fast. "Eh? Something in Luna II? But don't we already know about that? That it's a source of peculiar emanations or whatever?"

"Something like that." He shrugged helplessly, impatiently. "Maybe. I don't know. But when I was up there I felt it, and now it's starting to look like it felt me."

"It felt you?" Now he really *wasn't* making sense, had started to ramble.

"I don't know"—he shrugged again—"but it could be the answer to Everything—it could *be* Everything! Maybe there are lots of Luna IIs scattered through the universe, and they all have the power to change things. Like they're catalysts. They cause mutations—in space, in time. A couple of billion years ago the Earth felt it up there, felt its nearness, its effect. And it took this formless blob of mud hurtling through space and changed it, gave it life, brought micro-organisms awake in the soup of its oceans. It's been changing things ever since—and we've called *that* evolution! Do you see what I mean? It was The Beginning—and it might yet be The End."

"Smiler, I—"

He caught my arm, gave me what I suspect was the most serious look he'd ever given anyone in his entire life, and said: "Don't look at me like that, Peter." And there was just a hint of accusation.

"Was I?"

"Yes, you were!" And then he relaxed and laughed, and just as suddenly became excited. "Man, when something like this happens, you're bound to ask questions. So I've asked myself questions, and the things I've told you are the answers. Some of them, anyway. Hell, they may not even be right, but they're *my* answers!"

"These are your thoughts, then? Not the boffins'?" This was one of his Brit words I used, from the old days. It meant "experts."

"Mine," he said, seeming proud of it, "but grown at least in part from what the boffins have told me."

"So what *has* happened?" I asked him, feeling a little exasperated now. "What's going down, Smiler?"

"Not so much going down," he shook his head, "as coming out."

"Coming out?" I waited, not sure whether to smile or frown, not knowing what to do or say.

"Of me."

And still I waited. It was like a guessing game where I was supposed to come up with some sort of conclusion based on what he'd told me. But I didn't have any conclusions.

Finally he shrugged yet again, snorted, shook his head, and said: "But you do know about cancer, right? About the Big 'C'? Well, when I went up to Luna II, it changed my cancer. Oh, I still have it, but it's not the same any more. It's a separate thing existing in me, but no longer truly a part of me. It's in various cavities and tracts, all connected up by threads, living in me like a rat in a system of burrows. Or better, like a hermit crab in a pirated shell. But you know what happens when a hermit crab outgrows its shell? It moves out, finds itself a bigger home. So . . . this thing in me has tried to vacate—has experimented with the idea, anyway. . . ."

He shuddered, his whole body trembling like jelly.

"Experimented?" It was all I could find to say.

He gulped, nodded, controlled himself. And he sank what was left of his drink before going on. "In the night, a couple of nights ago, it started to eject—from both ends at once—from just about everywhere. Anus, throat, nostrils, you name it. I almost choked to death before they got to me. But by then it had already given up, re-treated, *retracted* itself. And I could breathe again. It was like it . . . like it hadn't wanted to kill me."

I was numb, dumb, couldn't say anything. The way Smiler told it, it was almost as if he'd credited his cancer with intelligence! But then a white movement caught my eye, and I saw with some relief that it was the boys from the ambulance coming for him. He saw them, too, and clutched my arm. And suddenly fear had made his eyes round in his round face. "Peter . . ." he said. "Peter . . ."

"It's OK," I grabbed his fist grabbing me. "It's all right. They have to know what they're doing. You said it yourself, remember? You're not going to die."

"I know, I know," he said. "But will it be worth living?"

And then they came and took him to the ambulance. And for a long time I wondered about that last thing he'd said. But of course in the end it turned out he was right. . . .

The car door slammed and the telephone rang at one and the same time, causing me to start. I looked out through the control shack's dusty window and saw Big "C" receding from the car. Apparently everything was OK. And when the telephone rang again I picked it up.

"OK, Peter," Smiler's voice seemed likewise relieved, "you can come on in now."

But as well as relieved I was also afraid. Now of all times—when it was inevitable—I was afraid. Afraid for the future the world might never have if I didn't go in, and for the future I certainly wouldn't have if I did. Until at last common sense prevailed: what the heck, I had no future anyway!

"Something wrong, old friend?" Smiler's voice was soft. "Hey, don't let it get to you. It will be just like the last time you visited me, remember?" His words were careful, innocent yet contrived. And they held a code.

I said "Sure," put the phone down, left the shack and went to the car. If he was ready for it then so was I. It was ominous out there, in Big "C"'s gloom; getting into the car was like entering the vacant lair of some weird, alien animal. The thing was no longer there, but I knew it had been there. It didn't smell, but I could smell and taste it anyway. You would think so, the way I avoided breathing.

And so my throat was dry and my chest was tight as I turned the lights on to drive. To drive through Big "C", to the core which was Ben "Smiler" Williams. And driving I thought:

I'm travelling down a hollow tentacle, proceeding along a pseudopod, venturing in an alien vein. And it can put a stop to me, kill me any time it wants to. By suffocation, strangulation, or simply by laying itself down on me and crushing me. But it won't because it needs Smiler, needs to appease him, and he has asked to see me.

As he'd said on the telephone, "Just like the last time." Except we both knew it wouldn't be like the last time. Not at all. . . .

The last time:

That had been fifteen months ago when we'd agreed on the boundaries. But to continue at that point would be to leave out what happened in between. And I needed to fill it in, if only to fix my mind on something and so occupy my time for the rest of the journey. It isn't good for your nerves, to drive down a mid-morning road in near darkness, through a tunnel of living, frothing, cancerous flesh.

A month after I'd seen Smiler on the beach, Big "C" broke out. Except that's not exactly how it was. I mean, it wasn't how you'd expect. What happened was this:

Back in 2002 when we went through a sticky patch with the USSR and there were several (as yet *still* unsolved) sabotage attempts on some of our missile and space research sites, a number of mobile ICBM and MIRV networks were quickly commissioned and established across the entire U.S.A. Most of these had been quietly decommissioned or mothballed only a year or two later, but not the one covering the Okeechobee region of Florida. That one still existed, with its principal base or railhead at La Belle and arms reaching out as far as Fort Myers in the west, Fort Drum north of the Lake, and Canal Point right on the Lake's eastern shore. Though still maintained in operational order as a deterrent, the rail network now carried ninety percent of hardware for the Space Center while its military functions were kept strictly low profile. Or they had been, until that night in late August 2024.

Smiler had a night nurse, but the first thing Big "C" did when he emerged was to kill him. That's what we later figured, anyway. The second thing that he did was derail a MIRV bogie on its way through Lakeport. I can't supply details; I only know he did it.

Normally this wouldn't matter much: seventy-five percent of the runs were dummies anyway. But this one was the real thing, one of the two or three times a year when the warheads were in position. And it looked like something had got broken in the derailment, because all of the alarms were going off at once!

The place was evacuated. Lakeport, Venus, Clewiston— all the towns around Lake Okeechobee—the whole shoot. Even the Okeechobee Space Center itself, though not in its entirety; a skeleton crew stayed on there; likewise at the La Belle silos. A decon team was made ready to go in and tidy things up . . . except that didn't happen. For through all of this activity, Smiler (or rather, Big "C") had somehow contrived to be forgotten and left behind. And what *did* happen was that Smiler got on the telephone to Okeechobee and told them to hold off. No one was to move. Nothing was to happen.

"You'd better listen and listen good," he'd said. "Big 'C' has six MIRVs, each one with eight bombs aboard. And he's got five of them lined up on Washington, London, Tokyo, Berlin and Moscow, though not necessarily in that order. That's forty nukes for five of the world's greatest capitals and major cities within radii of two hundred miles. That's a holocaust, a nuclear winter, the New Dark Age. As for the sixth MIRV: that one's airborne right now! But it won't hurt because he hasn't programmed detonation instructions. It's just a sign to let you all know that he's not kidding and can do what he says he can do."

The MIRV split up north of Jacksonville; bombs came down harmlessly in the sea off Wilmington, Cape Fear, Georgetown, Charleston, Savannah, Jacksonville, Cape Canaveral and Palm Beach. After that . . . while no one was quite sure just exactly who Big "C" was, certainly they all knew he had them by the short and curlies.

Of course, that was when the "news" broke about Smiler's cancer, the fact that it was different. And the cancer experts from the Lakeport Center, and the space medics, too, arrived at the same conclusion: that somehow alien "radiations" or emanations had changed Smiler's cancer into Big "C". The Lakeport doctors and scientists had intended that when it vacated Smiler they'd kill it, but now Big "C" was threatening to kill us, indeed the world. It was then that I remembered how Smiler had credited the thing with intelligence, and now it appeared he'd been right.

So . . . maybe the problem could have been cleared up right there and then. But at what cost? Big "C" had demonstrated that he knew his way around our weaponry, so if he was going to die why not take us with him? Nevertheless, it's a fact that there were some itchy fingers among the military brass right about that time.

Naturally, we had to let Moscow, London and all the other target areas in on it, and their reaction was about what was expected:

"For God's sake—placate the thing! Do as it tells you— *whatever* it tells you!" And the Sovs said: "If you let anything come out of Florida heading for Moscow, comrades, that's war!"

And then, of course, there was Smiler himself. Big "C" had Smiler in there—a hero, and one of the greatest of all time. So the hotheads cooled down pretty quickly, and for some little time there was a lot of hard, cold, calculated thinking going on as the odds were weighted. But always it came out in Big "C"'s favor. Oh, Smiler and his offspring were only a small percentage of life on Earth, right enough, and we could stand their loss . . . but what if we attacked and this monstrous growth actually *did* press the button before we nailed him? Could he, for instance, monitor incoming hardware from space? No, for he was at Lakeport and the radar and satellite monitoring equipment was at La Belle. So maybe we could get him in a pre-emptive strike! A lot of fingernails were chewed. But:

Smiler's next message came out of La Belle, before any-body could make any silly decisions. "Forget it," he warned us. "He's several jumps ahead of you. He made me drive him down here, to La Belle. And this is the deal: *Big 'C' doesn't want to harm anyone*—but neither does he want to be harmed. Here at La Belle he's got the whole world laid out on his screens—*his* screens, have you got that? The La Belle ground staff—that brave handful of guys who stayed on—they're . . . finished. They opposed him. So don't go making the same mistake. All of this is Big 'C''s now. He's watching everything from space, on radar . . . all the skills we had in those areas are now his. And he's nervous because he knows we kill things that frighten us, and he supposes that he frightens us. So the minute our defense satellites stop co-operating—the very *minute* he stops receiving information from his radar or pictures from space—he presses the button. And you'd better believe there's stuff here at La Belle that makes that derailed junk at Lakeport look like Chinese firecrackers!" And of course we knew there was.

So that was it: stalemate, a Mexican stand-off. And there were even groups who got together and declared that Big "C" had a right to live. If the Israelis had been given Is-rael, (they argued) the Palestinians Beirut and the Aborig-ines Alice Springs all the way out to Simpson Desert, then why shouldn't Big "C" have Lake Okeechobee? After all, he was a sentient being, wasn't he? And all he wanted was to live—wasn't it?

Well, that was something of what he wanted, anyway. Moisture from the Lake, and air to breathe. And Smiler, of course.

And territory. A lot more territory.

Big "C" grew fast. Very fast. The word "big" itself took on soaring new dimensions. In a few years Big "C" was into all the lakeside towns and spreading outwards. He seemed to live on anything, ate everything, and thrived on it. And it was about then that we decided we really ought to negotiate boundaries. Except "negotiate" isn't the right word.

Smiler asked to see me; I went in; through Smiler Big "C" told me what he wanted by way of land. And he got it. You don't argue with something that can reduce your planet to radioactive ashes. And now that Big "C" was into all the towns and villages on the Lake, he'd moved his nukes in with him. He hadn't liked the idea of having all his eggs in one basket, as it were.

But between Big "C"'s emergence from Smiler and my negotiating the boundaries, Christ knows we tried to get him! Frogmen had gone up the Miami, Hillsboro, and St. Lucie canals to poison the Lake—and hadn't come down again. A man-made anthrax variant had been sown in the fields and swamps where he was calculated to be spreading—and he'd just spread right on over it. A fire had started "accidentally" in the long hot summer of 2019, in the dried-out Okaloacoochee Slough, and warmed Big "C"'s hide all the way to the Lake before it died down. But that had been something he couldn't ignore.

"You must be crazy!" Smiler told us that time. "He's launched an ICBM to teach you a lesson. At ten megs its the smallest thing he's got—but still big enough!"

It was big enough for Hawaii, anyway. And so for a while we'd stopped trying to kill him, but we never stopped thinking about it. And someone thought:

If Big "C"'s brain is where Smiler is, and if we can get to that brain . . . will that stop the whole thing dead?

It was a nice thought. We needed somebody on the inside, but all we had was Smiler. Which brings me back to that time fifteen months ago when I went in to negotiate the new boundaries.

At that time Big "C" was out as far as ten miles from the Lake and expanding rapidly on all fronts. A big round nodule of him extended to cover La Belle, tapering to a tentacle reaching as far as Alva. I'd entered him at Alva as per instructions, where Big "C" had checked the car, then driven on through La Belle on my way to Lakeport, which was now his HQ. And then, as now, I'd passed through the landscape, which he opened for me, driving through his ever-expanding tissues. But I won't go into that here, nor into my conversation with Smiler. Let it suffice to say that Smiler intimated he would like to die now and it couldn't come quickly enough, and that before I left I'd passed him a note which read:

> Smiler,
>
> The next time someone comes in here he'll be a volunteer, and he'll be bringing something with him. A little something for Big "C". But it's up to you when that happens, good buddy. You're the only one who can fix it.
>
> > Peter

And then I was out of there. But as he'd glanced at the note there had been a look on Smiler's face that was hard to gauge. He'd *told* me that Big "C" only used him as a mouthpiece and as his . . . host. That the hideous stuff could only instruct him, not read his mind or get into his brain. But as I went to my car that time I could feel Big "C" gathering himself—like a big cat bunching its muscles—and as I actually got into the car something wet, a spot of slime, splashed down on me from overhead! *Jesus!* It was like the bastard was drooling on me!

"Jesus," yes. Because when I'd passed Smiler that note and he'd looked at me, and we'd come to our unspoken agreement, I hadn't known that *I* would be the volunteer! But I was, and for two reasons: my life didn't matter any more, and Smiler had asked for me—if I was willing. Now that was a funny thing in itself because it meant that he was asking me to die with him. But the thought didn't dawn on me that maybe he knew something that he shouldn't know. Nor would it dawn on me until I only had one more mile to go to my destination, Lakeport. When in any case there was no way I could turn back.

As for what that something was: it was the fact that I too was now dying of cancer.

It was diagnosed just a few weeks after I'd been to see him: the fast-moving sort that was spreading through me like a fire. Which was why I said: Sure, I'll come in and see you, Smiler. . . .

Ostensibly I was going in to negotiate the boundaries again. Big "C" had already crossed the old lines and was now out from the lake about forty miles in all directions, taking him to the Atlantic coast in the east and very nearly the Gulf of Mexico in the west. Immokalee had been my starting point, just a mile southwest of where he sprawled over the Slough, and now I was up as far as Palmdale and turning right for Moore Haven and Lakeport. And up to date with my morbid memories, too.

From Palmdale to Lakeport is about twenty-five miles. I drove that narrow strip of road with flaps and hummocks of leprous dough crawling, heaving and tossing on both sides—or clearing from the tarmac before my spinning wheels—while an opaque webbing of alien flesh pulsed and vibrated overhead. It was like driving down the funnel-trap of some cosmic trapdoor spider, or crossing the dry bed of an ocean magically cleared as by Moses and his staff. Except that *this* sea—this ocean of slime and disease—was its own master and cleared the way itself.

And in my jacket pocket my cigarette lighter, and under its hinged cap the button. And I was dying for a cigarette but couldn't have one, not just yet. But (or so I kept telling myself, however ridiculously) that was a good thing because they were bad for you!

The bomb was in the hollow front axle of the car, its two halves sitting near the wheels along with the propellant charges. When those charges detonated they'd drive two loads of hell into calamitous collision right there in the middle of the axle, creating critical mass and instant oblivion for anything in the immediate vicinity. I was driving a very special car: a kamikaze nuke. And ground zero was going to be Big "C"'s brain and my old pal Smiler. And myself, of course.

The miles were passing very quickly now, seeming to speed up right along with my heartbeat. I guessed I could do it even before I got there if I wanted to, blow the bastard to hell. But I wasn't going to give him even a split second's warning, because it was possible that was all he needed. No, I was going to park this heap right up his nose. Almost total disintegration for a radius of three or four miles when it went. For me, for Smiler, but especially for Big "C." Instantaneous, so that he wouldn't even have time to twitch.

And with this picture in mind I was through Moore Haven and Lakeport was up ahead, and I thought: *We've got him! Just two or three more miles and I can let 'er rip any time! And it's goodbye Big "C."* But I wouldn't do it because I wanted to see Smiler one last time. It was him and me together. I could smile right back at him (would I be able to? God, I hoped so!) as I pressed the button.

And it was then, with only a mile to go to Lakeport, that I remembered what Smiler had said the last time he asked for a visitor. He'd said: "Someone should come and see me soon, to talk about boundaries *if for nothing else.* I think maybe Peter Lancing . . . if he's willing."

The "if for nothing else" was his way of saying: "OK, bring it on in." And the rest of it. . . .

The way I saw it, it could be read two ways. That "if he's willing" bit could be a warning, meaning: "Of course, this is really a job for a volunteer." Or he could simply have been saying good-bye to me, by mentioning my name in his final communication. But . . . maybe it could be read a third way, too. Except that would mean that he *knew* I had cancer, and that therefore I probably would be willing.

And I remembered that blob of goo, that *sweat* or *spittle* of Big "C," which had splashed on me when I was last in here. . . .

Thought processes, and while they were taking place the mile was covered and I was in. It had been made simple: Big "C" had left only one road open, the one that led to the grounds of the Cancer Research Foundation. Some

irony, that this should be Big "C"'s HQ! But yes, just looking at the place I knew that it was.

It was . . . *wet*-looking, glistening, alive. Weakened light
filtered down through the layers of fretted, fretting webs
of mucus and froth and foaming flesh overhead, and the
Foundation complex itself looked like a gigantic, sup-
purating mass of decaying brick and concrete. Tentacles
of filth had shattered all the windows outwards, for all the
world as if the building's brain had burst out through its
eyes, ears and nostrils. And the whole thing was connected by writhing ropes of webbing to the far greater
mass which was Big "C"'s loathsome body.

Jesus! It was gray and green and brown and blue-tinged.
In spots it was even bright yellow, red, and splashed with
purple. It was Cancer with a capital C—Big "C" himself—
and it was alive!

"What are you waiting for, Peter?" Smiler's voice came
out of my radio, and I banged my head on the car roof
starting away from it. "Are you coming in, old friend . . .
or what?"

I didn't have to go in there if I didn't want to; my
lighter was in my pocket; I touched it to make sure. But
. . . I didn't want to go out alone. I don't just mean out
like out of the car, but out period. And so:

"I'm coming in, Smiler," I told him.

And somehow I made myself. In front of the main
building there'd been lawn cropped close as a crew-cut.
Now it was just soil crumbling to sand. I walked across it
and into the building, just looking straight ahead and nowhere else. Inside . . . the corridors were clear at least.
Big "C" had cleared them for me. But through each door
as I passed them I could see him bulking, pile upon pile of
him like . . . like heaped intestines. His brains? God, I
hoped so!

Finally, when I was beginning to believe I couldn't go
any further on two feet and would have to crawl—and
when I was fighting with myself not to throw up—I found
Smiler in his "office:" just a large room with a desk which
he sat behind, and a couple of chairs, telephones, radios.

And also containing Big "C," of course. Which is the part I've always been reluctant to talk about, but now have to tell just the way it was.

Big "C" was plugged into him, into Smiler. It was grotesque. Smiler sat propped up in his huge chair, and he was like a spider at the center of his web. Except the web wasn't of silk but of flesh, and it was attached to him. The back of his head was welded to a huge fan-shape of tentacles spreading outwards like some vast ornamental headdress, or like the sprawl of an octopus's arms; and these cancerous extensions or extrusions were themselves attached to a shuddering bulk that lay behind Smiler's chair and grew up the walls and out of the windows. The lower part of his body was lost behind the desk, lost in bulging gray sacks and folds and yellow pipes and purplish gelatinous masses of . . . Christ, of whatever the filthy stuff was! Only his upper body, his arms and hands, face and shoulders were free of the stuff. He was it. It was him—physically, anyway.

No one could have looked at him and felt anything except disgust, or perhaps pity if they'd known him like I had. And if they hadn't, dread and loathing and . . . yes, horror. Friendship didn't come into it; I knew that I wasn't smiling; I knew that my face must reflect everything I felt.

He nodded the merest twitch of a nod and husked: "Sit down, Peter, before you fall down! Hey, and you think I look bad, right?" Humor! Unbelievable! But his voice was a desiccated whisper, and his gray hands on the desk shook like spindly skating insects resting up after a morning's hard skimming over a stagnant pond.

I sat down on a dusty chair opposite him, perching myself there, feeling all tight inside from not wanting to breathe the atmosphere, and hypersensitive outside from trying not to touch anything. He noticed and said: "You don't want to contaminate yourself, right? But isn't it a bit late for that, Peter?"

From which I could tell that he knew—he *did* know—and a tingle started in my feet that quickly surged through my entire being. Could he see it in me? Sense it in me? Feel some sort of weird kinship with what was under my skin, burgeoning in me? Or was it worse than that? And right there and then I began to have this feeling that things weren't going according to plan.

"Smiler," I managed to get started at the second attempt, "it's . . . *good* to see you again, pal. And I . . ." And I stopped and just sat there gasping.

"Yes?" he prompted me in a moment. "And you—?"

"Nerves!" I gasped, forcing a sickly smile, and forced in my turn to take my first deep breath. "Lots of nerves. It was always the same. It's why I had to stay behind when you and the others went into space." And I took out my cigarettes, and also took out the lighter from my pocket. I opened the pack and shook out several cigarettes, which fell on the floor, then managed to trap one between my knees and transfer it shakily to my mouth. And I flipped back the top on my lighter.

Smiler's eyes—the only genuinely mobile parts he had left—went straight to the lighter and he said: "You brought it in, right?" But should he be saying things like that? Out loud, I mean? Couldn't Big "C" hear him or sense his mood? And it dawned on me just how little we knew about them, about Big "C" and Smiler—as he was now. . . .

Then . . . Smiler smiled. Except it wasn't his smile!

Goodbye, everything, I said to myself, pressing the button and holding my thumb down on it. Then releasing it and pressing it again, and again. And finally letting the fucking thing fall from my nerveless fingers when, after two or three more tries, *still* nothing had happened. Or rather, "nothing" hadn't happened.

"Peter, old buddy, let me tell you how it is." Smiler got through to me at last, as the cigarette fell from my trembling lips. "I mean, I suspect you now *know* how it is, but I'll tell you anyway. See, Big 'C' changes things. Just about anything he wants to change. He was nothing at first, or not very much—just a natural law of change, mutation, entropy if you like. An 'emanation.' Or on the other hand I suppose you could say he was everything—like Nature itself. Whichever, when I went up there to Luna II he got into me and changed my cancer into himself, since when he's become one hell of a lot. We can talk about that in a minute, but first I want to explain about your bomb. Big 'C' changed it. He changed the chemical elements of the explosive charges, and to be doubly sure sucked all the fizz out of the fissionable stuff. It was a firework and he dumped it in a bucket of water. So now you can relax. It didn't go off and it isn't going to."

"You . . . *are* him!" I knew it instinctively. Now, when it was too late. "But when? And why?"

"When did I stop being Smiler? Not long after that time you met him at the beach. And why the subterfuge? Because you human beings are a jumpy lot. With Smiler to keep you calm, let you think you had an intermediary, it was less likely you'd do something silly. And why should I care less you'd do something silly? Because there's a lot of life, knowledge, sustenance in this Earth and I didn't want you killing it off trying to kill me! But now you can't kill me, because the bigger I've got the easier it has become to change things. Missiles? Go ahead and try it. They'll be dead before they hit me. Why, if I got the idea you were going to try firing a couple, I could even kill them on the ground!

"You see, Peter, I've grown too big, too clever, too devious to be afraid any more—of anything. Which is why I have no more secrets, and why there'll be no more subterfuge. Subterfuge? Not a bit of it. Why, I'm even broadcasting all of this—just so the whole world will know what's going on! I mean, I *want* them to know, so no one will make any more silly mistakes. Now, I believe you came in here to talk about boundaries—some limits you want to see on my expansion?"

Somehow, I shook my head. "That's not why I'm here, Smiler," I told him, not yet ready to accept that there was nothing of Smiler left in there. "Why I'm here is finished now."

"Not quite," he said, but very quietly. "We can get to the boundaries later, but there is something else. Think about it. I mean, why should I want to see you, if there's nothing else and if I can make any further decisions without outside help?"

"I don't know. Why?"

"See, Smiler has lasted a long time. Him and the frogmen that came to kill me, and a couple of farmers who didn't get out fast enough when they saw me coming, oh, and a few others. And I've been instructed by them. Like I said: I've learned how to be devious. And I've learned anger, too, though there's no longer any need for that. No need for any human emotions. But the last time you came to see Smiler—and when you would have plotted with him to kill me—that angered me."

"And so you gave me my cancer."

"Yes I did. So that when I needed you, you'd *want* to be my volunteer. But don't worry . . . you're not going to die, Peter. Well, not physically anyway, and not just yet a while. For just like Smiler here, you're going to carry on."

"But no anger, eh? No human emotions? No . . . revenge? OK, so let me go free to live out what days I've got left."

"No anger, no revenge, no emotions—just need. I *can't* let you go! But let me explain myself. Do you know what happens when you find a potato sprouting in your vegetable rack and you plant it in the garden? That's right, You get lots of new potatoes! Well, I'm something like that. I'm putting out lots of new potatoes, lots of new me. All of the time. And the thing is this: when you dig up those potatoes and your fork goes through the old one, what do you find? Just a wrinkled, pulpy old sack of a thing all ready to collapse in upon itself, with nothing of goodness left in it—pretty much like what's left of Smiler here. So . . . if I want to keep growing potatoes, why, I just have to keep planting them! Do you see?"

"Jesus! *Jesus!*"

"It's nothing personal, Peter. It's need, that's all. . . . No, don't stand up, just sit there and I'll do the rest. And you can stop biting down on that clever tooth of yours, because it isn't poison any more, just salt. And if you don't like what's happening to Smiler right now, that's OK—just turn your face away. . . .

". . . There, that was pretty easy, now wasn't it?

"All you people out there, that's how it is. So get used to it. As for the new boundaries: there aren't any.
                              "This is Big 'C,' signing off."

Afterword

Me, "Big 'C'," and H. P. L.

When I started to write this story I could have sworn I didn't have a Lovecraftian thought in my head, and I wasn't even sure it would turn out to be a horror story. Not the sort I usually write, anyway. But for some time I'd been playing around with a handful of ideas for weird SF stories, and "BIG 'C'" was mainly something left over after I'd completed "The Man Who Felt Pain" for *Fantasy Tales.* Maybe the two stories had tried to be one but somehow got separated, I'm not sure.

Anyway, when one of the editors of this current volume wrote to me asking for a *Lovecraft's Legacy* story, I told him I didn't have one, wasn't working on anything H. P. hellish, and in any case didn't have the time, for I was into the last few chapters of my new novel. Which wasn't a brush-off, I assure you (hey, it's nice when someone thinks of you, and I can always use the work!), just the truth.

But then I thought of "Big 'C'" and wondered if I could maybe rework it into something Lovecraft might have inspired, only to discover that he sure as hell *had* inspired it! Well, and I mustn't complain about that . . . I'm just a little bit deeper in H. P. L.'s debt, that's all—as if I weren't in deep enough already!

So . . . while "Big 'C'" isn't pastiche—while it wasn't consciously written "after" H. P. L.—nevertheless he does seem to have had a hand in it. No prize for matching this up with Lovecraft's masterful original. That would be just too simple, for they're both pretty much the same alien color.

UGLY
Gary Brandner

Murray Kline was addicted to swap meets. Indoor, out-door, big, little, it did not matter. He was drawn to swap meets like a moth to flame. It was the only vice available to him as he was constitutionally unable to drink, and Phyllis forbade smoking in the house.

This one was not much as swap meets go. Just four rows of rickety stands set up in a high school parking lot. No matter, Murray pulled the Taurus over and parked across the street. You never knew what you might find among the tawdry new and the scuzzy old things for sale. And besides, stopping here allowed him to prolong the unpleasantness of going home for an hour.

He took his time strolling up and down the rows, in-specting the merchandise first on one side, then the other, while the vendors watched hopefully. There were boxes of paperback books, old record albums, stereo equipment that might as well have had STOLEN stenciled on each piece. There were fake leather luggage, incomplete sets of cheap china, T-shirts with rude remarks printed on them, video and audio cassettes with rubber-stamped labels. A hard-looking woman sold nothing but little plastic birds that repeatedly dipped their beaks in a saucer of water. An old man had stacks of yellow-covered *National Geographics* that looked to be in mint condition. There were the usual layouts of junk and jetsam that had come from attics and garages. There was the Gypsy family with racks of bright polyester shirts.

Murray bought a paperback copy of *Salem's Lot* to justify his presence there. He was headed down the last row and toward the street when he reached the hunchback's stand.

He felt a kinship with deformed people because of his face. He had long ago learned to live with the puckered scar that pulled his left eye down and lifted his lip away from his upper teeth. He was by now used to the range of reactions. He pretended to be unaffected by the frank stares of children and the sidelong glances of adults who thought they were unobserved. But never, not for one waking second, was Murray unaware of the way he looked. Probably worst was the false nonchalance of people trying to pretend his face was as acceptable as their own.

But while he could not deny his face, Murray had learned to live with it. The scar, after all, had been with him thirty-seven of his forty-four years. The pain it had caused him was balanced by the empathy it gave him for God's other deformed creatures.

The hunchback sat on his stool and watched as Murray poked through the trashy merchandise. There seemed to be no plan or organization to the display. Heaped together in bins were toy soldiers, old movie magazines, dusty beer mugs with football teams' logos, strings of cheap beads, small transistor radios, packets of screws and nails, a couple of shabby dolls. Nothing Murray Kline could possibly use.

He looked up into the dark unsmiling eyes of the hunchback and gave him a friendly shrug. There was no response.

Suddenly in a hurry to be out of there, Murray turned and started away from the stand. Then the lizard caught his eye. It was about eight inches long, including a stumpy tail, with fat little bowed legs that ended in sharp claws. The lizard was sealed in a block of clear plastic about the size of a brick. Its skin was an iridescent blue-green. The staring eyes were pea-size bulbs with vertical black slits for pupils. But what held Murray was the lizard's face. The left side seemed to have been punctured by some jagged instrument. Half of the mouth was drawn up to expose a double row of sharp little teeth. The eye on that side was sucked off line. It was the ugliest thing living or dead that Murray had ever seen. He had to have it.

The hunchback wanted twenty dollars for the lizard. Murray offered him ten. They settled on $17.50. Murray knew it was too much, but he had never been good at bargaining. And he *had* to have that lizard.

At home he hoped to smuggle the prize back to his tiny workroom before Phyllis saw it, but she was waiting for him at the door.

"What's that thing?" she demanded. "You've been to another of those swap meets, haven't you?"

"Just a small one. It was right on my way home."

Phyllis bent down for a better look at his purchase. Murray stared at the dark roots of her red hair.

"My God, that's ugly." She straightened suddenly and glared at him. "I hope you don't expect to keep it in the house."

Murray studied his wife's generous breasts, her solid stomach, her rounded hips. She may have added a few pounds during their marriage, but she was still a fine-looking woman. He had wondered, early in their relationship, what she saw in him, considering his distorted face. Finally, he had to admit that what she saw was security and a better life than she could have achieved working behind the counter at Denny's.

"Did you hear me?" she said, thrusting her face close to his.

"Yes, Phyllis, I heard you. And no, I won't keep it anywhere you have to look at it."

"I should hope not. If you had your way you'd want it in bed with us." She gave a snort to show what she thought of *that* idea, then added, "Since you took so long at your precious swap meet your dinner's cold."

"That's all right," he said. "I don't mind warming it up."

Phyllis immersed herself in a television game show where she shouted out the answers, trying to beat the contestants. Murray retreated to his workroom, a converted closet off the kitchen, and set his new acquisition on the work table under a bright light for a good look at it. It was not like any lizard he had ever seen in life or in pictures. The teeth, for one thing, were more like a baby shark's than an herbivorous reptile's. Then there was the skewed face, and the staring eyes that seemed to follow his movements.

How had someone gone about sealing the creature in its plastic coffin? he wondered. Could it have been alive at the time? It certainly looked lifelike now. What unspeakable pain must it have suffered as its body was submerged in molten plastic? Could the lizard's death agony account for the twisted face?

"Poor little thing," he said. "I wish I could help you. But I guess you're beyond help now. At least you have a home. And you really should have a name. We'll have to come up with one, won't we."

When at last he left the workroom and walked back through the house Phyllis was watching a sitcom wherein the family wisecracked constantly to a crackling laugh track.

"I'm going to bed now," he said.

She grunted, not bothering to turn from the screen. They hardly ever went to bed at the same time anymore.

Considering what little remained of their sex life, it hardly mattered.

Murray slipped easily into sleep. His dreams centered around the lizard, not as a plastic-encased paperweight, but as a living, breathing companion. He had never had a pet, man or boy. When he awoke in the morning and looked over at his softly snoring wife, he had a pang of regret that the dream was not real.

He switched off the alarm to let Phyllis sleep. Then, even before brushing his teeth, Murray went back through the kitchen to the workroom.

The tabletop was bare. The lizard was gone. There was no doubt he had left it right out in the center of his work table under the lamp. And now it was gone. He hurried back to the bedroom and gently squeezed Phyllis by the shoulder until, scowling and groaning, she awoke.

"Did you by any chance move my lizard?" he said.

Slowly her sleep-dissembled face came together. Her eyes became sly. "Why would I want to touch that ugly thing?"

Because it's mine, he thought, but he said nothing. He knew it would be fruitless to pursue the subject. He left her drifting back to sleep and proceeded to search the various trash receptacles in the house and outside. In the big plastic barrel behind the garage he found it.

The block with the lizard inside was crusted with coffee grounds and discarded scraps of paper, but undamaged. As Murray brushed it off he saw clinging to it one of his business cards—*Cash and Kline Consulting Services.* Printed in the lower corner was the name of his partner: *Benjamin Cash.* Odd. Murray turned the card over. Written on the back in a familiar hand was *Monday—2 p.m.* Monday? Something clicked in the back of Murray's head. He tucked the card into a pocket and carried the plastic brick back into the house to wash it off.

The hours of Friday dragged at Cash and Kline. Murray wanted to be at home looking at his lizard. But someone had to be here, and Ben Cash had taken one of his frequent days off. "Making contacts," Ben called it. He was the outside man, the one who dealt face-to-face with clients. For obvious reasons Murray stayed in the office. No one wanted to hire a firm represented by a gargoyle.

When at last five o'clock came Murray hurried home. He acknowledged Phyllis's cool greeting and went at once to his workroom.

He settled himself on the stool, pulled the plastic block to him, looked down at the lizard, and gasped.

The creature's right eye was closed. Surely they had both been open when he bought it. And again this morning. He could not be mistaken about that. And yet now the left, pulled-down eye stared at him while the right eye winked. Yes, *wink* was exactly the word. The row of sharp little teeth glinted as in a knowing smirk. The eye could not possibly have closed with the lizard sealed inside the plastic prison, and yet there it was.

Before he retired that night Murray put the lizard carefully away in a drawer he had installed under the table, and which only he knew about. Then, while Phyllis dozed in front of the late-night talk show host, he went to bed and dreamed he was being watched by one enormous green eye with a vertical slit for a pupil.

On Saturday morning he started the coffeemaker, then went directly to his tiny workroom, reached into the secret drawer, and took out his lizard. The first thing he checked was the state of the eyes. The right one still winked at him. He must have been mistaken, Murray decided, about both eyes being open when he bought it.

But wait! Surely the two clawed front feet had been planted firmly and parallel beneath its body. There was no room for doubt; he had spent enough time examining the lizard from all angles to know the position of the legs. Now the right foot was very definitely forward of the left, and elevated. As though the creature were reaching for . . . for *something.*

And then, as Murray Kline watched, impossible though it was, the lizard moved. The reptilian head jerked a fraction of an inch in his direction. The closed right eye popped open and looked at him.

Murray picked up the plastic block and held it to the light to be sure it was not an illusion. The lizard moved again. If there was an air bubble inside surrounding the creature, he could not see it. The short, thick tail twitched. Somehow, sealed within the brick of clear plastic, the creature was moving. Some weird post-mortem rictus? No. The head turned another tiny fraction. The lower jaw moved. The glossy green eyes watched him.

The lizard was alive.

Sweating in his excitement, Murray bolted the door to his workroom. He rummaged through his tools until he found a stout utility knife. Then he clamped the brick with the lizard inside firmly in a vise and carefully, very carefully, began carving away the plastic.

It was not an easy job. The plastic was dense and extremely hard. Each stroke of the knife blade shaved off only a fine translucent strip. Through the day he worked, and into the night. Several times Phyllis shouted a question at him through the door. He answered with a grunt and she went away.

Some time after midnight Murray had reduced the block to a sausage-shaped lump with the lizard inside watching him intently. Murray wanted nothing more than to finish the job, but his hand was cramped and his eyes ached from the strain. He had to have some sleep.

Early Sunday morning he was back at the task. The shaving away of plastic went even slower now, as he wanted to take no chances on cutting into the lizard. It was dusk when Murray finally leaned back on the stool to appraise his work and to massage his throbbing hand. There was now just a thin layer of plastic coating the lizard. He was eager to finish the job, but had trouble controlling his cramped and quivering hand. The long hours of cutting away its plastic prison had given him a strong feeling of kinship with the little animal, and he would not risk injuring it so close to freedom.

Before retiring he returned one last time to the workroom. The lizard with its thin coating of plastic waited for him in the secret drawer. Murray picked it up ever so carefully and held it close to his face. He made little chirping sounds to it. The lizard jerked in his hand. The plastic coating split like an old skin and fell away to the tabletop.

Murray gasped. The lizard's claws gripped his forearm, but gently, not breaking the skin. The little head turned this way and that in a series of small jerks as it surveyed the surroundings. Then it looked up at Murray. The shiny little eyes blinked once. The twisted mouth opened with a soft hiss and a forked tongue flickered like a tiny purple flame.

"You little devil," Murray said, "you're alive."

The lizard reached out a foreleg and very softly drew its claws down along the inside of Murray's arm, stroking him.

Murray smiled, for once not caring that it only made his face uglier. "And you like me, don't you," he said. "Well, you have a home now. You'll need a name. And we'll have to find out what you like to eat."

Using a soft old sweater, he made a bed for his pet in the secret drawer. That Sunday night, for one of the few times in his life, Murray Kline went to bed happy.

Ben Cash came into the office shortly before eleven Monday morning. Dark and good-looking in a surly way, Ben was six inches taller and seven years younger than Murray. For the next hour he examined his nails, flirted with the file clerk, flipped through the mail, and at noon locked up his desk.

"See you tomorrow, partner," he said, giving Murray a two-finger salute.

"Making contacts?" Murray said.

"Got a deadly lunch set up with the Boston people. Then some boring function at the Ridgecrest Club afterwards. You're lucky you don't have to go."

"Sure." Murray watched his partner go out the door. Under his breath he added, *"Some people don't know how lucky they are."*

Murray kept busy answering correspondence, calling clients, and checking figures. He gave the two women employees enough work to carry them through the day. At a quarter of two he locked his desk and left.

Murray drove away from the office in the opposite direction from his home. Ben Cash lived in an expensive new condominium on the other side of the city. The complex had tennis courts, babbling brooks, lots of greenery, and Tudor-style multilevel townhouses, each with its own private patio and hot tub.

Murray parked the Taurus a block away and walked back toward the condo complex. He found a bench that was screened from view by a laurel hedge. He did not have long to wait. At two minutes past two Phyllis's Cutlass rolled in. The double garage door behind Ben Cash's condo swung up and Phyllis pulled in beside Ben's BMW. The door came down with a soft thump. After several minutes Murray got up from the bench and walked back to his car and drove away.

His own house was empty. As empty as the great black hollow Murray felt inside himself. Lord knew Phyllis was not the perfect wife. Far from it. But she was *his* wife, dammit. And she had accepted him at, bitter phrase, face value.

His puckered, twisted countenance mocked him now from the mirror over the mantle. The reflection faded and he saw the voluptuous naked body of his wife intertwined with the lean, salon-tanned Ben Cash. He punched himself hard in the jaw with his fist. The taunting vision faded and his own sorry face returned.

Even a visit to his lizard could not cheer him. The little creature scrambled readily up his arm to his shoulder. It made chittering sounds in his ear.

"Are you hungry, little guy? I'll figure out something, but not right away, okay? My wife is fucking my partner, and I need some time to get the kinks out of my chest. And I must be losing it completely, telling my troubles to a lizard."

He set the little beast tenderly back in the drawer and

returned to his car. At a nearby shopping mall he bought a ticket at the multiscreen theater, not caring what was playing, and walked into the darkness where no one could see him cry.

The bubbles foamed around the naked couple in the hot tub. Ben Cash pulled Phyllis against him and wondered, not for the first time, if his ugly little partner appreciated the body on his wife. Probably not, or she wouldn't be here naked in Ben Cash's hot tub.

Phyllis reached for the glass of chilled white zinfandel on the rim of the tub. She laughed and gave Ben a playful swat as he did something with his hand down under the water. "Don't get in a hurry now, we've got all afternoon."

"You don't expect me to keep my hands off when you're this close to me, do you?"

Phyllis started to answer when something plopped into the hot water behind her. She gave a high-pitched squeal. "Ben?! What do you think you're doing?"

He held up both hands above the bubbles in a gesture of innocence. "Hey, I didn't—"

The sentence was never finished. Ben's face twisted into an agonized mask. He screamed hoarsely and plunged his hands down into the water. The bubbles foaming up crimson from between his legs. He doubled over and submerged, his scream drowned in the red froth.

Phyllis thrashed the water in horror. She grabbed the rim and fought to lift herself from the bloody cauldron. Something sharp sank into her under the water and stripped flesh and muscle away from the bone. Her agonized screech died as she was pulled under.

Murray sat through the entire movie twice without knowing what he had seen. Something about two cop buddies who shoot up half the city to make Los Angeles safe for honest folk.

The house was dark when he got home. Phyllis had not returned. He went straight to the workroom. The door was open. Inside, the concealed drawer was pulled out.

And empty. A black day. First he learns his wife is cheating on him with his partner, now his lizard was gone.

Out in the living room the telephone rang. Murray took his time getting there. Whoever was on the line was persistent. Seven rings, eight, ten. He picked up the instrument.

"Mr. Murray Kline?"

"Yes."

"This is Police Sergeant Dennis Hovey. I'm afraid I have some bad news."

Murray listened quietly as the policeman described in formal language what had been found in Ben Cash's hot tub. Murray thanked him, said he would come down to the police station right away. No, he did not need any assistance.

He hung up the phone thoughtfully. There would be a lot to do. Phyllis's things would have to be disposed of. And adjustments would be needed at the office. He went into the kitchen and made himself a sandwich.

Something scratched at the back door. Murray opened it and looked down to see the blue-green stumpy-tailed lizard. His lizard. He bent down and picked it up. The reptile chittered happily.

Holding the lizard up before his face Murray saw the flecks of dried blood along the twisted mouth.

"Well, Ugly," he said, "at least now we know what you eat."

Afterword

The first H. P. Lovecraft story I can remember reading was "The Color out of Space." I was maybe 12 years old. I didn't fully understand the story, but I understood the emotion. Fear. And I learned something that I would put to use many years later. Fear can be fun . . . when it is between the covers of a book, or up on a movie screen. Those of us who work in fiction with fear as our raw material owe a debt to the pioneers like Lovecraft, Edgar Allan Poe, Algernon Blackwood, and Bram Stoker. It is they who broke the ground for us.

True, I had my problems with Lovecraft's stories of the Old Ones with the unpronounceable names—Cthulhu and that bunch. However, I have not forgotten the emotional impact of his stories. My own story herein is my way of saying thank you to a master.

THE BLADE AND THE CLAW
Hugh B. Cave

Floating there in the dark, the thing might have been a cadaver's head dipped in some kind of red phosphorus. Its eyes blazed. Its mouth was a jagged hole that appeared to be voicing a scream of agony. But there was no sound.

And the head was bleeding. From its severed neck, which had been sliced off as neatly as though by a guillotine, drops of blood fell like rain to the concrete floor. They made no sound as they hit, but Cannon could see a red stain forming there.

Then Cannon heard words. They were barely louder than the sound of his own quickened breathing, but he could see the red mouth shaping them as it floated there.

"Tonton yo . . . Tonton Macoute yo . . ."

Over and over the words were repeated. And now two long-fingered hands were visible, reaching out to him.

Were they pleading for his help?

Or were they threatening him with some hideous form of death?

Before he and his wife had been in Haiti an hour, Mark Cannon realized he had made a mistake in urging Ellen to accompany him. She had not been with him during his earlier stay in that impoverished West Indian country, when he wrote his book about Haiti under the Duvaliers.

Heaven help him, he should have left her at home this time, too. Nothing he might do at this late date could possibly save their marriage.

Point One: they were met at the airport not by his old friend Edouard Bourand but by Eddie's sister, and Janine Bourand was a beauty. Ellen did not like women her own age who were more beautiful than she.

To be sure, after driving them to the house her brother had rented for them Janine departed, having other things to do. But it was a bad beginning.

Point Two: Although he had warned Ellen about the ghastly slums to be encountered on the ride from the airport to the city, for some reason they had been even more crowded, more smelly, and more depressing that day than he remembered them. And Ellen was the kind of woman who would walk out of a restaurant if she found a spot on the tablecloth.

Point Three: The house rented for them harbored a cat and three kittens, and Ellen despised cats. She was not allergic to them; she simply loathed them.

The house was impressive otherwise. Located at the end of a dead-end lane in one of the quieter parts of a city that, of course, was seldom very quiet, it was comfortably large and nicely furnished. It had a study in which he could work undisturbed on his new book—about life in Haiti after the end of the Duvaliers' long reign. It even had a sewing room, complete with a late-model Swiss machine, in which Ellen could pursue her favorite diversion of making clothes for herself. The country produced sea-island cotton, Cannon recalled, in designs nearly as color-

ful as its primitive art. That should excite her to a degree
that few things seemed to of late.

But, ah, the cat and kittens.

They were in an open closet in the master bedroom
when Ellen discovered them. She had followed the maid,
Lucille, into the room. Cannon, entering behind her, had
his attention captured by the image of her in a full-length
mirror on the wall. Though he had been married to this
former schoolteacher for seven years and thought he
knew her every mood, her face in the mirror suddenly
betrayed such—what was the word? Revulsion?—that it
stopped him in his tracks.

Then he heard her suck in a breath and cry out in a
voice that should have shattered the mirror, "What are
these monsters doing here?"

Eddie Bourand had hired a housekeeper and a cook
who spoke some English. (To find a yard boy who did
that had been impossible, his sister had explained, but
Creole-speaking Julien was at least reliable.) Lucille, the
housekeeper, responded to Ellen's outcry now by turning
to direct a questioning frown at her.

"Monsters, *madame?*" Lucille was a woman of about
thirty, tall, not unattractive, and apparently hard to ruffle.
Despite Ellen's outcry, her response was one of mere interest, not alarm.

"These cats! I hate cats! I will not have them in my
house!"

"Now, Ellen," Cannon said quickly, "this is a pleasant
house in a good location. Whatever little problems we
may have—"

"*Little* problems!" she exploded.

He tried to make a joke of it. "Well, God knows they're
not very big, are they? Not the kittens, anyway." He himself had always liked cats and regretted not being able to
have two or three around after his marriage to Ellen. Step-
ping past his wife and the Haitian woman, he hunkered
down in front of those in the closet and put out his hand.

The mother ignored him. One of her offspring came

forward at once and licked a finger, the scratchy little tongue sending a thrill up his arm. Kitten number two backed against the closet's rear wall with a snarl that revealed very small, very pointed teeth. The third had only one eye—its left appeared to be covered by an opaque white film—but used that eye most effectively to direct a defiant stare at him.

"Where did they come from, Lucille?" he asked.

"They were here yesterday when I came, *m'sié*. The former tenant must have left them."

"Well, for the time being they won't be much of a problem, I'm sure." Cannon looked at his wife. "Will they, dear?"

Ellen's dark eyes had acquired an all too familiar glitter. "You know how I feel about cats!"

"I do. And we'll find a home for them as soon as we're a bit more settled. Lucille, can you take them down to the kitchen for now and look after them there? Give them some milk or whatever we happen to have?" The maid and cook shared a one-room servants' cottage in the yard. He couldn't very well ask them to accommodate a cat and three kittens in that small space.

"Now, *m'sié?*" Lucille said. "This minute?"

"Yes, now. *Madame* and I will finish the grand tour by ourselves."

Cannon had already settled on the best way to get the material for his book. In the garage right now stood a jeep his friend Eddie Bourand had placed at his disposal. In it he would do Port-au-Prince, the capital, and its mountain suburb of Pétionville, talking to old acquaintances and anyone else who would talk to him. As a trained reporter he would of course double-check anything he heard before using it.

Then he would visit Cap Haïtien, Les Cayes, Jérémie, and Jacmel, Haiti's principal outlying towns, and talk to people there.

All of this would entail attendance at voodoo services, conversations with farmers, business people, politicians, and especially women. You learned a lot from women when you were six-foot-one and somewhat resembled John Wayne at the height of the Duke's career.

He spent the first day at home, however, helping Ellen do the house over the way she wanted it. Or, rather, helping the servants do it over while she supervised. His wife was not the kind of woman who could move into a furnished house and leave things the way she found them.

This took most of the day. Since daylight at this latitude was pretty much from six to six, darkness had fallen by the time the cook, Edita, had dinner ready. Yet despite her having spent most of the day dusting, polishing, and moving furniture about—chores no Haitian would have demanded of a cook—the meal was a good one.

Edita was a bright little thing, under thirty, with an ever-ready smile. The pumpkin soup was tasty, the chicken tender, the vegetables not overcooked, and the coffee . . . well, to connoisseurs of coffee, that produced in Haiti was right up there with Jamaica's famous Blue Mountain.

"What are these little black things in the rice, please?" Ellen asked.

"Dried mushrooms, *madame*. The dish is called *djon-djon et di-ri.*"

"It's uniquely Haitian, Ellen," Cannon put in.

"Well, if you say so. I don't think we'll want it again, Edita. Thank you."

"M'sié asked for it, *madame."*

The gaze Ellen directed at Cannon was one he knew well. "Did you, Mark?"

He had long since learned not to make an issue of small things when dealing with her. Big ones, yes—he had no intention of becoming a doormat—but unless there was something important at stake, to hell with it. He had been dazzled by Ellen's looks when he urged her to marry him. Much of what he would get along with that face and body beautiful he had not discovered until too late.

Dinner finished, the two Haitian women cleaned up the kitchen, asked if anything more was expected of them, and seemed more than glad to retire to their cottage. Cannon turned on a radio in the living room, happening to flip the switch just as an announcer began the station's call letters.

"Ici Radio Haiti . . ."

"French?" Ellen made a face as she rose from the chair she had settled in. "If that's all we can get here, I'm going to bed."

He did not try to dissuade her. There was a part of the house that he had barely glanced at during the day's activities. Apparently used as a storeroom, it contained some cardboard cartons, half hidden in a dark corner, that had waked his curiosity—either they went with the house, or the previous tenant had left them behind and the owner had failed to notice them. "I'll be up soon," he said casually. "Will the radio bother you?"

"Well . . . if you must listen to it, I'll shut the bedroom door."

"Thanks." Listening to the radio and reading the little French-language Haitian newspapers were part of what he had come here to do.

With a shrug, Ellen crossed the room and climbed a handsome, curving staircase that led to the bedrooms. There were three of those, all large and nicely furnished in Haitian mahogany. All, too, had windows that opened on a metal section of roof that sloped down to within a few feet of the ground, because the house had been built into an almost vertical hillside. Cannon had already made a mental note to make certain the screens at those windows were locked at night. Port-au-Prince was notorious for nighttime thieves who were very good at entering a home without disturbing its sleeping occupants.

When he heard Ellen close the door of the room they would be sharing, he turned the radio up a little louder and left the living room.

The veranda of this house he had rented was not an overhanging thing but rather like a ship's deck, and the area he wished to explore further was a walled tunnel or corridor or basement—he really had no idea what to call it—directly underneath. The door to that area was in the yard, under an end of the veranda. The key to it was one of those handed him by Eddie Bourand's lovely sister.

With a flashlight he had found in the kitchen, he made his way to the door and thrust the key into the lock. The flashlight's batteries were all but dead, but there was a light switch just inside the doorway. Opening the door, he flipped the switch.

Nothing happened. Something had happened earlier, activating three bare bulbs that dangled from the storeroom ceiling, but now the bulbs stayed dark. "Damn," Cannon said aloud, then "Damn" again when the flashlight in his hand gave up the ghost as well.

He stood there peering into the blackness of the cellarlike space confronting him. What to do? There were no spare light bulbs in the house that he knew of, and new ones probably wouldn't help anyway. All three of these would not have burned out at the same time. Something must have gone wrong with the wiring. A job for an electrician. Well, he would have to phone Eddie Bourand in the morning and—

Something moved in the darkness at the far end of the under-veranda basement, and Cannon saw the severed human head floating there. And the long-fingered hands reaching for him. And heard the voice.

"Tonton yo . . . Tonton Macoute yo . . ."

That was enough. Lurching back out of there, he slammed the door shut and turned the key with such force that it nearly broke in the lock. His teeth chattered. His whole body shook. He dropped the key and had to scramble for it on his knees in the dark before running to the veranda steps.

But he was not a man who yielded long to panic. By the time he reached the veranda he had himself under control again. Striding to the far end, he stood there with both hands on the concrete railing and frowned down at the basement door.

Would it open? Was the thing in there capable of opening a door? A locked one?

"Tonton Macoute yo." The Tonton Macoutes had been Papa Doc's private army of thugs and killers, taken over by his son Jean-Claude when Papa died and the son became President. After Baby Doc's forced flight into exile the people of Haiti, normally gentle, had turned on some of the worst of that murderous private army and obtained revenge for at least a few of the killings and tortures. But many other Tontons were still alive, in hiding.

Had this house been one of their hiding places?

Ellen was asleep when Cannon entered the bedroom. She had chosen the twin bed nearest the windows, he noticed. Those were open and moonlight glistened on the sloping metal roof. After checking the screens to be sure they were locked, he undressed quietly so as not to wake her and slid into his own bed. But sleep would not come. For a long time he lay there thinking about what he had seen, or thought he had seen, in the tunnel under the veranda.

A sea breeze whispered among tall, thin pines whose branches overhung the roof. Now and then a cone dropped, producing a loud thud followed by metallic ripples of vibration. Dogs barked in distant yards. At last he slept.

To his surprise, the three lights in that under-veranda tunnel went on when he clicked the switch in the morning. He clicked it several times; it worked each time. Had he somehow managed to fumble it in the dark last night?

Before turning his attention to the cartons, he sought an explanation of the floating head and hands that had dripped blood. His search turned up nothing. The answer had to be in the cartons, then. They were stacked at the tunnel's far end where he had seen the apparitions.

Lowering the first one to the floor, he used his jackknife to slit the tough brown tape that secured it. It contained clothing for a man, or men. Some red silk shirts. A green velvet jacket and pants to match. A black suit that brought to mind undertakers and funerals. He pushed the carton aside and opened the second one.

More of the same.

But the remaining two were more rewarding. As he lifted out their contents he was mentally back at voodoo ceremonies he had attended on his earlier visit. Both cartons contained objects used on that peasant religion's sacred altars.

Each item was wrapped in layers of newspaper. One by one he unwrapped and examined four of the special gourd rattles called *assons,* then eight of the decorated earthenware jars called *govis,* in which the spirits of gods and the dead were said to dwell, then a number of bowls designed to hold the cornmeal with which, at a service, the *houngan* or *mambo* would draw the gods' identifying *vèvés* on the floor of the peristyle. In addition he discovered a number of framed lithographs. One was of Mary, mother of Jesus, who in voodoo was revered as Erzulie Fréda, the goddess of love. Others depicted various saints of the Roman Catholic Church who also had their counterparts in voodoo.

But there was more.

At the very bottom of the second carton, wrapped not in newspaper but in layers of silk, were three very old glass bottles. At first glance they were green, but on closer examination other colors appeared—little rivers of red, gold and purple that appeared to be alive and actually flowing. He handled them with care and studied them a long time, remembering a day he had talked his way into one of the most secret *hounfors* in all Haiti and found similar bottles on the altar there. Most such bottles had been destroyed during the Catholic Church's relentless campaign to wipe out voodoo many years ago.

Priceless, he thought. Obviously they belonged to the previous tenant, not the landlord. The latter never would have stored such objects in a house to be rented. But why had they been left behind? Where was the previous tenant now?

Cannon repacked the cartons and stacked them again. Finding his wife in the room she already referred to as her sewing room, he told her he would be going out for a while. "I'll be calling on Eddie Bourand. Want to come along?"

She dismissed the idea with a shake of her head. "Not this morning. I want to try out this machine."

"Well, all right. I don't expect to be gone long."

Touching his lips to hers—one could hardly call it a kiss, but they still went through the motions—he went out to the garage. The yard boy, Julien, was wiping down the jeep. About eighteen, he was a good-looking youth who went home nights to wherever he lived. Probably a peasant *caille* somewhere.

Cannon tried out his Creole, found he could still make himself understood, and was pleased. No outsider, of course, ever wholly mastered that peasant tongue and besides, it differed in different parts of the country. "I'll talk to you when I get back," he said. Maybe Julien knew something about the former tenant.

Eddie Bourand and his sister lived on a tree-lined street of fine homes in the wealthy suburb of Turgeau. Janine herself opened the door, though servants hovered in the background. Her brother, she said, had gone to Les Cayes where he had recently opened a new store to complement his others in the capital and Cap Haïtien. "But do come in, Mark. Can I get you a drink?"

"Thanks, but I think I'm going to need a clear head." He did accept her gestured invitation to sit, though. And, as always, he gazed at her with pleasure as she seated herself. Janine Bourand, in her early thirties and still unmarried, was the most beautiful woman he had ever known. With those almost black eyes, that golden skin and exquisitely shaped body . . . just being in her presence was exciting.

"Is there something I can help you with?" she asked.

"I hope so. I need to know who owns the house Eddie rented for me."

"Raoul Valinare. Do you know him?"

Cannon shook his head.

"He has a lot of property. Lives in Canapé Vert. Seems

to be pretty deep in politics." She frowned. "Are you having some problems?

"I've a cat and some kittens that must have been left behind by the previous tenant." Cannon went into some detail about the three kittens and their apparently quite different personalities. "And there are some treasures in the cellar that must belong to him. Why he left them there I can't understand. Or why your Raoul Valinare didn't discover them when he got the place ready for me. But, of course, he probably had servants tidy it up, and that dark crypt under the veranda isn't a place they would have been eager to go into."

"You found treasures, you say?"

"Voodoo things that a folklore museum would put a high price on, I think. Some are very old. I know I'd give my eye teeth to own them, but—" He shrugged. Then he told her about the spectral head he thought he had seen in the tunnel where the treasure cartons were stacked.

Soberly she said, "A disembodied head? Outstretched hands that dripped blood? *Mon Dieu,* Mark . . . it sounds as though the owner of those cartons may still be there!"

"It does, doesn't it? In one form or another." Realizing he was learning nothing, Cannon stood up and thanked her for her hospitality.

"I will speak to Eddie when he returns," she said. "That will be tomorrow, I suppose. He didn't say. Anyway, I'll tell him to phone you."

Cannon drove around the city then, revisiting places he had written about before and would be writing about again: the waterfront, the Iron Market, the slums of Bel Air. His Creole was adequate, he discovered. He had long ago learned that the way to get an answer in that difficult tongue was to keep rephrasing the question until you were understood. When he returned to the house in mid-afternoon, he found Ellen in her sewing room, cutting out a dress of sea-island cotton on a collapsible ping-ping table that had been in another room.

"I guessed you'd be gone most of the day," she said

with a shrug, "so I called a taxi and went shopping. How
was your day?"

"Not bad." Knowing she was not interested in his work,
he never went into details any more. "I think the cat
problem will soon be solved, at least."

"It already is."

"Oh?"

"Lucille or Edita—I don't know which because neither
will admit it—left the kitchen door open and all four cats
have disappeared." She shrugged. "When you stop to
think about it, if they've been shut up in this house since
the last tenant left, they probably wanted out in the worst
kind of way." She crinkled her nose up. "They've been
around long enough to make parts of the house smell, I
can tell you. It's disgusting. God knows what they've been
living on. Mice, I suppose. Or rats. Or cockroaches. Whatever it is that makes the scurrying sounds I keep hearing."

"Have you looked for them?" Cannon asked with a
frown.

"Oh, we looked for them. But they could have been
miles away by the time I discovered they were gone." She
put down her scissors. "No doubt they'll survive. By the
way, do you know we have a swimming pool?"

So she had solved the cat problem by leaving the
kitchen door open, he thought. Of course, the former tenant could not have cared much about them or he would
not have left them here, but what would happen to them
now? The city was full of half-starved dogs. "A swimming
pool?" he said absently. "Where?"

"I'll show you."

The pool had not been used in a long time, Cannon saw
when she led him to it. At the far end of the yard, it held
water all right—in fact, was full to overflowing—but it
was layered with a surface scum full of red almond leaves
and frogs' eggs. Even as he stood scowling at it, a green
head popped up through the scum and bulbous eyes
stared at him.

"What do you think?" his wife said. "If you ask me, it's

too filthy to bother with. I know I won't be using it, even
if the yard boy cleans it out."

Cannon shrugged and turned away, still thinking of the
cats. Or more specifically of the three kittens, one so affectionate, the second so definitely not, the third with
only one eye.

That evening, when Cannon opened the door under the
veranda and fingered the light switch, the tunnel stayed
dark. He stood there until the head with the screaming
mouth glowed red near the four stacked cartons and the
dripping hands reached out toward him. Then he shut the
door and locked it.

When he went upstairs to bed, a second surprise
awaited him. Ellen was in his bed, awake and waiting for
him with her arms outstretched, and when he drew back
the sheet that covered her, he discovered she was naked.

"I thought you'd never come up," she whispered.
"Mark, darling, it's been such a long time since we made
love!"

Ellen was a beautiful woman—as stunningly so tonight
as she had been on their wedding night. His reaction to
her invitation was a wedding-night thing, too. Before he
knew it, he was naked beside her, eagerly returning her
ardent caresses.

Starved for the affection he was now being given, Cannon could think of nothing else for the next half hour.
Gone were those nagging questions about the cats, the
bloody head in the cellar, the contents of the cartons. He
made love to his wife with a passion that obliterated all
else and ended only when both of them were exhausted—though even then he was still breathing hard
and she still voiced sounds of pleasure remarkably like the
purring of a kitten. Then, pushing himself up on his elbows, he saw in the moonlight a thing that puzzled him.

He had never thought of his wife as having much body
hair, but she did, he suddenly realized. The V between
her thighs was covered with a soft, silky hair that re-

sembled fur. It was heavy in her armpits, too, and there were little tufts of it under her breasts.

Strange, he thought. But then he hadn't seen her naked in a long time, had he? And what difference did it make? She was still a lovely woman and now so wonderfully loving as well. . . .

He fell asleep feeling ten years younger and full of gratitude.

The day after his startling surprise in the bedroom, Cannon continued his research in the city. Returning in mid-afternoon, he found his old friend Eddie Bourand talking to Ellen on the veranda. As handsome as his sister Janine was lovely, Bourand explained that he was on his way home from Les Cayes and had stopped by to see if the house suited them. "Does it, old buddy?" A frown accompanied the question. "From talking with Ellen, I get a feeling you have some problems with it."

Surprised, Cannon turned to his wife. The look he had seen on her face last night and this morning was no longer there.

Ellen and Bourand were drinking rum punch. As Cannon pulled up a chair, Lucille came to the door to ask if he would like one. "Please," he replied, then with his hands on his knees leaned toward their caller.

"Tell me something, Eddie. When you rented this house from the owner—"

"Raoul Valinare," Bourand supplied.

"—you must have looked at it first."

"Of course. What actually happened, Valinare came into my store one day and I asked him if he knew of any nice house I could rent for you. He owns property all over the city. This one had just become available, he said, so I looked at it and rented it that same afternoon."

"Did you meet the man who lived here?"

"No. He'd gone."

"Can you tell me anything about him?"

"Only that he lived here alone. Which surprises me—a

house this big. I've no idea where he might be now. Why
the interest, old buddy?"

Lucille came with a rum punch for Cannon, and he
nodded his thanks. "He left some things behind, Eddie.
Unless . . . that is"—the thought seemed to come to Cannon from nowhere, perhaps even out of the drink as he
sipped it—"they belong to Valinare. But I hardly think
they do."

"What sort of things, Mark?"

"Voodoo articles. *Assons, govis,* some rare old bottles."

Ellen said sharply, "You didn't tell me that, Mark."

"Didn't I? It must have slipped my mind. I'll show you
later." Or should he? Mark asked himself. If that bleeding
head appeared, or those ghastly, dripping hands, Ellen
would probably insist on leaving. And good houses were
hard to find.

Nevertheless, soon after Eddie Bourand departed, he
took Ellen into the tunnel under the veranda and showed
her. Perhaps because it was still daylight, the light switch
worked, and the floating head did not appear.

But Ellen was quite unimpressed by the contents of the
cartons. "So far as I'm concerned, it's just a lot of old
junk," she said. "I can't understand why you're concerned
about it."

"You're not interested in voodoo?"

"Not in the slightest. In spite of what you've written
about it, I think it's a joke."

He looked at her. There was simply nothing of last
night left. What could have brought about a change so
soon? "It isn't a joke, you know," he said with a little sigh.
"Nor are these things in the boxes."

"Well, I disagree. Completely."

Ellen worked at her sewing machine until late that evening. Cannon sat at the dining room table with a portable
typewriter, putting down thoughts for the book he would
write. What, exactly, was the mood of this troubled country now that the Duvalier regime had turned to ashes?
Had he come too soon? It would seem so, from what he

had seen and heard so far. True, for the first time since 1957 someone other than a Duvalier occupied the palace. But things were still in a turmoil following Jean-Claude's middle-of-the-night ride to the airport, where a U.S. C-141 had been waiting to fly him into exile.

Well . . . he could only keep on working and hope for the best.

At eleven-thirty he put the typewriter away and went to the sewing room. "Hey," he said from the doorway, "you know what time it is, lady? How about going to bed?"

Ellen looked at her wristwatch. "I'll be a few minutes yet. Why don't you run along?"

"Will you lock up?" In this city, you or a servant made certain before retiring that the downstairs doors and windows, at least, were locked. Otherwise you might wake up in the morning to find your valuables missing. Or you might not wake up at all.

"I'll take care of it," Ellen said. "Go on."

Would it be like last night when she finally did come to bed? Her face and tone of voice hadn't said so, but those inner feelings had to be there still . . . didn't they? Naked in bed, he waited for her. Then as a kind of joke he pretended to be asleep when at last she came.

He had put the light out and she didn't turn it on, but the moonlight glistening on the metal roof outside the windows enabled him to watch her undress. Again he saw—and longed for—the exquisite body he had made love to the night before. But without even a glance in his direction she put on her pajamas and got into her own bed.

Was she, too, playing a game? He tried to make himself wait to find out, but impatience ruled and he went to her. "Hey." Drawing back the sheet that covered her, he leaned over, smiling, to kiss her mouth.

Her lips parted, but not the way he had expected them to. They curled apart in a snarl full of sound and spittle, and suddenly her arms flew up from her sides and her nails raked his face. An inch higher and they might have gouged out his eyes. With a howl of pain he flung himself backward.

"What the hell—!"

It was not his wife he was staring at. It was scarcely human. Like a huge cat she was suddenly on all fours, her eyes ablaze with hate as she glared at him. Dripping saliva from its corners, her mouth again voiced a snarling challenge. Fully expecting her to spring, Cannon flung up his arms to protect himself.

But the attack did not materialize. Instead, the snarling gradually ceased and after twice turning a slow circle on all fours Ellen lay down with her head on one curved arm. Her eyes closed. Though Cannon remained standing there with blood dripping from his gouged face, she did not move again.

When he had recovered enough to move, Cannon snatched up his pajamas and went to the bathroom to clean himself up. Then, still in shock, he paced along the upstairs hall to one of the other bedrooms. But not to sleep. Only to lie there trying in vain to make some sense out of what had happened. At times he felt like crying. At times he watched the door in dread that it might open. Not until the windows were gray with the first light did he at last fall asleep.

When he went down to breakfast, feeling he had been on a treadmill all night, he found Ellen already at the table. "You must have worked late last night," she observed cheerfully.

"What?"

"You used another bedroom, the way you do at home when you're up late."

"Oh. Well, yes." Suspiciously he looked at her.

Nothing in her expression indicated she was playing a game with him. Was she unaware of what she had done? And if so, did she also not remember having made love to him so long and hard the night before? What the hell was going on here anyway?

"Why the Band-Aids on your face?" she asked, frowning. "You look as if a cat scratched you."

"You don't know what they are?"

"Why should I?"

"Well"—he shrugged—"I guess I don't either. Something I did in my sleep, maybe."

Lucille, the housekeeper, had been waiting for a chance to interrupt. She did so now. "*M'sié,* do you know you left a window unlocked last night?"

"What?"

"In the living room. It is not wise to do that, *m'sié.*"

Ellen said sharply, "Now wait just a minute, please. I was the one who locked up last night, and I definitely did not overlook any window." Her voice would have scratched glass. "If you found one open, someone must have opened it!"

There was a brief but uncomfortable silence. Then Lucille, with a face of black stone, said, "Excuse me, please," and stiffly strode out of the room.

Cannon heard her go upstairs. After a moment her voice came shrilling down. *"M'sié, madame! Vini vite, souplé!"*

That command from a normally calm woman to "come quickly, please" was not to be taken lightly. Cannon's chair went over backward as he shot to his feet. Taking the stairs two at a time, he was at the top before Ellen even reached the bottom.

Lucille was at a window in the master bedroom. "Look!" She cried, reverting to English. "Look at this!"

Yes. Look at this, Cannon. See how someone on the roof last night cut a hole in the plastic screen and reached in to lift the hook that secured it. In this house the window screens were hinged on one side and they opened like casement windows.

"And look at this!" Lucille was pointing now at the sill. "Grease! They work naked and grease their bodies so that if you wake up and grab at them, you can't hold them."

Ellen, coming into the room, said, "What's this about grease?"

"On the sill here, Ellen." Cannon explained the meaning of the smear there. "Seems we had a prowler last night. He came in off the roof while you were sleeping and must have left by way of the living room window Lucille found open this morning."

"A prowler!" Ellen's voice cracked. "Oh, my God!"

"We'd better see what he took, then phone the police."

But by the time they had finished their tour of the house an hour later, Cannon was puzzled. *Had* it been a thief who slit the bedroom screen and left the living room window open? Why would one go to all that trouble— even to greasing himself—and not take anything? Because nothing was missing. Not even the radio, which surely would have been one of the first things to catch a thief's eye.

He shook his head in defeat. "I'm damned if I know how to explain this."

"You *are* going to call the police, aren't you?" his wife said.

"And tell them what? We found a screen slit and a window open, but nothing is missing?" He was angry enough to swing around and glare at her. "What's the matter with your eye?"

"What?"

"Your *eye*. Why are you rubbing it like that?"

She dropped her hand from her face, and he stepped forward to peer at her more closely. Her right eye was inflamed. "You must have got something in it," he said. "Don't rub it any more, for God's sake. Put something on it."

Almost contritely she said, "Yes . . . I suppose I'd better," and went to do so.

An hour later they had a caller.

Arriving in a Cadillac driven by a chauffeur, the man introduced himself as Raoul Valinare, the owner of the house. A massive man with an almost hairless head and abnormally large, protruding eyes, he lowered himself onto a veranda chair and, with his hands clasped over his belly, beamed at them. "I have been meaning to come by and ask if everything is to your liking. I apologize for being so tardy. Business, you know." His soprano voice came as a total surprise.

Everything was fine, Cannon assured him.

"Good. Good. But—ah—Edouard Bourand tells me the former tenant left some things behind. A bother to you, I am sure. I should have gone through the house myself after he left, of course, but foolishly I trusted one of my employees to do it." His tongue made clicking sounds as he shook his head. "If you will show me what was left, I will take it to him. Of course."

Cannon said, "You know, *M'sié* Valinare, I'm curious about this man who had the house before we came. What sort of fellow is he?"

"Well, he—ah—he is a painter. Yes, an artist from—ah—Furcy. A peasant, actually, but of course many of our peasant painters have become famous for their primitive art." The almost bald head bobbed up and down now. "He wished to live here in the city for a time, to paint city scenes."

"And now he's returned to—where did you say? Furcy?"

"Yes, he has gone home." The big man was beaming again. "And I will, of course, take to him whatever he left here. I consider it my duty. In fact, I will go there now, at once, even before returning home myself, so that we may consider this matter laid to rest."

"Excuse me a minute, then." Cannon rose. "Ellen, can you give me a hand, please?"

Ellen looked at him in surprise but correctly read the warning in his frown. With a murmured "of course" she followed him into the house, where Cannon did not stop to let her catch up to him until sure they would not be overheard.

He caught hold of her hands then. "Listen. There's something wrong here. When you see what I bring him, don't comment. Okay?"

Though obviously bewildered, she nodded.

"Wait here for me. I'm going out the back way."

He hurried around the house to the door under the veranda. In the tunnel he took up one of the cardboard cartons. Could the man above hear him? It was something to think about, and the thinking induced a sweat that stung the gouges inflicted by Ellen's fingernails. Clutching the carton, he hurried back the way he had come, and found Ellen waiting. Together they approached their caller.

With Ellen silent at his side, Cannon opened the carton on the veranda floor to show Valinare what was in it. "They appear to be costumes of some sort," he said, hoping he sounded convincing. "Something to do with his painting, no doubt. Anyway, they look expensive."

Valinare held up the red silk shirts, the outfit of green velvet, the black suit. His face hardened. "This is all?"

"Yes, of course."

"But your friend Bourand used the word 'treasures.'"

"Well, I guess that's the word *I* used when I talked to him. Perhaps a poor choice, but these *are* unusual clothes, don't you think?"

The almost bald man pushed himself to his feet and stooped to pick up the carton. He no longer beamed. His expression was one of anger and suspicion. Glowering at the Cadillac, he thrust out a hand and imperiously snapped his fingers. His chauffeur sprang from the car and ran up the steps to take the carton from him. Then with a muttered "I bid you good-day," Raoul Valinare departed.

"Do you mind telling me what that was all about?" Ellen demanded of Cannon.

He leaned against the veranda railing and looked at her. "Let me tell you about the last time I went to this Furcy he talked about. It's way up in the mountains and I was driving a jeep, not a Cadillac. And a good part of that road was so narrow and vertical, even for a jeep in four-wheel drive, that I had to ask Eddie Bourand to sit out front on the hood, with his feet on the front bumper, so we wouldn't tip over backward."

She had to think about that. "You mean he was lying?"

"His head off," Cannon said grimly. "The only thing is—I can't figure out why."

Puzzled and apprehensive about Valinare's visit, Cannon spent that day at home. But he had more than the Haitian's lying to think about. Throughout the day Ellen's eye worsened.

Lucille noticed it while serving the evening meal. *"Madame,* you should see a doctor," she advised, shaking her head in what had to be genuine concern for another's suffering. "It has become much worse since morning, *madame!"*

Ellen's response was a surprise even to Cannon, who had lived with her temper for years. His wife turned on the housekeeper in a fury. "Damn it, leave me alone! When I want your advice, I'll ask for it."

Lucille fled to the kitchen and Cannon heard her sobbing. Then Ellen turned on him.

"I suppose you and Edita want me to go to a doctor, too. All of you know what's best for me. Maybe I should ask the yard boy for his opinion."

"Ellen, cut it out," he begged. "There *is* something wrong with your eye and you *ought* to see a doctor."

"Well, I'm not trusting my eyes to any Haitian doctor, I can tell you! I want to go back to Florida!"

"Do you? Really?"

"Of course I do! I never should have come to this stupid country!"

No, Cannon thought, you never should have. But not just because of your eye. "All right. We'll get you on a plane tomorrow."

"Thank God." She pushed her chair back from the table and stood up. "I'll go upstairs and pack. Right now!"

Cannon forced himself to finish his dinner, then went into the living room and sat to think. He heard his wife upstairs, slamming closet doors in her anger. Heard Lucille and Edita in the dining room, clearing the table. Suddenly, to his surprise, the two Haitian women came into

the living room and approached his chair. "May we speak
to you *m'sié?*" Lucille asked.

"Of course."

"It is about *madame.*" They looked at each other, as
though half afraid to continue. Then Lucille plunged on.
"*M'sié,* it is not true that one of us left a door open and
the cats ran away!"

"I know." He nodded. "My wife left it open."

"No, *m'sié.*"

"What?" Bewildered, he studied their faces.

"She drowned them in the pool, *m'sié,*" Edita said. "We
saw her do it, both of us. She carried them one by one to
the pool in the yard and held them under the water until
they drowned. Then she threw them over the wall, and
we heard dogs fighting over them."

"My God," Cannon said in a whisper. "How could she?"

He had to confront his wife with this. Had to, absolutely.
But halfway up the stairs he decided not to. Those three
kittens, one so affectionate, one a snarler, one with only
one eye . . . Ellen was already paying a price for killing
them. A kind of price he did not quite understand, but this
was Haiti where all sorts of mysterious things happened.

With a shake of his head he returned to the living room
and switched on the radio. Then, remembering there was
something he wanted to do before Ellen and he retired,
he went into the kitchen. Edita was washing the dinner
dishes, Lucille drying them.

"I need an empty tin can. Do we have one?"

Edita fished an evaporated milk can out of the trash.
"Like this, *m'sié?*"

"Fine. And some string."

She produced a ball of thick sisal twine from which he
cut off a couple of feet with his jackknife.

He carried the can out to the driveway and half filled it
with pebbles, then took it up to the bedroom where Ellen
was packing. The tightness of her lips told him she was still
furious. Not wanting another demonstration of her temper,
he silently went about finishing what he had started.

With his knife he punched a hole in the can near the top, then fastened one end of the twine to it. The slashed screen, when closed on the other end, was snug enough to hold it. When he finished, the can dangled between window and floor where it could not be seen from the roof.

"What's that for?" Ellen demanded.

"A burglar alarm. If he pays us a return visit tonight, this can of pebbles will fall to the floor and the racket will wake us."

"How ingenious."

Ignoring the sarcasm, he turned to frown at her: "How is your eye?"

"Oh, go to hell."

Prepared for a return visit from the prowler, Cannon dispensed with pajamas that night and slept with his clothes on—not in the bed but on it. Sometime in the middle of the night the can of pebbles clattered to the floor and waked him.

The screen was open. On the floor in front of it crouched a glistening black shape apparently frozen in mid-motion by the alarm. When Cannon flung himself from the bed and lunged for it, the shape raced for the door.

Cannon tore down the stairs after it, losing ground when he stumbled and nearly fell headlong. Only a quick clutch at the mahogany railing saved him. But the prowler won no great advantage. At the foot of the stairs he hesitated, turning first to the window he had used as an exit before, then to the door. Racing to the door, he reached up to pull down one of the two bolts that held it shut, then seized the knob and yanked.

Before he could realize that in his panic he had forgotten the bolt at the bottom, Cannon was on him. And Cannon was bigger, stronger. When they went to the floor together, Cannon was the one who ended up on his knees with both hands at the other's throat, even though the other was naked and greased.

"Please, *m'sié*," the man under him begged in Creole. "Please . . . I meant you no harm. I did not come here to steal from you."

There was not much moonlight in that part of the room. Bewildered, Cannon had to bend lower to make sure he had identified the voice correctly. "Julien?" he said. The yard boy?

"*M'sié,* let me explain," the youth whispered. "Please. I will not try to get away again."

Cannon pulled him to his feet and led him to a chair. "All right, sit down." The grease would ruin the slipcover, but it could be cleaned, and anyway, he could not keep the fellow standing for as long as this would probably take, nor did he feel like standing that long himself. Pulling up another chair, he sat facing the boy. "Are you the one who broke in here last night?"

Julien nodded.

"Why? What are you after?"

"*M'sié,* let me show you." Hesitantly, the yard boy extended both hands. When they were not slapped away, he found courage enough to place his fingertips against Cannon's temples. "Now close your eyes," he said. "Please. I am your friend. I will not hurt you."

This was crazy, Cannon thought, but found himself obeying. His eyes closed. For a moment nothing happened except that he could feel the pressure of the fingers on his temples. Then in some way that he found completely bewildering he realized he was no longer in the living room but out in the yard. It was night but the yard was awash with moonlight. About twenty feet away stood a man he had never seen before—a black man of average height, average build, but one who would never see middle age again.

At the foot of the driveway was a car. A Cadillac. Four men were getting out of it. One was the big, almost bald man with bulging eyes who had come in the same car yesterday. Valinare. Raoul Valinare.

One of the other three swung a machete whose blade seemed to slice the moonlight into glittering shards as the intruders strode across the yard toward their quarry.

The four encircled the old man, effectively preventing any flight he might have had in mind, and Cannon was very much present, invisible to the others but a witness to what was happening. It was Valinare who spoke first.

"Sylvio, your presence is required at the palace."

"So you say." The old fellow lifted his small bony shoulders in a shrug. "I have already said I will not go."

"You must. They demand it."

"Let them demand. I am a respected *houngan.* I do not serve such people."

"Then we must change your mind for you, Sylvio. Because we do not leave here tonight without you. And unless you come with us, you will never go anywhere again." With a nod to the others, Valinare stepped back and folded his arms.

A man went behind Sylvio. Grasping the old man's left wrist, he jerked the arm up until a bone snapped and Sylvio's mouth opened in a scream of agony. Valinare said, "Now will you come with us?"

Staring back into these bulbous eyes, Sylvio shook his head.

The man behind him grasped his other wrist and jerked that arm up, too, until something broke. Again the old man screamed.

"Now?" Valinare said.

"No! I respect the *loa.* I will not debase them in such a way!"

Valinare nodded to the man with the machete. That one stepped forward and placed the edge of the blade against the old man's throat. "Old fool, this is your last chance!" the big man shouted. "Are you coming with us or do you wish to part with your head?"

"I serve only the *loa.*"

Valinare shrugged, then stepped aside to give the man with the machete more room. That one's left hand shot out to clench in Sylvio's hair. His other hand, holding the huge knife, swept back over his shoulder.

The blade flashed forward. When the *hougan's* body fell twitching to the ground, his head, gushing blood from the neck, still hung from his executioner's outstretched hand.

Valinard said, "Bring a sack," and one of the men, going
to the Cadillac, returned with an empty burlap bag. The
houngan's arms were chopped off and stuffed into it.
Then his legs. His head went in last. Then, with two men
sharing the weight of the sack between them, the intruders returned to the car and it disappeared down the road.

As the picture faded, Cannon found himself gazing again
into the face of his yard boy. "My God," he whispered as
the fingertips stopped pressing his temples. And then,
"How did you do that?"

"I was Papa Sylvio's protégé, *m'sié.* He taught me that
and more." Tears filled the boy's eyes. "He was one of the
most learned *houngans* in all Haiti, and a good man."

"After what you've just shown me, I believe you." Re-
covering, Cannon sat back on his chair. "So that's what
you are looking for, is it? His body?"

"No, not his body. I watched this whole thing happen
from a window, you understand. I know the body is not
here. What I seek is a *govi* the master made just before
they killed him. Do you know what a *govi* is, *m'sié?*"

"A jar in which he spirits of the dead reside, I believe."

"Well, yes—that is enough to know. And one of those he
made was to be the resting place of his own spirit. It was
blue, with Erzulie's heart of love painted on it in her other
colors of rose and white. That is what I seek, *m'sié*—Sylvio's
govi. Only that, so I can take it to his home in Furcy."

"He lived in Furcy?"

Julien nodded. "He was an artist. As good a one as Phi-
lomé Obin or Hector Hyppolite or any of those others
whose work, people say, is known all over the world
now." Tears trickled down the boy's cheeks. "That wonderful man . . . and you have seen what Valinare and those
Tonton Macoutes did to him."

"Why did they want him to go to the palace?"

Julien wiped his tears away. "Who knows for sure? But
one can guess, no? Those at the palace must have been
full of despair at that time, knowing the end was so near
unless they could persuade someone powerful to help
them. What does it matter now?" The youth struggled to

his feet. "All that matters is that Papa Sylvio must be re-
venged, *m'sié!* Those evil men must pay!"

From the foot of the stairs a voice interrupted. "Mark,
what is he saying?"

Startled, Cannon looked up and saw Ellen standing
there. The clatter of his tin can alarm must have waked
her.

He answered her question.

"I don't believe a word of it!" she sneered. "The boy is
a thief and you know it. This is just a cover-up!"

"Now, Ellen—"

"You mean you're not even going to call the police?"

He stood up and faced her. "If I call the police, Ellen, it
will be only to tell them what Valinare and his Tontons
did."

"You fool, must you believe everything you are told in
this stupid country? All I can say is—"

Cannon was no longer interested in what she was saying. The yard boy had grabbed at his sleeve and was making the hissing sound—"Psssst!"—that people used in this
country to attract attention.

"Listen!" the boy whispered. "In the road, *m'sié!* A car!"

Cannon heard nothing but stepped to a window. Lucien
was right. At the end of the driveway a car had stopped.
Was it the Cadillac? He thought it was. Its doors swung
open and four men stepped out. One of them Cannon
recognized as Raoul Valinare.

The boy had moved swiftly to Cannon's side. Peering
out, he said quietly, "Those are the same men, *m'sié!*"

Here for what? Cannon asked himself. The "treasures"
he had mentioned? That was it, of course. These monsters
who had butchered an innocent old man just for refusing
his services would undoubtedly put a high value on the
instruments of his power.

With his wife silent now and young Julien at his side,
he watched the men ascend the driveway. What time was
it? He glanced at his watch. Three-twenty. Thin clouds
formed a layer of gauze that diluted the moonlight, but
the men were visible enough. They went where he

thought they would go: straight to the door under the veranda. Because, of course, Valinare had heard him there when he went for the carton of clothing.

Cannon turned from the window. "Julien, come with me," he whispered. "Be very quiet." His wife also followed, but he was in too big a hurry to tell her not to.

He led the boy through the house and out the back way, then around the house to a high hibiscus hedge through which they could watch what was happening without being noticed.

Valinare and his thugs were at the door, one of them working on the lock. In a moment the door was open and they disappeared inside.

They were using flashlights, Cannon saw. Either the light switch hadn't worked—it never had at night—or they had chosen not to use it lest they attract attention to their intrusion. With a nod to Julien, he glided forward from the hedge, the boy only a step behind when they reached the doorway. By then the four intruders were at the far end of the tunnel.

They had no trouble opening the containers there; Cannon had seen no need to be careful in reclosing them. Bending over them, one of the men lifted out an earthenware jar—one of the *govis* the *houngan* had made—and handed it to Valinare. "Good!" Cannon heard the politician mutter. "How many are there?"

"Eight. And look! This one for Erzulie is a true beauty!" The fellow handed Valinare a second *govi.*

"Ah!" Those big, pudgy hands lifted the jar to the level of Valinare's bulging eyes while another Tonton shone a light on it.

Suddenly, without warning, a fiery head exploded from the jar and hung blazing in the space above it, dripping blood. A pair of disembodied hands followed.

Cannon had seen that head and those hands before, exactly as they were now—the mouth a jagged hole voicing a silent scream of agony while blood dripped from it like red rain, the hands a pair of bloody claws seemingly searching for a victim. But one of the hands now gripped a huge machete, the blade of which pulsed as though just snatched from a blacksmith's furnace.

With a hoarse cry Valinare let the *govi* fall. It hit the concrete floor with a sound like a clap of thunder and broke into two jagged pieces. From the bottom half a fiery shape resembling a cat leaped out, followed by three smaller such shapes. But the politician and his thugs were already in wild flight, desperately pawing and pushing one another in their rush to the door.

Cannon and young Julien quickly stepped aside to leave the doorway empty, lest they be knocked down and trampled. But they had nothing to fear. The floating face and hands of old Sylvio were faster than the intruders. Faster, in fact, than Cannon's eye could follow. Before Valinare and his thugs could reach the entrance, the fiery face and hands were there to block it.

Then the hand with the machete went to work.

Valinare was the first to feel the blade because, being heavier and more ruthless, he was the first to come within reach. It slashed across his skull horizontally with such force that the top part of his head—the part with the bulging eyes—sailed a yard through space before plopping to the floor like an inverted bowl. The second blow of the steel was a downward slash that stopped one of the Tontons in his tracks and made two vertical halves of him.

Then, like a bolt of fiery lightning gone mad, the blade continued its quest for vengeance, turning what had been four living men into bloody scraps of meat, bone, and clothing. The walls of the tunnel dripped with splatterings. The pile on the floor belonged in a slaughterhouse.

The last motion of the machete was like an afterthought. Through the eerie beams of dropped flashlights the blade or the spectral hand holding it seemed to seek some special target. Its point suddenly stabbed downward into the remains of a head. Something like a red ping-pong ball flew across the tunnel to splatter against a wall. A second one followed.

Though numb with horror, Cannon asked himself why.

Was it so that even in death the man with bulging eyes would exist in darkness as he deserved?

There was no time to ponder the question. Though the floating face and hands of old Sylvio had disappeared now, something else was happening. The four cat shapes from the *houngan's govi* were on the prowl. Their eyes glowed with a frightening brightness as they bounded toward the doorway as though they, too, sought vengeance.

After all, they were not ordinary cats . . . were they? They had been the companions of a voodoo priest. . . .

In the yard a woman was screaming. Not recognizing the voice, Cannon turned. Dim in the moonlight some ten yards away stood his wife, her hands rigidly outthrust as though she knew she was the prey being sought. A few yards away stood the housekeeper, Lucille, in a white nightgown.

Why was Lucille only standing there instead of trying somehow to help?

The answer flashed in Cannon's consciousness as though young Julien's fingertips were pressing his temples again. He was back in the dining room where with genuine concern Lucille had just said to Ellen, "*Madame,* you should see a doctor." And Ellen, having turned on her in a rage, was snarling, "Damn it, leave me alone! When I want your advice, I'll ask for it!"

Ah, Ellen, you are your own worst enemy!

In any case, it was too late now. With the mother cat in the lead, the spectral shapes had nearly reached their target. Cannon saw his wife lift a limp hand to her ailing eye as though accepting the truth for the first time. Facing them, retreating backward step by step, she seemed physically unable to turn and run.

Suddenly Cannon was aware of what her stalkers intended. "Ellen, look out!" he yelled. "Behind you!"

But there was no time. Even as he cried out, the largest of the spectral cats became larger—became a blazing apparition the size of a tiger—and leaped. Ellen's scream of terror split the night wide open as she flung up her arms.

One foot caught on the edge of the pool. Her attacker

crashed into her. Claws and fangs had already silenced the scream before tiger and victim disappeared together.

The three spectral kittens, on reaching the pool, committed themselves to it without hesitation, as though eager to play their part in what was happening below that floating layer of scum.

Cannon stumbled forward but was still a step away from the pool's edge when his wife's face reappeared, upturned in a mass of slime. He stopped then, knowing there was nothing he or anyone else could do.

As he sank to his knees he heard himself sobbing out the last words he would ever say to her. "Oh my God, Ellen . . . you could have left a door open and let them run away. . . . You didn't have to drown them. . . ."

He awoke in a bed, with faces hovering over him. One was that of his friend, Eddie Bourand, the other that of Eddie's lovely sister, Janine. Both were full of concern and compassion. Janine reached for one of his hands and held it.

"At last," she whispered. "Oh, Mark, at last! How do you feel?"

Struggling to sit up, he looked around. "Where am I?"

"The hospital," Eddie Bourand said.

"How long have I been here?"

"All day. Lucille phoned us at four this morning. We went and got you."

"Yes," Janine said. "And you've been babbling all that time about what happened." Her free hand began to stroke his forehead, and the touch was unmistakably a caress. "But you are not to worry, Mark. Julien and Lucille told the police everything. They won't be troubling you except perhaps to sign a statement. After all, they are Haitian. They understand these things."

Her brother said, "Mark, I'm so damned sorry. Forgive me."

"For what?"

"For renting a house from that bastard. I didn't know what he was."

"It's all right, old buddy. I know you didn't."

"Look, I have to go now. When you get out of here,
you'll be staying with us until you're over this. You hear?"
Eddie leaned over his sister to touch Cannon on the
shoulder. "See you both later," he said, and went out.

With Janine still sitting there, Cannon lay with his eyes
closed, thinking about what had happened. His unhappy
life with Ellen was over, he realized. She, not he, had
played the final card.

Then he looked up at the face of the woman beside his
bed and saw his future . . . as clearly as though young
Julien's fingertips were again pressing his temples.

Afterword

Many an aspiring writer tries to imitate the work of Howard
Phillips Lovecraft; we all know that. And it has been said by
certain editors and critics that some of those aspiring writers reach for the wrong gun in the Lovecraft arsenal.

In short, they attempt to emulate the Lovecraft style,
when they ought to be trying to scale the heights of his
imagination.

If this is so—and I think it may be—then I must have
been an exception to the rule. When I was a young writer
living in Lovecraft's Providence, writing poems for the
Evening Bulletin and short stories for the pulp-paper
magazines, I read H.P.L's work in *Weird Tales* and admired not his style, which in my youthful arrogance I dismissed as antique, but the aforementioned imagination.
Hey, look. This fellow wasn't writing about vampires and
werewolves and mummies and stuff; he was inventing a
whole new mythology and making you believe it!

He was doing something else, too, that I admired. He
knew how to grip the reader by the throat early on, then
develop a story slowly but suspensefully until he was
ready to lower the boom with an explosive ending. Very
good at this was Howard Lovecraft. We owe him.

SOUL KEEPER
Joseph A. Citro

The door was unlocked. He was sure of it. The old man had never turned the key!

Carl pressed his ear against its heavy wooden panels, listening. He touched the painted oak with his fingertips, touched the lock, the hinge, the frame itself, feeling for vibrations. Listening. . . .

Did he dare to open it?

No! It could be a trick. The old man might be waiting on the other side with a knife or a gun.

But that wasn't right. Carl had clearly heard him descend the stairs, his heavy footfalls unmistakable as they faded. And he hadn't come back up; Carl had been listening for hours. God, it must be almost midnight by now.

Eyes closed, forehead against the door, Carl tried to imagine how things had looked on the other side. He could recall the narrow unlighted stairway leading to the hall below. Was there carpet on the stairs? He didn't know; he just couldn't remember.

And what of the downstairs hall? Was *it* carpeted? Was the floor exposed wood and potentially noisy? Would he have to walk in his stocking feet so as not to be heard?

If he was lucky, he could make it down the stairs, across the hall, and to the safety of the outside. But wait; if he got out, he'd *need* his shoes. Trouble was, if he carried them, he'd have only one hand free to defend himself.

God, there were so many little details. Any one of them could mean the difference between life and death.

Carl took the doorknob in his hand, moved it minutely to the left and right. Did he dare?

Listening. . . .

Quiet on the other side. He sensed no vibration with his fingertips, heard nothing with his fine-tuned ears. All was still. Even the relentless squall of the televangelists was silenced for another day.

The old man must be in bed.

But was he sleeping?

Carl stood up. His back, still stiff from the accident, protested with a dull tug of pain. "Ahhh!" But his wounded leg was better; the swelling was down. Finally, he was able to bend it at the knee. He was certain he could walk on it with no trouble.

But could he run?

What if the old man heard him? Or saw him?

What if he *had* to run?

Would he be able to?

And how far?

It didn't matter; it was worth the risk. If he didn't leave tonight, now, he might be doomed to remain a captive in this tiny prison for another week, a month, maybe longer. In fact, he might never get another crack at escape. He'd have to wait—months maybe—until the old man forgot to lock the door again.

No. Now was the time. By God, he'd risk it.

His fingers tightened on the cold doorknob and—he took a deep breath—turned it.

Thank God! It really was unlocked! Oh, thank God.

Now, the problem was immediate. And simple. Could he open the door quietly, descend the stairs, make it all the way to the front door without waking the old man?

He didn't know; he wasn't confident.

Feeling the punch of his heart against the inside of his chest, Carl willed himself to be calm.

I'd better take another minute and think.

He had to remember everything, to picture precisely all the features of the old house. He wanted to anticipate every obstacle between here and freedom. Were there irregularities in the walls? Would he find furniture blocking his way in the darkness? Did the outside door open outward, or inward? He had to remember, he *had* to. . . .

His life depended on it.

Carl sat down on the carpet, his back to the door, and, for the millionth time, he ran through all of it in his memory.

The First Day

The fight with Lucy had been a stupid thing. *Tithing* for Christ sake! *Now* she wanted him to pledge twenty percent of his income to the church! Twenty percent!

"You're the one who 'got religion,' but I'm the one who's paying for it!"

Her eyes did their best Tammy Bakker imitation, filling quickly with sparkling tears. It was as if her pudgy body were sculpted from a wet sponge, and he was squeezing it.

His anger rose as he scanned their checkbook. April third, check number 215 paid to the Church of the Christian Soldiers, fifteen dollars. April tenth, twenty-five dollars. April 17, twenty-five dollars. Good God, he only earned $304.00 a week at the gas station! There was the rent, the car payments, Jilly's braces. Good God, there was food to buy!

"You're already giving away twenty-five dollars a week! Do you know how long it takes me to earn twenty-five dollars? Jesus, Lucy, we can't afford your religion!"

Her mouth opened. Her right hand fluttered up to her chest, perched like a dove upon her heart. She took a step backward. "I . . . I . . ."

Carl threw the checkbook at her. Though it missed her head by inches, it must have triggered her "ON" switch. "You're a Godless man, Carl Congdon. A Godless, selfish man. There are them whose need is greater than ours, there are them who . . ."

Her voice trailed off to a blessed whisper as he slammed the screen door and stomped across the rain-drenched yard to the car.

"You're bound for damnation, Carl Congdon," she called after him. "You're bound . . ."

The engine roared when he turned the key. His foot stomped mercilessly on the accelerator. Burning rubber in reverse, he screeched into the road, hit the clutch, the shift, and rocketed northward.

At first there were only a few other cars on the road. Then none at all. It was too dark, too rainy. Drops of water flattening against the windshield made the whole world look like it was wrapped in cellophane.

He took a moment to breathe deeply, willing himself to be calm. The best medicine, he knew, was tucked into the upholstered pocket behind the passenger's seat. He reached back—"Ah, got it!"—and pulled the pint to a place it would be more useful. Momentarily taking his hands from the wheel, he removed the cap and kissed the bottle.

Leaving East Burke and heading toward Burke Hollow, Carl started to relax. The Vermont hills, day or night, always made him feel better. God, he thought, her holy-rolling is getting way out of hand. She's gone crazy with it. I never gambled on something like that when I said for better or for worse.

He knew he had about a hundred dollars in his pocket, the money he'd been stashing away to buy Floyd Blount's Harley. "Fuck the Harley," he said out loud. "By Jesus, I'm going to Canada!"

With those simple words Carl had completely severed all the rotting fibers that joined him to his wife and family. It was over. Period. It was just that simple. The Lord could have her.

He continued north, drifting away from the better-traveled routes and on to the narrow pitted traces that crisscrossed Vermont's Northeast Kingdom like lines in the palm of a hand. The Kingdom was the most remote, least settled part of the state. The forests were vast, the roads were gravel, and the inhabitants were few and far between. As long as he headed north he'd be fine; he was in no hurry. He could be in Montreal before morning.

Trying to recap the pint, he lifted his hands from the wheel. Briefly. Just long enough to drift onto the soft shoulder of the dirt road. The engine roared as his wheels spat sand and fought for purchase. Wet saplings, resisting the metallic intrusion, swatted at the car as it bore into the bushes.

The last thing he saw was a tree rushing at him. God, it was going to hit—

The Second Day

Eyes.

Two eyes floated before him, staring from out of a mysterious undulating fog. They were like twin headlights in an infinite darkness.

A blink brought the man into focus—the man the eyes belonged to. Dressed in white . . . must be a doctor.

Carl shook his head, trying to wake up. The motion hurt. The fog swirled and throbbed and parted.

He was in a room. Not a hospital room. It was like a library, with books on long shelves made of dark wood.

Carl could smell those books, they had a musty odor like the magazines he used to read in the barn when he was a boy.

"You have been sent to me," said the man with the eyes, his voice a whisper. The moving lips were barely visible amid the gray thatch of his beard. "You are in my care now. I hope you are feeling better."

It *must* be a hospital?

The accident rushed back, filling his mind. The tree charging his car—

Remembering the impact shocked Carl to full alertness. Fog cleared as if blasted by sunlight.

It took a moment to find his voice, "Where . . . where am I?"

The eyes squinted, but didn't close. "You are at my house, high in the sky." The voice had a singsong quality that Carl didn't like. "Our Good Lord directed me to the wreckage of your vehicle on the road. It is fortunate you were thus chosen. No one would have found you. No one passes that way. And you were suffering, so I brought you here."

"Well . . . I . . . thank you, but—"

"No, don't thank me. It is my calling." Then the eyes widened to an unsettling fullness. "You're dead, you know."

Carl's nervous system seized up like a disc brake. Dead! He flexed his toes, his fingers. Other than the pounding in his head he could feel no pain, no discomfort.

"Dead?" he gulped. "What are you talking about?"

The old man's face, a bird's nest of hair and wrinkles, rearranged itself into a soothing smile. "You are but one step from the Heavenly Land—"

"Now wait a minute!" Carl sat up with a start. The sudden motion hammered in his temples. Settling back on the leather sofa, he waited for the pain to pass.

"W . . . what do you mean I'm . . . dead?"

The old man patted Carl's shoulder. He spoke like a stern parent. "My son, your life ended in the wreckage of your car on the road. Until you are finally at peace, it is my calling to make your time in transition—be it days, weeks, or even years—as pleasant for you as possible."

Carl studied the robed, long-haired figure. Only one word came to mind: *crazy.*

"I . . . what are you talking about?"

The ancient eyes were patient. "Your final reward, my son. Your days of peace. Come with me, let me show you."

Carl's fleeting thoughts of a fast escape ended when he saw a gun in the old man's hand.

"To where?" Carl said hopelessly, gazing at the barrel of the weapon.

"Why up, of course. Up to Heaven."

With the muzzle of the .38, the bearded man nudged Carl up a narrow, unlit stairway. Carl's back was so tense and numb that any attempt to straighten it resulted in sharp tearing pain. With every step, his injured leg shot bolts of electrical agony along his stooped spine.

At the top of the stairway Carl saw a huge wooden door, painted gold. They opened the heavy door, passed through, and into a foyer that connected four rooms. Carl looked around. This floor, like the one below, showed many indications of the old man's wealth.

Carl scanned the impressive paintings on the walls: sunny pastures, proud white stallions, ships under full sail. There were other pictures too, violent Biblical scenes with scarlet skies and sharp fingers of lightning that pinned wriggling sinners to an endless wall of skulls. There was a portrait of the smiling Jesus and behind him a white-bearded deity with merciless maniacal eyes.

Carl shivered. When his gaze came to rest on the hand-carved woodwork framing a nearby window, he gasped. His nerves flared at what he saw behind the glass: bars! They were so black they seemed like part of the night.

A soft sob of dread escaped his heaving lungs.

Carl couldn't pull his unwilling eyes from those bars as the old man continued, "Here you will have everything you may require to make your brief stay comfortable and pleasant. There is an excellent library—I've personally selected the titles. There is a color television set tuned to inspirational programming. And of course stereophonic equipment of rare and unmatched quality. Should there be anything not provided, you may make me aware of it in your prayers. I am a wealthy man, sir. Our Lord has generously provided for me to perform my special calling—I will provide for you just as generously. After all, it is your reward, is it not?"

"My reward?"

"Yes, my son, you have attained the Heavenly Land. Your stay in transition will be brief. I must prepare you for your journey to the final realm. And now, sir, you must rest." The old man smiled beatifically, "Bless you and good night."

Carl could not speak as he watched the heavy door close. He heard the solid sound of wood against wood. He heard the metal key turn in the lock. "Heaven . . ." he sighed, "with a big, fat lock on the pearly gates."

The Third Day

After the initial panic, after he'd had a little time to think, Carl began to realize the seriousness of his position. Gazing out the barred windows for hours had shown him how far away from civilization he was. All he could see were rolling pine-topped hills, distant pastures, and far far away to the south, what appeared to be a stream. He couldn't even see a road! Suppose he could figure a way out of here, how would he make his way back to civilization?

The alternative was apparently what the crazy old man had in mind: to hold him prisoner in this ersatz Heaven until he died of old age, or maybe worse, became was loony as his captor.

Carl had a clear idea what religious excess could do to the mind. He had seen the beginnings of some kind of mania in his wife Lucy. Helplessly, he had watched it take hold of her during the eighth year of their marriage. How quickly its stern hands had molded her, transforming her into a self-righteous stranger ping-ponging between frequent fits of scolding and tears.

Well, he had run away from Lucy, and he could run away from this lunatic as well.

But the time was not right.

Although his back pain had diminished, his leg was still stiff and sore. At first he had feared a fracture, but now he was convinced it was merely a sprain. In any event, running was out of the question. While he waited for it to heal, he would plan his escape.

He knew the bars on the windows and the heavy bolted door would be problems. Perhaps his only hope was to subdue the old man somehow and make a run for it. It wouldn't be easy; the old man never appeared without a Bible in one hand and a weapon in the other.

Two days worth of "classes" had given Carl plenty of insight into the old man's delusions. Apparently he thought he was "God's man," a modern-day prophet charged with the responsibility of preparing near-worthy souls for their ascent into the Second Heaven.

The First Heaven, the old man had explained, was the top floor of his house.

"Our Great God placed you into my hands," the old man was always quick to remind him. "He says you are nearly ready, but yet imperfect. That is why He did not take you in the crash. That is why He entrusted you to me. I shall put the final touches on your salvation."

The old man went on with his sermon as Carl's mind wandered. Vaguely, he heard resonant tones rendering passages from a book the old man had written. A book he'd added to the Bible between the Old and New Testaments. Carl had to fight tears of resignation with every lofty-sounding phrase.

The brutal realization hit him again and again: he was being held by a madman, and there was absolutely nothing he could do about it.

He feigned attention and dreamed of escape.

Today's "lesson" consisted of a few confusing remarks intended to clarify the Bible readings. The concluding statement showcased the prophet's skills as an orator, "Those of us placed above temptation are nearer yet to the Golden Light. All men must be guided by the prophet, as the wisdom of the prophet is guided by the Light. Yield not to temptation, for those who embrace its worldly rewards will never attain the Heavenly Land, and all will be lost."

The old man paused dramatically, looking at his congregation of one. He punctuated the lesson's end with a stiff nod of the head, then he left the room. His long black cassock flapped behind him like the wings of a crow.

In the silence that followed, Carl heard the familiar sound of the key turning in the lock.

He stared at the barred window and he wept.

The Fifth Day

His breakfast tray did not arrive. Noon came and passed, but there was no midday meal.

Could something have happened to the old man?

Carl's brief flash of hope quickly turned into a new terror: if the old man died or took off, Carl could waste away and starve to death.

He ran to the golden door. Tried it. Found it locked. He pounded until his hands throbbed and hollered till his throat was hoarse. Nothing.

Then he ran to the window and shouted some more.

Exhausted, sobbing, Carl settled into a fitful nap. When he awoke his dinner tray was on the table in the foyer. It was empty except for a note on his pewter plate. It said:

One must learn to accept God's gifts with
an attitude of restraint and moderation. For

today's lesson, you must learn the glory of self-denial.

The Fifteenth Day

By now Carl was convinced the old man was planning to kill him.

He suspected that when he had learned the lessons to the old man's satisfaction, a bullet to the head—or something—would propel him the rest of the way into Heaven.

Or maybe it would be nothing so rapid. He knew the once-a-day oatmeal was not enough to sustain him much longer. Was he fated to starve to death?

From somewhere he remembered a saying he had once heard, something about those who God will destroy He'd first make mad.

Well, madness was close at hand. He found himself praying that the bodily destruction to follow would be mercifully swift. A quick bullet to the brain would be preferable to this gradual starvation.

God, he was so weak; he slept ten to fourteen hours a day. His health and his sanity seemed to be draining away. Death. Sleep. Insanity. Anything would be preferable to another week of this imprisonment.

Death was beginning to seem like a friend.

The Twenty-First Day

Carl awoke on the floor when something jabbed his head. He opened his eyes. The shades in the room were drawn; it would have been completely black but for the light of the television. A profusely sweating Reverend Mercy paraded back and forth on the screen; luckily the sound was off.

Something jabbed Carl's head again. Eyes shifting left, he saw the old man kneeling beside him, poking his temple with the muzzle of the pistol.

"Hey!" Carl protested.

"Ssssh," said the old man. "It's time for our lesson."

As Carl started to get up he realized one foot was chained to the floor. "What's this? Why'd you do that?"

"Today you must learn to humble yourself before the Lord." There was repressed thunder in the old man's voice.

Carl was on his feet now. The eighteen-inch length of chain made walking impossible.

"Now you must kneel before the Lord!" The voice was loud, commanding. The eyes blazed with an unworldly light. "On your knees, sinner. On your knees and ask the good Lord to take you home."

Carl felt the strength drain from his legs. His knees turned to Jello. Weakened by irregular meals and the drugs he was sure the old man was giving him, Carl was afraid he'd fall. But even in his unrelenting state of fear, he'd be damned if he'd kneel before this lunatic.

"On your knees before me!"

"I won't."

The old man pushed Carl off-balance. The chain stiffened, snagged his untethered foot. He toppled, his face smashed against the wooden floor.

"On your knees. Now. Or know the vengeance of the Light."

A sob squeezed from his constricted throat.

Carl shifted his position, got one knee firmly under him before lifting himself onto both.

The Final Day

Carl feigned sleep there on the floor, pretending he'd passed out. The events which immediately followed were like the short precise acts of a tragic play: he felt the old man remove the chain, stomp to the door, unlock it, pull it open, close it, and descend the stairs.

He heard every footfall.

Only then did he dare to open his eyes. The room was

surreal in the unearthly blue light from the TV screen.
Rain beat against the window glass.

Carl crawled to the sofa and tried to pull himself up.
The chain was gone but the skin around his ankle was raw
and bleeding. His wounded leg throbbed.

When he was able to get to his feet, he walked unsteadily from room to room. He wanted to limber up and
to make sure he was alone.

As always, in an automatic part of his wandering ritual,
he listened at the door to the stairs. Then, absently, he
tried it.

It was unlocked!

He couldn't believe it!

In his rage the old man had forgotten to secure the
bolt.

Thunder crashed outside. Lightning lit the room with
flashbulb brilliance. Carl's mind worked the fastest it had
in weeks. He could get out now! He could hot-wire the
old man's car and be safe at home by morning. He could
leave the old man and his lunatic Heaven far behind.

Wait. No. Not so fast.

He sat by the door for a long time. Listening. Planning.
Gathering strength.

From somewhere downstairs, he heard the chime of a
faraway clock. Midnight.

Alertness splashed over him like a cold shower.

Yes, the old man must be asleep.

And Carl was ready.

He turned the knob. The door opened with a muffled
click.

Carl removed his shoes, tucked one into his belt and
carried the other—a weapon.

Okay! All set to go!

One deep calming breath and he started down the darkened stairway, advancing slowly, walking on the sides of
the steps, back against the wall, trying to minimize the
creaking of the ancient boards. There were fifteen steps in
all. Carl paused on each one, listening, watching, preparing his balance for the next.

Finally his groping right foot found the soft carpet of the downstairs hall. Home free! He permitted himself a tight smile in the darkness.

The main door, his exit, was at the end of the shadowy thirty-foot hallway. On either side of the door white moonlight shone through narrow panels of cut glass. So close to freedom.

He thought of Lucy. Maybe he could talk some sense into her now. He could tell her about the crazy old man whose religion made him believe Heaven was on the second floor of his house. What would Lucy say to that? What would the police say?

God, it was almost funny. . . .

Squinting down the dark hall, he was sure one of the doors along either side concealed the sleeping prophet. But which?

It didn't matter.

Now was the time. He'd make a run for it.

Carl began a graceless tiptoed sprint down the carpeted hall. He was pleased with himself for making no noise.

With the exhilaration of a front runner breaking the tape, he reached the door. His prize was waiting for him; he couldn't believe it. The key was in the lock!

He tugged at the door, turning the key at the same time.

Lightning flashed again, throwing the hall into painful light. But the light didn't go out.

Terror knotted Carl's face. He felt a lump moving in his stomach. Blood seemed to drain from his body, leaving him cold, weak and afraid as he faced the old man.

The prophet was dressed in a long gray robe. His white hair, wild and abundant, made him look like the mad artist's rendering of a violent Old Testament God.

Carl withered in the old man's stare. From the gnarled hand a revolver's barrel also stared, cold and unblinking.

The old man's voice was like thunder. "You have been a fool, and you've proven yourself a sinner. You have failed your test, revealed the kind of soul you possess. In spite of my warnings, my help, and my prayers, you have yielded to temptation, forever forsaking your place above."

He lifted the revolver with both hands, leveled it at Carl's forehead. "For your transgression, it is the calling of the prophet to see that you are punished. Damnation—that is your fate. Damnation for your sins, now and forever."

And so saying, the old man motioned with his weapon, and pulled open the heavy door to the basement.

Afterword

In "Soul Keeper," as in all my work to date, I owe a considerable debt to Lovecraft for my awareness of setting and atmosphere.

Although I am a lifelong New Englander, it took Lovecraft to show me what was directly under my feet: that searchers after horror need not haunt strange, far places. As he wrote in "The Picture in the House." ". . . the true epicure in the terrible . . . esteems most of all the ancient, lonely farmhouses of backwoods New England; for there the dark elements of strength, solitude, grotesqueness and ignorance combine to form the perfection of the hideous."

I started reading Lovecraft when I was in the fifth grade. I remember the added vividness each tale assumed when I realized, why, this could be happening right here in Vermont! Right in the forests behind my house!

In putting this yarn together, I thought about the mania that might grow unchecked behind the locked doors of some remote forgotten country mansion in what Lovecraft called, "the wild domed hills of Vermont," the hills right behind my house. The result is the story you just read, my tribute to my first writing teacher.

FROM THE PAPERS OF HELMUT HECKER

Chet Williamson

Letter to World Fantasy Convention:

November 12, 1986

Dear Sirs:

My agent, J. Arthur Pembroke, has notified me that you wish to give me an award for my novel, *The Dark Borders.* When I asked him to investigate the situation further before accepting said award, he told me of the nature of your organization and the titles of the other nominated works.

I do not wish, nor have I ever wished, my work to be compared with commercially written tales of vampires, werewolves, elves, unicorns, fairies, and other ragtag pseudo-creations of hack writers, and I am utterly disgusted to have it in some tawdry competition with the same. Likewise, I am appalled at the insinuation that I

would actually *welcome* such an award. I have been informed that Borges received this same "honor," but, after
seeing a photograph of the award itself (a staring, prog-
nathous monster of some sort, I assume), if I were to
learn that Borges's passing came only a short time after he
received it, I would not be surprised.

In short, I have received numerous awards, including the
Pulitzer Prize, the National Book Critics Circle Award, the
Faulkner Award, the National Book Award, and the Booker
Prize. I neither need nor desire your goggle-eyed ghoul.

Helmut Hecker

Journal entry (November 18, 1986):

I often wish it were possible to perpetrate some of the
more savage activities in my tales upon these so-called
"fans" of my work. (REMINDER: inform Arthur to refuse any
more offers of appearances on these absurd call-in shows,
both television and radio.) It is annoying enough that I
should be expected to go on one of these "book tours," as if I
need flaunt myself to become any more popular, but on top
of it that I should be subjected to the ignorant commentary
of ignorant readers who buy my works for their own ignorant purposes is beyond imagining.

For example, today in a B. Dalton here in (what god-
awful town is this today? Ah yes—) Providence, Rhode
Island, I signed a book for some fool in a baseball cap,
who then asked me if I feel I've been influenced by Lovekraft. I looked at him like the dunce he was, and asked
who or *what* was a Lovekraft, and he replied, with mis-
placed and feeble pride, that this Lovekraft was a "horror
writer" who had lived in the very city we were in. I responded that I have never been influenced by these
dreadful, so-called "horror writers" for the simple fact
that I have never wasted my time or energy or intellect
reading any of their formulaic and puerile work, that I
knew only the names of a few with whom I have been
forced to share the bestseller list, told this clod that their

presence thereon was further proof of the execrable taste of that portion of the American public who still read, and reiterated what I have proclaimed in every interview I have ever given in the so-called "popular" press, that I am *not* a "horror writer," but deal with the dark side of humanity in the tradition of Hesse, Mann, Borges, and others for whom this Lovekraft and others I could name would not be fit to sharpen pencils, and that if he wanted to understand my work and its influences (as much influence as can be had upon a writer of supreme originality such as myself), that he should read the articles and interviews with me that have appeared in *The New York Review of Books, The Antioch Review, The Yale Review, Sewanee Review,* and others that would in all likelihood be far too challenging for his limited mental capacity. I further told him that I abhorred the idea of being read by readers such as he, who would buy Picasso nudes in order to masturbate, and would never be able to understand the politically allegorical aspects of my work, and I deplored a marketing situation that made it possible for such pearls as mine to be thrown before the misunderstanding eyes of swine like himself.

The cretin stood there, nodding placidly at all this, as though I had merely complimented him on his baseball cap (it bore a "B"—I assume for "Boeotian"), then said, and I quote his exact words, "Yeah, I don't really get all that stuff, but, man, I love the way you carve up the bitches."

I hurled the book I had just signed at his head, missing in my rage. The manager of the store ended the signing early, of course, but I have remained livid with fury for the remainder of the day. To bystanders, I am sure that my reaction must have been viewed as a simple and justified attack on a Philistine. But I am not certain that the verminous pig did not touch on the truth.

Ever since I was a child in Hamburg, I have felt an amount of pleasure in the sufferings of others, and—

My Freudian musings must cease now, for Heuer has just begun to rub against my legs. He is the newest addition to my small retinue, a poor replacement for Jenny, perhaps, but not nearly as difficult to care for. Yes, Heuer is content with a saucer of milk and some tinned food (chicken or beef only—he turned up his nose at the fish). But then cats, male of female, seem so much more easily pleased—and more intelligent—than females of the human species. Indeed, if women did not whimper so marvelously when in pain, I swear I should have nothing to do with them at all. Foolish Jenny. I always knew when to stop. I never *truly* hurt her, never beyond recovery.

But enough thoughts of her. I must remark on finding Heuer. While in Boston several days ago, I received a call from Fritz, who told me my old cat, Jorg, died in its sleep. I loved Jorg dearly, having brought him from Germany when I moved to America fifteen years ago, and the news of the animal's passing deeply saddened me.

So it was, I felt, fate that placed the pet shop next to the B. Dalton, and that placed Heuer, a handsome and fully grown cat, in its window. As I walked by, he looked at me with such wise and knowing eyes that I knew immediately that he would be Jorg's replacement. I marched into the shop, the publisher's representative who accompanied me howling that we were late for the signing (and indeed the line already wound out the door and down the block), paid the small amount required, and told the manager to hold Heuer until I returned.

Why Heuer? I must confess that the name struck me immediately upon seeing the cat. It was the name of one of my mother's lovers, the only one I ever liked. There was something about the eyes that reminded me of Heuer, I believe, so Heuer he is. . . .

Journal entry (January 14, 1987):

Heuer is such a glorious creature. His thick yellow fur glimmers like gold in the sun that pours through my study window. He seems to love this old city as much as I do now, and sits for hours at the window, looking at me and then at the peaceful skyline of Providence. Though its age pales before the long history of the town in which I grew up, there is at the same time a sense of great antiquity here. I did not realize how much I admired it before I had left it, gone back to New York with Heuer. He seemed to languish, poor beast, and it was not long before I realized that his soulsickness only reflected my own.

There had been something about Providence that had captured my spirit in the two short days I was there—the tang of the sea air coming up from the wharfs, the quaint gambrel roofs that line Benefit Street, the inspiring steeple of the First Baptist Church, St. John's Churchyard—so much so that it is astonishing that it took as long as two weeks before I ordered Fritz to Rhode Island to secure us lodgings on College Hill. The house in which the three of us now reside dates back to the American Revolution. The yard is large, and filled with old shade trees. When spring comes, Heuer and I shall spend our afternoons out there when our writing mornings are ended, cozily ensconced behind the massive brick wall that encloses our estate and insures our privacy.

I say *our* writing, because Heuer sits near me all morning, never sleeping, merely watching the sky outside or watching me. What a fine comrade he is. Soon, I trust, all the disjointed thoughts I have concerning my next book shall coalesce into a magnificent whole. . . .

Journal entry (February 6, 1987):

The day has been a long one, but at last I have in mind my next book. It shall be a group of related stories, perhaps four or five of them, all long novelettes. The theme shall be the effects of huge, primal institutions upon modern man, allegorized by—

No. My working notes will reflect all the details. I have filled pages with them today, and tomorrow I begin the long work of actual writing. And it *shall* be long. I see the years stretching out before me. My mind is stuffed with ideas, and I burn to begin.

But Heuer, who rubs up against my leg, is correct. The

time has come to rest. Schnapps for me, and a dish of ice cream for dear Heuer, then an early bedtime. I feel even too weary for a woman. Strange that my desires have not forced me to roam Providence's seamier streets. Perhaps the sedateness of this town is having an effect on me after all. . . .

Journal entry (July 24, 1987):

Five months after beginning it, the work is going splendidly. It is slow and painstaking, but the vision taking shape is one of both human and cosmic significance. I truly feel that it is the finest work I have yet done, and should firmly establish me as one of the great masters of world literature. This book shall insure my immortality.

I have begun working more and more by night, my faithful friend Heuer by my side. My mind seems clearer somehow, more receptive to the marvelous and terrifying visions that assail me on every side. My style, too, seems to be changing. Whereas before I have cut my phrases to the bone, creating a clean economy of prose, I have now become more verbose, grandiloquent even, as though my previous terse style was incapable of communicating the altogether *fantastic* and *bizarre sense of outsideness* and *cosmicism* that flows from my pen.

Ah yes, I have retired my trusty typewriter for the nonce. It was simply impossible to use the machine on this book. The clattering drove me insane, until I realized that, for the first time, the noise truly was disabling my cognitive processes. When I took up a pen, however, the words ran onto the paper with the speed of some jellyish ichor heated to mad liquidity. . . .

Letter to J. Arthur Pembroke:

From the Nethermost Wells of Hali Hour of the Dim Moaning of the Wailing Bells, in the year of F'Thagn

Dear T'chei-Ahrp-Ahmb:

Although you have not heard from me in many months, I have not been idle. Indeed, the work is nearly finished! And it is, with all my usual humility, a masterpiece. It consists of four long novelettes, and ends with a short novel. They are interconnected thematically, though no characters appear in more than one tale. No *human* characters, at any rate. Dear Gawd, Arthurius, the vistas of cosmic terror I have opened in this work dwarf all my previous puny attempts at showing my readers the truth about this world. I have done nothing less than create a *Weltanschauung* that contains the *universe*!

I expect to complete the final tale within a month. Revision should take several more. As you well know, this opus has taken me over three years to create, but had it taken twenty, it could be no greater a work.

Yrs. for the Black Testament of Thog,

Ait'ch-Ait'ch

Letter from J. Arthur Pembroke:

April 30, 1990

Dear Helmut:

You may wonder why I choose to respond to your manuscript by mail rather than by telephone or a personal visit. It's simply that I know that Teutonic temper of yours, and I wish to spare myself its lightning bolts. All this is leading up to the fact that my reaction to *The Night Testaments* is not at all positive.

I suppose there is a possibility, first of all, that this is all a gigantic and clever hoax on your part, done in order to give me a minor stroke. If so, you have nearly succeeded. Please congratulate yourself, laugh sadistically for several hours, and then send me ASAP the actual manuscript you have been working on these past forty months.

If this is *not* the case, if what I have on my desk is truly your next work that you expect me to market, I must confess that the task is impossible. I know you work in secrecy, that you prefer to say next to nothing about works in progress, even to me, and that you refuse to sell your work until it is completed to your satisfaction. I have accepted all these quirks, feeling confident that you would continue to produce not only marketable work, but work that will garner excellent reviews, spots on the bestseller lists, and prestigious awards (by the way, the Horror Writers of America wish to present you with a Life Achievement Award again—refuse as usual?). This time, however, you would have done well to take me into your confidence, so that I could have kept you from making such a terrible *faux pas.*

Helmut, I'll make this as quick and painless as possible. Neither the market, the editors, the public, nor the critics will accept plagiarized work, not even from a writer of the stature of Helmut Hecker. I admit, your reworking of H. P. Lovecraft is extraordinarily well done, but you surely must know that it is nothing more than a reworking, as if Lovecraft himself had revised his own pieces years later. In fact, that's *precisely* what it's like. I compared Lovecraft's stories to your versions, and your writing is indeed better than Lovecraft's. But I already knew that, and it is small compensation for over three years' work. What on earth were you trying to prove? I didn't even know you'd ever *read* Lovecraft, let alone were obsessed by him.

For the life of me, Helmut, I don't know what to do with this. I can not and will not present it to Knopf. It's all so obviously a swipe that I can't even suggest that it be published under a pseudonym. Even if we were to find a publisher ignorant of Lovecraft, Arkham House, the small house that publishes his works, would sue instantly.

So. I am entirely at a loss. If you wish to seek other representation, you're free to do so, but frankly, Helmut, I know of no agent, respectable or not, who would be willing to market this manuscript, which I reluctantly and sadly return. I am, as always, at your service.

Sincerely,
Arthur

Journal entry (April 6, 1990):

I have just gotten off the phone from talking to Arthur, the greatest liar on the face of the earth! How in God's name, I asked him, can a man plagiarize from a book he has never read, written by an author of whom he has never heard, except for the occasional idiot in a B. Dalton or a Waldenbooks asking if this Lovecraft influenced him? Be reasonable, I told Arthur. Three and a half years rewriting another man's work? It is impossible! I never would have done it, and told him that the joke had gone far enough. He tried to patronize me, of all things, and I fired him on the spot. All right, he said, all right, so you haven't read Lovecraft. But read him now, he said, and you'll see. *Patronizing* me, as if I were a child! Bastard! He is lying to me somehow, lying about all of this, and I shall prove it. I am going out and batter my way into bookstores until I find a book by this Lovecraft. Can such a volume be found in Providence, I wonder? No matter—I shall find it!

Journal entry:

It is true.

I do not know how, but everything Arthur said is true. I went through the town, searching for bookstores until I found one open near Brown University. There I demanded volumes of Lovecraft, and was given two thick books with absurdly juvenile illustrations on their jackets. I purchased them immediately, and stepped out onto the street, where I opened one of the volumes and began to peruse it by the light of a street lamp.

I found nothing in the first few stories to support Arthur's claim, as they were mere bagatelles, stories for little boys to frighten each other with around a campfire—one about a ghost who bites off a man's feet, another about a monster who poses for an artist—the stupidest things I have ever read. I clapped the book shut, carried it home, and began to go through the rest of the stories, reading only the first few lines of each, until I arrived at the seventh tale, the one entitled "The Haunter of the Dark." When I read the first paragraph I knew.

It was nothing less than a paraphrase of my own new tale, "That Which Came by Darkness."

I was stunned, and turned to look at the copyright page, thinking the only thing I *could* think, that this Lovecraft had somehow broken into my home, copied my manuscript, rewritten it, and had it published while I was working on the related stories. But then I saw that the copyright for the volume was 1963, and that the *story* was copyrighted *1936.*

I continued to look frenziedly through the volume, and found therein my allegory of thought control, "Encased Minds," under the title of "The Whisperer in Darkness," complete with nearly identical situations and characters. My "Submersible God" was called "The Call of Cthulhu," and my "Of Deepest Knowledge" was now given the pulpish title, "The Shadow Out of Time." With shaking hands, I opened the second volume, and learned that my crowning achievement, my short novel entitled *What We Have Inherited,* has already existed for sixty years as *At the Mountains of Madness.*

Madness indeed. What have I done? Or what has been done to me. . . ?

Journal entry:

I know now. I know. I went back to that bookstore and found one more volume of Lovecraft's work, and bought a biography of the man as well. I have spent half the night reading as much as I can, and it has been enough. Still, I must write everything down so that I can examine the logic of it all, or what little logic there may be:

Facts about Hecker

1. I have never before read any work by or any books about H. P. Lovecraft.
2. I began to write *The Night Testaments* after coming to Providence to live.
3. Changes that have lately occurred in me are:
  A. I now write at night rather than in the day.
  B. My style has changed tremendously, even my correspondence, as in my salutations and signatures (e.g. Ait'ch-Ait'ch).
  C. As much as it pains me to write it down, I have been unconsciously plagiarizing the work of a dead writer.

Facts about Lovecraft

1. Lovecraft lived for most of his life in Providence, and loved the city deeply.
2. Lovecraft liked to write at night, and wrote in a style far more verbose than mine.
3. Lovecraft's letters were replete with tiresome "in-jokes," such as signing himself E'ch-Pi-El.
4. Lovecraft loved cats.
5. Lovecraft loved ice cream and detested sea food.

Facts about Heuer

1. Heuer was bought in Providence, and seemed to blossom when we returned here.
2. Heuer is a cat.
3. Heuer loves ice cream, but, unlike most cats, detests fish.
4. Heuer was in my study with me whenever I worked on *The Night Testaments.*

It seems clear. But before I draw the logical conclusion, I must make one experiment. Leaving Heuer in the room, I shall try to begin a new story. Then, after a line or two, I shall take Heuer to the basement, shut him in, and try to write again. . . .

Fragments (on single crumpled page):

West of Fenton the hills rise wild, and there are valleys with deep woods no axe has cut. . . .
I have been asked before why I fear a draught of cool air. . . .
The most merciful thing in the world is the inability of the mind to correlate its contents. . . .

Fragment (on second page):

Blood the color of roses screens my vision.
Her blood, shed for my sin, for the sin of men, of man, of mandarin manipulators of manacles, maniac mangel-wurzels, and yes, I said yes how I would mangle her wurzel. . . .

Journal entry:

No doubt lingers. The first page bears slight rewrites of the beginnings of Lovecraft tales, while the second shows no trace of that simple-minded Puritan. It is Hecker, Hecker, pure Hecker and no one else.
My conclusion then? That cat who now is shut up in the basement is nothing less than the reincarnated spirit of Howard Phillips Lovecraft.
Does not Heuer sound like Howard? And the distaste for seafood, the love of Providence—it all fits, does it not? Of course! While in the presence of this reincarnate mind, I was telepathically affected by it to the point of revising its own blasted work. I know it sounds ridiculous—a reincarnate telepathic cat!—but no more so than some of

these egregious and incestuous theme anthologies I am always being asked to participate in. If an entire book of tales about lesbian vampire dolphins is acceptable to the great unwashed, how much more easily can my own present situation be believed!

One thing remains—the death of that creature who has caused me to waste a great part of my creative life. To think that I, Hecker, have thrown away years of talent merely rewriting the work of a man whose idea of a climax was to have the narrator write down his screams as a monster destroys him! Whose idea of wordplay and alliteration was to write of ghouls and gugs and ghasts! Whose poetry was even more noxious than his prose, and whose work could only find publication in the shabby pages of *pulp magazines!*

I shall destroy that beast with orgasmic pleasure. I shall literally rend it apart with my hands, breaking its paws first of all so that it shall scratch me as little as possible. Then I shall pluck out its yellow fur in great lumps, revealing the skin beneath, sodden with blood; I shall pluck out its whiskers one by one, then its teeth, and finally its eyes, mashing them to jelly on the floor. Then I shall yank out its tongue, that demonic tongue that never meows. And then—then I shall have some *real* fun. . . .

Journal entry:

It got away.

A cellar window was open, and the damned beast must have pushed the screen aside and squeezed through. What a disappointment! But no matter. It is gone from my life. All that remains of it is that chasm of desire for its destruction that still gapes within me. It must be filled and satiated, if not with that monster's guts, then with the whimpers of another victim. Tonight I shall find a woman, some whore who, for enough money, will acquiesce to my demands. There must be junkies in Providence, yes? And then, when I am finished, when she leaves, exhausted, terrified, bleeding, then I shall sleep, and when I awake I shall begin again with my work.

But first I shall pillory Lovecraft.

I shall write an attack on him that will rattle the teeth of his idiotic admirers, that will insure that his damned name will never appear within the pages of any learned journal, that will make it an intellectual *crime* even to admit to having *read* the man's tripe! I shall—

I don't know why I broke off just then. I felt as though—but no, that's impossible—as though I was being watched, not only by eyes, but by . . . another mind.

Absurd.

But then why do I write on? When everything within me wishes to fling down the pen, rise, shake off this feeling, go out and find a slut, why do I remain here scribbling these words? Get up, Hecker! Arise, I tell myself! But I cannot!

And now I turn my head toward the doorway while I write on, and I see the source of my scrivening—

There sits Heuer! His tail wrapped around him, staring at me with huge, green eyes! All within me rages—I would leap up, grasp my chair, and smash him into a shattered mass of bone, muscle, and fur—but instead I *sit* here! *Scribbling*, like one of that damned Lovecraft's narrators!

I shall not let this creature steal my mind! My will is stronger! For I am Hecker! Hecker!

Hecker!

Hecker

Heuer

Heuer

Howard.

No! I shall break this spell if I must die to do it! I shall throw down the pen—now! And escape!

The beast comes closer—closer—it leaps up onto my desk, sits directly in front of me, its eyes blazing!

No! It shall not take me! I tear my eyes away from its gaze!

Now—if only I could drop this cursed pen from my paw. . . .

My *paw?*

Letter to J. Arthur Pembroke:

The Ancient Hill
May 30th, 1990

Dear Arthurius,

Many thanks for your inquiry as to Heuer's health. His temperament, as you know from your last visit when he scratched you, had been gradually worsening, so it was with sorrow but no little surprise that I found his torn body in the back yard the other day. I assume that the other cats of the neighborhood had had quite enough of his bullying, and joined forces to end his violent career.

I am indeed glad that the most recent chapters of *The Night Testaments* were to your liking, and enclosed are several more for your perusal. Again, I render my deepest apologies for that abysmal first draft, and my unforgivable burst of temper when you recognized it as the grossly derivative work it was. It seems as though my humble scribblings had to find their proper voice. I'm only sorry that it took so long to establish it. I'm quite content now, working from the philosophical core of that, if you will, "posthumously collaborative" effort, and am pleased that you find it not only marketable, but meritorious. I sincerely hope the editors will agree with your kindly opinion, as it is quite unlike my previous published work. Perhaps we can speak of any revisions you feel necessary when I visit those Cyclopean modern towers of Manhattan Island next month to attend the fête thrown by the Horror Writers of America, whom I have recently joined.

Which reminds me—I have written to those running the World Fantasy Convention to be held in Providence this fall, and have informed them that I would be delighted to assist in any way possible. I offered specifically to aid in the bus tour of "Lovecraft's Provience," since I feel that I might be able to show them some associational sites in the city of which they may not have been otherwise aware.

Yr. obt. Servnt.—
E'ch-E'ch

Afterword

To 'From the Papers of Helmut Hecker'

I am *bound* to Lovecraft, like it or not. My first exposure to him was the 1963 Lancer *Dunwich Horror.* The grisly green face and the clutching hands on the cover drew my adolescent attention, but what was inside made me an acolyte. I read every bit of HPL I could find, became a serious collector, and in 1973 joined the Esoteric Order of Dagon, a Lovecraft amateur press association in which I remained for ten years. Yet none of my fiction has been "Lovecraftian"—no Cthulhu Mythos tales lurk in my trunk. In fact, I've always felt a sort of pride that my fiction bears no traces of Lovecraft. Or so I thought.

When the Arkham House corrected texts came out, I reread some of the stories I'd read as a kid, and was struck by the scene in "The Picture in the House" in which the narrator sees on the ceiling, "a large irregular spot of wet crimson." I realized I had used the same image in my novel, *Dreamthorp:* "a large, irregular, dark patch on the ceiling, from which the blood was slowly dripping" onto a red velvet hat. Good Lord, I thought, unconscious plagiarism! But then I recalled that that particular image had come from a dream of mine years before, which I had written down in my own "Commonplace Book," and eventually used in *Dreamthorp.* So it seems that Lovecraft not only entered my prose, but my dreams as well!

As I say, I am bound to Lovecraft, and "From the Papers of Helmut Hecker" is my tongue-in-cheek examination of and thank you for that pleasant bondage.

MERYPHILLIA
Brian McNaughton

"For a ghoul is a ghoul, and at best an unpleasant companion for man."
—*H. P. Lovecraft*
The Dream Quest of Unknown Kadath

Meryphillia was the least typical ghoul in the graveyard. No man would ever have called her a beauty, but her emaciation was less extreme, her pallor less ghastly, and her gait less grotesque than those of her sisters.

Untypically tender-hearted, she would sometimes shed a tear for a dead infant that her nature compelled her to devour. She was considerate of her fellows, too, and her feeding habits were all but mannerly. Least typical of all, for ghouls love to laugh, was her inextinguishable sorrow for the world of sunlight and human warmth she had lost.

Traditional wisdom holds that ghouls bring their condition upon themselves by indulging morbid interests in adolescence. Gluttriel, God of Death, takes note of such youngsters and offers them the knowledge of the corpses they will eat in return for their lives.

Others assert that ghoulism is a disease, called Porfat's Distemper after the physician who described it, and who later vanished under circumstances of suggestive peculiarity. Before the transformation becomes obvious to those grieving at the sickbed, their grief compounded by the loved one's growing taste for perverse wit and unseemly laughter, a hunger for dead flesh impels the victim to the nearest burial ground. The first meal induces physical changes that destroy all hope of return to human society.

Either explanation might apply in Meryphillia's case. As a girl nearing womanhood in Crotalorn, she knew the necropolis called Dreamers' Hill better than the malls and ballrooms where her peers flocked. She wandered among the tombs of the rich and the ditches of the poor in all weathers. Her clothing, lacking style to begin with, suffered from these rambles, and it never quite fit: perhaps because a pocket would always be weighted down with a volume of Asteriel Vendren's tales, malign carbuncles of that madman's diseased fancy.

Perched on some collapsed slab that might well have capped a ghoul pit, innocently ascribing the scratches and titters she heard to the creak of trees and rustle of weeds, she would play an air of Umbriel Fronn on her recorder, a cherished gift from her late mother. Often she would pause to ponder questions that the healthy young person is well advised to leave to priests and philosophers.

Her father strove to cure her moping and put some meat on her bones in the hope of marrying her into one of the Great Houses. He would regularly purge her library, castigating her preference for tales of terror to worthwhile literature, for Umbriel's cerebral nocturnes to the cheery ditties of the day. He would pinch her cheeks into smiles as he bellowed for food, wine and happy tunes. Unfortunately his business as a timber merchant kept him often from the city and their home on Hound Square, and Meryphillia would resume her unhealthy habits as soon as he had breezed out the door.

When he held up her stepmother as an example to emulate in his absence, she would only hang her head and mumble. A giddy Frotherine not much older than the girl herself, Meryphillia's father's second wife filled the house with robust athletes and ditty-strummers in what she claimed was an effort to cheer her daughter up. But she never seemed to notice when Meryphillia fled to the nearby cemetery to escape their din and their importunities.

Whether she fled into the arms of Gluttriel, or whether vapors of the corpse-crammed and claw-mined earth afflicted her with Porfat's Distemper, the result was the same: shortly before her eighteenth birthday, she vanished irretrievably into the burrows of the ghouls.

For all their laughter, ghouls are a dull lot. Hunger is the fire in which they burn, and it burns hotter than the hunger for power over men or for knowledge of the gods in a crazed mortal. It vaporizes delicacy and leaves behind only a slag of anger and lust. They see their fellows as impediments to feeding, to be mauled and shrieked at when the mourners go home. They are seldom alone, not through love of one another's company, but because a lone ghoul is suspected of concealing food. Their copulation is so hasty that distinctions of sex and identity are often ignored.

Just as she had once yearned to know the secrets of the grave, Meryphillia now longed to penetrate the mysteries of friendship and love. Mostly she wanted to know about love. She believed that it must transcend her bony collisions with Arthrax, least unfeeling of all the male ghouls, whom she untypically clove to.

"Why are you crying?" he once asked while their coupling rattled the slats of a newly emptied coffin.

"It's nothing. Dust in my eyes."

"That happens."

His question and comment were the nearest a ghoul could come to sympathy, but it fell so far short of the standard she imagined to be human that she wept all the more.

*   *   *

She sought answers from the dead, for the ghoul acquires the memories of what it feeds upon, but her strength was no match for the giants of the underground in the battle for mnemonic bits. Studying human experience from the scraps she got was like learning about painting by spinning on her toes through a museum. She hugged vivid glimpses: the smell of orange spice-cake and a childish song that evoked a long-gone celebration of Polliel's Birthday; the creaking leather and muscular embrace of someone's beloved brother, home safe at last from a forgotten war; a shrine ablaze with stolen candles, a wan face among borrowed blankets, the words, "The fever has broken."

Others did far better. Feeding lustily, they would recall great chunks of lives. For a while they would assume a likeness to their meal and give those satiric impersonations of human beings that are a favorite entertainment of their kind. Even Meryphillia screamed with laughter when Lupox and Glottard disputed which of them was Zuleriel Vogg, the notorious grave-robber, whose execution the ghouls had cheered only less gleefully than the disposal of his pieces in an unguarded pit.

Scroffard once wolfed down an old beggar woman so completely that his performance lost its satirical edge. He alternately whined for spare coins, complained of the dark and damp and smell, and quavered, "Who is that? Who's there?" at every furtive patter and stifled giggle.

Most shunned the mock woman, hoping that Scroffard, when he recovered and found no one else on whom to exercise his temper, would tear off his own head for a change; but Meryphillia, who would formerly have crossed the street to avoid such a wretch, was drawn to caress the fragile face. She seemed beautiful, not least of all for her intensely feeling eyes.

Handicapped with human vision, Scroffard was at first unable to make out the young ghoul by the glow of the niter-crusted tunnel. When he saw what pawed his human face, he screamed his way to the surface, where he was

battered about the head by the shovels of two grave-rob-
bers. To their dismay, for they thought they were dealing
with the routine nuisance of a prematurely buried hag,
the beating restored the most irascible of ghouls to his
roaring self. He wrenched from the luckless men the vengeance he might otherwise have wrested from Meryphillia.

She treasured what happy moments she could retrieve,
but murder, disease and madness were the staples of her
diet, with the manifold agonies of death for dessert. The
fond memories of the rich were locked away in tombs of
marble and bronze, while souvenirs of poverty and despair lay everywhere for the taking. The very poorest
corpses, unloved, unmourned, unwanted by either medical students or necrophiliacs, were thrown directly into a
riddled pit that the gravediggers called Gluttriel's Lunch-
Bucket. No matter how full the hole was filled by nightfall, by morning its rocky bottom would be licked clean as
a dutiful child's porridge-bowl.

One day word chattered through the mines that a man
of substance, sleek as a pig and skewered cleanly in a
duel, had just been laid in a plain grave. His widow, no
native of Crotalorn, had conceived the notion that its
ghouls were a myth. As the box dropped into the earth of
an unfashionable quarter, she was overheard to assure the
attentive victor in the duel that bronze-bound tombs of
stone were vulgar.

No ghoul resumed his sleep that day. The ground of the
thrilling burial was too quaggy for tunneling; the meat
must be extracted from above. Digging should begin at
the first blink of darkness, before human thieves could
cheat the underground of its due. As the watchmen would
still be reasonably sober, as mourners might be dawdling,
the daring of the raiders would set new limits for legend.
Debate over tactics grew so heated that the crows of the
necropolis took wing and blackened the dome of Ash-
tareeta's temple, which was seen as a fearful omen by her
clergy, and cause for an emergency collection.

Meryphillia knew the debate was a farce. Plans would be trampled in a general stampede for the grave. Her own best hope was to creep out at twilight and work her way among the hedges and headstones until she had found a hiding place near the target. Her intention was not to get there first: whoever claimed that honor would be run over by a monster like Glottard or Lupox. She would wait for one of them to make his dash and cling to the bristles of his dorsal ridge while he punished the early starters. Sticking close as the warts on his rump, she would snatch what scraps she could.

When the moment came, Clamythia, wiliest of ghouls, usurped the shadow of Lupox. It pained Meryphillia to trip her sister and emboss the mud with her venerable muzzle, but protocol had foundered in howling chaos. Lupox savaged the first arrivals like a fighting-dog set on rats, uncaring that two of the obstructions he flung from his path were human watchmen. Whimpering mindlessly, they left their broken bills where they lay and staggered to the safety of their lodge.

The grave erupted in a fountain of dirt, pumped pluming into the twilight by a frenzy of ghoulish talons. The geyser soon began to spray crushed flowers, splinters of wood, then tattered silk and trinkets of gold that a robber would have wept to see so treated. Without undue effort, Meryphillia found herself hugging a whole quarter of a head, with the coveted eye adhering.

This was the ghoulish equivalent to a delicacy that a banquet-guest would have exclaimed over before daintily sampling; but Meryphillia, with claws scraping her back, elbows gouging her ribs and jaws stretching over her shoulders to seize her prize, could only stuff it into her mouth, grind it hastily, and gulp it down.

Hunched between Lupox's gnarly knees, she then beheld the strangest vision: of herself, standing up straight, as her father had so often told her to; with her hair pushed out of her eyes, as he had so often pushed it; and with an unlikely smile dimpling cheeks not nearly so gaunt as they had been. The vision glowed with love, tinged only slightly by the acid of vexation and fixed forever beneath a glaze of sorrow.

She realized whose grave she crouched in, but, being what she was, could only scrabble for more and leave her feelings to sort themselves out. Her next find was a hand, one that held a far clearer imprint of her stepmother's buttocks. It proved a timely antidote to the first course.

In her preoccupation with life, Meryphillia relapsed into her solitary ways. She was allowed to. No one suspected her of hiding food. The ghouls thought her as odd as humans once had. Like them, her new companions were grateful for a respite from her brooding silences, her inappropriate observations and her reluctance to join in a good laugh.

Lurching one night along a path she used to glide with her recorder, she nearly stumbled over a man who had come neither to loot tombs nor kill himself. He was declaiming verses to the full moon with such rapt fervor that he failed to notice her slip hastily into the tent of a willow's branches.

This was the poet Fragador, which she learned from his own lips, for he gave himself credit for each poem as if afraid the moon would confuse him with someone else: "*On the Hands of Therissa Sleith,* a sonnet by Fragador of Fandragord," he would announce, or, "*For Therissa Sleith on Her Birthday,* an ode by Fragador, poet and tragedian, lately of Fandragord."

It would be an unobservant moon indeed, she thought, that would forget his name. He was the most beautiful man she had ever seen; but she viewed him with the eyes of a ghoul, unaware that many people thought him ghoulishly pale and thin. Her heart, so still even before her present state, startled her like a hammering visitor at her breast.

His subject pleased less than his voice. Therissa Sleith was the darling of Crotalorn, and had often been held up to her as an example of what she was not. Fragador desired her as ardently, though perhaps not quite so hopelessly, as Meryphillia desired him.

He visited the graveyard as often as she used to, and always with a new batch of poems praising the wit, grace and beauty of the same unsuitable person. When the moon had other obligations, he would recite his verses to a statue of Filloweela that reclined complaisantly on one of her cleric's tombs, unaware that the lavish form of the goddess hid a quivering horror that yearned to give him everything Therissa withheld.

How she loathed that name! It figured in every verse he wrote, and his voice would falter and throb on its shaky nastiness. She learned to anticipate its occurrence, and she would whisper her own name just loudly enough to bar the syllables from her ears, even though this lamed his elegant scansion. Sometimes she would speak too vehemently, and he would clear his throat, clean his ear, or peer uneasily into the shadows.

His heart heard her name imperfectly, however, for one night he thrilled her by declaiming a poem to "Morthylla," whom his poetic intuition identified as a lurking spirit of night and death, and whose help he invoked in softening Therissa before her lithe limbs should go to feed the ghouls. Meryphillia would recite the lines to herself while wishing that those limbs were in fact within reach of her coffin-cracking jaws.

They were so alike, or had been, she and Fragador, with their delight in horror, their flirtation with death, their love of shadow and solitude. If only she had met him—but she withered her wish: even if she had stood up straight and combed her hair, even if she had twittered pleasantries and smiled now and then, no man drawn to the pert face and nubile form of Therissa Sleith would have spared her a glance.

His verses swerved into delirium when the cruel ninny was betrothed to another. The corruption that had always festered beneath his sunniest images tore off its mask as he raved of murder and suicide. Not just a beautiful man, not merely a gifted poet, he was a genius, Meryphillia avowed, one who gazed even more deeply into the abyss than had Asteriel Vendren. She loved him, she worshiped him, and now that the incongruous object of his desire had shown herself an even worse fool than had been obvious, she timidly hoped for him. She hardly ate, she never slept, she grew so listless that rats began to eye her with an impudent surmise. She pictured her brain as crawling with busy ants, each ant a notion for declaring her love, until she could have smashed her skull to exterminate them.

The full moon returned, but the poet did not. She fretted, pacing from the favored statue to the willow and back again. At last she broke the circle and loped to the main gate, to the very fringe of life and light. Springing atop the wall, she peered up and down Citron Street, then leaned perilously far to scan Hound Square, descrying no one but unremarkable stragglers and lurkers. So great was her concern for her beloved that the sight of her festively lit home, the first she had had of it since her transformation, gave her no slightest pang.

The first note of a shriek told her she had been seen, but she slipped into the darkness so swiftly that it lost conviction and ended as an embarrassed laugh.

She feared that Fragador had made good the threat of his latest poems and killed himself, but her fear was superseded by fearful desire. She had longed for union with him. What union could be more complete than to be the man himself?

His grumbled asides had told her that he would be granted no impregnable crypt. She would raid his grave at high noon to beat the greater ghouls to his dear relics. Watchmen be damned! What finer way to end her hated existence than in the form of her love, to remember the pain of his death even as she saw her own coming, and saw it coming through his very eyes? No passion had ever been so fully consummated. It would cry out in vain for the immortalizing pen of Fragador.

Fatigued, distraught, but now ever so dimly cheered, she found her way to his favorite tomb and lay down in the moon-shadow of the Goddess of Love, where she slept.

She was woken by sobbing so bitter that she thought it must be her own. The fat and ruddy moon had decayed to a ghoulish disc above her. Rubbing her eyes, she felt no tears, but the sobs continued. It was he, and her joy nearly drove her to embrace him before she thought what effect this might produce.

"Ghouls!" he suddenly screamed. "Fiends and demons of the dark, attend me! Morthylla, come to me!"

Before others could respond, she rose.

"By Cludd!" he gagged, and half his sword appeared like silver lightning from its scabbard. In a like flash, she saw herself in his loathing grimace. A wheel revolved ponderously inside her, leaving something crushed. She crossed her hands to her shoulders and hung her head in suppliance.

"I did call you," he said after a long silence. "Your promptness startled me."

"Forgive me."

"Offense and forgiveness have no meaning, for meaning itself is nonsense. Therissa Sleith is no more."

"I'm sorry," she lied.

"You would be, of course. Not even a ghoul's dream could penetrate the sepulcher of the Sleiths."

She looked up to protest this misunderstanding, but his face silenced and melted her. Something like wonder crossed it as he saw her eyes. Her father had always praised them as her best feature, and now they were the most vividly yellow globes in the underground.

"Are you really. . . ?" he began. "No, it would be mad to ask if you are a symptom of my madness."

"You are the sanest man since Asteriel Vendren."

"Sleithreethra spare us from literate ghouls!"

She shuddered. Not even a ghoul would speak the name of that Goddess in a graveyard at midnight, and certainly not with a laugh. He was indeed mad, and it thrilled her. No more to be held than a sob or a last breath, it burst out: "I love you!"

He stepped forward boldly. "Come down from the tomb, then, Morthylla, and let us speak of love."

Her claws clicked with their shaking until they rested in his firm clasp. She whispered, "Don't mock me." She added, "And it's *Meryphillia.*"

Correction seemed to irk him, but he took it. "I have heard that a ghoul who eats the heart and brain of a person becomes that person."

"I have seen it."

"I mean no offense, but this restoration would have no added characteristics? No redundancy of teeth, no odor, no urge to laugh at odd moments?"

She averted her misting eyes. "The personation is perfect." She flared. "My odor offends you?"

She was instantly sorry, having forgotten that her new face and voice translated petulance as demoniacal fury.

"Please," he said when he could speak again. "I meant nothing like that. A dead body, you know. You have an inner beauty, Meryphillia. I see it through your eyes."

"Really?"

"Please don't laugh, I'm unused to it." She was unaware that she had laughed. He thrilled her by taking her hand in both of his. "Dear ghoul, I have acquired the key to the tomb of the Sleiths, where Therissa will be interred tomorrow. I wish you to do with her as we said."

"But that's monstrous!"

His look clearly told her that the word was inappropriate on her nominal lips, but she pressed on: "She would be just as she was in life. If she denied you then—"

"Her parents denied me, her position denied me, her name denied me; never her heart. If she had but one hour, she might listen to her heart. If I could have a word with her, a look—dare I hope for a kiss?"

A perverse impulse to refuse seized her. She desired him as she had never desired anyone, but the price he demanded, to transform herself into the sort of person her father and stepmother had wanted her to be, seemed too high.

"Please, Meryphillia," he murmured, and he shocked her by touching his lips to her cheek.

She took the key he pressed into her callused palm.

Near the hour of the tryst, she crept through the flowering precincts of the richest tombs with ghoulish stealth, which makes the hovering owl seem rowdy. Her ears were extended to gather the whispers of moths and the mutter of coffin-worms. Her nasal pits gaped to the fullest, so that each encrypted corpse around her, however desiccated by ages uncounted, announced its discrete presence: none more brightly than that of Therissa Sleith, its decay just a sigh beneath the salt tears and scented soaps of the servants who had primped her for the last time.

No other ghouls blighted the air with their rancid breath, nor watchmen with their wine, but she crept nonetheless, horrified by a vision of the underground host bursting over her to fill the tomb of the Sleiths, ransacking bones inviolate for a thousand years and scattering Therissa's shreds into a thousand greedy gullets. If that happened, she could never face Fragador. No, she would creep up from behind, fight down her distaste for unripe flesh, and eat him. Denied the looks and sighs and touches of his love, she would at least know him from the inside of his being.

She rose to her full height only in the shadow of the doorway, where the terrible motto of Therissa's tribe was incised beneath an image of Sleithreethra: WHO TOYS WITH US, SHE SHALL FONDLE. The brass key that Fragador had given her slipped from quivering fingers to clatter as loudly, it seemed, as the head of a watchman's bill, nor could her scrabbling claws at once fit themselves to the human device. She was sobbing with frustration by the time she succeeded in juggling it up to the keyhole and jamming it in.

The bronze leaves swung inward on oiled hinges. The chain to a gong in the tower had been cut by a watchman with a taste for Fragador's poetry and an even greater gusto for opium, who had been persuaded that the poet contemplated no unusual indecencies with the dead darling of Crotalorn.

She was lovely, Meryphillia had to admit when she had ripped the massive lid from the sarcophagus, especially now that the pink tinge of her skin had been replaced with hints of violet. The fatal twist of her head had been all but straightened; she could have been a sleeper who would wake with nothing to complain of but a stiff neck.

She paused for a moment to admire that elfin nose, so unlike the assertive one she had worn, before biting it off. Uncoiling her razorish tongue, she slipped it in to shred the brain into manageable morsels. Dainty swirls of her smallest claw served to scoop out the eyes. She savored them with restrained whimpers of pleasure before proceeding to the large and tasty breasts.

Therissa heard her sisters chattering as they returned from the regimental review of Cludd's Whirlwind. It was their custom to tease the Holy Soldiers with inviting smiles and restless wiggles. The celibate warriors were charged to be on their sternest behavior, and the girls' object was to make one drop his pike or, worse, raise his staff, offenses that earned the culprit a flogging and a night spent kneeling on pebbles. Why had Meryphillia never had such fun, never even thought of it? She almost wept for her wasted life before recalling that she had done it, as Therissa Sleith.

Ripping down to bare ribs, she opened them like a book: the Book of Love. She gobbled the tough, lean heart.

How that heart had leaped when, whirling at the head of the stairs to show off her bridal gown, Therissa had felt the hem snag her heel! The floor tilted, the ceiling spun, but she was spared from terror by the knowledge that this could never happen to her. Even if it did (and there could be no doubt that she was plunging headlong down the stairs) she would suffer only inconvenient bruises. She pitied the chorus of screamers. She wanted to assure them that she was Therissa Sleith, whose youth and beauty were invulnerable, who was dead.

Meryphillia raged at the unfairness, the tiresome untimeliness. Most of all she regretted the graceless exit she had made, and right in front of her sisters, of all people. Examining these thoughts, she knew that the moment was upon her, and she rushed her meal. She had hardly started on the tangy kidneys when she glanced at her hand and was shaken by that mixture of emotions few other creatures can know.

The sight of her own hand sickened her, its tiny, maggot-plump fingers so unlike the talons she had grown used to. At the same time Therissa gagged with loathing to see what her dainty hand clutched, what smeared her arm to the elbow.

It took more than a moment to calm themselves. Therissa accepted her death more gracefully than Meryphillia did the alien will that made her wash in the wine and oil provided for a differently envisioned afterlife. Drying herself on an unsullied corner of her gown, Therissa scolded her for not having taken better care of it, for now they had nothing to wear. The ghoul was reminded of her stepmother.

Therissa unwound the clattering bones of an ancient Sleith from their wrapping and swirled it around her. She succeeded in looking more stylish than Meryphillia once would have in her newest clothes.

"I believe in making do," Therissa said. "Even if I were a filthy ghoul, I'd make the best of it. And I don't want to waste my brief resurrection moping in a smelly tomb, so let's go, shall we?"

Part of her wanted to linger over her unfinished remains, but another part refused even to look into the sarcophagus, and both were parts of the same person: who called herself, in her inmost thoughts, Therissa Sleith, but who felt an almost uncontrollable urge to laugh when she did.

Fragador had sacrificed for it and fully expected it, but Therissa's emergence from the tomb shocked him speechless. She tossed her hair in exactly that heart-stopping way of hers and gazed around the cemetery before spotting him in the shadow of a stone demon. When her face lit up, his heart woke like a sunrise choir of birds.

"You're not dead!" He laughed wildly. "I knew they had to be wrong, you . . ."

The pity in her eyes stopped him even before she said, "No, they were right. Nor am I entirely as I seem."

"Nerythillia?"

"Please get her name right. Her love for you makes mine seem shallow."

Love had brought him here, yes, but anger, too, anger with her for slavishly heeding the rules of society; anger with himself for breaking those rules by being poor, and a poet. She had planned to marry a man who had won a contract to build public conveniences for the city.

"You can't wear sonnets or eat odes," she had said, "but you can build a fragrant palace from urinals."

In his maddest moments, he had wanted to resurrect her so he could strangle her. At very least he had meant to ask her, with a suitable flourish at the moon-blazing marble of her tomb, what she thought of her fragrant palace now. In the presence of wonder, however, spite was impossible.

And there was that other to consider, that monstrous but magical being that animated her. In a strange part of himself, he loved her even more than Therissa. Unlike Therissa, she appreciated his art. She had even compared him to Asteriel Vendren, whom the dear, dead dunce had never heard of.

"Meryphillia," he enunciated clearly as he took her into his arms.

Now that she had known the soft sighs and shouted transports of human love, Meryphillia wept more bitterly than ever her exile to the underground.

"Why are you crying?" Fragador asked tenderly.

"Nothing. Dust in my eyes."

"That happens," he said from the depth of his human wisdom and sympathy, and she wept all the more.

"What if I was vain and frivolous by your absurd standards?" said the voice in her head. "I knew life and love and happiness. Now I shall know peace. Will you ever say such things?"

She was unsure whether those were the words of the fast-fading Therissa or the words she would have put into her mouth. Whatever they were, they bit like truth.

She rose before the transformation could become complete, unwilling to show her true form again to the poet and blight his memory of love. Turning for one last look, she found herself staring into the grinning face of Arthrax.

"Now I can write poems for you," he said. "*We shall know what the darkness discovers*—how's that for a start?"

The sight of him had speeded Therissa's evaporation. Meryphillia scanned the necropolis with all her senses for Fragador, but he, too, had vanished. She demanded, "What have you done with him? Where is he?"

"He contracted with two of us," Arthrax said. "You, last night. Me, tonight, just before he drank poison." He grimaced so horribly that even she retreated.

She had learned from Therissa. No longer inclined to weep, she turned and smiled at the gaping, unguarded sepulcher of the Great House of Sleith. Far off she heard the cackling of creatures like herself born on the night wind, and for the first time she held back nothing as she joined in their laughter.

Afterword

I can reread only a few authors from year to year with unabated pleasure: Shakespeare, Joyce, Boswell, Gibbon, and Lovecraft. It may seem unlikely company for HPL, but similarities can be traced: Boswell was obsessed, Gibbon was a snob, Joyce didn't give a damn for the average reader, and Shakespeare had looked into the abyss.

Those qualifications on their own may never make a great writer, but they combined in Lovecraft to make an American original. Many have conjectured about what he saw in the abyss, so I won't. It's enough to know that it scared him, and that the narrow focus and obsessive force of his art allowed him to give us all a taste of his terror.

A popular writer of horror novels who shall remain nameless—most likely to posterity as well—once told the moderator of a televised discussion that no one over twelve years of age can read Lovecraft with pleasure. This slander contains a distorted truth, for the qualities I have cited are childish; in any activity but art, they might be considered disabling flaws.

Who else is like that? Kafka, yes, Poe, okay, but then the list comes to a shuddery halt. The sane and sensible may write horror stories, but not all the Koontzes and Kings of this world can infect us with the cancerous dread of a haunted genius.

"All life," Lovecraft once wrote in his endearingly wrong-headed way, "is only a set of pictures in the brain, among which there is no difference betwixt those born of real things and those born of inward dreamings, and no cause to value the one above the other."

I hope he really believed that. If so he may have been spared the pain of the neglect and rejection that he knew too well. However belatedly and inadequately, I offer my story in homage to his spirit.

LORD OF THE LAND
Gene Wolfe

The Nebraskan smiled warmly, leaned forward, and made a sweeping gesture with his right hand, saying, "Yes indeed, that's exactly the sort of thing I'm most interested in. Tell me about it, Mr. Thacker, please."

All this was intended to keep old Hop Thacker's attention away from the Nebraskan's left hand, which had slipped into his left jacket pocket to turn on the miniature recorder there. Its microphone was pinned to the back of the Nebraskan's lapel, the fine brown wire almost invisible.

Perhaps old Hop would not have cared in any case; old Hop was hardly the shy type. "Waul," he began, "this was years an' years back, the way I hear'd it. Guess it'd have been in my great granpaw's time, Mr. Cooper, or mebbe before."

The Nebraskan nodded encouragingly.

"There's these three boys, an' they had an old mule,

wasn't good fer nothin' 'cept crowbait. One was Colonel
Lightfoot—course didn't nobody call him colonel then.
One was Creech an' t'other 'un . . ." The old man paused,
fingering his scant beard. "Guess I don't rightly know. I
did know. It'll come to me when don't nobody want to
hear it. He's the one had the mule."

The Nebraskan nodded again. "Three young men, you
say, Mr. Thacker?"

"That's right, an' Colonel Lightfoot, he had him a new
gun. An' this other 'un—he was a friend of my grandpaw's
or somebody—he had him one everybody said was jest
about the best shooter in the county. So this here Laban
Creech, he said *he* wasn't no bad shot hisself, an' he went
an' fetched his'un. He was the 'un had that mule. I recollect now.

"So they led the ol' mule out into the medder, mebbe
fifty straddles from the brake. You know how you do.
Creech, he shot it smack in the ear, an' it jest laid down
an' died, it was old, an' sick, too, didn't kick or nothin'. So
Colonel Lightfoot, he fetched out his knife an' cut it up
the belly, an' they went on back to the brake fer to wait
out the crows."

"I see," the Nebraskan said.

"One'd shoot, an' then another, an' they'd keep score.
An' it got to be near to dark, you know, an' Colonel Lightfoot with his new gun an' this other man that had the
good 'un, they was even up, an' this Laban Creech was
only one behind 'em. Reckon there was near to a hundred
crows back behind in the gully. You can't jest shoot a
crow an' leave him, you know, an' 'spect the rest to come.
They look an' see that dead 'un, an' they say, Waul, jest
look what become of *him*. I don't calc'late to come any-
wheres near *there*."

The Nebraskan smiled. "Wise birds."

"Oh, there's all kinds of stories 'bout 'em," the old man
said. "Thankee, Sarah."

His granddaughter had brought two tall glasses of
lemonade; she paused in the doorway to dry her hands on

her red-and-white checkered apron, glancing at the Nebraskan with shy alarm before retreating into the house.

"Didn't have a lick, back then." The old man poked an ice cube with one bony, somewhat soiled finger. "Didn't have none when I was a little 'un, neither, till the TVA come. Nowadays you talk 'bout the TVA an' they think you mean them programs, you know." He waved his glass. "I watch 'em sometimes."

"Television," the Nebraskan supplied.

"That's it. Like, you take when Bud Bloodhat went to his reward, Mr. Cooper. Hot? You never seen the like. The birds all had their mouths open, wouldn't fly fer anything. Lost two hogs, I recollect, that same day. My paw, he wanted to save the meat, but 'twasn't a bit of good. He says he thought them hogs was rotten 'fore ever they dropped, an' he was 'fraid to give it to the dogs, it was that hot. They was all asleepin' under the porch anyhow. Wouldn't come out fer nothin'."

The Nebraskan was tempted to reintroduce the subject of the crow shoot, but an instinct born of thousands of hours of such listening prompted him to nod and smile instead.

"Waul, they knowed they had to git him under quick, didn't they? So they got him fixed, cleaned up an' his best clothes on an' all like that, an' they was all in there listenin', but it was terrible hot in there an' you could smell him pretty strong, so by an' by I jest snuck out. Wasn't nobody payin' attention to *me,* do you see? The women's all bawlin' an' carryin' on, an' the men thinkin' it was time to put him under an' have another."

The old man's cane fell with a sudden, dry rattle. For a moment as he picked it up, the Nebraskan glimpsed Sarah's pale face on the other side of the doorway.

"So I snuck out on the stoop. I bet it was a hundred easy, but it felt good to me after bein' inside there. That was when I seen it comin' down the hill t'other side of the road. Stayed in the shadow much as it could, an' looked like a shadow itself, only you could see it move, an' it was always blacker than what they was. I knowed it

was the soul-sucker an' was afeered it'd git my ma. I took
to cryin', an' she come outside an' fetched me down the
spring fer a drink, an' that's the last time anybody ever did
see it, far's I know."

"Why do you call it the soul-sucker?" the Nebraskan
asked.

"'Cause that's what it does, Mr. Cooper. Guess you know
it ain't only folks that has ghosts. A man can see the ghost of
another man, all right, but he can see the ghost of a dog or a
mule or anythin' like that, too. Waul, you take a man's, 'cause
that don't make so much argyment. It's his soul, ain't it? Why
ain't it in Heaven or down in the bad place like it's s'posed
to be? What's it doin' in the haint house, or walkin' down the
road, or wherever 'twas you seen it? I had a dog that seen a
ghost one time, an' that'n was another dog's, do you see? *I*
never did see it, but he did, an' I knowed he did by how he
acted. What was it doin' there?"

The Nebraskan shook his head. "I've no idea, Mr.
Thacker."

"Waul, I'll tell you. When a man passes on, or a horse or
a dog or whatever, it's s'pposed to git out an' git over to
the Judgment. The Lord Jesus Christ's our judge, Mr.
Cooper. Only sometimes it won't do it. Mebbe it's afeared
to be judged, or mebbe it has this or that to tend to down
here yet, or anyhow reckons it does, like showin' somebody some money what it knowed about. Some does that
pretty often, an' I might tell you 'bout some of them
times. But if it don't have business an' is jest feared to go,
it'll stay where 'tis—that's the kind that haints their
graves. They b'long to the soul-sucker, do you see, if it
can git 'em. Only if it's hungered it'll suck on a live person, an' he's bound to fight or die." The old man paused
to wet his lips with lemonade, staring across his family's
little burial plot and fields of dry cornstalks to purple hills
where he would never hunt again. "Don't win, not particular often. Guess the first 'un was a Indian, mebbe.
Somethin' like that. I tell you how Creech shot it?"

"No you didn't, Mr. Thacker." The Nebraskan took a

swallow of his own lemonade, which was refreshingly
tart. "I'd like very much to hear it."

The old man rocked in silence for what seemed a long
while. "Waul," he said at last, "they'd been shootin' all
day. Reckon I said that. Fer a good long time anyhow. An'
they was tied, Colonel Lightfoot an' this here Cooper was,
an' Creech jest one behind 'em. 'Twas Creech's time next,
an' he kept on sayin' to stay fer jest one more, then he'd
go an' they'd all go, hit or miss. So they stayed, but wasn't
no more crows 'cause they'd 'bout kilt every crow in
many a mile. Started gittin' dark fer sure, an' this Cooper,
he says, Come on, Lab, couldn't nobody hit nothin' now.
You lost an' you got to face up.

"Creech, he says, waul, 'twas my mule. An' jest 'bout
then here comes somethin' bigger'n any crow, an' black,
hoppin' 'long the ground like a crow will sometimes, do
you see? Over towards that dead mule. So Creech ups
with his gun. Colonel Lightfoot, he allowed afterwards he
couldn't have seed his sights in that dark. Reckon he jest
sighted 'longside the barrel. 'Tis the ol' mountain way, do
you see, an' there's lots what swore by it.

"Waul, he let go an' it fell over. You won, says Colonel
Lightfoot, an' he claps Creech on his back, an' let's go.
Only this Cooper, he knowed it wasn't no crow, bein' too
big, an' he goes over to see what 'twas. Waul, sir, 'twas
like to a man, only crooked-legged an' wry neck. 'Twasn't
no man, but like to it, do you see? Who shot me? it says,
an' the mouth was full of worms. Grave worms, do you
see?

"Who shot me? An' Cooper, he said Creech, then he
hollered fer Creech an' Colonel Lightfoot. Colonel Lightfoot says, boys, we got to bury this. An' Creech goes back
to his home place an' fetches a spade an' a ol' shovel,
them bein' all he's got. He's shakin' so bad they jest rattled together, do you see? Colonel Lightfoot an' this
Cooper, they seed he couldn't dig, so they goes hard at it.
Pretty soon they looked around, an' Creech was gone, an'
the soul-sucker, too."

The old man paused dramatically. "Next time anybody

seed the soul-sucker, 'twas Creech. So he's the one I seed, or one of his kin anyhow. Don't never shoot anythin' without you're dead sure what 'tis, young feller."

Cued by his closing words, Sarah appeared in the doorway. "Supper's ready. I set a place for you, Mr. Cooper. Pa said. You sure you want to stay? Won't be fancy."

The Nebraskan stood up. "Why, that was very kind of you, Miss Thacker."

His granddaughter helped the old man rise. Propped by the cane in his right hand and guided and supported by her on his left, he shuffled slowly into the house. The Nebraskan followed and held his chair.

"Pa's washin' up," Sarah said. "He was changin' the oil in the tractor. He'll say grace. You don't have to get my chair for me, Mr. Cooper, I'll put on till he comes. Just sit down."

"Thank you." The Nebraskan sat across from the old man.

"We got ham and sweet corn, biscuits, and potatoes. It's not no company dinner."

With perfect honesty the Nebraskan said, "Everything smells wonderful, Miss Thacker."

Her father entered, scrubbed to the elbows but bringing a tang of crankcase oil to the mingled aromas from the stove. "You hear all you wanted to, Mr. Cooper?"

"I heard some marvelous stories, Mr. Thacker," the Nebraskan said.

Sarah gave the ham the place of honor before her father. "I think it's truly fine, what you're doin', writin' up all these old stories 'fore they're lost."

Her father nodded reluctantly. "Wouldn't have thought you could make a livin' at it, though."

"He don't, pa. He teaches. He's a teacher." The ham was followed by a mountainous platter of biscuits. Sarah dropped into a chair. "I'll fetch our sweet corn and potatoes in just a shake. Corn's not quite done yet."

"O Lord, bless this food and them that eats it. Make us thankful for farm, family, and friends. Welcome the stranger 'neath our roof as we do, O Lord. Now let's eat."

The younger Mr. Thacker rose and applied an enormous butcher knife to the ham, and the Nebraskan remembered at last to switch off his tape recorder.

Two hours later, more than filled, the Nebraskan had agreed to stay the night. "It's not real fancy," Sarah said as she showed him to their vacant bedroom, "but it's clean. I just put those sheets and the comforter on while you were talkin' to Grandpa." The door creaked. She flipped the switch.

The Nebraskan nodded. "You anticipated that I'd accept your father's invitation."

"Well, he hoped you would." Careful not to meet his eye, Sarah added, "I never seen Grandpa so happy in years. You're goin' to talk to him some more in the mornin'? You can put the stuff from your suitcase right here in this dresser. I cleared out these top drawers, and I already turned your bed down for you. Bathroom's on past Pa's room. You know. I guess we seem awful country to you, out here."

"I grew up on a farm near Fremont, Nebraska," the Nebraskan told her. There was no reply. When he looked around, Sarah was blowing a kiss from the doorway; instantly she was gone.

With a philosophical shrug, he laid his suitcase on the bed and opened it. In addition to his notebooks, he had brought his well-thumbed copy of *The Types of the Folktale* and Schmit's *Gods Before the Greeks,* which he had been planning to read. Soon the Thackers would assemble in their front room to watch television. Surely he might be excused for an hour or two? His unexpected arrival later in the evening might actually give them pleasure. He had a sudden premonition that Sarah, fair and willow-slender, would be sitting alone on the sagging sofa, and that there would be no unoccupied chair.

There was an unoccupied chair in the room, however; an old but sturdy-looking wooden one with a cane bottom. He carried it to the window and opened Schmit, determined to read as long as the light lasted. Dis, he knew,

had come in his chariot for the souls of departed Greeks,
and so had been called the Gatherer of Many by those too
fearful to name him; but Hop Thacker's twisted and almost pitiable soul-sucker appeared to have nothing else in
common with the dark and kingly Dis. Had there been
some still earlier deity who clearly prefigured the soul-
sucker? Like most folklorists, the Nebraskan firmly believed that folklore's themes were, if not actually eternal,
for the most part very ancient indeed. *Gods Before the
Greeks* seemed well indexed.

Dead, their mummies visited by An-uat, 2.

The Nebraskan nodded to himself and turned to the
front of the book.

> An-uat, Anuat, "Lord of the Land (the Nec-
> ropolis)," "Opener to the North." Though
> frequently confused with Anubis, to whom
> he lent his form, it is clear that An-uat the
> jackal-god maintained a separate identity
> into the New Kingdom period. Souls that had
> refused to board Ra's boat (and thus to ap-
> pear before the throne of the resurrected Os-
> iris) were dragged by An-uat, who visited
> their mummies for this purpose, to Tuat, the
> lightless, demon-haunted valley stretching
> between the death of the old sun and the
> rising of the new. An-uat and the less threat-
> ening Anubis can seldom be distinguished in
> art, but where such distinction is possible,
> An-uat is the more powerfully muscled fig-
> ure. Van Allen reports that An-uat is still in-
> voked by the modern (Moslem or Coptic)
> magicians of Egypt, under the name Ju'gu.

The Nebraskan rose, laid the book on his chair, and
strode to the dresser and back. Here was a five-thousand-

year-old myth that paralleled the soul-sucker in function. Nor was it certain by any means that the similarity was merely coincidental. That the folklore of the Appalachians could have been influenced by the occult beliefs of modern Egypt was wildly improbable, but by no means impossible. After the Civil War the United States Army had imported not only camels but camel drivers from Egypt, the Nebraskan reminded himself; and the escape artist Harry Houdini had once described in lurid detail his imprisonment in the Great Pyramid. His account was undoubtedly highly colored—but had he, perhaps, actually visited Egypt as an extension of some European tour? Thousands of American servicemen must have passed through Egypt during the Second World War, but the soul-sucker tale was clearly older than that, and probably older than Houdini.

There seemed to be a difference in appearance as well; but just how different were the soul-sucker and this Ju'gu, really? An-uat had been depicted as a muscular man with a jackal's head. The soul-sucker had been . . .

The Nebraskan extracted the tape recorder from his pocket, rewound the tape, and inserted the earpiece.

Had been "like to a man, only crooked-legged an' wry neck." Yet it had not *been* a man, though the feature that separated it from humanity had not been specified. A dog-like head seemed a possibility, surely, and An-uat might have changed a good deal in five thousand years.

The Nebraskan returned to his chair and reopened his book, but the sun was already nearly at the horizon. After flipping pages aimlessly for a minute or two, he joined the Thackers in their living room.

Never had the inanities of television seemed less real or less significant. Though his eyes followed the movements of the actors on the screen, he was in fact considerably more attentive to Sarah's warmth and rather too generously applied perfume, and still more to a scene that had never, perhaps, taken place: to the dead mule lying in the field long ago, and to the marksmen concealed where the woods began. Colonel Lightfoot had no doubt been a historical person, locally famous, who would be familiar to the majority of Mr. Thacker's hearers. Laban Creech might or might not have been an actual person as well. Mr. Thacker had—mysteriously, now that the Nebraskan came to consider it—given the Nebraskan's own last name, Cooper, to the third and somewhat inessential marksman.

Three marksmen had been introduced because numbers greater than unity were practically always three in folklore, of course; but the use of his own name seemed odd. No doubt it had been no more than a quirk of the old man's failing memory. Remembering *Cooper,* he had attributed the name incorrectly.

By imperceptible degrees, the Nebraskan grew conscious that the Thackers were giving no more attention to the screen than he himself was; they chuckled at no jokes, showed no irritation at even the most insistent commercials, and spoke about the dismal sitcom neither to him nor to one another.

Pretty Sarah sat primly beside him, her knees together, her long legs crossed at their slender ankles, and her dishwater-reddened hands folded on her apron. To his right, the old man rocked, the faint protests of his chair as regular, and as slow, as the ticking of the tall clock in the corner, his hands upon the crook of his cane, his expression a sightless frown.

To Sarah's left, the younger Mr. Thacker was almost hidden from the Nebraskan's view. He rose and went into the kitchen, cracking his knuckles as he walked, returned with neither food nor drink, and sat once more for less than half a minute before rising again.

Sarah ventured, "Maybe you'd like some cookies, or some more lemonade?"

The Nebraskan shook his head. "Thank you, Miss Thacker; but if I were to eat anything else, I wouldn't sleep."

Oddly, her hands clenched. "I could fetch you a piece of pie."

"No, thank you."

Mercifully, the sitcom was over, replaced by a many-colored sunrise on the plains of Africa. There sailed the boat of Ra, the Nebraskan reflected, issuing in splendor from the dark gorge called Tuat to give light to mankind. For a moment he pictured a far smaller and less radiant vessel, black-hulled and crowded with the recalcitrant dead, a vessel steered by a jackal-headed man: a minute fleck against the blazing disk of the African sun. What was that book of Von Daniken's? *Ships*—no, *Chariots of the Gods.* Spaceships none the less—and that was folklore, too, or at any rate was quickly passing into folklore; the Nebraskan had encountered it twice already.

An animal, a zebra, lay still upon the plain. The camera panned in on it; when it was very near, the head of a huge hyena appeared, its jaws dripping carrion. The old man turned away, his abrupt movement drawing the Nebraskan's attention.

Fear. That was it, of course. He cursed himself for not having identified the emotion pervading the living room sooner. Sarah was frightened, and so was the old man—horribly afraid. Even Sarah's father appeared fearful and restless, leaning back in his chair, then forward, shifting his feet, wiping his palms on the thighs of his faded khaki trousers.

The Nebraskan rose and stretched. "You'll have to excuse me. It's been a long day."

When neither of the men spoke, Sarah said, "I'm 'bout to turn in myself, Mr. Cooper. You want to take a bath?"

He hesitated, trying to divine the desired reply. "If it's not going to be too much trouble. That would be very nice."

Sarah rose with alacrity. "I'll fetch you some towels and stuff."

He returned to his room, stripped, and put on pajamas and a robe. Sarah was waiting for him at the bathroom door with a bar of Zest and half a dozen towels at least. As he took the towels the Nebraskan murmured, "Can you tell me what's wrong? Perhaps I can help."

"We could go to town, Mr. Cooper." Hesitantly she

touched his arm. "I'm kind of pretty, don't you think so? You wouldn't have to marry me or nothin', just go off in the mornin'."

"You are," the Nebraskan told her. "In fact, you're very pretty; but I couldn't do that to your family."

"You get dressed again." Her voice was scarcely audible, her eyes on the top of the stairs. "You say your old trouble's startin' up, you got to see the doctor. I'll slide out the back and 'round. Stop for me at the big elm."

"I really couldn't, Miss Thacker," the Nebraskan said.

In the tub he told himself that he had been a fool. What was it that girl in his last class had called him? A hopeless romantic. He could have enjoyed an attractive young woman that night (and it had been months since he had slept with a woman) and saved her from . . . what? A beating by her father? There had been no bruises on her bare arms, and he had noticed no missing teeth. That delicate nose had never been broken, surely.

He could have enjoyed the night with a very pretty young woman—for whom he would have felt responsible afterward, for the remainder of his life. He pictured the reference in *The Journal of American Folklore:* "Collected by Dr. Samuel Cooper, U. Neb., from Hopkin Thacker, 73, whose granddaughter Dr. Cooper seduced and abandoned."

With a snort of disgust, he stood, jerked the chain of the white rubber plug that had retained his bath water, and snatched up one of Sarah's towels, at which a scrap of paper fluttered to the yellow bathroom rug. He picked it up, his fingers dampening lined notebook filler.

Do not tell him anything grandpa told you. A woman's hand, almost painfully legible.

Sarah had anticipated his refusal, clearly; anticipated it, and coppered her bets. *Him* meant her father, presumably, unless there was another male in the house or another was expected—her father almost certainly.

The Nebraskan tore the note into small pieces and flushed them down the toilet, dried himself with two towels, brushed his teeth and resumed his pajamas and robe, then stepped quietly out into the hall and stood listening.

The television was still on, not very loudly, in the front room. There were no other voices, no sound of footsteps or of blows. What had the Thackers been afraid of? The soul-sucker? Egypt's mouldering divinities?

The Nebraskan returned to his room and shut the door firmly behind him. Whatever it was, it was most certainly none of his business. In the morning he would eat breakfast, listen to a tale or two from the old man, and put the whole family out of his mind.

Something moved when he switched off the light. And for an instant he had glimpsed his own shadow on the window blind, with that of someone or something behind him, a man even taller than he, a broad-shouldered figure with horns or pointed ears.

Which was ridiculous on the face of it. The old-fashioned brass chandelier was suspended over the center of the room; the switch was by the door, as far as possible from the windows. In no conceivable fashion could his shadow—or any other—have been cast on that shade. He and whatever he thought he had glimpsed would have to have been standing on the other side of the room, between the light and the window.

It seemed that someone had moved the bed. He waited for his eyes to become accustomed to the darkness. What furniture? The bed, the chair in which he had read—that should be beside the window where he had left it—a dresser with a spotted mirror, and (he racked his brain) a nightstand, perhaps. That should be by the head of the bed, if it were there at all.

Whispers filled the room. That was the wind outside; the windows were open wide, the old house flanked by stately maples. Those windows were visible now, pale rectangles in the darkness. As carefully as he could he crossed to one and raised the blind. Moonlight filled the bedroom; there was his bed, here his chair, in front of the window to his left. No puff of air stirred the leaf-burdened limbs.

He took off his robe and hung it on the towering bedpost, pulled top sheet and comforter to the foot of the bed, and lay down. He had heard something—or nothing. Seen something—or nothing. He thought longingly of his apartment in Lincoln, of his sabbatical—almost a year ago now—in Greece. Of sunshine on the Saronic Gulf. . . .

Circular and yellow-white, the moon floated upon stagnant water. Beyond the moon lay the city of the dead, street after narrow street of silent tombs, a daedal labyrinth of death and stone. Far away, a jackal yipped. For whole ages of the world, nothing moved; painted likenesses with limpid eyes appeared to mock the empty, tumbled skulls beyond their crumbling doors.

Far down one of the winding avenues of the dead, a second jackal appeared. Head high and ears erect, it contemplated the emptiness and listened to the silence before turning to sink its teeth once more in the tattered thing it had already dragged so far. Eyeless and desiccated, smeared with bitumen and trailing rotting wrappings, the Nebraskan recognized his own corpse.

And at once was there, lying helpless in the night-shrouded street. For a moment the jackal's glowing eyes loomed over him; its jaws closed, and his collarbone snapped. . . .

The jackal and the moonlit city vanished. Bolt upright, shaking and shaken, he did not know where. Sweat streamed into his eyes.

There had been a sound.

To dispel the jackal and the accursed, sunless city, he rose and groped for the light switch. The bedroom was—or at least appeared to be—as he recalled it, save for the damp outline of his lanky body on the sheet. His suitcase stood beside the dresser; his shaving kit lay upon it; *Gods Before the Greeks* waited his return on the cane seat of the old chair.

"You must come to me."

He whirled. There was no one but himself in the room, no one (as far as he could see) in the branches of the maple or on the ground below. Yet the words had been

distinct, the speaker—so it had seemed—almost at his
ear. Feeling an utter fool, he looked under the bed. There
was nobody there, and no one in the closet.

The doorknob would not turn in his hand. He was
locked in. That, perhaps, had been the noise that woke
him: the sharp click of the bolt. He squatted to squint
through the old-fashioned keyhole. The dim hallway outside was empty, as far as he could see. He stood; a hard
object gouged the sole of his right foot, and he bent to
look.

It was the key. He picked it up. Somebody had locked
his door, pushed the key under it, and (possibly) spoken
through the keyhole.

Or perhaps it was only that some fragment of his dream
had remained with him; that had been the jackal's voice,
surely.

The key turned smoothly in the lock. Outside in the
hall, he seemed to detect the fragrance of Sarah's perfume,
though he could not be sure. If it had been Sarah, she had
locked him in, providing the key so that he could free
himself in the morning. Whom had she been locking out?

He returned to the bedroom, shut the door, and stood
for a moment staring at it, the key in his hand. It seemed
unlikely that the crude, outmoded lock would delay any
intruder long, and of course it would obstruct him when
he answered—

Answered whose summons?

And why should he?

Frightened again, frightened still, he searched for another light. There was none: no reading light on the bed,
no lamp on the nightstand, no floorlamp, no fixture upon
any of the walls. He turned the key in the lock, and after a
few seconds' thought dropped it into the topmost drawer
of the dresser and picked up his book.

> Abaddon. The angel of destruction dis-
> patched by God to turn the Nile and all its
> waters to blood, and to kill the first-born
> male child in every Egyptian family. Abad-

don's hand was averted from the Children of Israel, who for this purpose smeared their doorposts with the blood of the paschal lamb. This substitution has frequently been considered a foreshadowing of the sacrifice of Christ.

Am-mit, Ammit, "Devourer of the Dead." This Egyptian goddess guarded the throne of Osiris in the underworld and feasted upon the souls of those whom Osiris condemned. She had the head of a crocodile and the forelegs of a lion. The remainder of her form was that of a hippopotamus, Figure 1. Am-mit's great temple at Henen-su (Herakleopolis) was destroyed by Octavian, who had its priests impaled.

An-uat, Anuat, "Lord of the Land (the Necropolis)," "Opener to the North." Though frequently confused with Anubis—

The Nebraskan laid his book aside; the overhead light was not well adapted to reading in any case. He switched it off and lay down.

Staring up into the darkness, he pondered An-uat's strange title, Opener to the North. Devourer of the Dead and Lord of the Land seemed clear enough. Or rather Lord of the Land seemed clear once Schmit explained that it referred to the necropolis. (That explanation was the source of his dream, obviously.) Why then had Schmit not explained Opener to the North? Presumably because he didn't understand it either. Well, an opener was one who went before, the first to pass in a certain direction. He (or she) made it easier for others to follow, marking trails and so on. The Nile flowed north, so An-uat might have been thought of as the god who went before the Egyptians when they left their river to sail the Mediterranean. He himself had pictured An-uat in a boat earlier, for that matter, because there was supposed to be a celestial Nile. (Was it the Milky Way?) Because he had known that the

Egyptians had believed there was a divine analog to the Nile along which Ra's sun-boat journeyed. And of course the Milky Way actually was—really is in the most literal sense—the branching star-pool where the sun floats. . . .

The jackal released the corpse it had dragged, coughed, and vomited, spewing carrion alive with worms. The Nebraskan picked up a stone fallen from one of the crumbling tombs, and flung it, striking the jackal just below the ear.

It rose upon its hind legs, and though its face remained that of a beast, its eyes were those of a man. "This is for you," it said, and pointed toward the writhing mass. "Take it, and come to me."

The Nebraskan knelt and plucked one of the worms from the reeking spew. It was pale, streaked and splotched with scarlet, and woke in him a longing never felt before. In his mouth, it brought peace, health, love, and hunger for something he could not name.

Old Hop Thacker's voice floated across infinite distance: "Don't never shoot anythin' without you're dead sure what 'tis, young feller."

Another worm and another, and each as good as the last.

"We will teach you," the worms said, speaking from his own mouth. "Have we not come from the stars? Your own desire for them has wakened, Man of Earth."

Hop Thacker's voice: "Grave worms, do you see?"

"Come to me."

The Nebraskan took the key from the drawer. It was only necessary to open the nearest tomb. The jackal pointed to the lock.

"If it's hungered, it'll suck on a live person, an' he's bound to fight it or die."

The end of the key scraped across the door, seeking the keyhole.

"Come to me, Man of Earth. Come quickly."

Sarah's voice had joined the old man's, their words mingled and confused. She screamed, and the painted figures faded from the door of the tomb.

The key turned. Thacker stepped from the tomb. Behind him his father shouted, "Joe, boy! Joe!" And struck him with his cane. Blood streamed from Thacker's torn scalp, but he did not look around.

"Fight him, young feller! You got to fight him!"

Someone switched on the light. The Nebraskan backed toward the bed.

"Pa, DON'T!" Sarah had the huge butcher knife. She lifted it higher than her father's head and brought it down. He caught her wrist, revealing a long raking cut down his back as he spun about. The knife, and Sarah, fell to the floor.

The Nebraskan grabbed Thacker's arm. "What is this!"

"It is love," Thacker told him. "That is your word, Man of Earth. It is love." No tongue showed between his parted lips; worms writhed there instead, and among the worms gleamed stars.

With all his strength, the Nebraskan drove his right fist into those lips. Thacker's head was slammed back by the blow; pain shot along the Nebraskan's arm. He swung again, with his left this time, and his wrist was caught as Sarah's had been. He tried to back away; struggled to pull free. The high, old-fashioned bed blocked his legs at the knees.

Thacker bent above him, his torn lips parted and bleeding, his eyes filled with such pain as the Nebraskan had never seen. The jackal spoke: *"Open to me."*

"Yes," the Nebraskan told it. "Yes, I will." He had never known before that he possessed a soul, but he felt it rush into his throat.

Thacker's eyes rolled upward. His mouth gaped, disclosing for an instant the slime-sheathed, tentacled thing within. Half falling, half rolling, he slumped upon the bed.

For a second that felt much longer, Thacker's father stood over him with trembling hands. A step backward, and the older Mr. Thacker fell as well—fell horribly and awkwardly, his head striking the floor with a distinct crack.

"Grandpa!" Sarah knelt beside him.

The Nebraskan rose. The worn brown handle of the butcher knife protruded from Thacker's back. A little blood, less than the Nebraskan would have expected, trickled down the smooth old wood to form a crimson pool on the sheet.

"Help me with him, Mr. Cooper. He's got to go to bed."

The Nebraskan nodded and lifted the only living Mr. Thacker onto his feet. "How do you feel?"

"Shaky," the old man admitted. "Real shaky."

The Nebraskan put the old man's right arm about his own neck and picked him up. "I can carry him," he said. "You'll have to show me his bedroom."

"Most times Joe was just like always." The old man's voice was a whisper, as faint and far as it had been in the dream-city of the dead. "That's what you got to understand. Near all the time, an' when—when he did, they was dead, do you see? Dead or near to it. Didn't do a lot of harm."

The Nebraskan nodded.

Sarah, in a threadbare white nightgown that might have been her mother's once, was already in the hall, stumbling and racked with sobs.

"Then you come. An' Joe, he made us. Said I had to keep on talkin' an' she had to ask you fer supper."

"You told me that story to warn me," the Nebraskan said.

The old man nodded feebly as they entered his bedroom. "I thought I was bein' slick. It was true, though, 'cept 'twasn't Cooper, nor Creech neither."

"I understand," the Nebraskan said. He laid the old man on his bed and pulled up a blanket.

"I kilt him didn't I? I kilt my boy Joe."

"It wasn't you, Grandpa." Sarah had found a man's bandana, no doubt in one of her grandfather's drawers; she blew her nose into it.

"That's what they'll say."

The Nebraskan turned on his heel. "We've got to find that thing and kill it. I should have done that first." Before he had completed the thought, he was hurrying back toward the room that had been his.

He rolled Thacker over as far as the knife handle permitted and lifted his legs onto the bed. Thacker's jaw hung slack; his tongue and palate were thinly coated with a clear, glutinous gel that carried a faint smell of ammonia; otherwise his mouth was perfectly normal.

"It's a spirit," Sarah told the Nebraskan from the doorway. "It'll go into Grandpa now, 'cause he killed it. That's what he always said."

The Nebraskan straightened up, turning to face her. "It's a living creature, something like a cuttlefish, and it came here from—" He waved the thought aside. "It doesn't really matter. It landed in North Africa, or at least I think it must have, and if I'm right, it was eaten by a jackal. They'll eat just about anything, from what I've read. It survived inside the jackal as a sort of intestinal parasite. Long ago, it transmitted itself to a man, somehow."

Sarah was looking down at her father, no longer listening. "He's restin' now, Mr. Cooper. He shot the old soulsucker in the woods one day. That's what Grandpa tells, and he hasn't had no rest since, but he's peaceful now. I was only eight or 'bout that, and for a long time Grandpa was 'fraid he'd get me, only he never did." With both her thumbs, she drew down the lids of the dead man's eyes.

"Either it's crawled away—" the Nebraskan began.

Abruptly, Sarah dropped to her knees beside her dead parent and kissed him.

When at last the Nebraskan backed out of the room, the dead man and the living woman remained locked in that kiss, her face ecstatic, her fingers tangled in the dead man's hair. Two full days later, after the Nebraskan had crossed the Mississippi, he still saw that kiss in shadows beside the road.

Afterword

I first encountered Poe's stories when I was enrolled in Edgar Allan Poe Elementary School, where they were required reading. A few years later I discovered Lovecraft in the pages of *Weird Tales*. He seemed to me then—as he seems to me now—Poe's only successor, the only writer of stature to extend the tradition in horror Poe created. Like Poe, he made full use of scientific developments. (I remember writing August Derleth about twenty years ago to explain Lovecraft's use of vector multiplication.) Like Poe, he valued atmosphere above everything else, yet gave delighted readers everything fiction *can* give.

By an irony rather too familiar, the academic critics who in Lovecraft's day deplored Poe's neglect themselves neglected Lovecraft; and in all honesty, neither writer provides what such people crave: exquisitely unsatisfying stories with characters like themselves, written by one of themselves. Instead, Poe was a working journalist for most of his too-brief life; and though we seldom think of his narrators, when we do we will generally conclude that they too must be sad, down-at-heels journalists. Lovecraft was a consulting writer, just as the Sherlock Holmes of the first and best stories is a consulting detective. That most of his narrators are, beneath their various names, somewhat glamorized Lovecrafts cannot have escaped many readers.

Both lacked professorial tenure and formal schooling in the humanities, the sine qua nons for critical acceptance in their days as in ours; but each possessed a darkness of vision so deep that the unsophisticated have supposed them mad. Neither was, to be sure. (Did you know that Poe's family called him Eddie? Or that Lovecraft was pampered by two doting aunts?) Rather, each kept, like Shakespeare, a spark of the God-given fire that illuminates the lightless places. If the "Lord of the Land" owes too much to Lovecraft, remember please that even Scotland Yard did not scruple to beg a brighter lamp in darkest need.

H.P.L.

Gahan Wilson

"I was far from home, and the spell of the eastern sea was upon me."
　　　　　　　　　　—H.P. Lovecraft

And it was, it *was*!

Smelling deeply the rich, time-abiding scent of the coastal marshes, I greedily read juicily exotic names at random from the road map clutched in my hand—Westerly, Narragansett, Apponaug—and to the north, drawing nearer every minute as the bus trundled efficiently along the upward curve of the coastal road, was Providence!

There could be no doubting it at all—absolutely incontrovertible evidence was all about me in the form of swooping gulls and salty surf and bleached piers in varying states of Innsmouthian decay—I, Edward Haines Vernon, born and bred in and frustrated by the flat, flat flatlands of the Midwest, having grown up by one shore of Lake Michigan with the sure and certain knowledge that its other, opposite shore was only a sunny day's excursion away, and that it would only be another boring Midwestern shore with more boring people talking about more boring things if I'd bothered to go there—that I, the aforementioned Edward Haines Vernon, was now actually on the coast of the great Atlantic, *the eastern sea* itself, on whose other coast would be nothing less magnificent than Europe, for God's sake!

I sat back, letting a bone-deep, noisy sigh of satisfaction escape simultaneously from my mouth and nostrils and shook my fist in the air before me with triumph; then I saw I'd alarmed the thin, grey lady sitting next to me. But after being irritated with her for the tenth part of a second, I realized that—of course—she was a fine, old, *New England* lady, and would be upset by the crude, un-cultured ways of a clumsy, ill-bred Midwesterner such as myself, God bless her withered old heart, God bless her pale blue, disapproving eyes!

"Excuse me," I said, gently, "But I am new to your country and do not fully understand its ways. Please be kind enough to pardon my outburst."

She regarded me steadily for a long moment over the steel rims of her glasses, then sniffed and turned back to her perusal of *Prevention* magazine, God bless her again, as I, in turn, turned back to my wide-eyed gazing out of the window of the bus.

It had not—I realized that now—it had not really so far hit me that all of this was actually happening! I had dreamed of it and planned and schemed for it so many long years, for such a large part of my life, that I had grown entirely accustomed to thinking of it as lurking (I hoped) in the future. It was always going to happen later on, but suddenly it was happening now! Suddenly it was all here! And so was I!

Carefully, so as not to alarm my dear New England lady once more with any further *gaucherie,* I pulled my little overnight bag (though I planned to stay in these regions far longer than overnight—by God, I planned to *live* here!) from under my seat and zipped it open and carefully lifted out the neatly folded letter which rested inside it on top of everything else. Reverently, like a priest with some holy artifact, I opened the precious thing and scanned its tiny letters penned in that spidery, small hand, and the words swam in my eyes for a moment before I blinked the tears away and I could reread that golden first paragraph for the thousandth, perhaps the ten thousandth, time.

"Of course you must come and visit me. Edwardius—by all means. And please do stay in my house, a handsome structure which I am sure one gifted with your knowledge and admiration of the antique will be able to appreciate fully. In the past, because of painfully reduced circumstances, I was not able to play the host to favored correspondents in the style I would have wished. Perhaps the greatest pleasure attendant to my present state of prosperity is that now I can fully indulge myself in grandfatherly welcomings!"

This totally unanticipated invitation had come in response to a wistfully timid outburst in my preceding letter to him wherein I'd confessed I dreamed of one day walking the streets which he and Poe had walked, and told him how I indulged myself sometimes with fantasies of sitting on some tomb in St. John's Churchyard, during an appropriately Gothic night of fog or lightning flashes, and building poems and stories with him about the worms which crawled and fed in the mouldy ground beneath our feet.

After that first, dazzling paragraph, he made a little joke to the effect that the Churchyard was really a very pleasant place, not mouldy at all, and then went on to practical specifics as to my visit, even volunteering to pay for my transportation, if that should present a problem.

"Please do not take offense at this offer," he wrote. "You know, being familiar with my history, that I am only too well acquainted with the perils and varied embarrassments which poverty afflicts on those who, like yourself, affront the common herd by daring to value art above commerce."

I sent back a reply in the affirmative as soon as I could get a proper one on paper—it took me about a week and, I think, about a ream's worth of drafts!—and I was careful to explain that I had put aside sufficient funds to make the trip providing I employed economical means. His reply to that included a line or two of touchingly old-fashioned praise for my thrift and industry, and after a short exchange of correspondence, we had settled all the dates and details.

Suddenly my eyes widened and I shook myself from this reverie of past events, leaned forward in my seat, and found myself actually pressing my nose against the window (doubtless to the further horrification of my seat mate) because beyond the glass, before and above me, seeming to appear with the abruptness of a mystic's vision of a paradise long deferred, unexpectedly loomed the hoary spires and domes of College Hill—lost in dreams of anticipation, I had, all unknowing, been driven into Providence itself!

I stared out nervously as we pulled into the bus station. He'd said I would be met but had not, I suddenly realized, given me any clues to help me identify the person he planned to send to fetch me.

Then my heart stopped and I actually gasped aloud (earning another audible sniff of disapproval from my neighbor), for there, in the flesh, standing with a positively jaunty air on the platform, was Howard Phillips Lovecraft, H.P.L., himself!

I had thought that, because of his enormous age, he would have the gravest difficulties in moving about, that it was highly likely he was now permanently housebound, or possibly confined to some beloved antique wingback, or even permanently ensconced in a quaint canopied bed, but it was quite obvious I had severely underestimated his durability. Though he did seem just a tiny bit stooped, and there was some small trace of that cautious slowness in his movements usually associated with considerable age, he leaned only lightly on his cane and stood his ground easily against the push and press of the crowd as he peered up into the windows of the bus with a lively curiosity sparkling in his eyes.

Of course his long, gaunt, Easter Island face with its aquiline nose and hollow cheeks and overpowering jaw was as instantly recognizable to me as that of my father or mother since I'd lovingly studied every photograph of Lovecraft I could get my hands on over the years, going from those black-and-white snaps taken in the twenties and thirties and bound into the old Arkham House collections, all the way on up to the underexposed—and therefore humorously greenish—Polaroid he'd enclosed with his letter of invitation: ". . . in order to prepare you for the shock of seeing Grandpa in his present corpselike condition."

I waved at him through the window with the eagerness of a child and as his teeth flashed in a smile and he gave me exactly the sort of friendly little salute of recognition I had hoped for, I clumsily hauled my bag for the last time from its lair under the seat, and emerged from the bus directly behind my New England lady.

And then she stepped primly away from before me, leaving me exposed in full view, and I turned suddenly from the happiest of young men to one of the most miserable wretches in the world, for though he did his gentlemanly best to hide it, I caught the almost instantly extinguished, kindly amusement in Lovecraft's eyes as he took me in from head to toe, and, for the first time, standing before this man who had been my idol through the bulk of my formative years, the full extent of the incredible idiocy, the grotesque absurdity, the horrible *presumption* of my short, plump, silly self, affecting the mode of attire he'd taken up in his later years, the black cape and wide-brimmed hat, dawned on me with a fierce, merciless clarity which threatened to crush me to the ground, then and there, under its weight.

Frozen in my pose before the doorway of the bus, unable even to breathe, totally humiliated, I only barely managed to fight down a mad, desperate urge to turn and flee into the vehicle's dark interior and cower there until it should drive me back to my hated flatlands.

Then Lovecraft's face lit with that kindly radiance which one sees only rarely in his photos, and he moved toward me with his hand extended.

"I confess I am very touched, Edwardius," he said, speaking quickly and precisely in a high-pitched, gentle voice. "It truly is—as I am only now able to appreciate fully for the first time—the *sincerest* form of flattery. Please accept my gratitude."

He paused and gave my hand one brief, firm, friendly squeeze in what I realized must be a very Yankee form of handshake, then turned and waved his cane to indicate a large, black, very elegant old Rolls which, even under the grey, lowering sky, gleamed and glistened like a fine old British beetle in the parking lot by the side of the station.

"And now," he said, giving my shoulder a light, comradely pat, and studiously keeping his eyes from mine so that I might have sufficient privacy to put myself together, "Let us saunter forth from this hub of public transport, you and I, and enjoy a form of locomotion more suitable to the gentry."

The driver's door of the Rolls opened as we approached and a tall, thin, bearded man emerged gracefully. He was wearing a very elegantly tailored blazer and his perfect ascot evoked my idea of Saint Tropez more than Providence. He watched the approach of Lovecraft and myself in our identical capes and hats with no visible sign of hilarity save for a slightly ironic tilt to his head, but I came to learn that cranial attitude was habitual with him.

"This, Edwardius, is my valued associate, Mr. Smith," said Lovecraft as we reached the thin man's side. "Mr. Smith, please allow me to present Mr. Vernon, the young fantiste whose work we have discussed so much of late."

Mr. Smith favored me with a shy, deeply wrinkled smile, and though his handshake was not particularly strong, he delivered it more along the lines of the heartier Midwestern style to which I was accustomed.

But then, from the unobtrusive alacrity with which he gently withdrew his hand and carefully placed it out of sight in the pocket of his blazer, I realized I had not managed altogether to cover my wince of distaste when I'd touched his flesh. It was singularly dry and oddly unyielding, and though he was so refined and physically delicate in every other aspect of his appearance that he put me instantly in mind of an Elizabethan dandy in some elegant portrait, the texture of his skin was shockingly coarse. It was obvious the poor man suffered from a hideously incongruous illness.

"I found myself particularly admiring your management of the worm king in 'The Enshrouding,'" he said, speaking softly in an accent obviously foreign to this region, and, to all appearances, completely unaware of the little pantomime which had just taken place between us. "But I must confess my special favorite so far has been your notion of a displeased god presenting its followers with a poisoned idol made in its own image."

As I thanked him for his gracious comments I found myself looking at him with an increasingly awed puzzlement because, even though I could not at this moment connect it with any specific association, I was now absolutely certain that I knew his face well and had seen its wise eyes looking out at me from their wrinkled settings many times.

By now Lovecraft had entered the back of the car—again with no visible sign that the burden of his great age was more than a trifling inconvenience—and he waved me in beside him as Mr. Smith arranged himself in the driver's seat in order to play the chauffeur while H.P.L. gave us a brief tour of his beloved Providence. He pointed out various landmarks significant in the old town's history and his own, spinning little stories about them all with numerous brilliant asides, and I did not even try to deny myself the gleeful delight of anticipating the envy my telling and retelling of this adventure would produce in my listeners' hearts down through the years to come. And so it has!

However, with each sidewise glance I stole at my host my astonishment at his remarkable preservation increased. Looking at him one had no doubt that he was extraordinarily old, but there was also no doubt he was astoundingly—even eerily—fit and spry for a gentleman hovering around the century mark.

Also, the ravages of time seemed, in his case, to have

followed some weird progression which differed significantly from the common patterns. He was not, for example, actually *wrinkled,* because instead of the deep fleshly canyons one is used to seeing, his face was covered with a sort of web of fine lines, thin as cobwebs and shallow as the cracklings in a quaint old doll. Also there were none of the standard grotesqueries associated with the very old, no enlargement of the ears, no wattling of the throat, and absolutely no thinning of the hair at all. The truth was that if you squinted your eyes, he looked very much as he had in those old photos taken back in the late '30s.

He finished his tour by pointing out the house he'd lived in during the last period of his "obscurity," as he called it.

"It was moved from its original location to Meeting Street," he said, "But, as you see, I managed to arrange to have it carefully brought back here to 66 College Street, where it belongs. And I saw to it that my aunts had the use of it, not just part of it, but the run of the whole building, until their deaths."

"That must have been very satisfying to you," I said.

"It was, Edwardius," he said with a smile that began a little grimly but then broadened. "However it was nothing next to the restoration, the recreation, you might even fairly say the glorification of my grandfather's place at 454 Angell Street, which is where Mr. Smith has now almost driven us. There it is, just ahead."

We paused briefly before a high, wrought-iron gate which opened smoothly when a button was pushed in the Rolls's dashboard, then rolled up the curve of a driveway and came to a gliding stop before a large, most imposing house.

"I admit to improving on its architecture," Lovecraft observed, exiting from the car with a light step and no use of his cane whatsoever. "Even to transforming it entirely. Whipple Van Buren Phillips' house was a simple clapboard affair, though of substantial size, and not at all the splendid Georgian manor which you see before you. I suppose I could be accused of being a trifle Williamsburgian in all this, but it's both esthetically and emotionally authentic, and the material, garnered by my agents from all points in a quite Hearstian manner, is entirely period."

"It sounds just like the creation of the mansion in your story, 'The Rats in the Walls,'" I said, looking about at all this splendor more than a little wide-eyed.

"Of course it does," said Lovecraft, with a smile. "Of course it does. Good heavens, wasn't it painfully obvious my whole notion of that American millionaire creating an ideal ancestral home was the pathetic dream of an impoverished romantic? Ah, but I see from your expression that does not seem to have crossed your mind. Well then, perhaps that little tale of mine isn't quite as embarrassing as I'd feared all these years, after all."

By now Mr. Smith had opened and was standing by the many-paneled front door, tall and richly gleaming beneath its glorious fanlight. Lovecraft led the way inside, laid his cape and hat on a handsome Wedgwood table and waited until I had done the same with mine.

"They look quite natural there, side by side, do they not?" he asked. "Perhaps, Edwardius, where I have failed to do so on my own, the two of us together may bring capes and broad-brimmed trilbies back in style!"

He walked to a handsome double door, paused with his hand on one of its brightly polished knobs, then turned back to me with a mildly vexed expression.

"Please do accept my apologies," he said, "I have grown thoughtless in my solitary, self-indulgent ways. I was about to drag you on through an extended tour of the house as I know there is much you will want to see, particularly in the library—oh, just wait 'til you see the library!—but it completely slipped my mind that you've only just climbed off that obviously uncomfortable bus and would doubtless very much enjoy some freshening up."

He paused to snap open and consult a wonderfully quaint old watch which he'd extracted from a pocket in his vest.

"It's a little over an hour to four," he said. "If Mr. Smith will be kind enough to show you to your room, you'll have plenty of time for a wash-up and perhaps even a short nap before tea, which is a custom we have taken to observing in recent years. Also, quite frankly, it will give your grandpa a chance for a little nod as well!"

Mr. Smith led me to my quarters and introduced me to its quirks, most helpfully the involved controls on an imported shower in the bathroom. After he left I spent a few minutes gaping in wonder at the room's marvelous antique furnishings, including a dazed, indeterminate period of time standing before a huge, lovely, glowing landscape which I took to be a Turner until I bent to examine the small gold plate fixed to its bottom frame and read that it portrayed the fabled realm of Ooth-Nargai from Lovecraft's novel *Beyond the Walls of Sleep* and that its artist was "unknown."

Standing back from the painting I felt a slight dizziness and finally realized that Lovecraft had been quite right: I *was* exhausted (my prim New England lady would be shocked to learn how loudly she snored). So I hung up my one spare suit, washed some of the grime of travel from my hands and face, and it seemed to me I had barely stretched out on the bed when I found myself suddenly being dragged out of a profound slumber by a gentle tapping and Mr. Smith's voice informing me from the other side of the door that tea would shortly be served.

I reared up on my elbows and lay there for a second or two trying to pull back the vanishing recollections of what must have been a spectacularly interesting nightmare. It had been quite Lovecraftian, which was, of course, appropriate. I'd been in a harsh landscape, cold, windy and mountainous, and seen bits and pieces of something huge and grey with an appalling wingspan come flapping down toward me through the snowy air, clacking its teeth horribly and ever more eagerly with each lurching drop in its descent. Its small red eyes burned piercingly down at me with an intent interest which somehow struck me as hideously *personal*, and I heard it caw tremendously: "Perfect, ah, but you're *perfect!*" just before it reached out its claws and I felt the first taloned squeeze of its inescapable grip. "You're next!" it cawed, "You're next! You're next!"

Some important aspect of the dream seemed determined to evade me but I pursued it determinedly until I felt my stomach contract with the peculiarly horrible recollection that I'd been looking up at the monster from the very stalks and bracken of the creature's nest.

I shook my head without clearing it all that much, did another quick wash, tightened my tie and started down the softly carpeted steps, but my downward progress was slowed considerably by the wonderful discovery that the ancestor portraits which lined the wall of the landing and stairway and which I'd only dimly noticed on my way up were, in fact, quite marvelous oil paintings of some of the principal villains in Lovecraft's novels and stories, each one of their names and birth and death dates neatly engraved on little golden plaques mounted at the bottoms of their frames.

Along the wall of the landing was hung a triptych of portraits, the center one being the slim, subtly gruesome figure of Joseph Curwin, the resurrected necromancer from *The Case of Charles Dexter Ward,* and it was flanked by the likenesses of the two ghastly, grinning ancients who were his mentors and assistant magicians in the novel, Simon Orne, originally of Salem, and Edward Hutchinson, later known as Baron Ferenczy of Transylvania. Among the other wonderfully sinister villains depicted in paintings descending the handsome staircase, I came across the hunched and leering Keziah Mason from "Dreams in the Witch House," with her horrendous familiar, Brown Jenkin, curling nastily round her feet, and an enormous, towering oil of Wilbur Whateley, the hybrid sorcerer of "The Dunwich Horror," seemingly all unaware that his vest had come slightly open and the viewer had an appalling peek at the writhing monstrosity which was his chest.

The front part of the ground floor was deserted, but I

heard a cozy clatter coming from the rear of the house and soon found my way to an exceptionally comfortable, sunny and obviously well-equipped kitchen where I came across Mr. Smith leaning over a counter and humming to himself, serenely engaged in cutting tiny triangular sandwiches for tea.

"Ah, Mr. Vernon," he said, looking up at my entrance and smiling. "Did you have a pleasant rest?"

I smiled back at him and had actually opened my mouth to make some insignificant joke about my nightmare of being in the monster's nest, when the sunlight shone on his cheek in a certain way, and I recognized him at last.

He stopped his cutting and began to observe me with some concern because my expression most certainly had abruptly turned very odd indeed, and I'm sure I must have gone pale as a corpse.

"Is there something wrong?" he asked. "Can I get you a glass of water, Mr. Vernon?"

"Edwardius," I said, then realized I had barely croaked the name, so I cleared my throat and swallowed before continuing. "I should be very honored if you would call me Edwardius, just as Lovecraft does. After all, he has always acknowledged you as his peer."

"His peer?" asked Mr. Smith.

"You," I said, "Because you are Clark Ashton Smith, poet, author, artist, and honored friend of Lovecraft, of H.P.L. Please don't deny it because I'm sure of it."

I paused, and then, aware of my heart beating in my chest, I said the other part.

"Of course I know it's impossible because you are dead."

He stared at me for a moment, then he frowned slightly and went back thoughtfully to his cutting. He made about three more little sandwiches and stacked them carefully on a silver tray with the rest, then he lay the knife on the counter.

"I suppose it was bound to happen one day, sooner or

later," he murmured to the sandwiches, and then he gave a tiny shrug and looked up directly into my eyes.

"Very well, you're right," he said. "About both those things. I *am* Clark Ashton Smith, and I *am* dead. As you see, it turned out not to be impossible."

I stared at him, then groped forward and took hold of the counter with both hands because, to my great embarrassment, I appeared to be on the verge of fainting.

"There's a stool there, by your side, to your left," said Smith gently. "From the look of you, it might be a good idea if you sat on it. Carefully and slowly. It was quite thoughtless of me to be so abrupt."

I sat, carefully and slowly as he had said, and the pounding in my ears and the dancing spots of light before my eyes began to fade and dim.

"I thought you'd spotted me back at the bus terminal, you know," he said, handing me a glass of water which he had somehow filled without my noticing. "Then I saw you hesitate and falter into indecision, and I figured we'd got away with it again."

I took a long drink of the water, then another, and after a deep breath or two I decided I would probably be able to talk.

"I couldn't place you until just now," I said, speaking a little clearer with each word. "Then I saw the sun shining through your beard, and I knew."

He glanced at the window behind him and nodded with the relieved air of one who has solved a minor puzzle.

"Ah, yes. That *would* weaken its effect," he said. "It's the square cut extending from the sides of the jaw that does the job, you see. I thought it up myself and must admit I'm quite proud of the way it effectively obscures the essential triangularity of my face. Unless, as I now learn, the sun shines through it from behind."

"Of course it's particularly difficult to recognize someone in disguise when you think they're in their grave," I said, taking another sip of water.

"Naturally. That was our basic working assumption," he

said. Then, with a small, resigned sigh, he added: "Not that I'm all that well known. It isn't as though we've been trying to conceal someone really famous."

The kettle on the burner started to whistle and he reached up, took two canisters from a shelf, then turned to me.

"What tea would you care for, Mr.—ah—Edwardius? We've finally managed to wean Howard away from sugar with a little coffee to a simple English breakfast blend. I, always the exotic, am attached to an odd Japanese concoction brewed from twigs, but it's not, confessedly, for every taste."

"I've never ventured out further than Lipton's in a bag," I admitted.

"None of that here, I'm afraid," Smith said. "Far too common for the likes of us. Let's start you out with a Darjeeling; the highest quality, but quite undemanding."

He lost himself for a moment or two in contentedly and efficiently assembling pots and cups and saucers, but then he stared at his hands, stopped still, and looked up at me from a neatly squared little stack of napkins with an expression of concern on his face which was more than a little pathetic.

"I hope you're not apprehensive about these hands of mine spreading some contagion," he said, holding them up before himself like two foreign objects. "They look this way, *I* look this way, because of an essential crudeness in my construction. It's not a disease, you know. It's nothing you can catch."

"I'm sorry I pulled my hand away from yours back at the bus station," I said, after a pause.

"Oh, no, you had every right to. They're horrible," he said. *"Horrible!"*

He turned towards the window and rotated his hands on his wrists so that they caught the sunlight this way and that.

"I'm like this all over, you know," he said. "Every inch of me. And it's not just my skin, worse luck, it's the same with my insides. My bowels, my heart, no doubt my brain itself must be made of this repellent, defective stuff."

He rubbed his hands as if he were trying to smooth them, to reduce their gaping pores, and then looked back at me over his shoulder.

"You must forgive him," he said. "He was lonely, you see. I know it's difficult for one as young as yourself to begin to imagine how impossibly isolating it is to have the world one was born in die off with the passage of the years. *Along* with all of its inhabitants, mind. People and things keep vanishing only to be replaced by other people and things which vanish in their turn until even the *memories* of everything and everybody you grew up with and held dear are reduced to tiresome, passé jokes."

He had turned back to the tea tray, busying and calming himself with a final supply and inventory of its contents as he talked.

"You said it yourself, Edwardius," he said, filling the creamer with a hand that betrayed only the tiniest tremble. "I was one of the very few people he considered his peer. I was also, very importantly, an inhabitant of his original world; a contemporary. Unfortunately for him, I was also dead. But H.P.L. had, some time ago, hit on a way past that. He'd purloined the basic notion from a book by none other than good old Cotton Mather—the idea of raising the dead from their 'essential salts'—attributed it to the French scholar Borellus, and used it as the basic modus operandi for his scurvy Frankensteins in *The Case of Charles Dexter Ward.* My present resurrection represents his second practical application of the technique."

"That's horrible!" I cried.

"Yes," he said. "I confess that now and then I find myself wishing he hadn't done it, as death was really quite a relief. But, as I say, he was lonely. And eventually I will die again. I need only be patient."

A faint sigh sounded from the back of the kitchen.

"Well, well, Klarkash-Ton," said Lovecraft softly, employing the eerie nickname he'd concocted for his friend during their famous correspondence in the thirties. He stood framed by the doorway, leaning forward slightly with both hands interlaced atop the handle of his cane. "Things seem to have moved along smartly during Grandpa's nap."

I jumped to my feet as clumsily as a startled calf, but Smith merely turned his head and nodded as Lovecraft advanced into the room, looking carefully first at one and then the other of us.

"The boy has so far exceeded our most hopeful expectations. He recognized me, Howard," Smith said, "He recognized me—thereby setting himself apart from all previous visitors—and being a meticulous scholar of our little literary circle, he knew of my generally unheralded demise."

"So you went ahead and told him the truth without overmuch preamble, as we planned," he said, then walked slowly over to my side. "And you, Edwardius? Have you believed him? From the look of you it would appear you have."

"My presence is difficult to refute," observed Smith. "As are my grisly looks. More importantly than all that, our friend appears to have taken the complete and sudden overturning of reality as he knew it with commendable equanimity. It seems our speculations based on the promise of his tales were quite correct and that—unlike the common herd—Edwardius is blessed with an open mind."

Lovecraft rubbed his huge jaw thoughtfully, studied me silently for a long moment.

"Excellent," he said at length, and, after a moment more, he added, "The two of us have for some time felt the growing need for a knowledgeable assistant, Edwardius. Also, certain signs which have cropped up repeatedly in my studies and experiments indicate strongly that our establishment is on the brink of some important transformation and that new blood will very shortly be required. We have been studying your writings and been impressed by them, not only because of their obvious literary merit, but because they seem to tell us that there is something remarkably *right* about you for the sort of activities in which we are engaged. We have both, in short, come to the conclusion that you would fit nicely into our little association."

I was amazed, even dazzled by this totally unexpected turn. For a space I could only gape at the two of them—with my mouth wide open I am sure—but eventually I managed to gather myself together enough to speak.

"I'm honored," I said, "more honored than I can say, that you would even consider such a thing!"

"Very well, then, let us see how things work out," said Lovecraft with a small nod as he studied me intently, eye to eye. "Your ability to accept Klarkash-Ton's resurrection was the passing of an important test. Perhaps after we've all enjoyed a little tea, Edwardius, you'll be up to accepting a few other things. But be warned, please *do* be warned, they'll be a lot harder to swallow than our ghostly Mr. Smith!"

The sandwiches tasted even better than they had looked, an almond cake which Smith had purchased from a Portuguese bakery was superb, and the Darjeeling demonstrated clearly that my accustomed bag of Lipton's, though perfectly serviceable, by no means exhausted the subject of tea.

"Delightful," said Lovecraft, leaning back comfortably into exactly the sort of leather wing chair I'd hoped he have. "And now that we're sated, thanks to the efforts of Klarkash-Ton and his foreign baker friend, I think it's time we quit this lovely, sunny Georgian parlor and give Edwardius a little tour of the premises."

We rose and Lovecraft headed for one of the tall white doors with me in his wake, but Smith produced the silver tray and began collecting cups and saucers.

"I'll think I'll stay behind and tidy up," he said. "Am I to assume you won't be giving our young friend the usual restricted and misleading tour?"

"He shall see every trap door and secret panel," said Lovecraft, smiling. "Events have proceeded rather more quickly than I'd planned, thanks to Edwardius' astute perceptions and flexibility, so things are ahead of schedule. I believe the time has well and truly arrived to enlighten him as fully as possible about his present company. I'll begin the job in the library, rather than putting it off for a final treat, since I believe its atmosphere and impressive contents will go a long way towards lending credence to the admittedly implausible information I plan to impart."

Smith, nodding, said no more, and as he bent to sorting china with his usual mild but interested bemusement, I followed Lovecraft through the door and soon found myself being led down a handsome hallway which, like so much of the house, was lined with paintings associated with my host's works. These, however, were far more disturbing than the ones I'd seen heretofore, since they were all depictions of various fabulous monsters described in his tales.

"I'm quite pleased with myself for coming up with the idea of hanging these huge oils in such a constricted area," said Lovecraft, grinning at me over his shoulder and casually indicating a remarkably horrific visualization of what—from its fanged, vertical mouth and jutting pink eyes—could only be one of the gigantic, ever-ravenous Gugs which prowled the pages of his *Dream Quest of Unknown Kadath*. "It renders them particularly overpowering, does it not? And forces one into a threatening intimacy with the creatures which the timid viewer could avoid in the space provided by a room."

I glanced—a little nervously, I'm not ashamed to admit—this side and that at the looming horrors that towered so very oppressively near to us as we passed, and I freely confess that I actually started and drew back when the sleeve of my jacket accidentally brushed against an almost fiendishly well-executed painting of that shifting conglomeration of iridescent globes which is Yog-Sothoth, one of the most puissant and awful gods in Lovecraft's mythos.

Eventually he paused before a large, elaborately paneled door made of almost ebon teak and, producing a heavy gold chain loaded with formidable-looking keys, operated no less than three locks before turning a huge brass knob sculpted to resemble an unwinking, octopoid eye framed with undulating tentacles, and pushed the portal open.

"My library," he said simply, but with obvious pride, and led the way inside.

Of course I had realized some time ago that everything about this house far surpassed all aspects of that one owned by Whipple Van Buren Phillips, but I felt certain nothing about this dream version of Lovecraft's favorite childhood home would have awed his grandfather more than the library which I now found myself entering.

There were shelves upon shelves of books, two full stories of them. Outside of the space taken up by the three tall windows on the side of the room facing the entrance, absolutely every available inch of wall above and below the encircling balcony was filled with books, and there were piles more of them on the two long tables, and on the high-backed chairs, and stacks more yet were on the floor and heaped in the corners. It was a collector's wonder, a scholar's marvel, and I burned to feel the bindings and turn the pages and read the words.

"Impressive, isn't it?" said my host. "I fancy it is by far the best collection in the entire world of volumes dealing with the macabre and the fantastic. Over there, for instance, under that Grecian niche containing a pallid bust of Pallas, is the sort of marvelous accumulation of first editions and manuscripts—along with other, rather more exotic artifacts—of Poe which I had never dared even hope to see, let alone touch, let alone own, back in the days of my obscurity."

He walked slowly down the long room, pointing his cane towards this or that fabulous rarity and contentedly describing their queer particulars and complex histories, and I stumbled after him in a sort of daze, gaping with increasing astonishment at all these legendary treasures, astounded to see books by giants such as Arthur Machen and Ambrose Bierce and Arthur Conan Doyle which I, a specialist in the field, did not even know existed.

Eventually we reached the far wall of the room and, standing by one of the curling steel stairways leading to the balcony, Lovecraft placed his hand carefully on the head of a tiny gargoyle carved into the shelving beside him and regarded me with an extremely solemn and serious expression on his long, lean face.

"You must promise me, most earnestly," he said, speaking quite severely with all trace of banter gone from his voice, "that you will never reveal anything of what you are about to see next unless you have my clear permission to do so."

I studied him for some sign which would indicate that this sudden extreme sternness was some sort of amusing pose, but then I realized he really was, indeed, deadly serious and nodded my head affirmatively.

"I'm afraid I need more than a nod on this," he said, with no trace of humor in his voice.

"I promise I'll keep secret whatever you're going to show me," I said. "I do, really."

He searched my face for a long moment, then smiled, gave the little gargoyle a precise poke on its nose, and—without a whisper of sound—the shelving slid smoothly aside to reveal an even deeper layer of rows and rows of books hidden a yard or two behind. There was a smaller—and, I could tell it at once, far more sinister—second library hidden craftily within the first!

"These books, too, are related to the macabre fantastic," observed Lovecraft entering into this mysteriously revealed little room with something of a saunter. He still preserved traces of that new solemnity, but with his much more familiar tone of underlying mockery once again apparent. "The essential event is that we have now passed beyond the fiction department of my little collection and have moved into that portion concerned with fact, and though a great many of its facts would be vehemently denied by this world's contemporary wisdom, there is much here which would be approved of by the staidest investigators."

He waved his fingers at the section of newer-looking books which nearly filled one side wall, and a quick scan of them revealed a multitude of names well known to anyone pretending to the slightest familiarity with modern physics.

"Of course even in this supposedly safer area I have a

number of items which might very seriously disturb the present scientific community," he said. "The formulae scrawled in that little notebook of Einstein's just in front of your nose, for instance. But I think that a scholar of your particular tastes, Edwardius, will be more interested in having a look at those volumes over there."

I stared at the far side of the room which he had indicated and was puzzled because it seemed to me that there was something very strange and wrong about the sight of it. I could not quite pin down what it was save to say that the whole area seemed oddly dark, as if it were somehow veiled—a distasteful and highly disturbing image of horribly sticky spider webs out of focus floated into my mind—and it seemed, in some weird fashion, as if that corner of the little library was disproportionately far away. I had the most peculiar notion that I would never be able to walk the whole distance if I spent hours or even weeks at it, and that I would very likely die under hideous circumstances somewhere along the journey if I undertook to try it.

But obviously none of this made sense, so I pulled myself together and had taken a step towards the shelves Lovecraft had indicated when he laid a hand gently on my arm to stop me, then sidled past me and—with his back turned scrupulously in my direction so as to block my view—he appeared neatly and efficiently to execute a brief series of ritualistic gestures before standing aside, almost with a little bow, and indicating I should pass. I looked at the corner again and had to smile at all my previous imaginings because now there was no sign of any odd darkness there at all, and if there ever had been that strange spatial distortion and I hadn't fantasized it completely, it had entirely disappeared.

But as I approached those shelves and began to be able to read some of the titles of the books resting on them, I felt my smile vanishing rapidly. I reached out with a hand gone suddenly clammy, plucked a worm-eaten volume from the shelf before me, and nervously turned several of its pages—which were not paper, but something disgustingly thick, almost *flabby*, which seemed to flop

mockingly from my fingertips with a life quite their own—
before total revulsion overcame me completely and I hur-
riedly stuffed it back into its place with a violent shudder. I
turned to Lovecraft and saw that he was leaning forward on
his cane with both hands and smiling at me with the air of
one who has pulled off a marvelous jest.

"It can't be," I gasped, and then I swallowed and
seemed to understand. "I see . . . you're smiling because
you've fooled me, because the thing's a wonderful forgery
and you've frightened me with it!"

"No, not at all," he said, still grinning. "I smile because
it's real, because your fear is well founded, because you
remind me so much of myself and my horror when I first
came across that book."

"But—*De Vermiis Mysteriis!*" I cried. "There isn't any
such book! It was made up by Robert Bloch in the mid-
thirties for a story in *Weird Tales* when you and he and all
those other authors were playing that wonderful literary
game of making up a world of monsters and their cults.
The book was just a black-magical prop for his fictitious
magicians. You even helped Bloch create it when you
wrote him a letter and told him how to Latinize the title!"

Lovecraft nodded solemnly, but the grin never left his
face.

"True, all true," he said. "And in my letters I often ad-
dressed Robert as Ludvig, after Ludvig Prinn, the bizarre
scholar who authored the *grimoire,* and Robert and I and
all of us firmly believed he'd made the old boy up out of
whole wool."

Lovecraft leaned back and laughed, and the echoes of
his laughter whispered back, bounced off the spines of all
those books.

"Oh, we were all taken in, Edwardius, it's really quite
amusing. We all thought we knew so much, but we were
only cocky, clever children toying with Yog-Sothothery—
your old Grandpa included—and it turned out we didn't
know a thing."

Then he paused and actually cackled.

"But we were right!" he said, looking up at me, twinkling. "Somehow, all along—we were *right!*"

Then he paused, took a deep breath, let it out slowly, and I saw him visibly gather himself before he continued.

"Edwardius, you are truly—as Klarkash-Ton observed—a formidable scholar of that small group of macabre writers with whom Smith and I are proud to be associated. You know much of all our histories, including my own particular, personal history, but I must tell you now that there are many turnings of considerable importance in that latter history which you do *not* know for the very good reason that I have gone to great lengths, and employed many ingenious stratagems, to keep them carefully hidden."

He made his way out of the small library and we sat on opposite sides of the nearest table in the larger room. Lovecraft shoved aside a jumble of stuff including a battered metal box, some yellowed newspaper clippings and a dusty slab of dried clay to clear the space between us, and then he leaned forward on his elbows, settled himself, and began to talk.

"You know of my severe illness in 1937. I had been pursued by an increasingly distressing digestive trouble for years which I had stoically and foolishly ignored, but by degrees I apprehended the seriousness of my condition, and in February of that year I had very little doubt that I was dying. My diagnosis was confirmed by a specialist in March, and I soon found myself full of morphine in Jane Brown Memorial Hospital with nothing to do but write up my symptoms in the faint hope it might be of help to my physician.

"Some time during the dark hours of the thirteenth the pain woke me in spite of my medication, and as I lay there, staring up at the ceiling and trying to isolate myself from the agony in my gut, a part of my mind which had been almost entirely repressed for my life's whole duration until that moment, suddenly loosened its bindings and began to speak to the rest of me with such eager intensity and desperate emphasis that it almost seemed I could actually hear it whispering in my ear, whispering so distinctly that I began to grow concerned that the nurses might hear it and somehow shush it, and I didn't want that to happen as it was telling me some remarkably interesting things."

He paused and looked at me, and in the darkening shadows of the library he seemed to be positively glowing with an air of excitement which made him look even younger than he'd seemed before.

"What if those awesome entities I had spent my whole life conjuring up and writing about—all those terrifying ancient monsters who'd wandered in from other planets and dimensions and whose powers were so vast and overwhelming— what if they were *real?* Suppose my minutely detailed, precise visualizations of all their horrendous particulars down to their last tentacle and claw, had not been my creation at all, but a slow unveiling of actual, existing beings?"

"It's a matter of record that I had toyed with such notions before, but only as teasing, intellectual diversions. However I think I must have known even then—though I surely would have denied it most righteously if pressed— that they spoke to something very deep within me, for they never failed to give me a profound and highly satisfactory ghoulish *frisson.* Could it be that I had been using talents and abilities which this sly whispering part of my mind had been aware of all along, but which my poor, strait-laced conscious mind, so pleased with limitations, had studiously—no doubt affrightedly—ignored? Had I all unknowing groped through the barriers which separated Them from us and *made an opening in the time and space between our different worlds?*"

He leaned forward, rattling the clay slab slightly on the table, and stared at me intently as if judging whether or not I was ready for what he was about to tell me next.

"I undertook a little experiment, Edwardius," he said. "A rather gaudy one for a quiet, reclusive author fond of his aunts, I'll admit, but, after all, I *was* dying. I wouldn't have another chance."

"I located a thin, spidery crack running in the ceiling

over my bed and I stared and stared at that crack as hard as I could until I saw its central edges start to bulge. Then I found I was able to stare harder yet, and I saw those same central edges begin to separate, and then, incredibly, but with an odd feeling of relief which I cannot even possibly begin to describe, I observed two delicate black tentacles writhe out and pull the crack open just a little bit wider so that a small chunk of the ceiling dislodged and I felt it land with a soft little plunk on the coverlet over my chest."

"Now the whisperer within me employed my whole mind to speak to that Entity above, commanding it with the certain confidence of an experienced wizard, and I was aware of an enormous stirring behind the entire ceiling and extending down along the upper portions of the walls. Faint scratchings and brushings—something like the scurryings of a thousand furtive rats and something like the coilings of a vast multitude of swollen worms—seemed to sound from every point, and now the crack in the ceiling widened even further, and oozing out from between those smaller tentacles emerged a long, complex serpentine appendage terminating in a complex swirl of undulating filaments. As I stared with bulging eyes it swayed lower and I observed the filaments sink smoothly through my coverings and glide inside my flesh."

"I watched my cancer leave me, Edwardius, I saw it being taken away, sucked up through that living tube in a steady, bloody stream, and only when it was entirely gone, every last molecule of it—and I *knew* it was gone, Edwardius!—did that remarkable thing detach itself from my body and glide up again and vanish."

"As I stared up into the crack after it I saw, hovering in the darkness behind the ceiling, a glowing red eye with a slit pupil, and it winked at me, and I winked at it, and the small tentacles curled back in again, out of sight, exactly like inhaled smoke, and the crack closed almost as tight shut as it was before my little experiment, but not quite."

He paused a long moment, and then he grinned and chuckled softly.

"It was all such an exactly perfect, hilarious travesty of a fresco by Giotto—the bony, dying author on his staid Memorial Hospital bed staring up with glistening eyes at a vision of a portion of Shub-Niggurath emerging from on high—that I began to laugh, Edwardius. Quietly at first, then louder and louder, and soon the ward seemed full of puzzled nurses brushing plaster off of Mr. Lovecraft and wishing he would shut up, and I wouldn't or couldn't because ever since I'd been a child I'd burned to play with jinns and dryads and now, only barely in the nick of time, the whisperer had shown me how to do it!"

He sighed happily, let himself sag back into his chair, and gave an expansive wave with both arms at the library about us.

"It's helped me build and buy this house, too," he said, "since I could have in no way afforded it—could have afforded *none* of this—save for the great, the astounding success my small literary efforts have had, in themselves and in the films and the extraordinary variety of other enterprises, worthwhile and puerile, which have spun off from them. I think it's fair to say that that dreadful Saturday morning animated television program for children which the network has loathsomely entitled *Cthulhu Kiddies* alone covers our ordinary daily expenses. All of that success has occurred since my recovery on that most eventful night, and its origins trace back clearly to the contract I made on that occasion."

I stared at him, my mind in a whirl, and stuttered out the burning question.

"Then those monsters you and Smith and Bloch and the others wrote about were real all along!"

"Just so!" he said. "But they weren't real in *our* reality. They were cut off from it, helpless in limbo, just like poor old Cthulhu in my stories. Our writings and dreamings touched and wakened them, but it was only after I'd actually pulled one of them out of the ceiling in order to save my life—dragged the thing out into this world of ours by a force of will absurdly magnified by the threat of imminent death—that they could start to manifest. They have been busily and ceaselessly continuing to follow up that first breakthrough into this dimensional knot of space and time wherein we make our home ever since, Edwardius, and, I must say, they have gone about it in the drollest way imaginable!"

He turned over the slab of clay and then pushed it across the table so that its face looked up at me.

"Do you recognize that?" he asked.

I studied it with growing astonishment. It was a rough rectangle less than an inch thick and about five by six inches in area. On its upper surface, in a sort of cross between cubist and art deco styles, very obviously out of the twenties or thirties, someone had modeled a remarkably disturbing low bas relief of a winged, octopoid monster squatting evilly before a multi-angled, Picassoid building.

"It's the dream-inspired sculpture of the artist Wilcox from "The Call of Cthulhu," I said, excitedly. "It's the first tangible clue given in your mythos stories that the old gods exist!"

"Precisely," said Lovecraft, nodding, "But not *quite* precisely. You'll notice the signature of the artist cut into the slab's back is Wilton, not Wilcox, and the date is 1938, not 1925, as it is in the story. And though the withered newspaper clippings you see here follow the same general pattern I created in *Call,* they are all *variations* on that pattern; they all concern real people with names which vary—sometimes subtly, sometimes quite widely—from the names I gave my fictitious characters, and they all date from after my medical adventures in Jane Brown Memorial Hospital."

"It is the same with these tattered old notebooks. You will observe that they are not written by the dear old Professor George Gammell Angell whom I first dreamed up during the miseries of my Brooklyn exile in 1925, but that they are the desperate scrawlings of a flesh-and-blood gentleman who is also a professor—of Physics, not Semitic Languages, it is interesting to note—named Horace Parker Whipple. Both of these gentlemen, however, real and fictitious, *did* die after being mysteriously jostled by a sailor. The strange forces shaping this ongoing realization of my fictitious world always adhere quite closely to my stories' more sinister original details."

"Along those lines it is also interesting to observe that—like those of my entirely imaginary Professor Angell—Whipple's notebooks show that he had come across a cult whose god's name *is,* indeed, Cthulhu. Though everything else in this continuing process of materializing the creatures and basic notions of my imaginary mythos and incorporating them into our universe seems subject to sometimes even whimsical change when needed, the names of all the deities and their servitors never vary by a letter from my original suggestions."

"But the books," I said, "If this changing of reality is all your doing, then how about the books? *De Vermiis Mysteriis* and the others—I glimpsed some of the rest!—all those ancient tomes of black magic which I'd thought you and the others'd all made up for your stories—*Cultes des Goules, Unaussprechlichen Kulten*—those books are old! They're ancient! They were here long before you were born!"

Lovecraft smiled.

"Yes, they were," he said. "And all the hoary dates which Smith and Bloch and I and the others ascribed to them have turned out to be accurate. Oh, it's true enough we were all only naive paupers, scribblers for the pulps with pathetic pretensions to scholarship, and none of us were near sophisticated enough to have a clue that what we were writing down might actually be the truth. But those books existed, all right, and they were very carefully hidden under lock and key by scholars, exactly as we thought; mainly, I think to protect presumptuous upstarts such as ourselves in the old *Weird Tales* gang from getting our uncultured paws on 'em! It's been quite a joke on us, not to mention our little planet, that the whole library of them turned out to be just as we'd made it up!"

He indulged himself once more in that rather unpleasant, somewhat witch-like cackle and leaned forward in a confidential manner.

"The only problem with those books, Edwardius," he whispered with a wink, "was that until I and the others wrote about them, and that until I made contact with the forces behind them on my supposed deathbed—the problem was they didn't work!"

He paused and leaned back with his fingers spread out on the dark wood of the table before him, and that stern solemnity I'd observed before fell over him, momentarily, like a shroud. Then, in a wink, it had lifted, and he was grinning triumphantly ear to ear.

"But now they work," he whispered. *"Now they work!"*

I sat like something carved in stone, groping unsuccessfully in the confused whirl of my brain for something solid to cling to. Then I heard a gently discreet rapping at the library door and jumped as if someone had fired off a cannon by my ear.

"That will be Smith," murmured Lovecraft, then called out, "Come in, Klarkash-Ton."

The door opened and Smith glided in quietly. He studied me with an interested expression on his lean, wrinkled face and then turned to Lovecraft.

"I see by our young friend's stunned expression that his initiation continues apace," he said. Then he turned back to me, examining me further in a kindly but penetrating manner. "Do not be too hard on yourself, Edwardius, it is all very difficult to grasp. I certainly found it was when H.P.L. tried to explain the state of affairs to me after he'd chanted Borellus' formula of evocation over my essential salts and brought me back to this simulacrum of my living self. And you are fortunate in that—when you finally do manage to grasp the situation's colorful implications— you will be able to console yourself with the knowledge that you are not among those responsible for its coming about. At least you had no part, as did Howard and myself, in setting these monsters free."

Lovecraft straightened in his chair, snorted softly, and glanced up at Smith with quiet disapproval.

"*Monsters,* Klarkash-Ton?" he asked. "Surely that is more than a little judgmental?"

"Monsters," said Smith, clearly and firmly, smiling at Lovecraft a little grimly, then turning to me still smiling. "Howard is never slow with the implication that I am cosmically xenophobic."

"I am not making an implication," said Lovecraft firmly. "I am stating a simple fact. These beings are in no way malevolent regarding life on our plant—I have said it all along in my stories and it has turned out to be the simple truth—they are merely indifferent to it."

Smith gazed at his old friend and sighed.

"When are you going to face it, Howard?" he asked. "These creatures we have let loose *are* monsters. They were monsters in whatever hell they came from, they are monsters here on Earth, and they will be monsters wherever they happen to go next. My good fortune is that I happen to be unfond enough of my fellow men and women not to be that overly disturbed at what we have unleashed upon them. Please don't take my attitude to be one of moral disapproval. It is not the sure and certain domination and destruction of my dreadful species which troubles me, it's embarrassment that my contribution was merely the accidental result of personal ineptness and ignorance. I would much rather have doomed my miserable race on purpose."

Lovecraft grimaced with distaste, waved Smith's comments aside with a weary gesture indicating he had done so many times before, and then looked at me from across the table with the air of a man who has suddenly had a very good idea.

"Since things are moving along so well and you've shown such a remarkable aptitude for expansion, Edwardius," he said, "I believe I've thought of a simple, reasonable way of putting to rest any little fears or nagging doubts which Klarkash-Ton's dreary speechifying may have roused within you regarding these visitors in our midst. It is, quite simply, to allow me to introduce one of them to you, in person, so that you can see it, talk with it, and then judge for yourself whether or not you think that it is a monster. Also, if you are to become involved with our continuing activities, it is important to discover whether or not they find *you* are tolerable. It is an obvious risk. Are you willing to take it?"

I gaped at him, my head spinning with the escalation of this whole affair.

"You're suggesting that you'll call one of these beings up?" I gasped.

"I do it all the time," said Lovecraft casually. "There's nothing simpler, once you've got the hang of it."

Smith stirred and I saw his expression had become even more ironic than usual.

"I think it only fair, H.P.L.," he said, "to explain to Edwardius the little reason *why* you have such frequent occasion to summon up your chums."

Lovecraft glanced up at him with a small frown, then shrugged and turned to me with a small spreading of his hands.

"As an accomplished student of our literary efforts," said Lovecraft, coolly, "you are, of course, aware that Klarkash-Ton is ever a lover of irony. The fact is that in order to continue on here in the luxury to which we have become accustomed, it is necessary, now and then, to offer up a little sacrifice. A human sacrifice, to be exact. Mind you, we have always been meticulously careful to offer up individuals whose loss will either not be missed or will actually be gratefully received by the thoughtful and intelligent. Arrogant or obtuse book critics, for instance, or some of those responsible for the cruder pastiches of my writings."

"And of mine," said Smith, with a grim little smile. "But, our good intentions aside, you must understand that if you allow Howard to make this proposed introduction you will be running the risk of becoming such a sacrifice yourself through misadventure. I am not sure these creatures can differentiate a bad critic from a good writer."

Lovecraft stood.

"What Klarkash-Ton says is perfectly true, Edwardius," he said. "This encounter will not be devoid of risk. But, unlike him, I can and do enthusiastically presume to recommend that you run that risk and undertake this adventure. I really think there is nothing I would not have gladly given if someone had proffered me an invitation such as this when *I* was a young man! So, then, Edwardius, are you game? Shall we do it?"

I hesitated a moment longer, then I rose and nodded firmly.

"I would never forgive myself if I didn't," I said.

Lovecraft and I left the library with a dubious Smith and made our way through halls and down stairways, myself always conscious of a painted villain or monster looking down at us from some wall. Lovecraft and I paused at the entrance to retrieve our capes and hats since a fine, gusting drizzle had begun to fall, then the two of us were outside walking through grass as Lovecraft led the way into a wooded area. After we'd made our way between its trees for some time more than I thought was likely in a property as small as this corner of Providence had seemed to be—especially when I noticed that those trees had turned from relatively new growth to wide-trunked, wizened old giants which were totally improbable in such an area—I turned to my host in some puzzlement.

"You are quite correct, Edwardius." He smiled at me and nodded. "All this is much larger and older than it has any right to be, but then we've cheated a little with its time and space. On this excursion we shall only penetrate a little bit into the forest's western edge. There is much more here, believe me, much for you to savor and explore once you've settled in with us. There's an ancient ruined city, for example, and a wonderfully gloomy swamp, and caves and grottos beneath which I haven't begun to explore. In any case, we've reached our goal."

We'd entered a clearing and I was thrilled to find myself standing dwarfed amidst the primitive spires of a small but impressive circle of monoliths. Lovecraft walked up to a grey standing stone which towered twice his height and stroked the damp undulations of its mossy side affectionately.

"These old rocks were carefully removed from a high, lonely mountaintop in the real world's very nearly exact equivalent of Dunwich, which was, of course, the locale of my fictitious Wizard Whateley and his dangerous, not altogether human, brood," he said. "I had them removed, then carefully arranged here in exactly the same sinister circular formation they originally enjoyed, and I'm pleased to say they've lost none of their awesome powers."

He pointed at a formidable flat slab of granite in the center of the formation.

"That is the stone of sacrifice," he said. "It was baptized long before the witches came from Europe to claim it for their own. The Indians used it in their rituals since ancient times, and recent contacts I have made assure me that older, much weirder entities gave it what it wanted during previous millennia. Walk up to it, Edwardius. Feel it. Not just its texture, but its mood. It has been involved in countless potent workings and sopped up much blood of many different kinds."

The drizzle had now turned to a steady, windswept rain, and the smooth runnels carved into the stone caught the fallen water so that it gurgled suggestively as it was guided and poured into an insatiable, sloping pit dug into the stone's center. I reached down with my hand and at the instant my fingers made contact with the spreading, lichen-specked discoloration surrounding the opening, the ground itself was jarred by the impact of an ear-shattering clap of thunder overhead.

"Oh, that's excellent," said Lovecraft, peering up at the sky, totally unaware of the rain cascading down his face, "Oh, that's very good. Look at the clouds, Edwardius— how smoothly they circle in from all horizons so as to form a single, larger cloud at that point overhead. Amusingly like witches scuttling to form a coven, isn't it?"

The wind had furiously increased and was whipping

our legs and the bases of the stones with the tall grass of the clearing, and snapping our capes about our bodies. Lightning angled everywhere across the sky and soon each thunderclap overlapped the one before so that there was only a perpetual, steady roaring.

But I was only dimly aware of all that for it was slowly coming clear to me that I was observing a phenomenon unparalleled by anything I'd seen or heard of in the natural world. I stared up at it, fully as intently as Lovecraft did beside me, and the more I watched of its unfoldments, the more my terrified awe turned unexpectedly into a kind of reverence.

The clouds had merged into one huge thing above us which, as I watched, swiftly took on a highly discomforting solidity while the lightning—flashing about it and in its depths—began revealing innumerable, increasingly clear details which I could easily see now were no longer mere gaseous swirlings, but the conscious movements of a vast multitude of living organs—first crudely formed, but soon swiftly sculpted and refined—each one born in frantic, greedy motion.

The insane range and variety of these members became clearer as their shapes clarified and their outlines grew more distinct. Some of them bore varying degrees of resemblance to the organs of creatures dwelling on our planet, but others were so totally alien to anything of Earth that they seemed to offer no possible relationship to any species or function I had ever seen or heard of.

Among those limbs and extensions at least somewhat identifiable I could make out claws and pincers of all possible descriptions snapping hungrily at the air; a seething mass of spidery legs groping with obscene curiosity in every direction, and innumerable wings—some webbed, some scaled, some raggedly and darkly feathered, but all of enormous span—which completely surrounded the thing's entire body in a huge, vast ring, each one flapping in perfect time with all the rest.

Dominating all of this was an enormous, staring eye surrounded by four huge, quivering lids made up of thousands of smaller eyes, each one peering in a different direction from its own twisting stalk, with the result that the momentous entity above us would be all-seeing.

I jumped as Lovecraft's hand suddenly grasped my shoulder.

"What do you think of it, Edwardius?" he shouted over the thunder. "Isn't it magnificent? Isn't it *beautiful*? Monster, indeed!"

I could think of no reply. I seemed momentarily beyond reply, and, besides, the overpoweringly steady roar of the thunder seemed to mock any little noises I might make.

Then I stiffened as I realized the sound of the thunder had begun to change and modulate. It was awhile before I understood what I was hearing: the thunder was shaping itself, much as the cloud's form had done before. It was steadily progressing from the random to the organic; it was starting to develop, in effect, a kind of mouth.

"You've grasped what's happening, haven't you, Edwardius?" said Lovecraft.

I started and turned and stared at him. I felt my legs tremble and leaned against the sacrificial stone for support. He frowned when he saw the gesture, and took hold of me and pulled me back.

"No," he said, "That's a mistake the victims always make. You stand by me."

"It's forming words," I said, "It's speaking!"

He cocked his head and listened critically.

"Well, not *quite,* not yet," he said. "But any minute now!"

Keeping one hand on my shoulder he stood a little ahead, peering upward.

"This is Edwardius," he called out loud and clear. "He is a friend. He is to work with us. He is not a sacrifice."

He repeated my name again, shouting out its syllables one by one and sounding them carefully.

"Ehd-ward-dee-uhs," he called out. "Ehd-ward-dee-uhs!"

I stared up at the thing and saw with a new thrill of horror that a sort of titanic convulsion had started taking place in the center of its underside, a spreading writhing and untangling of tentacles and jointed legs, not to mention pseudopods and spiny, telescopic horrors, and other, totally incomprehensible things—it was like watching a sea of knots untie itself!

And, at that moment, the creature found its voice.

"AAAAAY!" it roared in thunder. "AAAAAY!"

I felt Lovecraft stiffen slightly and look up in some concern.

"Odd," he said, sounding mildly puzzled and, for the first time, just the tiniest bit unsure of himself. "That doesn't sound right at all."

Then, freed of their entanglement with one another, all those awful organs stretched farther and impossibly farther out, until they extended even beyond the confines of their gigantic body. The whole thing looked like a horrible parody of a rayed, glistening star floating over a saint in a Russian icon.

"AAAAAY-CHaaa!" roared the voice, and I saw Lovecraft squint thoughtfully upwards. "AAAAAY-CHaaa!"

"Ehd-ward-dee-uhs!" he shouted up at it, then turned to me with a mildly irritated shrug. "It's got your name wrong. You can imagine how difficult our language is to manage for something with its vocal apparatus."

The stretched limbs extending from the creature began a slow, very ominous, downward curving and I cringed in spite of myself. Then they came lower yet, all those different graspers and clutchers and suckers and biting things, thousands of them coming closer and closer in a thousand different ways, and as they smoothly and inevitably continued their lowering swoop what was at first only a terrible guess on my part slowly and surely hardened into a certainty.

"It's reaching for me, isn't it?" First I said it calmly, then not quite so calmly. *"It's reaching for me, isn't it?"*

"Now don't panic, don't panic," Lovecraft whispered in my ear, and then he shouted upwards once again: "Ehd-ward-dee-uhs, he is a friend—*Ehd-ward-dee-uhs!*"

"AAAAAAAY-CHaaa PEEEEEEEE!" roared the voice from

overhead, and the mighty circle of stones seemed to quiver at the sound.

Lovecraft's face suddenly paled, then reddened, and then his eyes widened in absolute astonishment.

"My goodness, I think I understand what that stanza in Geoffrey's *People of the Monolith* means at last," he said to himself, and then he turned to me. "What is the date, Edwardius?"

"September the fifteenth."

"Aha," he said, "I thought so. Don't worry, my boy; you're quite safe."

Then he gazed gently up with a shy wistfulness which was totally incongruous on his bony Easter Island face, and extraordinarily moving. "It's really quite extraordinarily touching," he said.

Then he turned to me and pointed overhead.

"It *is* beautiful, is it not?" he asked me.

"Yes," I said, calmed by his calmness. "It is. Klarkash-Ton's wrong about them."

"He can't help it; there's a bitterness about him. You must forgive him."

"AAAAAAAAY-CHaaa PEEEEEEEEE EHLLLLLLLLLLLL!" boomed the voice, and the stones reeled and tottered in their sockets of earth.

He took his hand away from my shoulder and advanced a pace or two, then, with a little leap executed with the ease and unconscious gracefulness of a small boy, he hopped onto the center of the sacrificial stone.

"I'm here," he called up in his high, thin voice to the enormous roiling on high. "I'm here!"

"AAAAAAAAY-CHaaa PEEEEEEEEE EHLLLLLLLLLLLL!" boomed the thing again, and then: "ff—ff—ff—FATHER! FATHER!"

Lovecraft stood quietly, looking up wide-eyed at the huge business looming above him, at the tentacles and claws and oddly jointed fingers reaching for him. One of the monoliths, uprooted by the omnipresent roaring, fell with a great crash behind him, missing him only by inches, but he did not so much as notice.

"Ff—FATHER!" the voice boomed again as all those strange, horrific limbs tenderly took hold of Lovecraft, each one gentle in its separate way, according to its own bizarre anatomy, and together they lifted him carefully from the ground as he lay unresistingly in their grasps, their coilings, their enfoldments, as he stared upwards and above them at the great eye of the thing which was raising him higher and even higher, and the last I saw of H.P.L., the expression on his lean, long, solemn face had the strange, uncanny, loving peace of a babe in its crib.

The door of the house was open when I came back and Smith was standing just inside, holding two glasses of wine, and watching my solitary approach without a trace of any visible surprise.

"How strange," he said, "How very strange. I knew, I absolutely *knew* it would be you instead of Howard coming back. I don't know why. Certainly the possibility never occurred to me with any of the others. Perhaps it's those quotes from the *Pnakotic Manuscripts* he's been dropping lately."

"It's the anniversary of 'The Dunwich Horror,'" I said. "It's the day Wilbur Whateley's brother went home at last."

He stared at me thoughtfully.

"So it turned out to be a sacrifice, after all," he said, "And it worked. There's no doubt of that. You've changed."

And at that moment I realized for the first time that I *had* changed, that there was something very different in the way I felt from any way I'd ever felt before. It was a kind of glowing, a kind of power. A very deep kind of power which I liked very much.

"We always drink a toast after the sacrifices," said Smith, handing me one of the glasses. "It's become a tradition."

We touched the rims in a toast and the crystal made a magic little ringing. Smith tossed his wine back with one long, smooth swallow, but I just took a first sip. It was Amontillado, of course.

"I've got dinner ready for us whenever you're hungry," he said.

And that's the way it's been ever since, without either one of us feeling the slightest need for any discussion or agreement. Klarkash-Ton continues to be the sexton, I have taken over the position of wizard, and we've carried on the sacrifices with very little difficulty; there seems to be no foreseeable shortage of victims. We'd have a sufficiency with the disparaging researchers alone. I will admit I was startled to learn that they are ordinarily very bloody affairs, full of rippings and tearings and meltings down which bear small resemblance to the reverential ascension accorded H.P.L.

That first evening, however, Smith disappeared discreetly in the direction of the kitchen, pouring himself another glassful on the way, and I found myself walking with a quiet purposefulness towards the library. I was soon standing in the secret alcove at its back, reaching out for the tall, dark spine of the *Necronomicon,* which I had seen before but not quite dared to mention. My hand was still inches from the shelf when the book stirred like a gently wakened cat and glided into my fingers all on its own, settling softly into them as a bird settles into its nest.

It's bound in some sort of black pelt with long, thick hair, and after I'd held it a moment or two, I noticed that some of the longer strands had twined affectionately about my fingers. They still do it to this day, whenever I take the *Necronomicon* up, and sometimes they hold them very tightly. Particularly when I'm chanting.

Afterword

I was a kid on a Florida Christmas vacation with my folks and it was a long time ago and the cells in my head were even softer and more malleable than they are now when I bought the Bart House paperback of Lovecraft's *The Weird Shadow Over Innsmouth* in a ratty, dusty Key West drugstore.

I still have the book. I keep it carefully in a plastic bag even though it is in far from mint condition. Its cover is faded and dirty with both lower corners bent; there are many stains and smudges on its pages with lots of funny little bits of things lurking between them and, worst of all, it has an extremely embarrassing EX LIBRIS bookplate pasted in it featuring the drawing of a mouse which I tried to tell my twelve-year-old self was really a rat, staring vaguely at a book which I desperately attempted to believe looked at least something like the dreaded *Necronomicon.*

I am sure a good many Lovecraft connoisseurs would laugh it to scorn and they have my full sympathy, but to me it's far and away the most valuable item in my H.P.L. collection—even more treasured than the beloved bound first edition of *Innsmouth* with its Utpatel illustrations and errata slip which I acquired many, many years later—because I vanished into that paperback after reading just a few of its paragraphs during that ancient Key West afternoon, and I've never entirely come out since.

There's always something of me wandering along the tilty docks of "Innsmouth," or night-snooping in the dark, dead New York of "He;" I shall forever partly be "The Outsider," and an awed harkener to "The Whisperer in Darkness," and—most certainly and joyfully—a traveler enthusiastically riding a hybrid winged thing that no sound eye could ever wholly grasp, flapping my way through twisting, pitch-dark tunnels to "The Festival."

I suppose, in a way, it's a kind of curse, but I wouldn't have it any other way, and I'm terribly grateful to you for it, Mr. Lovecraft.

Please accept this story as a kind of thanks.

THE ORDER OF THINGS UNKNOWN

Ed Gorman

"I experience the horror of everything that is, to the point of longing for death."
                    —*Guy de Maupassant*

1

In memory, the street was a perfect image from a song by Elvis early on, or Chuck Berry, or Little Richard—a street where chopped and channeled '51 Mercs and '53 Oldsmobiles ferried dazzling pony-tailed girls and carefully duck-tailed boys up and down the avenue, where corner boys dangled Lucky Strikes from their lips and kept copies of *The Amboy Dukes* in the back pockets of Levi's from which the belt loops had been cut away with razor blades. The sounds: glas-pak mufflers rumbling, jukeboxes thundering Fats Domino's "Ain't That A Shame," police sirens cutting the night and sounding somehow cool and threatening at the same time (like a sound effect from one of the juvenile delinquent movies that always played on the double bill at the State); Italian babies screaming from the tiny apartments above the various storefronts; Irish babies screaming; black babies screaming; an argument ending "Fuck you!", "Well, fuck you, too!" as one corner boy walks away from another not really wanting to get into it (unlike movie pain, real pain can hurt); and talk talk talk, wives and husbands, lovers, little kids having just glutted themselves on "Captain Video" and imitating the Cap'n now, and old lonely ladies saying prayers for somebody in the parish, heart attack or cancer suddenly striking. And the smells: "Evening in Paris" on the girls and Wildroot Hair Oil on the boys and cigarette smoke and Doublemint gum and bus exhaust and smoky autumn and cheeseburgers and night itself, the neon of it, the Indian summer heat of it, and the vast harrowing potential of it (a guy could get laid; a guy could get knifed; it was great giddy fun and it was spooky as hell).

This then was Hanlon's memory of the street and it was completely fictitious, or so it seemed the only time he came back here, twenty-seven years after leaving.

Richard Hanlon gave the package of Luckies to the Oriental man behind the counter of the reeking little grocery store and the man smiled at him with rotten teeth and spoke in a language Hanlon understood not at all.

"How much?" Hanlon asked.

The man, leathery-skinned and ancient in a way almost sinister, punched up the price on the aged cash register and pointed to the amount showing in the machine's oblong window up top.

Hanlon pulled two singles from his pocket and handed the money across. The man gave something like a bow, smiling again with his bad teeth, and rang up the purchase. Hanlon got eight cents in change back.

As he left the store, Hanlon recalled the days when a flush-faced mick named Sullivan owned this little store. It didn't stink of dead meat and rotting produce in those days and Sullivan—despite the fact that he wouldn't sell you cigarettes until you were eighteen and could prove it—Sullivan at least spoke English.

Hanlon went out and stood on the pavement, thinking of all the times he used to do this in the old days. He'd been a corner boy for sure. Man, the hours he'd spent here, after school till dinner and then after dinner till nine or ten at night, eleven or twelve in the summers. Talking about who was cooler, James Dean or Robert Mitchum (he'd always opted for Mitch), talking about screwing Doris Cosgrove (hell, he would have been happy just to get a quick little kiss from her), talking about how he was going to be a writer some day (always toting a James T. Farrell book in his back pocket) and live in New York, the old man's union having a college fund which would insure all these dreams.

But now; now.

In the dirty street light, in the dirty night, the rusted and battered cars of the underclass dragged by like creatures without the wit or luck to simply die. On the sidewalk hookers leaned against paint-peeling storefronts and comic-book pimps manicured their nails with switchblades. Two cops parked in a squad car ate hamburgers and two men holding hands walked down the street. And always there was the language—Vietnamese, he supposed—crackling through the dirty air. He knew he was being racist and he tried not to be. But he had come back to a world he had always considered his and found it no longer his at all.

He smoked two Luckies, all the time staring up at the apartment over the Laundromat across the street. In the old days, the blind man with the gnarled hands and the garlic breath had always sat in his rocking chair at the window and looked out on the street below. As if he could see.

The blind man sat there now, staring, staring. Hanlon could make out his shape in the shadows.

Hanlon dropped his cigarette to the pavement and put it out with the toe of his black oxford.

So the blind man was expecting him.

Hanlon wasn't sure how he knew this; only that it was true. Taking a deep breath, he crossed the street.

2

Hanlon was blessed with one of those boyish, handsome faces that even people who should know better trust immediately. This was why he had no trouble luring women into his car and killing them.

He killed his first woman on the night of August 14, 1964. He had just left a local Democratic rally for President Lyndon Baines Johnson—who was running against the devil himself, Barry Morris Goldwater—when he saw a somewhat plump but very pretty woman in a pink waitress uniform standing in front of a somewhat battered 1956 Ford Fairlane, the hood up, steam poring out of the radiator. She seemed so helpless and disconsolate that she looked positively fetching. The image of a helpless woman appealed to him enormously.

He pulled in behind where she'd parked just off the road, got out and went over to her.

"Pretty hot night for car trouble," he said, smiling sympathetically.

"It sure is." She rolled a slender wrist to her face, reading a tiny cheap watch. "I'm supposed to be at a party in twenty minutes. Bridal shower."

"Why don't we take a look?" he said, sounding like a doctor about to peek in at a sore throat.

He saw the problem immediately. A hole in her radiator. A rock could have put it there or kids sabotaging cars in a parking lot.

He leaned back from inside the hood. "Tell you what. Why don't I give you a ride? There's a Standard station down the way. They can come back and tow your car in and if it's not too far out of my way, I can give you a ride to your party."

"Jeeze, it's gonna need towing?"

He smiled again. "Afraid so."

She didn't say thanks for the offer of a ride; thanks for looking at my car. She was as cheap as her watch.

"So what's wrong with it?"

"Hole in your radiator."

"Jeeze, why does this crap always happen to me?"

"My name's O'Rourke," he said. The odd thing was, the false name surprised him. He had no idea why he'd used it. No idea yet what he really had in mind. He put out a slender hand (he'd always hated his hands, tiny as a fourteen-year-old girl's, the wrists reedy no matter how long he lifted weights) and she took it.

"Paula. Stufflebeam."

"Now there's a sturdy name for you."

"Hah. Sturdy. Shitty is what you mean."

They got in the car and started driving. The radio played. When "Oh, Pretty Woman" by Roy Orbison came on she started sort of finger-popping and bopping with her hips and asked if he could maybe turn it up a little.

He smiled and complied.

When the song was finished, she said, "I like this car. What kind of monthly payments you have to make on it, anyway?"

"It was a gift."

"Huh?"

"My uncle gave it to me." He actually had a rich uncle.

"Jeeze, it must be nice."

The night was busy with traffic. Mosquitos slapped against the windshield. Mary Wells sang "My Guy." Two blocks from the Standard station, he suddenly veered right, still not knowing why. A sign said WARNER PARK, TWO BLOCKS EAST.

"Hey," she said.

"Pardon me?"

"This ain't the way to that gas station."

"No?"

"No."

He increased his speed. He was going forty miles per

hour. He had to be careful. He could get stopped by a cop.

"Don't get no ideas," she said. "About me, I mean."

"Wouldn't you like to look over the city? Just sort of take a break?"

"I don't even know you."

He turned toward her. He had an altar boy innocence. "I'm not going to put the make on you, if that's what you're afraid of." He frowned. "I'll be honest with you."

"Oh, yeah?"

"Yeah. My girlfriend—" He sighed and then steeled himself, as if saying the words were painful beyond belief. "My fiancée, to be precise, told me last night that she's in love with somebody else."

"Jeeze," Paula Stufflebeam said, "and you was going to be married and everything?"

"And everything."

"Jeeze."

"So right now I could use some company, you know? Just—a friend. A friend and nothing more."

"Jeeze."

"So I just thought it'd be nice if we could go up to Steep Rock and look out over the city."

"Nothin' more?"

"Nothing."

"You promise?"

"I promise."

She sighed. "Yeah, why not? I guess I'm late already, what's another hour anyway?"

Steep Rock was a red clay promontory that looked out over the city below. Over the hundred years the city had been here, Steep Rock had been used variously for seduction, bird watching and suicide.

After he parked the car, they got out and went to the edge. The night air was slow and hot, filled with fireflies and mosquitos. Below the city lay like a vast marijuana dream, unreal in the way it sprawled shimmering over the landscape and then ended abruptly, giving way to the plains and the forests again. Next to him, Paula Stufflebeam smelled of sweat and faded perfume and sexual juices. She had a run in her stockings so bad he could see it even in the moonlit darkness and oddly it made him feel sorry for her. She wasn't cheap, she was poor and uneducated and there was a difference.

"So who'd she dump you for?" Paula said after they'd looked at the city for a time.

"Somebody named Steve."

Where was this stuff coming from (and so fluidly)? He had no girl friend, let alone a fiancée, let alone one who'd dumped him for somebody named Steve.

"She give you the ring back?"

"The ring?"

"Engagement ring. Didn't you give her one?"

"Oh. The ring. Yes. She gave it back."

"Well at least she did that much for you."

He knew then he'd have to lure her. In the clearing where they stood ringed by the dark shapes of oaks and elms and pines, he put his head down abruptly, as if somebody had just stabbed him.

"You all right?" Paula Stufflebeam asked.

"Just—lonely, I guess. I'm sorry." He looked at her. "Maybe I'd better take you back."

"Jeeze, you're really strung out, aren't ya?"

"I'm afraid I am. I—"

And she accepted. He put his arms out wide and she came into them. And he held her tightly, feeling the shift of her breasts beneath the cotton of her uniform, smelling her bubble-gum-colored lipstick and the faint wisp of hairspray. They didn't kiss, merely embraced, one friend comforting another.

And he knew, then. Knew why he'd stopped for her. Knew why he'd brought her here.

Easing his hands from around her back, he quickly found her throat.

"Oh, God!" she shouted.

But before she could say anything else, his hands found their true place, and she squirmed against him almost carnally, and tried to get her arms up to push him away but he was too fast and strong, and then she sagged against him, spent, and then he lowered her to the ground and smelled the way she'd fouled herself.

Oh my God.

Oh. My. God.

What had he done?

And my God, why?

Why had he done this?

Why?

He stood in the clearing, moonlight-glazed, the city lights below so alien. He looked at his hands. They seemed to be strange tools that belonged to someone else.

Her uniform skirt was up over her thighs. He could see the tops of her stockings and her garters. She was as lurid as a cover of a true detective magazine. He could smell her sex and smell her bowels, one sweet, the other sour. He thought of how it would all look in the paper, the details.

Why? My God, why?

The darkness came then and it was chilling—literally, goosebumps and hackles standing on end—a darkness different from night, different from unconsciousness, a darkness in which voices in the unfathomable gloom whispered words he heard only teasingly. It was inward-turning, this darkness; it was pleasure-denying, this darkness; and it would be forever more.

He stood as if naked in the moonlight and looked up and saw the moon and the stars and sensed for the first time that beyond them, somehow, there was another reality, one few ever glimpsed, one that filled early graves and asylums alike.

When he put the girl in the trunk, he was careful to set her on the tarpaulin. She had begun to leak.

Richard Christopher Hanlon graduated from Illinois State University two years later with a degree in business administration. At that time he got a job working as a salesman for General Mills out of Minneapolis and he married a fellow graduate named Susan Anne Todd. At the time of their wedding Susan was four months pregnant, a

fact that displeased both of their parents greatly. Only on
August 6, 1966 did the parents smile. This was not just
the day of the wedding but the day Susan miscarried.
Now there would be no baby to embarrass them. The dig-
nity of both families would be intact. Susan and Richard
tried again, of course, and a year later the first of three
daughters was born to them.

Richard was these things: an amiable and compliant
worker for the great corporation, an attentive husband
and doting father, a good Democrat despite the fact that
he had begun to see that the lower classes weren't always
interested in helping themselves even when they had the
chance, a tireless watcher of Cubs and Bears games, a tender and inventive lover when his wife was not unduly
pregnant and then a champion masturbator, a golfer who
would never be any good, a tireless reader of political
biographies, and a troubled Catholic who felt that the
Church had lost all sense of Jesus. At thirty-one, he had
prostate problems. At thirty-three, he began to bald. At
thirty-five, he developed this little tumor of a pot belly
that no amount of exercise could quite quell. At thirty-six,
he saw his eldest daughter win a national essay contest
and go on the CBS Evening News and talk to Dan Rather.
At thirty-nine, he was promoted to a divisional sales manager and his salary, with perks and bonuses, exceeded one
hundred and fifty thousand per annum, which wasn't bad
for a former corner boy. At forty-one he had a brief cancer scare that turned out to be an eminently treatable
throat problem. His hair continued to fall out and by his
mid-forties he tended to identify himself as bald. During
all these years he was unfaithful only once (with a stew-
ardess from Peoria), was threatening to his wife only once
(he'd had a head cold and his irritability from the cold
caused him to erupt when she made some minor grousing
remark), and embarrassed his children only once (he insisted that he could do a good impersonation of a certain
rock star and did so at Katie's ninth birthday party; Katie,
ashamed, blushed so deeply it seemed a rash had broken
out on her face).

Of course he continued murdering women, too.

In all, from the night with the waitress to the time he returned to his old neighborhood, he killed seventeen women. Some were strangled, some shot, some slashed very, very badly. The murders took place in Minnesota, Iowa, Illinois and Missouri and always when he was on the road for Mother corporation. He scarcely remembered them, actually. They always took place during a merciful fog, a blood frenzy that left few details to be recalled later on. He would see a bloody breast, a bloody thigh, a bloody buttock, but then the image would recede, recede and be forgotten utterly. If he'd recalled in any detail what he'd done, he would have gone crazy, literally, and been put in an institution.

In his mid-forties, the dreams began, and it was the dreams that brought him back to the old neighborhood this night.

3

At the top of the long dusty staircase was a fire door. The moon was framed perfectly in it as Hanlon ascended the worn and tilting steps. The narrow passage upward smelled of heat and garbage left too long and of time itself, that taint of dust and decay.

When Hanlon reached the top of the stairs, he stopped. Three dark doors stood to his right, each opening on a sleeping room not much bigger than a prison cell and every bit as drab. He remembered the blind man's room. Hanlon and some of the other corner boys used to come up here sometimes when they heard the blind man playing his accordian. In those days his music—which ran to polkas rather than popular tunes—gave the boys great pleasure. How he tapped his foot, the blind man, when the tune quickened and swelled; how he rolled his dead milk-of-magnesia eyes when the tune turned somber. As if in lament; as if in lament. But soon enough the blind man became just another joke to the boys, one of those half-hateful, half-pitiful figures who were fun to tell huge lies about when lights went out and tales were told. As he passed beneath the window on his way to this girl's or that girl's, Hanlon often heard the blind man playing and even once or twice was tempted to go up in the room and watch the blind man strap on the dazzling cumbersome Excelsior and play the "Too Fat Polka" or "The Blue Danube Waltz," the room smelling of Kool cigarettes and Vicks and rubbing alcohol.

Now Hanlon sneezed. The dusty stairway had incited his sinuses. The noise he made was as sharp as a gunshot in the dusty gloom.

He took two steps forward to the middle door, raised a hand, and let it fall loud and sharp—one rap only—against the dying wood.

No response.

Hanlon sneezed again.

Sonofabitch. What a time to stir his allergies up.

This time he knocked three times, quickly, and with a certain air of irritation.

A cane tapped the floor in the silence.

The door opened faster than he imagined it would and the blind man leaned over the threshold. "Yes, Richard, what is it?"

The blind man's skull seemed to be a shrunken head on top of which wild strands of white hair had been affixed. In the moonlight, his dead eyes rolled white and his slack mouth ran with silver spittle. He smelled unclean, like an animal that has been sick for a long time. The ragged white shirt he wore on his bony frame was stained as if from wounds that excreted not only blood but pus. He kept his knobby hands on top of the same knobby black cane he'd had when Hanlon was a boy. When he breathed in Hanlon's direction, Hanlon had to hold his breath. The stink of it literally made him nauseous.

"Come in," the blind man said.

And so Hanlon followed.

He noticed the window first, the framed portrait of the street below inside the window frame, streetlights and neon. To the right of the window the early American style rocking chair sat faintly squeaking, as if waiting impatiently for the old man to return.

"How do you know who I am?" Hanlon asked.

Something like a grin played at the old man's mouth. "Oh, Richard, I've known about you since the first day you came up here with the other little boys."

He moved then through the filth and shadows of the tiny room, the old man, back to his place in the rocking chair, back to his place at the window. From a stand next to the chair he rummaged in a half-eaten bag of Oreos, lifting a cookie with the reverence of a priest lifting a communion wafer. The old man sniffed the cookie before he tossed it into his mouth and began to crunch with loud enjoyment, smacking his lips every few moments.

When he had completely swallowed the cookie, he wiped the back of his mouth with his hand and said, "Forgive an old man his only pleasure." He tapped the cookie package. It rattled like tin in a hailstorm.

Then he farted.

"That's the only trouble with 'em," the old man said. "They give me gas, believe it or not."

The old man seemed amused with his farting and Hanlon wondered if he hadn't done it on purpose.

Hanlon went to the window and looked down at the street. He could almost see the ghost of his boyhood on the street below. Hear his own summer shouting.

Hanlon turned back from the window to the old man. "You know about me, don't you?"

The old man began to rock. The chair sounded like rusty metal that needed oil. "Yes."

"About the killings."

"Ummm-hmmm."

"And the dreams?"

The old man stopped rocking.

The room was dust and silence.

"The dreams?" Hanlon repeated. "You know about them?"

The old man resumed his rocking. After a time he said, "Yes, I know about the dreams."

"What do they mean?"

"That you have been selected."

"Selected?"

"By the god that inspires the dream. I can't even pronounce its name. It is a vile god. A very vile god."

The old man rattled the Oreo package again. Brought a cookie to his lips. Chomped down on it. Quit rocking.

This time he talked as he ate, gesturing with the cookie the way some people gesture with a cocktail glass.

"The first time you ever came here, I had this sense about you. I recognized myself in you. You see, forty years ago, I wasn't blind and I did what you're doing now."

"Killing?"

"Yes, oh my God; yes. I think there were thirty of them in fact." He finished the cookie and wiped his mouth again. He resumed his rocking. Loudly.

Hanlon went back to the window, sighed. "I didn't start having the dreams until after I'd killed several of the women. And then I realized that I wasn't killing the women at all—that it was this god I saw and heard in my dreams—who was killing them. It just used me as a human instrument. Then I wondered if I was insane."

"Just as it used me," the old man said.

Hanlon looked back at the old man. "I don't want to kill anymore. I won't."

The old man snorted. "That's very noble, Richard, and I made the same statement many times back when I—when I was doing its bidding. But I'm afraid you don't have much choice."

Hanlon said, "Where did it come from?"

The old man rocked for a long time, his head down. "Several centuries ago, a Druid cult made human sacrifices here, where the neighborhood is now. They buried bones in satanic formations and prayed to this god. Ever since then, the god has selected people from here as its tools. That's what you're doing to those women, Richard. You're offering sacrifice."

"Not any more."

"That's what I said."

"But obviously you stopped."

The old man sighed again. "Yes, I stopped."

"How?"

The old man rocked some more, reached over after a time and snatched a cookie, and began eating noisily again.

"I quit taking my medicine."

"What medicine?"

"For my eyes. Blindness is often hereditary. I knew that given my family history, I needed to take a certain medicine as I got into my thirties. But I stopped." He paused. "I went blind in six months."

"My God, on purpose?"

"Of course. What good would a blind man be as a killer?"

Hanlon listened to the old man rock. "Did you ever write their families letters?"

"Indeed."

"I even started sending some of them money—to try and make up for what I'd done. I never identified myself, of course. I've tried to turn myself in."

The old man snorted again. "No, I'm afraid that doesn't work, does it? The one time I tried to walk into a police station and hand myself over, I had a heart attack and was rushed to the hospital. For a year and a half I was unable to move or speak and was comatose most of the time. That was when I plotted my idea for blindness."

"There's one woman, I even visit her grave. She was very young. Seventeen."

"It's not your fault, Richard. Knowing what you know now, you can't blame yourself. It uses us till it's done with us."

Hanlon said nothing. Turned back to the window. To the boy of him in the streets below. So innocent, then. But as always thoughts of blood intruded and he saw their faces, their eyes so shocked and afraid, and knew that even if he was only an instrument, still he was guilty.

"I appreciate your talking with me," Hanlon said, pushing away from the window.

"Where are you going?"

"I'm not sure," Hanlon said, though of course he was sure. Quite sure.

Rocking, reaching again for an Oreo, the blind man with his milk-of-magnesia eyes stared out the window. "The neighborhood has changed, hasn't it?"

"Too much."

"Even the smells are different now."

Hanlon was at the door.

The old man starting chewing again.

Hanlon opened the door.

"Don't run away, Richard," the old man said. "There's no place to run to."

Hanlon closed the door softly behind him and started down the stairs again. By the time he was halfway down, he began sneezing.

"Hi, hon."

"Hi. You about ready to come home?"

"Soon as I finish with that paperwork."

"Sara was disappointed you weren't able to be at her recital tonight."

"It's just all this damn paperwork," Hanlon said to his wife.

"I know, honey. I know."

Hanlon stood inside a lighted phone booth. The phonebook had been torn from its protective cover and the shelf beneath the phone was covered with four-letter-word graffiti.

"I just wanted to tell you how much I love you and the girls," Hanlon said.

There was a pause on the other end. "Richard?"

"What?"

"Are you all right?"

"Sure. Why?"

"You just sound—funny, I guess."

"I'm fine. I just wanted to tell you that."

"You're probably just feeling guilty that you missed Sara's recital. You know how guilty you Catholics get." She laughed.

"I'm sure that's it."

"I made a chocolate cake for the girls. If you're nice to me, I'll cut you a slice when you get home." She paused again. This time there was a certain urgency in her tone, as if she were still troubled by something in his voice. "Why don't you come home right now, hon?"

"Soon as I can." Pause. "Be sure and tell the girls how much I love them."

"See you soon," she said.

"Soon," he whispered, and hung up.

He had parked his car three blocks from the blind man's. After hanging up, he went straight there.

Because he was parked in a fairly well-lighted area, he drove awhile until he found an area that was mostly rubble, and lay completely in gloom.

He pulled up to the curb, shut off the engine, leaned over to the glove compartment and took the gun out.

He had planned this so many times that he was able to accomplish it without any reluctance or hesitation.

He lay his head back against the seat rest.

He opened his mouth wide the way he used to for communion.

He thought of the death and grief he'd brought to this world.

And then he thought purely and lovingly of his family, the girls and his wife.

I love you.

I love you.

The finger he used had a hangnail. But that didn't slow it from its course, pulling the trigger back, firing the bullet that would excise a small ragged circle from the rear of his skull.

4

At least twice a day, different people—a friend, a nurse, a doctor—would lean into his vision and tell him how lucky he was.

His wife, sensing that this sentiment displeased him in some way, said it only once and then quit.

On the sixth afternoon, his wife brought him a box of chocolates—he'd always had a sweet tooth—and the latest Tom Clancy novel. He thanked her for them.

Afterwards, they sat in the sunny white room, her hand on his. They didn't speak. There was nothing to say. Their hands were eloquent enough.

Around four, the phone next to his bed rang. She started to pick it up but he waved her away and got it himself.

He recognized the blind man immediately. "I admire you for trying, Richard."

"Is that one of the girls?" his wife smiled. "They said they'd call after school."

Hanlon shook his head, which was wrapped in startling white gauze.

"But it's not through with you, Richard. It's not through with you. Not yet. That's why you didn't die." He paused. "I'm sorry, Richard."

The blind man hung up.

After a time, their hands still touching, the sunny white room darkening with wintry dusk, he began crying, huge silver difficult tears and knowing better than to ask why, his wife simply kissed his tear-hot cheeks and held his hand the tighter.

5

In the spring, Hanlon was in Buffalo, New York at a sales conference. It was here he met a hotel hostess named Sally Wedmore. They had a few drinks and some conversation and he offered to give her a ride back to her apartment.

In the morning, she was found strangled with her own pantyhose, her stomach ripped away with a knife.

When Hanlon spoke to his wife long distance that evening, she assumed he sounded depressed because he was tired and when she mentioned this he agreed.

"Yes," Hanlon said, sighing. "I wish I could tell you just how tired I am."

Afterword

I first read Lovecraft seriously when I was in my mid-thirties. Till then he'd struck me as overly ornate and too quaint by half. But when I read "The Colour Out of Space" again I heard those particular resonances and echoes so many other people find in his stories. He was the great paranoid and it was his paranoia that gave him his concept of the universe, all those gears and levers, all that machinery of fate, operating in the cold shadows that keep hidden the real truths. In that respect, Lovecraft will be a modern no matter what age he's read in because we'll never be sure exactly what existence means—if it means anything at all—and old H.P.'s guess is a lot more fun than any other I've come by.

THE BARRENS

F. Paul Wilson

1. In Search of a Devil

I shot my answering machine today. Took out the old twelve gauge my father left me, and blew it to pieces. A silly, futile gesture, I know, but it illustrates my present state of mind, I think.

And it felt good. If not for an answering machine, my life would be completely different now. I would have missed Jonathan Creighton's call. I'd be less wise but far, far happier. And I'd still have some semblance of order and meaning in my life.

He left an innocent enough message:

"The office of Kathleen McKelston and Associates! Sounds like big business! How's it going, Mac? This is Jon Creighton calling. I'm going to be in the area later this week and I'd like to see you. Lunch or dinner—whatever's better. Give me a buzz." And he left a number with a 212 area code.

So simple, so forthright, giving no hint of where it would lead.

You work your way through life day by day, learning how to play the game, carving out your niche, making a place for yourself. You have some good luck, some bad luck, sometimes you make your own luck, and along the way you begin to think that you've figured out some of the answers—not all of them, of course, but enough to make you feel that you've learned something, that you've got a handle on life and just might be able to get a decent ride out of it. You start to think you're in control. Then along comes someone like Jonathan Creighton and he smashes everything. Not just your plans, your hopes, your dreams, but *everything*, up to and including your sense of what is real and what is not.

I'd heard nothing from or about him since college, and had thought of him only occasionally until that day in early August when he called my office. Intrigued, I returned his call and set a date for lunch.

That was my first mistake. If I'd had the slightest inkling of where that simple lunch with an old college lover would lead, I'd have slammed down the phone and fled to Europe, or the Orient, anywhere where Jonathan Creighton wasn't.

We'd met at a freshmen mixer at Rutgers University back in the sixties. Maybe we each picked up subliminal cues—we called them "vibes" in those days—that told us we shared a rural upbringing. We didn't dress like it, act like it, or feel like it, but we were a couple of Jersey hicks. I came from the Pemberton area, Jon came from another rural zone, but in North Jersey, near a place called Gilead. Despite that link, we were polar opposites in most other ways. I'm still amazed we hit it off. I was career-oriented while Jon was . . . well, he was a flake. He earned the name Crazy Creighton and he lived up to it every day. He never stayed with one thing long enough to allow anyone to pin him down. Always on to the Next New Thing before the crowd had tuned into it, *always* into the exotic and esoteric. Looking for the Truth, he'd say.

And as so often happens with people who are incompatible in so many ways, we found each other irresistible and fell madly in love.

Sophomore year we found an apartment off campus and moved in together. It was my first affair, and not at all a tranquil one. I read the strange books he'd find and I kept up with his strange hours, but I put my foot down when it came to the Pickman prints. There was something deeply disturbing about those paintings that went beyond their gruesome subject matter. Jon didn't fight me on it. He just smiled sadly in his condescending way, as if disappointed that I had missed the point, and rolled them up and put them away.

The thing that kept us together—at least for the year we were together—was our devotion to personal autonomy. We spent weeks of nights talking about how we had to take complete control of our own lives, and brainstorming how we were going to go about it. It seems so silly now, but that was the sixties, and we really discussed those sorts of things back then.

We lasted sophomore year and then we fell apart. It might have gone on longer if Creighton hadn't got in with the druggies. That was the path toward loss of *all* autonomy as far as I was concerned, but Creighton said you can't be free until you know what's real. And if drugs might reveal the Truth, he had to try them. Which was hippie bullshit as far as I was concerned. After that, we rarely ran into each other. He wound up living alone off campus in his senior year. Somehow he managed to graduate, with a degree in anthropology, and that was the last I'd heard of him.

But that doesn't mean he hadn't left his mark.

I suppose I'm what you might call a feminist. I don't belong to NOW and I don't march in the streets, but I don't let anyone leave footprints on my back simply because I'm a woman. I believe in myself and I guess I owe some of that to Jonathan Creighton. He always treated me as an equal. He never made an issue of it—it was simply implicit in his attitude that I was intelligent, competent, worthy of respect, able to stand on my own. It helped shape me. And I'll always revere him for that.

Lunch. I chose Rosario's on the Point Pleasant Beach side of the Manasquan Inlet, not so much for its food as for the view. Creighton was late and that didn't terribly surprise me. I didn't mind. I sipped a chablis spritzer and watched the party boats roll in from their half-day runs of bottom fishing. Then a voice with echoes of familiarity broke through my thoughts.

"Well, Mac, I see you haven't changed much."

I turned and was shocked at what I saw. I barely recognized Creighton. He'd always been thin to the point of emaciation. Could the plump, bearded, almost cherubic figure standing before me now be—?

"Jon? Is that you?"

"The one and only," he said and spread his arms.

We embraced briefly, then took our seats in a booth by the window. As he squeezed into the far side of the table, he called the waitress over and pointed to my glass.

"Two Lites for me and another of those for her."

At first glance I'd thought that Creighton's extra poundage made him look healthy for the first time in his life. His hair was still thick and dark brown, but despite his round, rosy cheeks, his eyes were sunken and too bright. He seemed jovial but I sensed a grim undertone. I wondered if he was still into drugs.

"Almost a quarter century since we were together," he said. "Hard to believe it's been that long. The years look as if they've been kind to you."

As far as looks go, I suppose that's true. I don't dye my hair, so there's a little gray tucked in with the red. But I've always had a young face. I don't wear make-up—with my high coloring and freckles, I don't need it.

"And you."

Which wasn't actually true. His open shirt collar was frayed and looked as if this might be the third time he'd worn it since it was last washed. His tweed sport coat was worn at the elbows and a good two sizes too small for him.

We spent the drinks, appetizers, and most of the entrées catching up on each other's lives. I told him about my small accounting firm, my marriage, my recent divorce.

"No children?"

I shook my head. The marriage had gone sour, the divorce had been a nightmare. I wanted off the subject. "But enough about me," I said. "What have you been up to?"

"Would you believe clinical psychology?"

"No," I said, too shocked to lie. "I wouldn't."

The Jonathan Creighton I'd known had been so eccentric, so out of step, so self-absorbed, I couldn't imagine him as a psychotherapist. Jonathan Creighton helping other people get their lives together—it was almost laughable.

He was the one laughing, however—good-naturedly, too.

"Yeah. It *is* hard to believe, but I went on to get a Master's, and then a Ph.D. Actually went into practice."

His voice trailed off.

"You're using the past tense," I said.

"Right. It didn't work out. The practice never got off the ground. But the problem was really within myself. I was using a form of reality therapy but it never worked as it should. And finally I realized why: I don't know—really *know*—what reality is. Nobody does."

This had an all too familiar ring to it. I tried to lighten things up before they got too heavy.

"Didn't someone once say that reality is what trips you up whenever you walk around with your eyes closed?"

Creighton's smile showed a touch of the old condescension that so infuriated some people.

"Yes, I suppose someone would say something like that. Anyway, I decided to go off and see if I could find out what reality really was. Did a lot of traveling. Wound up in a place called Miskatonic University. Ever heard of it?"

"In Massachusetts, isn't it?"

"That's the one. In a small town called Arkham. I hooked up with the anthropology department there—that was my undergraduate major, after all. But now I've left academe to write a book."

"A book?"

This was beginning to sound like a pretty disjointed life. But that shouldn't have surprised me.

"What a deal!" he said, his eyes sparkling. "I've got grants from Rutgers, Princeton, the American Folklore Society, the New Jersey Historical Society, and half a dozen others, just to write a book!"

"What's it about?"

"The origins of folk tales. I'm going to select a few and trace them back to their roots. That's where you come in."

"Oh?"

"I'm going to devote a significant chapter to the Jersey Devil."

"There've been whole books written about the Jersey Devil. Why don't you—"

"I want real sources for this, Mac. Primary all the way. Nothing second-hand. This is going to be definitive."

"What can I do for you?"

"You're a Piney, aren't you?"

Resentment flashed through me. Even though people nowadays described themselves as "Piney" with a certain amount of pride, and I'd even seen bumper stickers touting "Piney Power," some of us still couldn't help bristling when an outsider said it. When I was a kid it was always used as a pejorative. Like "clam-digger" here on the coast. Fighting words. Officially it referred to the multigenerational natives of the great Pine Barrens that ran south from Route 70 all the way down to the lower end of the state. I've always hated the term. To me it was the equivalent of calling someone a redneck.

Which, to be honest, wasn't so far from the truth. The true Pineys are poor rural folk, often working truck farms and doing menial labor in the berry fields and cranberry bogs—a lot of them do indeed have red necks. Many are uneducated, or at best undereducated. Those who can afford wheels drive the prototypical battered pick-up with the gun rack in the rear window. They even speak with an accent that sounds southern. They're Jersey hillbillies.

Country bumpkins in the very heart of the industrial Northeast. Anachronisms.

Pineys.

"Who told you that?" I said as levelly as I could.

"You did. Back in school."

"Did I?"

It shook me to see how far I'd traveled from my roots. As a scared, naive, self-deprecating frosh at Rutgers I probably had indeed referred to myself as a Piney. Now I never mentioned the word, not in reference to myself or anyone else. I was a college-educated woman; I was a respected professional who spoke with a colorless Northeast accent. No one in his right mind would consider me a Piney.

"Well, that was just a gag," I said. "My family roots are back in the Pine Barrens, but I am by no stretch of the imagination a Piney. So I doubt I can help you."

"Oh, but you can! The McKelston name is big in the Barrens. Everybody knows it. You've got plenty of relatives there."

"Really? How do you know?"

Suddenly he looked sheepish.

"Because I've been into the Barrens a few times now. No one will open up to me. I'm an outsider. They don't trust me. Instead of answering my questions, they play games with me. They say they don't know what I'm talking about but they know someone who might, then they send me driving in circles. I was lost out there for two solid days last month. And believe me, I was getting scared. I thought I'd never find my way out."

"You wouldn't be the first. Plenty of people, many of them experienced hunters, have gone into the Barrens and never been seen again. You'd better stay out."

His hand darted across the table and clutched mine.

"You've got to help me, Kathy. My whole future hinges on this."

I was shocked. He'd always called me "Mac." Even in bed back in our college days he'd never called me "Kathy." Gently, I pulled my hand free, saying, "Come on, Jon—"

He leaned back and stared out the window at the circling gulls.

"If I do this right, do something really definitive, it may get me back into Miskatonic where I can finish my doctoral thesis."

I was immediately suspicious.

"I thought you said you 'left' Miskatonic, Jon. Why can't you get back in without it?"

"'Irregularities,'" he said, still not looking at me. "The old farts in the antiquities department didn't like where my research was leading me."

"This 'reality' business?"

"Yes."

"They told you that?"

Now he looked at me.

"Not in so many words, but I could tell." He leaned forward. His eyes were brighter than ever. "They've got books and manuscripts locked in huge safes there, one-of-a-kind volumes from times most scholars think of as prehistory. I managed to get a pass, a forgery, that got me into the vaults. It's incredible what they have there, Mac. *Incredible!* I've got to get back there. Will you help me?"

His intensity was startling. And tantalizing.

"What would I have to do?"

"Just accompany me into the Pine Barrens. Just for a few trips. If I can use you as a reference, I know they'll talk to me about the Jersey Devil. After that, I can take it on my own. All I need is some straight answers from these people and I'll have my primary sources. I may be able to track a folk myth to its very roots! I'll give you credit in the book, I'll pay you, anything, Mac, just don't leave me twisting in the wind!"

He was positively frantic by the time he finished speaking.

"Easy, Jon. Easy. Let me think."

Tax season was over and I had a loose schedule for the summer. And even if I was looking ahead to a tight sched-

ule, so what? Frankly, the job wasn't anywhere near as satisfying as it once had been. The challenge of overcoming the
business community's prejudice and doubts about a
woman accountant, the thrill of building a string of clients,
that was all over. Everything was mostly routine now. Plus,
I no longer had a husband. No children to usher toward
adulthood. I had to admit that my life was pretty empty at
that moment. And so was I. Why not take a little time to
inspect my roots and help Crazy Creighton put his life on
track, if such a thing was possible? In the bargain maybe I
could gain a little perspective on my own life.

"All right, Jon," I said. "I'll do it."

Creighton's eyes lit with true pleasure, a glow distinct
from the feverish intensity since he'd sat down. He thrust
both his hands toward me.

"I could kiss you, Mac! I can't tell you how much this
means to me! You have no idea how important this is!"

He was right about that. No idea at all.

2. The Pine Barrens

Two days later we were ready to make our first foray into
the woods.

Creighton was wearing a safari jacket when he picked me
up in a slightly battered four-wheel-drive Jeep Wrangler.

"This isn't Africa we're headed for," I told him.

"I know. I like the pockets. They hold all sorts of things."

I glanced in the rear compartment. He was surprisingly
well equipped. I noticed a water cooler, a food chest,
backpacks, and what looked like sleeping bags. I hoped he
wasn't harboring any romantic ideas. I'd just split from
one man and I wasn't looking for another, especially not
Jonathan Creighton.

"I promised to help you look around. I didn't say anything about camping out."

He laughed. "I'm with you. Holiday Inn is my idea of

roughing it. I was never a Boy Scout, but I do believe in being prepared. I've already been lost once in there."

"And we can do without that happening again. Got a compass?"

He nodded. "And maps. Even have a sextant."

"You actually know how to use one?"

"I learned."

I dimly remember being bothered then by his having a sextant, and not being quite sure why. Before I could say anything else, he tossed me the keys.

"You're the Piney. You drive."

"Still Mr. Macho, I see."

He laughed. I drove.

It's easy to get into the Pine Barrens from northern Ocean County. You just get on Route 70 and head west. About halfway between the Atlantic Ocean and Philadelphia, say, near a place known as Ongs Hat, you turn left. And wave bye-bye to the twentieth century, and civilization as you know it.

How do I describe the Pine Barrens to someone who's never been there? First of all, it's big. You have to fly over it in a small plane to appreciate just how big. The Barrens runs through seven counties, takes up one-fourth of the state, but since Jersey's not a big state, that doesn't tell the story. How does 2,000 square miles sound? Or a million acres? Almost the size of Yosemite National Park. Does that give you an idea of its vastness?

How do I describe what a wilderness this is? Maps will give you a clue. Look at a road map of New Jersey. If you don't happen to have one handy, imagine an oblong platter of spaghetti; now imagine what it looks like after someone's devoured most of the spaghetti out of the middle of the lower half, leaving only a few strands crossing the exposed plate. Same thing with a population density map—a big gaping hole in the southern half where the Pine Barrens sits. New Jersey is the most densely populated state in the U.S., averaging a thousand bodies per square mile. But the New York City suburbs in north Jersey teem with forty thousand per square mile. After

you account for the crowds along the coast and in the
cities and towns along the western interstate corridor,
there aren't too many people left over when you get to
the Pine Barrens. I've heard of an area of over a hundred
thousand acres—that's in the neighborhood of 160 square
miles—in the south-central Barrens with twenty-one
known inhabitants. *Twenty-one.* One human being per
eight square miles in an area that lies on the route
through Boston, New York, Philadelphia, Baltimore, and
D.C.

Even when you take a turn off one of the state or fed-
eral roads that cut through the Barrens, you feel the isola-
tion almost immediately. The forty-foot scrub pines close
in behind you and quietly but oh so effectively cut you off
from the rest of the world. I'll bet there are people
who've lived to ripe old ages in the Barrens who have
never seen a paved road. Conversely, there are no complete topographical maps of the Barrens because there are
vast areas that no human eyes have ever seen.

Are you getting the picture?

"Where do we start?" Creighton asked as we crawled
past the retirement villages along Route 70. This had been
an empty stretch of road when I was a kid. Now it was
Wrinkle City.

"We start at the capital."

"Trenton? I don't want to go to Trenton."

"Not the state capital. The capital of the pines. Used to
be called Shamong Station. Now it's known as Chatsworth."

He pulled out his map and squinted through the index.

"Oh, right. I see it. Right smack in the middle of the
Barrens. How big is it?"

"A veritable Piney megalopolis, my friend. Three hundred souls."

Creighton smiled, and for a second or two he seemed
almost . . . innocent.

"Think we can get there before rush hour?"

3. Jasper Mulliner

I stuck to the main roads, taking 70 to 72 to 563, and we were there in no time.

"You'll see something here you won't see in any place else in the Barrens," I said as I drove down Chatsworth's main street.

"Electricity?" Creighton said.

He didn't look up from the clutter of maps on his lap. He'd been following our progress on paper, mile by mile.

"No. Lawns. Years ago a number of families decided they wanted grass in their front yards. There's no topsoil to speak of out here; the ground's mostly sand. So they trucked in loads of topsoil and seeded themselves some lawns. Now they've got to cut them."

I drove past the general store and its three gas pumps out on the sidewalk.

"Esso," Creighton said, staring at the sign over the pumps. "That says it all, doesn't it."

"That it do."

We continued on until we came to a sandy lot occupied by a single trailer. No lawn here.

"Who's this?" Creighton said, folding up his maps as I hopped out of the wrangler.

"An old friend of the family."

This was Jasper Mulliner's place. He was some sort of an uncle—on my mother's side, I think. But distant blood relationships are nothing special in the Barrens. An awful lot of people are related in one way or another. Some said he was a descendant of the notorious bandit of the pines, Joseph Mulliner. Jasper had never confirmed that, but he'd never denied it, either.

I knocked on the door, wondering who would answer. I wasn't even sure Jasper was still alive. But when the door opened, I immediately recognized the grizzled old head that poked through the opening.

"You're not sellin' anything, are you?" he said.

"Nothing, Mr. Mulliner," I said. "I'm Kathleen Mc-Kelston. I don't know if you remember me, but—"

His eyes lit as his face broke into a toothless grin.

"Danny's girl? The one who got the college scholarship? Sure I remember you! Come on in!"

Jasper was wearing khaki shorts, a sleeveless orange tee shirt, and duck boots—no socks. His white hair was neatly combed and he was freshly shaved. He'd been a salt hay farmer in his younger days and his hands were still callused from it. He'd moved on to overseeing a cranberry bog in his later years. His skin was a weathered brown and looked tougher than saddle leather. The inside of the trailer reminded me more of a low-ceilinged freight car than a home, but it was clean. The presence of the television set told me he had electricity but I saw no phone nor any sign of running water.

I introduced him to Creighton and we settled onto a three-legged stool and a pair of ladderback chairs as I spent the better part of half an hour telling him about my life since leaving the Barrens and answering questions about my mother and how she was doing since my father died. Then he went into a soliloquy about what a great man my father was. I let him run on, pretending to be listening, but turning my mind to other things. Not because I disagreed with him, but because it had been barely a year since Dad had dropped dead and I was still hurting.

Dad had not been your typical Piney. Although he loved the Barrens as much as anyone else who grew up here, he'd known there was a bigger though not necessarily better life beyond them. That bigger world didn't interest him in the least, but just because he was content with where he was didn't mean that I'd be. He wanted to allow his only child a choice. He knew I'd need a decent education if that choice was to be meaningful. And to provide that education for me, he did what few Pineys like to do: he took a steady job.

That's not to say that Pineys are afraid of hard work. Far from it. They'll break their backs at any job they're doing. It's simply that they don't like to be tied down to the same job day after day, month after month. Most of them have grown up flowing with the cycle of the Barrens. Spring is for gathering sphagnum moss to sell to the florists and nurseries. In June and July they work the blueberry and huckleberry fields. In the fall they move into the bogs for the cranberry harvest. And in the cold of winter they cut cordwood, or cut holly and mistletoe, or go "pineballing"—collecting pine cones to sell. None of this is easy work. But it's not the same work. And that's what matters.

The Piney attitude toward jobs is the most laid back you'll ever encounter. That's because they're in such close harmony with their surroundings. They know that with all the pure water all around them and flowing beneath their feet, they'll never go thirsty. With all the wild vegetation around them, they'll never lack for fruit and vegetables. And whenever the meat supply gets low, they pick up a rifle and head into the brush for squirrel, rabbit, or venison, whatever the season.

When I neared fourteen, my father bit the bullet and moved us close to Pemberton where he took a job with a well-drilling crew. It was steady work, with benefits, and I got to go to Pemberton High. He pushed me to take my schoolwork seriously, and I did. My high grades coupled with my gender and low socioeconomic status earned me a full ride—room, board, and tuition—at Rutgers. As soon as that was settled, he was ready to move back into the Barrens. But my mother had become used to the conveniences and amenities of town living. She wanted to stay in Pemberton. So they stayed.

I still can't help but wonder whether Dad might have lived longer if he'd moved back into the woods. I've never mentioned that to my mother, of course.

When Jasper paused, I jumped in: "My friend Jon's doing a book and he's devoting a chapter to the Jersey Devil."

"Is that so?" Jasper said. "And you brought him to me, did you?"

"Well, Dad always told me there weren't many folks in the Pines you didn't know, and not much that went on that you didn't know about."

The old man beamed and did what many Pineys do: he repeated a phrase three times.

"Did he now? Did he now? Did he really now? Ain't that somethin'! I do believe that calls for a little jack."

As Jasper turned and reached into his cupboard, Creighton threw me a questioning look.

"Applejack," I told him.

He smiled. "Ah. Jersey lightning."

Jasper turned back with three glasses and a brown quart jug. With a practiced hand he poured two fingers' worth into each and handed them to us. The tumblers were smudged and maybe a little crusty, but I wasn't worried about germs. There's never been a germ that could stand up to straight jack from Jasper Mulliner's still. I remember siphoning some off from my father's jug and sneaking off into the brush at night to meet a couple of my girlfriends from high school, and we'd sit around and sing and get plastered.

I could tell by the way the vapor singed my nasal membranes that this was from a potent batch. I neglected to tell Creighton to go slow. As I took a respectful sip, he tossed his off. I watched him wince as he swallowed, saw his face grow red and his eyes begin to water.

"Whoa!" he said hoarsely. "You could etch glass with that stuff!" He caught Jasper looking at him sideways and held out his glass. "But delicious! Could I have just a drop more?"

"Help yourself," Jasper said, pouring him another couple of fingers. "Plenty more where this came from. But down it slow. This here's sippin' whiskey. You go puttin' too much of it down like that and you'll get apple palsy. Slow and leisurely does it when you're drinking Gus Sooy's best."

"This isn't yours?" I said.

"Naw! I stopped that long time ago. Too much trouble and gettin' too civilized 'round here. Besides, Gus's jack is as good as mine ever was. Maybe better."

He set the jug on the floor between us.

"About that Jersey Devil," I said, prompting him before he got off on another tangent.

"Right. The ol' Devil. He used to be known as the Leeds' Devil. I'm sure you've heard various versions of the story, but I'll tell you the real one. That ol' devil's been around a spell, better'n two and a half centuries. All started back around 1730 or so. That was when Mrs. Leeds of Estellville found herself in the family way for the thirteenth time. Now she was so fed up and angry about this that she cried out, 'I hope this time it's the Devil!' Well now, Someone must've been listenin' that night, because she got her wish. When that thirteenth baby was born, it was an ugly-faced thing, born with teeth like no one'd ever seen before, and it had a curly, sharp-pointed tail, and leathery wings like a bat. It bit its mother and flew out through the window. It grew up out in the pine wilds, stealing and eating chickens and small piglets at first, then graduating to cows, children, even growed men. All they ever found of its victims was their bones, and they was chipped and nicked by powerful sharp teeth. Some say it's dead now, some say it'll never die. Every so often someone says he shot and killed it, but most folks think it can't be killed. It gets blamed for every missing chicken and every pig or cow that wanders off, and so after a while you think it's just an ol' Piney folk tale. But it's out there. It's out there. It's surely out there."

"Have you ever seen it?" Creighton asked. He was sipping his jack with respect this time around.

"Saw its shadow. It was up on Apple Pie Hill, up at the top, in the days before they put up the firetower. Before you was born, Kathleen. I'd been out doing some summer hunting, tracking a big ol' stag. You know what a climb Apple Pie is, dontcha?"

I nodded. "Sure do."

It didn't look like much of a hill. No cliffs or precipices, just a slow incline that seemed to go on forever. You didn't have to do much more than walk to get to the top, but you were bushed when you finally reached it.

"Anyways, I was about three-quarters the way up when it got too dark to do any more tracking. Well, I was tired and it was a warm summer night so's I just settled down on the pine needles and decided I'd spend the night. I had some jerky and some pone and my jug." He pointed to the floor. "Just like that one. You two be sure to help yourselves, hear me?"

"I'm fine," I said.

I saw Creighton reach for the jug. He could always handle a lot. I was already feeling my two sips. It was getting warmer in here by the minute.

"Anyways," Jasper went on, "I was sitting there chewing and sipping when I saw some pine lights."

Creighton started in mid-pour and spilled some applejack over his hand. He was suddenly very alert, almost tense.

"Pine lights?" he said. "You saw pine lights? Where were they?"

"So you've heard of the pine lights, have you?"

"I sure have. I've been doing my homework. Where did you see them? Were they moving?"

"They were streaming across the crest of Apple Pie Hill, just skirting the tops of the trees."

Creighton put his tumbler down and began fumbling with his map.

"Apple Pie Hill . . . I remember seeing that somewhere. Here it is." He jabbed his finger down on the map as if he were driving a spike into the hill. "Okay. So you were on Apple Pie Hill when you saw the pine lights. How many were there?"

"A whole town's worth of them, maybe a hunnert, more than I've ever seen before or since."

"How fast were they going?"

"Different speeds. Different sizes. Some gliding peacefully, some zipping along, moving past the slower ones. Looked like the turnpike on a summer weekend."

Creighton leaned forward, his eyes brighter than ever. "Tell me about it."

Something about Creighton's intensity disturbed me. All of a sudden he'd become an avid listener. He'd been listening politely to Jasper's retelling of the Jersey Devil story, but he'd seemed more interested in the applejack than in the tale. He hadn't bothered to check the location of Apple Pie Hill when Jasper had said he'd seen the Jersey Devil there, but he'd been in a rush to find it at the first mention of the pine lights.

The pine lights. I'd heard of them but I'd never seen one. People tended to catch sight of them on summer nights, mostly toward the end of the season. Some said it was ball lightning or some form of St. Elmo's fire, some called it swamp gas, and some said it was the souls of dead Pineys coming back for periodic visits. Why was Creighton so interested?

"Well," Jasper said, "I spotted one or two moving along the crest of the hill and didn't think too much of it. I spot a couple just about every summer. Then I saw a few more. And then a few more. I got a little excited and decided to get up to the top of Apple Pie and see what was going on. I was breathing hard by the time I got there. I stopped and looked up and there they was, flowing along the treetops forty feet above me, pale yellow, some ping-pong sized and some big as beach balls, all moving in the same direction."

"What direction?" Creighton said. If he leaned forward any farther, he was going to fall off his stool. "Which way were they going?"

"I'm getting to that, son," Jasper said. "Just hold your horses. So as I was saying, I was standing there watching them flow against the clear night sky, and I was feeling this strange tightness in my chest, like I was witnessing something I shouldn't. But I couldn't tear my eyes away. And then they thinned out and was gone. They'd all passed. So I did something crazy. I climbed a tree to see where they was going. Something in my gut told me not to, but I was filled with this wonder, almost like holy rapture. So I climbed as far as I could, until the tree started to bend with my weight and the branches got too thin to hold me. And I watched them go. They was strung out in a long trail, dipping down when the land dipped down, and moving up when the land rose, moving just above the tops of the pines, like they was being pulled along strings." He looked at Creighton. "And they was heading southwest."

"You're sure of that?"

Jasper looked insulted. "Course I'm sure of that. Bear Swamp Hill was behind my left shoulder, and everybody knows Bear Swamp is east of Apple Pie. Those lights was on their way southwest."

"And this was the summer?"

"Nigh on to Labor Day, if I 'member correct."

"And you were on the crest of Apple Pie Hill?"

"The tippy top."

"Great!" He began folding his map.

"I thought you wanted to hear about the Jersey Devil."

"I do, I do."

"Then how come you're asking me all these questions about the lights and not asking me about my meeting with the Devil?"

I hid a smile. Jasper was as sharp as ever.

Creighton looked confused for a moment. An expression darted across his face. It was only there for a second, but I caught it. Furtiveness. Then he leaned forward and spoke to Jasper in a confidential tone.

"Don't tell anybody this, but I think they're connected. The pine lights and the Jersey Devil. Connected."

Jasper leaned back. "You know, you might have something there. Cause it was while I was up that tree that I spotted the ol' Devil himself. Or at least his shadow. I was watching the lights flow out of sight when I heard this noise in the brush. It had a slithery sound to it. I looked down and there was this dark shape moving below. And you know what? It was heading in the same direction as the lights. What do you think of that?"

Creighton's voice oozed sincerity.

"I think that's damn interesting, Jasper."

I thought they both were shoveling it, but I couldn't decide who was carrying the bigger load.

"But don't you go getting too interested in those pine lights, son. Gus Sooy says they're bad medicine."

"The guy who made this jack?" I said, holding up my empty tumbler.

"The very same. Gus says there's lots of pine light activity in his neighborhood every summer. Told me I was a fool for climbing that tree. Says he wouldn't get near one of those lights for all the tea in China."

I noticed that Creighton was tense again.

"Where's this Gus Sooy's neighborhood?" he said. "Does he live in Chatsworth?"

Jasper burst out laughing.

"Gus live in Chatsworth? That's a good 'un! Gus Sooy's an old Hessian who lives way out in the wildest part of the pines. Never catch him *near* a city like this!"

City? I didn't challenge him on that.

"Where do we find him then?" Creighton said, his expression like a kid who's been told there's a cache of M&M's hidden somewhere nearby.

"Not easy," Jasper said. "Gus done a good job of getting himself well away from everybody. He's well away. Yes, he's well away. But if you go down to Apple Pie Hill and head along the road there that runs along its south flank, and you follow that about two mile and turn south onto the sand road by Applegate's cranberry bog, then follow that for about ten-twelve mile till you come to the fork where you bear left, then go right again at the cripple beyond it, then it's a good ten mile down that road till you get to the big red cedar—"

Creighton was scribbling furiously.

"I'm not sure I know what a red cedar looks like," I said.

"You'll know it," Jasper said. "Its kind don't grow naturally around here. Gus planted it there a good many year ago so people could find their way to him. The *right* people," he said, eyeing Creighton. "People who want to buy his wares, if you get my meaning."

I nodded. I got his meaning: Gus made his living off his still.

"Anyways, you turn right at the red cedar and go to the end of the road. Then you've got to get out and walk about a third of the way up the hill. That's where you'll find Gus Sooy."

I tried to drive the route across a mental map in my

head. I couldn't get there. My map was blank where he was sending us. But I was amazed at how far I did get. As a Piney, even a girl, you've got to develop a good sense of where you are, got to have a store of maps in your head that you can picture by reflex, otherwise you'll spend most of your time being lost. Even with a good library of mental maps, you'll still get lost occasionally. I could still travel my old maps. The skill must be like the proverbial bicycle—once you've learned, you never forget.

I had a sense that Gus Sooy's place was somewhere far down in Burlington County, near Atlantic County. But county lines don't mean much in the Pinelands.

"That's *really* in the middle of nowhere!" I said.

"That it is, Kathy, that it is. That it surely is. It's on the slope of Razorback Hill."

Creighton shuffled through his maps again.

"Razorback . . . Razorback . . . there's no Razorback Hill here."

"That's because it ain't much of a hill. But it's there all right. Just 'cause it ain't on your diddly map don't mean it ain't there. Lots of things ain't on that map."

Creighton rose to his feet.

"Maybe we can run out there now and buy some of this applejack from him. What do you say, Mac?"

"We've got time."

I had a feeling he truly did want to buy some of Sooy's jack, but I was sure some questions about the pine lights would come up during the transaction.

"Better bring your own jugs if you're goin'," Jasper said. "Gus don't carry no spares. You can buy some from the Buzbys at the general store."

"Will do," I said.

I thanked him and promised I'd say hello to my mom for him, then I joined Creighton out at the Wrangler. He had one of his maps unfolded on the hood and was drawing a line southwest from Apple Pie Hill through the emptiest part of the Barrens.

"What's that for?" I asked.

"I don't know just yet. We'll see if it comes to mean anything."

It would. Sooner than either of us realized.

4. The Hessian

I bought a gallon-sized brown jug at the Chatsworth general store; Creighton bought two.

"I want this Sooy fellow to be *real* glad to see me!"

I drove us down 563, then off to Apple Pie Hill. We got south of it and began following Jasper's directions. Creighton read while I drove.

"What the hell's a cripple?" he said.

"That's a spong with no cedars."

"Ah! That clears up everything!"

"A spong is a low wet spot; if it's got cedars growing around it, it's a cripple. What could be clearer?"

"I'm not sure, but I know I'll think of something. By the way, why's this Sooy fellow called a Hessian? Mulliner doesn't really think he's—?"

"Of course not. Sooy's an old German name around the Pine Barrens. Comes from the Hessians who deserted the British Army and fled into the woods after the battle of Trenton."

"The Revolution?"

"Sure. This sand road we're riding on now was here three hundred odd years ago as a wagon trail. It probably hasn't changed any since. Might even have been used by the smugglers who used to unload freight in the marshes and move it overland through the Pines to avoid port taxes in New York and Philly. A lot of them settled in here. So did a good number of Tories and Loyalists who were chased from their land after the Revolution. Some of them probably arrived dressed in tar and feathers and little else. The Lenape Indians settled in here, too, so did Quakers who were kicked out of their churches for taking up arms during the Revolution."

Creighton laughed. "Sounds like Australia! Didn't anyone besides outcasts settle here?"

"Sure. Bog iron was a major industry. This was the center of the colonial iron production. Most of the cannon
balls fired against the British in the Revolution and the
War of 1812 were forged right here in the Pine Barrens."

"Where'd everybody go?"

"A place called Pittsburgh. There was more iron there
and it was cheaper to produce. The furnaces here tried to
shift over to glass production but they were running out
of wood to keep them going. Each furnace consumed
something like a thousand acres of pine a year. With the
charcoal industry, the lumber industry, even the cedar
shake industry all adding to the daily toll on the tree population, the Barrens couldn't keep up with the demand.
The whole economy collapsed after the Civil War. Which
probably saved the area from becoming a desert."

I noticed the underbrush between the ruts getting
higher, slapping against the front bumper as we passed, a
sure sign that not many people came this way. Then I
spotted the red cedar. Jasper had been right—it didn't
look like it belonged here. We turned right and drove
until we came to a cul-de-sac at the base of a hill. Three
rusting cars hugged the bushes along the perimeter.

"This must be the place," I said.

"This is not a place. This is *no*where."

We grabbed our jugs and walked up the path. About a
third of the way up the slope we broke into a clearing with a
slant-roofed shack in the far left corner. It looked maybe
twenty feet on a side, and was covered with tarpaper that
was peeling away in spots, exposing the plywood beneath.
Somewhere behind the shack a dog had begun to bark.

Creighton said, "Finally!" and started forward.

I laid a hand on his arm.

"Call out first," I told him. "Otherwise we may be duck-
ing buckshot."

He thought I was joking at first, then saw that I meant it.
"You're serious?"

"We're dressed like city folk. We could be revenuers. He'll shoot first and ask questions later."

"Hello in the house!" Creighton cried. "Jasper Mulliner sent us! Can we come up?"

A wizened figure appeared on the front step, a twelve gauge cradled in his arms.

"How'd he send you?"

"By way of the red cedar, Mr. Sooy!" I replied.

"C'mon up then!"

Where Jasper had been neat, Gus Sooy was slovenly. His white hair looked like a deranged bird had tried to nest in it; for a shirt he wore the stained top from a set of long johns and had canvas pants secured around his waist with coarse rope. His lower face was obscured by a huge white beard, stained around the mouth. An Appalachian Santa Claus, going to seed in the off season.

We followed him into the single room of his home. The floor was covered with a mismatched assortment of throw rugs and carpet remnants. A bed sat in the far left corner, a kerosene stove was immediately to our right. Set about the room were a number of Aladdin lamps with the tall flues. Dominating the scene was a heavy-legged kitchen table with an enamel top.

We introduced ourselves and Gus said he'd met my father years ago.

"So what brings you two kids out here to see Gus Sooy?"

I had to smile, not just at the way he managed to ignore the jugs we were carrying, but at being referred to as a "kid." A long time since anyone had called me that. I wouldn't let anyone call me a "girl" these days, but somehow I didn't mind "kid."

"Today we tasted some of the best applejack in the world," Creighton said with convincing sincerity, "and Jasper told us you were the source." He slammed his two jugs on the table. "Fill 'em up!"

I placed my own jug next to Creighton's.

"I gotta warn you," Gus said. "It's five dollars a quart."

"Five dollars!" Creighton said.

"Yeah," Gus added quickly, "but seein' as you're buying so much at once—"

"Don't get me wrong, Mr. Sooy. I wasn't saying the price is too high. I was just shocked that you'd be selling such high-grade sipping whiskey for such a low price."

"You were?" The old man beamed with delight. "It is awful good, isn't it?"

"That it is, sir. That it is. That it surely is."

I almost burst out laughing. I don't know how Creighton managed to keep a straight face.

Gus held up a finger. "You kids stay right here. I'll dip into my stock and be back in a jiffy."

We both broke down into helpless laughter as soon as he was gone.

"You're laying it on awful thick," I said when I caught my breath.

"I know, but he's lapping up every bit."

Gus returned in a few minutes with two gallon jugs of his own.

"Hadn't we ought to test this first before you begin filling our jugs?" Creighton said.

"Not a bad idea. No, sir, not a bad idea. Not a bad idea at all."

Creighton produced some paper cups from one of the pockets in his safari jacket and placed them on the table. Gus poured. We all sipped.

"This is even smoother than what Jasper served us. How do you do it, Mr. Sooy?"

"That's a secret," he said with a wink as he brought out a funnel and began decanting from his jugs into ours.

I brought up Jon's book and Gus launched into a slightly different version of the Jersey Devil story, saying it was born in Leeds, which is at the opposite end of the Pine Barrens from Estellville. Otherwise the tales were almost identical.

"Jasper says he saw the Devil once," Creighton said as Gus topped off the last of our jugs.

"If he says he did, then he did. That'll be sixty dollar."

Creighton gave him three twenties.

"And now I'd like to buy you a drink, Mr. Sooy."

"Call me Gus. And I don't mind if I do."

Creighton was overly generous, I thought, with the way he filled the three paper cups. I didn't want any more, but I felt I had to keep up appearances. I sipped while the men quaffed.

"Jasper told us about the time he saw the Jersey Devil. He mentioned seeing pine lights at the same time."

I sensed rather than saw Gus stiffen.

"Is that so?"

"Yeah. He said you see pine lights around here all the time. Is that true?"

"You interested in pine lights or the Jersey Devil, boy?"

"Both. I'm interested in all the folktales of the Pines."

"Well, don't get too interested in the pine lights."

"Why not?"

"Just don't."

I watched Creighton tip his jug and refill Gus's cup.

"A toast!" Creighton said, lifting his cup. "To the Pine Barrens!"

"I'll drink to that!" Gus said, and drained his cup.

Creighton followed suit, causing his eyes to fill with tears. I sipped while he poured another round.

"To the Jersey Devil!" Creighton cried, hoisting his cup again.

And again they both tossed off their drinks. And then another round.

"To the pine lights!"

Gus wouldn't drink to that one. I was glad. I don't think either of them would have remained standing if he had.

"Have you seen any pine lights lately, Gus," Creighton said.

"You don't give up, do you, boy," the old man said.

"It's an affliction."

"So it is. All right. Sure. I see 'em all the time. Saw some last night."

"Really? Where?"

"None of your business."

"Why not?"

"Because you'll probably try to do something stupid like catch one, and then I'll be responsible for what happens to you and this young lady here. Not on my conscience, no thank you."

"I wouldn't dream of trying to catch one of those things!" Creighton said.

"Well, if you did you wouldn't be the first. Peggy Clevenger was the first." Gus lifted his head and looked at me. "You heard of Peggy Clevenger, ain't you, Miss McKelston?"

I nodded. "Sure. The Witch of the Pines. In the old days people used to put salt over their doors to keep her away."

Creighton began scribbling.

"No kidding? This is great! What about her and the pine lights?"

"Peggy was a Hessian, like me. Lived over in Pasadena. Not the California Pasadena, the Pines Pasadena. A few miles east of Mount Misery. The town's gone now, like it never been. But she lived thereabouts by herself in a small cabin, and people said she had all sorts of strange powers, like she could change her shape and become a rabbit or a snake. I don't know about that stuff, but I heard from someone who should know that she was powerful interested in the pine lights. She told this fella one day that she had caught one of the pine lights, put a spell on it and brought it down."

Creighton had stopped writing. He was staring at Gus. "How could she. . . ?"

"Don't know," Gus said, draining his cup and shaking his head. "But that very night her cabin burned to the ground. They found her blackened and burned body among the ashes the next morning. So I tell you, kids, it ain't a good idea to get too interested in the pine lights."

"I don't want to capture one," Creighton said. "I don't even want to see one. I just want to know where other people have seen them. How can that be dangerous?"

Gus thought about that. And while he was thinking, Creighton poured him another cupful.

"Don't s'pose it would do any harm to show you where they was," he said after a long slow sip.

"Then it's settled. Let's go."

We gathered up the jugs and headed out into the late afternoon sunshine. The fresh air was like a tonic. It perked me up but didn't dissipate the effects of all the jack I'd consumed.

When we reached the Wrangler, Creighton pulled out his sextant and compass.

"Before we go, there's something I've got to do."

Gus and I watched in silence as he took his sightings and scribbled in his notebook. Then he spread his map out on the hood again.

"What's up?" I said.

"I'm putting Razorback Hill on the map," he said.

He jotted his readings on the map and drew a circle. Before he folded everything up, I glanced over his shoulder and noticed that the line he had drawn from Apple Pie Hill ran right by the circle that was Razorback Hill.

"You through dawdlin'?" Gus said.

"Sure am. You want to ride in front?"

"No thanks," Gus said, heading for the rusty DeSoto. "I'll drive myself and you kids follow."

I said, "Won't it be easier if we all go together?"

"Hell no! You kids have been drinkin'!"

When we stopped laughing, we pulled ourselves into the Wrangler and followed the old Hessian back up his private sand road.

5. The Firing Place

"I used to make charcoal here when I was young," Gus said.

We were standing in a small clearing surrounded by young pines. Before us was a shallow sandy depression, choked with weeds.

"This used to be my firing place. It was deeper then. I

made some fine charcoal here before the big companies started selling their bags of 'brick-*ettes.*'" He fairly spat the word. "Ain't no way any one of those smelly little things was ever part of a tree, I'll tell you that."

"Is this where you saw the lights, Gus?" Creighton said. "Were they moving?"

Gus said, "You got a one-track mind, don't you, boy?" He glanced around. "Yeah, this is where I saw them. Saw them here last night and I saw them here fifty years ago, and I seen them near about every summer in between. Lots of memories here. I remember how while I was letting my charcoal burn I'd use the time to hunt up box turtles."

"And sell them as snail hunters?" I said.

I'd heard of box turtle hunting—another Pinelands mini-industry—but I'd never met anyone who'd actually done it.

"Sure. Folks in Philadelphia'd buy all I could find. They liked to let them loose in their cellars to keep the snails and slugs under control."

"The lights, Gus," Creighton said. "Which way were they going?"

"They was goin' the same way they always went when I seen them here. That way."

He was pointing southeast.

"Are you sure?"

"Sure as shit, boy." Gus's tone was getting testy, but he quickly turned to me. "'Scuse me, miss," then back to Creighton. "I was standing back there right where my car is when about a half dozen of them swooped in low right overhead—not a hunting swoop, but a floaty sort of swoop—and traveled away over that pitch pine there with the split top."

"Good!" said Creighton, eyeing the sky.

A thick sheet of cloud was pulling up from the west, encroaching on the sinking sun. Out came the sextant and compass. Creighton took his readings, wrote his numbers, then took a bearing on the tree Gus had pointed out. A slow, satisfied smile crept over his face as he drew the latest line on his map. He folded it up before I had a chance to see where that line went. I didn't have to see. His next question told me.

"Say, Gus," he said offhandedly. "What's on the far side of Razorback Hill?"

Gus turned on Creighton like an angry bear.

"Nothing! There's nothing there! So don't you even think about going over there!"

Creighton's smile was amused. "I was only asking. No harm in a little question, is there?"

"There is. There is. Yes, there surely is! Especially when those questions is the wrong ones. And you've been asking a whole lot of wrong questions, boy. Questions that's gonna get you in a whole mess of bad trouble if you don't get smart and learn that certain things is best left alone. You hear me?"

He sounded like a character from one of those old Frankenstein movies.

"I hear you," Creighton said, "and I appreciate your concern. But can you tell me the best way to get to the other side of that hill?"

Gus threw up his hands with an angry growl.

"That's it! I'm havin' no more to do with the two of you! I've already told you too much as it is." He turned to me, his eyes blazing. "And you, Miss McKelston, you get yourself away from this boy. He's headed straight to hell!"

With that he turned and headed for his car. He jumped in, slammed the door, and roared away with a spray of sand.

"I don't think he likes me," Creighton said.

"He seemed genuinely frightened," I told him.

Creighton shrugged and began packing away his sextant.

"Maybe he really believes in the Jersey Devil," he said. "Maybe he thinks it lives on the other side of Razorback Hill."

"I don't know about that. I got the impression he thinks the Jersey Devil is something to tell tall tales about while sitting around the stove and sipping jack. But those pine lights . . . he's scared of them."

"Just swamp gas, I'm sure," Creighton said.

Suddenly I was furious. Maybe it was all the jack I'd consumed, or maybe it was his attitude, but I think at that particular moment it was mostly his line of bull.

"Cut it, Jon!" I said. "If you really believe they're swamp gas, why are you tracking them on your map? You got me to guide you out here, so let's have it straight. What's going on?"

"I don't know what's going on, Mac. If I did, I wouldn't be here. Isn't that obvious? These pine lights mean something. Whether or not they're connected to the Jersey Devil, I don't know. Maybe they have a hallucinatory effect on people—after they pass overhead, people think they see things. I'm trying to establish a pattern."

"And after you've established this pattern, what do you think you'll find?"

"Maybe Truth," he said. "Reality. Who knows? Maybe the meaning—or meaninglessness—of life."

He looked at me with eyes so intense, so full of longing that my anger evaporated.

"Jon. . . ?"

His expression abruptly shifted back to neutral and he laughed.

"Don't worry, Mac. It's only me, Crazy Creighton, putting you on again. Let's have another snort of Gus Sooy's best and head for civilization. Okay?"

"I've had enough for the day. The *week!*"

"You don't mind if I partake, do you?"

"Help yourself."

I didn't know how he could hold so much.

While Creighton uncorked his jug, I strolled about the firing place to clear my fuzzy head. The sky was fully overcast now and the temperature was dropping to a more comfortable level.

He had everything packed away by the time I completed the circle.

"Want me to drive?" he said, tossing his paper cup onto the sand.

Normally I would have picked it up—there was something sacrilegious about leaving a Dixie cup among the pines—but I was afraid to bend over that far, afraid I'd keep on going head-first into the sand and become litter myself.

"I'm okay," I said. "You'll get us lost."

We had traveled no more than a hundred feet or so when I realized that I didn't know this road. But I kept driving. I hadn't been paying close attention while following Gus here, but I was pretty sure it wouldn't be long before I'd come to a fork or a cripple or a bog that I recognized, and then we'd be home free.

It didn't quite work out that way. I drove for maybe five miles or so, winding this way and that with the roads, making my best guess when we came to a fork—and we came to plenty of those—and generally trying to keep us heading in the same general direction. I thought I was doing a pretty good job until we drove through an area of young pines that looked familiar. I stopped the Wrangler.

"Jon," I said. "Isn't this—?"

"Damn right it is!" he said, pointing to the sand beside the road. "We're back at Gus's firing place! There's my Dixie cup!"

I turned the Jeep around and headed back the way I came.

"What are you doing?" Creighton said.

"Making sure I don't make the same mistake twice!" I told him.

I didn't know how I could have driven in a circle. I usually had an excellent sense of direction. I blamed it on too much Jersey lightning and on the thickly overcast sky. Without the sun as a marker, I'd been unable to keep us on course. But that would change here and now. I'd get us out of here this time around.

Wrong.

After a good forty-five minutes of driving, I was so embarrassed when I recognized the firing place again that I actually accelerated as we passed through, hoping Creighton wouldn't recognize the spot in the thickening dusk. But I wasn't quick enough.

"Hold it!" he cried. "Hold it just a damn minute! There's my cup again! We're right back where we started!"

"Jon," I said, "I don't understand it. Something's wrong."

"You're stewed, that's what's wrong!"

"I'm not!"

I truly believed I wasn't. I'd been feeling the effects of the jack before, true, but my head was clear now. I was sure I'd been heading due east, or at least pretty close to it. How I'd come full circle again was beyond me.

Creighton jumped out of his seat and came around the front of the Wrangler.

"Over you go, Mac. It's my turn."

I started to protest, then thought better of it. I'd blown it twice already. Maybe my sense of direction had fallen prey to the "apple palsy," as it was known. I lifted myself over the stick shift and dropped into the passenger seat.

"Be my guest."

Creighton drove like a maniac, seemingly choosing forks at random.

"Do you know where you're going?" I said.

"Yeah, Mac," he said. "I'm going whichever way you *didn't!* I think."

As darkness closed in and he turned on the headlights, I noticed that the trees were thinning out and the underbrush was closing in, rising to eight feet or better on either side of us. Creighton pulled off to the side at a widening of the road.

"You should stay on the road," I told him.

"I'm lost," he said. "We've got to think."

"Fine. But it's not as if somebody's going to be coming along and want to get by."

He laughed. "That's a fact!" He got out and looked up at the sky. "Damn! If it weren't for the clouds we could figure out where we are. Or least know where north is."

I looked around. We were surrounded by bushes. It was the Pine Barrens' equivalent of an English hedge maze. There wasn't a tree in sight. A tree can be almost as good as a compass—its moss faces north and its longest branches face south. Bushes are worse than useless for that, and the high ones only add to your confusion.

And we were confused.

"I thought Pineys never get lost," Creighton said.

"Everybody gets lost sooner or later out here."

"Well, what do Pineys do when they get lost?"

"They don't exhaust themselves or waste their gas by running around in circles. They hunker down and wait for morning."

"To hell with that!" Creighton said.

He threw the Wrangler into first and gunned it toward the road. But the vehicle didn't reach the road. It lurched forward and rocked back. He tried again and I heard the wheels spinning.

"Sugar!" I said.

Creighton looked at me and grinned.

"Stronger language is allowed and even encouraged in this sort of situation."

"I was referring to the sand."

"Don't worry. I've got four-wheel drive."

"Right. And all four wheels are spinning. We're in a patch of what's known as 'sugar sand.'"

He got out and pushed and rocked while I worked the gears and throttle, but I knew it was no use. We weren't going to get out of this super-fine sand until we found some wood and piled it under the tires to give them some traction.

And we weren't going to be able to hunt up that kind of wood until morning.

I told Creighton that we'd only waste what gas we had left and that our best bet was to call it a night and pull out the sleeping bags. He seemed reluctant at first, worrying about deer ticks and catching Lyme disease, but he finally agreed.

He had no choice.

6. The Pine Lights

"I owe you one, Jon," I said.

"How was I to know we'd get lost?" he said defensively. "I don't like this any more than you!"

"No. You don't understand. I meant that in the good sense. I'm glad you talked me into coming with you."

I'd found us a small clearing not too far from the jeep. It surrounded the gnarled trunk of an old lone pine that towered above the dominant brush. We'd eaten the last of the sandwiches and now we sat on our respective bedrolls facing each other across the Coleman lamp sitting between us on the sand. Creighton was back to sipping his applejack. I would have killed, or at least maimed, for a cup of coffee.

I watched his face in the lamplight. His expression was puzzled.

"You must still be feeling the effects of that Jersey lightning you had this afternoon," he said.

"No. I'm perfectly sober. I've been sitting here realizing that I'm glad to be back. I've had a feeling for years that something's been missing from my life. Never had an inkling as to what it was until now. But this is it. I'm . . ." My throat constricted around the word. "I'm home."

It wasn't the jack talking, it was my heart. I'd learned something today. I'd learned that I loved the Pine Barrens. And I loved its people. So rich in history, so steeped in its own lore, somehow surviving untainted in the heart of twentieth-century urban madness. I'd turned my back on it. Why? Too proud? Too good for it now? Maybe I'd thought I'd pulled myself up by my bootstraps and gone on to bigger and better things. I could see that I hadn't. I'd taken the girl out of the Pinelands but I hadn't taken the Pinelands out of the girl.

I promised myself to come back here again. Often. I was going to look up my many relatives, renew old ties. I wasn't ready to move back here, and perhaps I never would, but I'd never turn my back on the Pinelands again.

Creighton raised his cup to me.

"I envy anyone who's found the missing piece. I'm still looking for mine."

"You'll find it," I said, crawling into my bedroll. "You've just got to keep your eyes open. Sometimes it's right under your nose."

"Go to sleep, Mac. You're starting to sound like Dorothy from *The Wizard of Oz.*"

I smiled at that. For a moment there he was very much like the Jonathan Creighton I'd fallen in love with. As I closed my eyes, I saw him pull out a pair of binoculars and begin scanning the cloud-choked sky. I knew what he was looking for, and I was fairly confident he'd never find them.

It must have been a while later when I awoke, because the sky had cleared and the stars were out when Creighton's shouts yanked me to a sitting position.

"They're coming! Look at them, Mac! My God, they're coming!"

Creighton was standing on the far side of the lamp, pointing off to my left. I followed the line of his arm and saw nothing.

"What are you talking about?"

"Stand up, damn it! They're coming! There must be a dozen of them!"

I struggled to my feet and froze.

The starlit underbrush stretched away in a gentle rise for maybe a mile or two in the direction he was pointing, broken only occasionally by the angular shadows of the few scattered trees. And coming our way over that broad expanse, skimming along at treetop level, was an oblong cluster of faintly glowing lights. *Lights.* That's what they were. Not glowing spheres. Not UFOs or any of that nonsense. They had no discernible substance. They were just light. Globules of light.

I felt my hackles rise at the sight of them. Perhaps because I'd never seen light behave that way before—it didn't seem right or natural for light to concentrate itself in a ball. Or perhaps it was the way they moved, gliding through the night with such purpose, cutting through the dark, weaving from tree to tree, floating by the topmost branches, and then forging a path toward the next. Almost as if the trees were signposts. Or perhaps it was the silence. The awful silence. The Pine Barrens are quiet as far as civilized sounds are concerned, but there's always the noise of the living things, the hoots and cries and rustlings of the animals, the incessant insect susurration. That was all gone now. There wasn't even a breeze to rustle the bushes. Silence. More than a mere absence of noise. A holding of breath.

"Do you see them, Mac? Tell me I'm not hallucinating! Do you see them?"

"I see them, Jon."

My voice sounded funny. I realized my mouth was dry. And not just from sleep.

Creighton turned around in a quick circle, his arms spread.

"I don't have a camera! I need a picture of this!"

"You didn't bring a camera?" I said. "My God, you brought everything else!"

"I know, but I never dreamed—"

Suddenly he was running for the tree at the center of our clearing.

"Jon! You're not really—?"

"They're coming this way! If I can get close to them—!"

I was suddenly afraid for him. Something about those lights was warning me away. Why wasn't it warning Creighton? Or was he simply not listening?

I followed him at a reluctant lope.

"Don't be an idiot, Jon! You don't know what they are!"

"Exactly! It's about time somebody found out!"

He started climbing. It was a big old pitch pine with no branches to speak of for the first dozen feet or so of its trunk, but its bark was knobby and rough enough for Creighton's rubber-soled boots to find purchase. He slipped off twice, but he was determined. Finally he made it to the lowest branch, and from there on it looked easy.

I can't explain the crawling sensation in my gut as I

watched Jonathan Creighton climbing toward a rendezvous with the approaching pine lights. He was three-quarters of the way to the top when the trunk began to shake and sway with his weight. Then a branch broke under his foot and he almost fell. When I saw that he'd regained safe footing, I sighed with relief. The branches above him were too frail to hold him. He couldn't go any higher. He'd be safe from the lights.

And the lights were here, a good dozen of them, from baseball to basketball size, gliding across our clearing in an irregular cylindrical cluster perhaps ten feet across and twenty feet long, heading straight for Creighton's tree.

And the closer they got, the faster my insides crawled. They may have been made up of light but it was not a clean light, not the golden healthy light of day. This was a wan, sickly, anemic glow, tainted with the vaguest hint of green. But thankfully it was a glow out of Creighton's reach as the lights brushed the tree's topmost needles.

I watched their glow limn Creighton's upturned face as his body strained upward, and I wondered at his recklessness, at this obsession with finding "reality." Was he flailing and floundering about in his search, or was he actually on the trail of something? And were the pine lights part of it?

As the first light passed directly above him, not five feet beyond his outstretched hand, I heard him cry out.

"They're humming, Mac! High-pitched! Can you hear it? It's almost musical! And the air up here tingles, almost as if it's charged! This is fantastic!"

I didn't hear any music or feel any tingling. All I could hear was my heart thudding in my chest, all I could feel was the cold sweat that had broken out all over my body.

Creighton spoke again, he was practically shouting now, but in a language that was not English and not like any other language I'd ever heard. He made clicks and wheezes, and the few noises that sounded like words did not seem to fit comfortably on the human tongue.

"Jon, what are you doing up there?" I cried.

He ignored me and kept up the alien gibberish, but the

lights, in turn, ignored him and sailed by above him as if he didn't exist.

The cluster was almost past now, yet still I couldn't shake the dread, the dark feeling that something awful was going to happen.

And then it did.

The last light in the cluster was basketball-sized. It seemed as if it was going to trail away above Creighton just like the others, but as it approached the tree, it slowed and began to drop toward Creighton's perch.

I was panicked now.

"Jon, look out! It's coming right for you!"

"I see it!"

As the other lights flowed off toward the next treetop, this last one hung back and circled Creighton's tree at a height level with his waist.

"Get down from there!" I called.

"Are you kidding? This is more than I'd ever hoped for!"

The light suddenly stopped moving and hovered a foot or so in front of Creighton's chest.

"It's cold," he said in a more subdued tone. "Cold light."

He reached his hand toward it and I wanted to shout for him not to but my throat was locked. The tip of his index finger touched the outer edge of the glow.

"*Really* cold."

I saw his finger sink into the light to perhaps the depth of the fingernail, and then suddenly the light moved. It more than moved, it *leapt* onto Creighton's hand, engulfing it.

That's when Creighton began to scream. His words were barely intelligible but I picked out the words "cold" and "burning" again and again. I ran to the base of the tree, expecting him to lose his balance, hoping I could do something to break his fall. I saw the ball of light stretch out and slide up the length of his arm, engulfing it.

Then it disappeared.

For an instant I thought it might be over. But when Creighton clutched his chest and cried out in greater agony, I realized to my horror that the light wasn't gone—it was inside him!

And then I saw the back of his shirt begin to glow. I watched the light ooze out of him and reform itself into a globe. Then it rose and glided off to follow the other lights into the night, leaving Creighton alone in the tree, sobbing and retching.

I called up to him. "Jon! Are you all right? Do you need help?"

When he didn't answer, I grabbed hold of the tree trunk. But before I could attempt to climb, he stopped me.

"Stay there, Mac." His voice was weak, shaky. "I'm coming down."

It took him twice as long to climb down as it had to go up. His movements were slow, unsteady, and three times he had to stop to rest. Finally, he reached the lowest branch, hung from it by one hand, and made the final drop. I grabbed him immediately to keep him from collapsing into a heap, and helped him back toward the lamp and the bedrolls.

"My God, Jon! Your arm!"

In the light from the lamp his flesh seemed to be smoking. The skin on his left hand and forearm was red, almost scalded-looking. Tiny blisters were already starting to form.

"It looks worse than it feels."

"We've got to get you to a doctor."

He dropped to his knees on his bedroll and hugged his injured arm against his chest with his good one.

"I'm all right. It only hurts a little now."

"It's going to get infected. Come on. I'll see if I can get us to civilization."

"Forget it," he said, and I sensed some of the strength returning to his voice. "Even if we get the jeep free, we're still lost. We couldn't find our way out of here when it was daylight. What makes you think we'll do any better in the dark?"

He was right. But I felt I had to do something.

"Where's your first aid kit?"

"I don't have one."

I blew up then.

"Jesus Christ, Jon! You're crazy, you know that? You could

have fallen out of that tree and been killed! And if you don't
wind up with gangrene in that arm it'll be a miracle! What on
God's earth made you do something so stupid?"

He grinned. "I knew it! You still love me!"

I was not amused.

"This is serious, Jon. You risked your life up there! For
what?"

"I have to know, Mac."

"'Know?' What do you have to 'know?' Will you stop
giving me this bullshit?"

"I can't. I can't stop because it's true. I have to know
what's real and what's not."

"Spare me—"

"I mean it. You're sure you know what's real and so
you're content and complacent with that. You can't imagine what it's like not to know. To sense there's a veil
across everything, a barrier that keeps you from seeing
what's really there. You don't know what it's like to spend
your life searching for the edge of that veil so you can lift
it and peek—just peek—at what's behind it. I know it's
out there, and I can't reach it. You don't know what that's
like, Mac. It makes you crazy."

"Well, that's one thing we can agree on."

He laughed—it sounded strained—and reached for his
jug of applejack with his good hand.

"Haven't you had enough of that tonight?"

I hated myself for sounding like an old biddy, but what
I had just seen had shaken me to the core. I was still
trembling.

"No, Mac. The problem is I haven't had enough. Not
nearly enough."

Feeling helpless and angry, I sat down on my own bedroll and watched him take a long pull from the jug.

"What happened up there, Jon?"

"I don't know. But I don't ever want it to happen again."

"And what were you saying? It almost sounded as if you
were calling to them."

He looked up sharply and stared at me.

"Did you hear what I said?"

"Not exactly. It didn't even sound like speech."

"That's because it wasn't," he said, and I was sure I detected relief in his voice. "I was trying to attract their attention."

"Well, you sure did that."

Across the top of the Coleman lamp, I thought I saw him smile.

"Yeah. I did, didn't I?"

In the night around us, I noticed that the insects were becoming vocal again.

7. The Shunned Place

I'd planned to stay awake the rest of the night, but somewhere along the way I must have faded into sleep. The next thing I knew there was sunlight in my eyes. I leaped up, disoriented for a moment, then I remembered where I was.

But where was Creighton? His bedroll lay stretched out on the sand, his compass, sextant, and maps upon it, but he was nowhere in sight. I called his name a couple of times. He called back from somewhere off to my left. I followed the sound of his voice through the brush and emerged on the edge of a small pond rimmed with white cedars.

Creighton was kneeling at the edge, cupping some water in his right hand.

"How'd you find this?" I said.

"Simple." He pointed out toward a group of drakes and mallards floating on the still surface. "I followed the quacking."

"You're becoming a regular Mark Trail. How's the water?"

"Polluted." He pointed to a brownish blue slick on the surface of the pond, then held up a palmful of clear, brownish water. "Look at that color. Looks like tea."

"That's not polluted," I told him. "That's the start of some bog iron floating over there. And this is cedar water. It gets brown from the iron deposits and from the cedars but it's as pure as it comes."

I scooped up a double handful and took a long swallow. "Almost sweet," I said. "Sea captains used to come into these parts to fill their water casks with cedar water before long voyages. They said it stayed fresher longer."

"Then I guess it's okay to bathe this in it," he said, twisting and showing me his left arm.

I gasped. I couldn't help it. I'd half convinced myself that last night's incident with the pine light had been a nightmare. But the reddened, crusted, blistered skin on Creighton's arm said otherwise.

"We've got to get you to a doctor," I said.

"It's all right, Mac. Doesn't really hurt. Just feels hot."

He sank it past his elbow into the cool cedar water.

"Now *that* feels good!"

I looked around. The sun shone from a cloudless sky. We'd have no trouble finding our way out of here this morning. I stared out over the pond. Water. The sandy floor of the Pine Barrens was like a giant sponge that absorbed a high percentage of the rain that fell on it. It was the largest untapped aquifer in the northeast. No rivers flowed into the Pinelands, only out. The water here was glacial in its purity. I'd read somewhere that the Barrens held an amount of water equivalent to a lake with a surface area of a thousand square miles and an average depth of seventy-five feet.

This little piece of wetness here was less than fifty yards across. I watched the ducks. They were quacking peacefully, tooling around, dipping their heads. Then one of them made a different sound, more like a squawk. It flapped its wings once and was gone. It happened in the blink of an eye. One second a floating duck, next second some floating bubbles.

"Did you see that?" Creighton said.

"Yeah, I did."

"What happened to that duck?" I could see the excitement starting to glow in his eyes. "What's it mean?"

"It means a snapping turtle. A big one. Fifty pounds or better, I'm sure."

Creighton pulled his arm from the pond.

"I do believe I've soaked this enough for now."

He dipped a towel in the water and wrapped it around his scorched arm.

We walked back to the bedrolls, packed up our gear, and made our way through the brush to the Wrangler.

The jeep was occupied.

There were people inside, and people sitting on the hood and standing on the bumpers as well. A good half-dozen in all.

Only they weren't like any people I'd ever seen.

They were dressed like typical Pineys, but dirty, raggedy. The four men in jeans or canvas pants, collared shirts of various fabrics and colors or plain white tee-shirts; the two women wore cotton jumpers. But they were all deformed. Their heads were odd shapes and sizes, some way too small, others large and lopsided with bulbous protrusions. The eyes on a couple weren't lined up on the level. Everyone seemed to have one arm or leg longer than the other. Their teeth, at least in the ones who still had any, seemed to have come in at random angles.

When they spotted us, they began jabbering and pointing our way. They left the Wrangler and surrounded us. It was an intimidating group.

"Is that your car?" a young man with a lopsided head said to me.

"No." I pointed to Creighton. "It's his."

"Is that your car?" he said to Creighton.

I guessed he didn't believe me.

"It's a jeep," Creighton said.

"Jeep! Jeep!" He laughed and kept repeating the word. The others around him took it up and chorused along.

I looked at Creighton and shrugged. We'd apparently come upon an enclave of the type of folks who'd helped turn "Piney" into a term of derision shortly before World War I. That was when Elizabeth Kite published a report titled "The Pineys" which was sensationalized by the press and led to the view that the Pinelands was a bed of alcoholism, illiteracy, degeneracy, incest, and resultant "feeble-mindedness."

Unfair and untrue. But not entirely false. There has always been illiteracy and alcoholism deep in the Pinelands. Schooling here tended to be rudimentary if at all. And as for drinking? The first "drive-thru" service originated before the Revolution in the Piney jug taverns, allowing customers to ride up to a window, get their jugs topped off with applejack, pay, and move on without ever dismounting. But after the economy of the Pine Barrens faltered, and most of the workers moved on to greener pastures, much of the social structure collapsed. Those who stayed on grew a little lax as to the whys, hows, and to-whoms of marriage. The results were inevitable.

All that had supposedly changed in modern times, except in the most isolated area of the Pines. We had stumbled upon one of those areas. Except that the deformities here were extraordinary. I'd seen a few of the inbreds in my youth. There'd been something subtly odd about them, but nothing that terribly startling. These folk would stop you in your tracks.

"Let's head for the jeep while they're yucking it up," I said out of the corner of my mouth.

"No. Wait. This is fascinating. Besides, we need their help."

He spoke to the group as a whole and asked their aid in freeing the jeep.

Somebody said, "Sugar sand," and this was repeated all around. But they willingly set their shoulders against the Wrangler and we were on hard ground again in minutes.

"Where do you live?" Creighton said to anyone who was listening.

Someone said, "Town," and as one they all pointed east, toward the sun. It was also the direction the lights had been headed last night.

"Will you show me?"

They nodded and jabbered and tugged on our sleeves, anxious to show us.

"Really, Jon," I said. "We should get you to—"

"My arm can wait. This won't take long."

We followed the group in a generally uphill direction along a circuitous footpath unnavigable by any vehicle other than a motorcycle. The trees thickened and soon we were in shade. And then those trees opened up and we were in their "town."

A haze of blue woodsmoke hung over a ramshackle collection of shanties made of scrap lumber and sheet metal. Garbage everywhere, and everyone coming out to look at the strangers. I'd never seen such squalor.

The fellow with the lopsided head who'd asked about the jeep before pulled Creighton toward one of the shacks.

"Hey, mister, you know about machines. How come this don't work?"

He had an old TV set inside his one-room hut. He turned the knobs back and forth.

"Don't work. No pictures."

"You need electricity," Creighton told him.

"Got it. Got it. Got it."

He led us around to the back to show us the length of wire he had strung from a tree to the roof of the shack.

Creighton turned to me with stricken eyes.

"This is awful. No one should have to live like this. Can we do anything for them?"

His compassion surprised me. I'd never thought there was room for anyone else's concerns in his self-absorbed life. But then, Jonathan Creighton had always been a motherlode of surprises.

"Not much. They all look pretty content to me. Seem to have their own little community. If you bring them to the government's attention they'll be split up and most of them will probably be placed in institutions or group homes. I guess the best you can do is give them whatever you can think of to make the living easier here."

Creighton nodded, still staring around him.

"Speaking of 'here,'" he said, unshouldering his knapsack, "let's find out where we are."

The misshapen locals stared in frank awe and admiration as he took his readings. Someone asked him, "What is that thing?" a hundred times. At least. Another asked "What happened to your arm?" an equal number of times. Creighton was heroically patient with everyone. He knelt on the ground to transfer his readings to the map, then looked up at me.

"Know where we are?"

"The other side of Razorback Hill, I'd say."

"You got it."

He stood up and gathered the locals around him.

"I'm looking for a special place around here," he said.

Most of them nodded eagerly. Someone said, "We know every place there is around here, I reckon."

"Good. I'm looking for a place where nothing grows. Do you know a place like that?"

It was as if all of these people had a common plug and Creighton had just pulled it. The lights went out, the shades came down, the "Open" signs flipped to "Closed." They began to turn away.

"What'd I say?" he said, turning his anxious, bewildered eyes on me. "What'd I *say?*"

"You're starting to sound like Ray Charles," I told him. "Obviously they want nothing to do with this 'place where nothing grows' you're talking about. What's this all about, Jon?"

He ignored my question and laid his good hand on the shoulder of one of the small-headed men.

"Won't you take me there if you know where it is?"

"We know where it is," the fellow said in a squeaky voice. "But we never go there so we can't take you there. How can we take you there if we never go there?"

"You *never* go there? Why not?"

The others had stopped and were listening to the exchange. The small-headed fellow looked around at his neighbors and gave them a look that asked how stupid could anyone be? Then he turned back to Creighton.

"We don't go there 'cause nobody goes there."

"What's your name?" Creighton said.

"Fred."

"Fred, my name is Jon, and I'll give you . . ." He patted his pockets, then tore the watch off his wrist. "I'll give you this beautiful watch that you don't have to wind—see how the numbers change with every second?—if you'll take me to a place where you *do* go and point out the place where nothing grows. How's that sound?"

Fred took the watch and held it up close to his right eye, then smiled.

"Come on! I'll show you!"

Creighton took off after Fred, and I took off after Creighton.

Again we were led along a circuitous path, this one even narrower than before, becoming less well defined as we went along. I noticed the trees becoming fewer in number and more stunted and gnarled, and the underbrush thinning out, the leaves fewer and curled on their edges. We followed Fred until he halted as abruptly as if he had run into an invisible wall. I saw why: the footpath we'd been following stopped here. He pointed ahead through what was left of the trees and underbrush.

"The bald spot's over yonder atop that there rise."

He turned and hurried back along the path.

Bald spot?

Creighton looked at me, then shrugged.

"Got your machete handy, Mac?"

"No, Bwana."

"Too bad. I guess we'll just have to bull our way through."

He rewrapped his burned arm and pushed ahead. It wasn't such rough going. The underbrush thinned out quickly and so we had an easier time of it than I'd anticipated. Soon we broke into a small field lined with scrappy weeds and occupied by the scattered, painfully gnarled trunks of dead trees. And in the center of the field was a patch of bare sand.

. . . a place where nothing grows . . .

Creighton hurried ahead. I held back, restrained by a sense of foreboding. The same something deep within me that had feared the pine lights feared this place as well. Something was wrong here, as if Nature had been careless, had made a mistake in this place and had never quite been able to rectify it. As if . . .

What was I thinking? It was an empty field. No eerie lights buzzing through the sky. No birds, either, for that

matter. So what? The sun was up, a breeze was blowing—
or at least it had been a moment ago.

Overruling my instincts, I followed Creighton. I
touched the tortured trunk of one of the dead trees as I
passed. It was hard and cold, like stone. A petrified tree.
In the Pinelands.

I hurried ahead and caught up to Creighton at the edge
of the "bald spot." He was staring at it as if in a trance.
The spot was a rough oval, maybe thirty feet across. Nothing grew in that oval. Nothing.

"Look at that pristine sand," he said in a whisper. "Birds
don't fly over it, insects and animals don't walk on it. Only
the wind touches and shapes it. That's the way sand
looked at the beginning of time."

It had always been my impression that sand wasn't yet
sand at the beginning of time, but I didn't argue with him.
He was on a roll. I remembered from college: You don't
stop Crazy Creighton when he's on a roll.

I saw what he meant, though. The sand was rippled like
water, like sand must look in areas of the Sahara far off the
trade routes. I saw animal tracks leading up to it and then
turning aside. Creighton was right: nothing trod this soil.

Except Creighton.

Without warning he stepped across the invisible line
and walked to the center of the bald spot. He spread his
arms, looked up at the sky, and whirled in dizzying circles. His eyes were aglow, his expression rapturous. He
looked stoned out of his mind.

"This is it! I've found it! This is the place!"

"*What* place, Jon?"

I stood at the edge of the spot, unwilling to cross over,
talking in the flat tone you might use to coax a druggie
back from a bad trip, or a jumper down from a ledge.

"Where it all comes together and all comes apart!
Where the Truth is revealed!"

"What the hell are you talking about, Jon?"

I was tired and uneasy and I wanted to go home. I'd

had enough, and I guessed my voice showed it. The rapture faded. Abruptly, he was sober.

"Nothing, Mac. Nothing. Just let me take a few readings and we're out of here."

"That's the best news I've heard this morning."

He shot me a quick glance. I didn't know if it conveyed annoyance or disappointment. And I didn't care.

8. Spreading Infection

I got us back to a paved road without too much difficulty. We spoke little on the way home. He dropped me off at my house and promised to see a doctor before the day was out.

"What's next for you?" I said as I closed the passenger door and looked at him through the open window.

I hoped he wouldn't ask me to guide him back into the Pines again. I was sure he hadn't been straight with me about his research. I didn't know what he was after, but I knew it wasn't the Jersey Devil. A part of me said it was better not to know, that this man was a juggernaut on a date with disaster.

"I'm not sure. I may go back and see those people, the ones on the far side of Razorback Hill. Maybe bring them some clothing, some food."

Against my will, I was touched.

"That would be nice. Just don't bring them toaster cakes or microwave dinners."

He laughed. "I won't."

"Where are you staying?"

He hesitated, looking uncertain.

"A place called the Laurelton Circle Motor Inn."

"I know it."

A tiny place. Sporting the name of a traffic circle that no longer existed.

"I'm staying in room five if you need to get hold of me but . . . can you do me a favor? If anybody comes looking for me, don't tell them where I am. Don't tell them you've even seen me."

"Are you in some sort of trouble?"

"A misunderstanding, that's all."

"You wouldn't want to elaborate on that, would you?"

His expression was bleak.

"The less you know, Mac, the better."

"Like everything else these past two days, right?"

He shrugged. "Sorry."

"Me, too. Look. Stop by before you head back to Razorback. I may have a few old things I can donate to those folks."

He waved with his burnt hand, and then he was off.

Creighton stopped by a few days later on his way back to Razorback Hill. His left arm was heavily bandaged in gauze.

"You were right," he said. "It got infected."

I gave him some old sweaters and shirts and a couple of pairs of jeans that no longer fit the way they should.

A few days later I bumped into him in the housewares aisle at Pathmark. He'd picked up some canned goods and was buying a couple of can openers for the Razorback folks. His left arm was bandaged as before, but I was concerned to see that there was gauze on his right hand now.

"The infection spread a little, but the doctor says it's okay. He's got me on this new antibiotic. Sure to kill it off."

Looking more closely now in the supermarket's fluorescent glare, I saw that he was pale and sweaty. He seemed to have lost weight.

"Who's your doctor?"

"Guy up in Neptune. A specialist."

"In pine light burns?"

His laugh was a bit too loud, a tad too long.

"No! Infections."

I wondered. But Jon Creighton was a big boy now. I couldn't be his mother.

I picked out some canned goods myself, checked out behind Creighton, and gave the bagful to him.

"Give them my best," I told him.

He smiled wanly and hurried off.

At the very tail end of August I was driving down Brick Boulevard when I spotted his Wrangler idling at the Burger King drive-thru window. I pulled into the lot and walked over.

"Jon!" I said through the window and saw him jump.

"Oh, Mac. Don't ever do that!"

He looked relieved, but he didn't look terribly glad to see me. His face seemed thinner, but maybe that was because of the beard he had started to grow. A fugitive's beard.

"Sorry," I said. "I was wondering if you wanted to get together for some *real* lunch."

"Oh. Well. Thanks, but I've got a lot of errands to run. Maybe some other time."

Despite the heat, he was wearing corduroy pants and a long-sleeved flannel shirt. I noticed that both his hands were still wrapped in gauze. An alarm went off inside me.

"Isn't that infection cleared up yet?"

"It's coming along slowly, but it's coming."

I glanced down at his feet and noticed that his ankles looked thick. His sneakers were unlaced, their tongues lolling out as the sides stretched to accommodate his swollen feet.

"What happened to your feet?"

"A little edema. Side effect of the medicine. Look, Mac, I've got to run." He threw the Wrangler into gear. "I'll call you soon."

It was a couple of weeks after Labor Day and I'd been thinking about Creighton a lot. I was worried about him, and was realizing that I still harbored deeper feelings for him than I cared to admit.

Then the state trooper showed up at my office. He was big and intimidating behind his dark glasses; his haircut came within a millimeter of complete baldness. He held out a grainy photo of Jon Creighton.

"Do you know this man?" he said in a deep voice.

My mouth was dry as I wondered if he was going to ask me if I was involved in whatever Creighton had done; or worse: if I'd care to come down and identify the body.

"Sure. We went to college together."

"Have you seen him in the past month."

I didn't hesitate. I did the stand-up thing.

"Nope. Not since graduation."

"We have reason to believe he's in the area. If you see him, contact the State Police or your local police immediately."

"What's he done, officer?"

He turned and started toward the door without deigning to answer. That brand of arrogance never failed to set something off in me.

"I asked you a question, *officer*. I expect the courtesy of a reply."

He turned and looked at me, then shrugged. Some of the Dirty Harry facade slipped away with the shrug.

"Why not?" he said. "He's wanted for grand theft."

Oh, great.

"What did he steal?"

"A book."

"A *book*?"

"Yeah. Would you believe it? We've got rapes and murders and armed robberies, but this book is given a priority. I don't care how valuable it is or how much some university in Massachusetts wants it, it's only a book. But the Massachusetts people are really hot to get it back. Their governor got to our governor and . . . well, you know how it goes. We found his car abandoned out near Lakehurst a while back, so we know he's been through here."

"You think he's on foot?"

"Maybe. Or maybe he rented or stole another car. We're running it down now."

"If he shows up, I'll let you know."

"Do that. I get the impression that if he gives the book back in one piece, all will be forgiven."

"I'll tell him that if I get the chance."

As soon as he was gone, I got on the phone to Creighton's motel. His voice was thick when he said hello.

"Jon! The state cops were just here looking for you!"

He mumbled a few words I didn't understand. Something was wrong. I hung up and headed for my car.

There are only about twenty rooms in that particular motel. I spotted the Wrangler backed into a space at the far end of the tiny parking lot. Number five was on a corner of the first floor. A DO NOT DISTURB sign hung from the knob. I knocked on the door twice and got no answer. I tried the knob. It turned.

It was dark inside except for the daylight I'd let in. And that light revealed a disaster area. The room looked like the inside of a dumpster behind a block of fast-food stores. Smelled like one, too. There were pizza boxes, hamburger wrappers, submarine sleeves, Chinese food cartons, a sampling from every place in the area that delivered. And it was hot. Either the air conditioner had quit or it hadn't been turned on.

"Jon?" I flipped on the light. "Jon, are you here?"

He was in a chair in a corner on the far side of the bed, huddled under a pile of blankets. Papers and maps were piled on the night table beside him. His face, where visible above his matted beard, was pale and drawn. He looked as if he'd lost thirty pounds. I slammed the door closed and stood there, stunned.

"My God, Jon, what's wrong?"

"Nothing. I'm fine." His hoarse, thick voice said otherwise. "What are you doing here, Mac?"

"I came to tell you that the State Police are cruising around with photos of you, but I can see that's the least of your problems! You're really sick!" I reached for the phone. "I'm calling an ambulance."

"*No!* Mac, please *don't!*"

The terror and soul-wrenching anguish in his voice

stopped me. I stared at him but still kept a grip on the receiver.

"Why not?"

"Because I'm begging you not to!"

"But you're sick, you could be dying, you're out of your head!"

"No. That's one thing I'm not. Trust me when I say that no hospital in the world can help me—because I'm not dying. And if you ever loved me, if you ever had any regard for who I am and what I want from my life, then you'll put down that phone and walk out that door."

I stood there in the hot, humid squalor of that tiny room, receiver in hand, smelling the garbage, detecting the hint of another odor, a subtle sour foulness that underlay the others, and felt myself being torn apart by the choice that faced me.

"Please, Mac," he said. "You're the only person in the world who'll understand. Don't hand me over to strangers." He sobbed once. "I can't fight you. I can only beg you. Please. Put down the phone and leave."

It was the sob that did it. I slammed the receiver onto its cradle.

"Damn you!"

"Two days, Mac. In two days I'll be better. You wait and see."

"You're damn right I'll see—I'm staying here with you!"

"No! You can't! You have no right to intrude! This is *my* life! You've got to let me take it where I must! Now leave, Mac. Please."

He was right, of course. This was what we'd been all about when we'd been together. I had to back off. And it was killing me.

"All right," I said around the lump in my throat. "You win. See you in two days."

Without waiting for a reply, I opened the door and stepped out into the bright September sunlight.

"Thanks, Mac," he said. "I love you."

I didn't want to hear that. I took one last look back as I

pulled the door closed. He was still swaddled from his neck to the floor in the blankets, but in the last instant before the door shut him from view, I thought I saw something white and pointed, about the circumference of a garden hose, snake out on the carpet from under the blankets and then quickly pull back under cover.

A rush of nausea slammed me against the outer wall of the motel as the door clicked closed. I leaned there, sick and dizzy, trying to catch my breath.

A trick of the light. That was what I told myself as the vertigo faded. I'd been squinting in the brightness and the light had played a trick.

Of course, I didn't have to settle for merely telling myself. I could simply open the door and check it out. I actually reached for the knob, but couldn't bring myself to turn it.

Two days. Creighton had said two days. I'd find out then.

But I didn't last two days. I was unable to concentrate the following morning and wound up canceling all my appointments. I spent the entire day pacing my office or my living room; and when I wasn't pacing, I was on the phone. I called the American Folklore Society and the New Jersey Historical Society. Not only had they not given Creighton the grants he'd told me about, they'd never heard of him.

By nightfall I'd taken all I could. I began calling Creighton's room. I got no answer. I tried a few more times, but when he still hadn't picked up by eleven o'clock, I headed for the motel.

I was almost relieved to see the Wrangler gone from the parking lot. Room five was still unlocked and still a garbage dump, which meant he was still renting it—or hadn't been gone too long.

What was he up to?

I began to search the room. I found the book under the bed. It was huge, heavy, wrapped in plastic with a scrawled note taped to the front:

Please return to Miskatonic U. archives

I slipped it out of the plastic. It was leather-bound and

handwritten in Latin. I could barely decipher the title—something like *Liben Damnatus*. But inside the front cover were Creighton's maps and a sheaf of notes in his back-slanted scrawl. The notes were in disarray and probably would have been disjointed even if arranged in proper order. But certain words and phrases kept recurring: *nexus point* and *equinox* and *the lumens* and *the veil*.

It took me a while but eventually I got the drift of the jottings. Apparently a section of the book Creighton had stolen concerned "nexus points" around the globe where twice a year at the vernal and autumnal equinoxes "the veil" that obscures reality becomes detached for a short while, allowing an intrepid soul to peek under the hem and see the true nature of the world around us, the world we are not "allowed" to see. These "nexus points" are few and widely scattered. Of the four known, there's one near each pole, one in Tibet, and one near the east coast of North America.

I sighed. Crazy Creighton had really started living up to his name. It was sad. This was so unlike him. He'd been the ultimate cynic, and now he was risking his health and his freedom pursuing this mystical garbage.

And what was even sadder was how he had lied to me. Obviously he hadn't been searching for tales of the Jersey Devil—he'd been searching for one of these "nexus points." And he was probably convinced he'd found one behind Razorback Hill.

I pitied him. But I read on.

According to the notes, these "nexus points" can be located by following "the lumens" to a place shunned equally by man, beast, and vegetation.

Suddenly I was uneasy. "The lumens." Could that refer to the pine lights? And the "bald spot" that Fred had showed us—that was certainly a place shunned by man, beast, and vegetation.

I found a whole sheet filled with notes about the Razorback folk. The last paragraph was especially upsetting:

> The folks behind Razorback Hill aren't deformed from inbreeding, although I'm sure

that's contributed its share. I believe they're misshapen as a result of living near the nexus point for generations. The semi-annual lifting of the veil must have caused genetic damage over the years.

I pulled out Creighton's maps and unfolded them on the bed. I followed the lines he had drawn from Apple Pie Hill, from Gus's firing place, and from our campsite. All three lines represented paths of pine lights, and all three intersected at a spot near the circle he had drawn and labeled as Razorback Hill. And right near the intersection of the pine light paths, almost on top of it, he had drawn another circle, a tiny one, penciled in the latitude and longitude, and labeled it *Nexus!*

I was worried now. Even my own skepticism was beginning to waver. Everything was fitting too neatly. I looked at my watch. Eleven thirty-two. The date read "21." September 21. When was the equinox? I grabbed the phone and called an old clam-digger who'd been a client since I'd opened my office. He knew the answer right off:

"The autumnal equinox. That's September twenty-second. 'Bout a half hour from now."

I dropped the phone and ran for my car. I knew exactly where to find Jon Creighton.

9. The Hem of the Veil

I raced down the Parkway to the Bass River exit and tried to find my way back to Gus Sooy's place. What had been a difficult trip in the day proved to be several orders of magnitude more difficult in the dark. But I managed to find Gus's red cedar. It was my plan to convince him to show me a short way to the far side of Razorback Hill, figuring the fact that Creighton was already there might make him more tractable. But when I rushed up to Gus Sooy's clearing, I discovered that he wasn't alone.

The Razorback folk were there. All of them, from the looks of the crowd.

I found Gus standing on his front step, a jug dangling from his hand. He was obviously shocked to see me, and was anything but hospitable.

"What do you want?"

Before I could answer, the Razorback folks recognized me and a small horde of them crowded around.

"Why are they all here?" I asked Gus.

"Just visiting," he said casually, but did not look me in the eye.

"It wouldn't have anything to do with what's happening at the bald spot on the other side of Razorback Hill, would it?"

"Damn you! You've been snoopin' around, haven't you? You and your friend. They told me he was coming around, askin' all sorts of questions. Where's he now? Hidin' in the bushes?"

"He's over there," I said, pointing to the top of Razorback Hill. "And if my guess is correct, he's standing right in the middle of the bald spot."

Gus dropped his jug. It shattered on the boards of his front step.

"Do you know what'll happen to him?"

"No," I said. "Do you?" I looked around at the Razorback folk. "Do they?"

"I don't think anyone knows, leastmost them. But they're scared. They come here twice a year, when that bald spot starts acting up."

"Have you ever seen what happens there?"

"Once. Never want to see it again."

"Why haven't you ever told anyone?"

"What? And bring all sorts of pointyheads here to look and gawk and build and ruin the place. We'd all rather put up with the bald spot craziness twice a year than pointy-head craziness every day all year long."

I didn't have time to get into Creighton's theory that the bald spot was genetically damaging the Razorback folks. I had to find Creighton.

"How do I get there? What's the fastest way?"

"You can't—"

"*They* got here!" I pointed to the Razorback folks.

"All right!" he said with open hostility. "Suit yourself. There's a trail behind my cabin here. Follow it over the left flank of the hill."

"And then?"

"And then you won't need any directions. You'll know where to go."

His words had an ominous ring, but I couldn't press him. I was being propelled by a sense of enormous urgency. Time was running out. Quickly. I already had my flashlight, so I hurried to the rear of his shanty and followed the trail.

Gus was right. As I crossed the flank of the hill I saw flashes through the trees ahead, like lightning, as if a very tiny and very violent electrical storm had been brought to ground and anchored there. I increased my pace, running when the terrain would allow. The wind picked up as I neared the storm area, growing from a fitful breeze to a full-scale gale by the time I broke through the brush and stumbled into the clearing that surrounded the bald spot.

Chaos. That's the only way I can describe it. A nightmare of cascading lights and roaring wind. The pine lights—or *lumens*—were there, hundreds of them, all sizes, unaffected by the rushing vortex of air as they swirled about in wild arcs, each flaring brilliantly as it looped through the space above the bald spot. And the bald spot itself—it glowed with a faint purplish light that reached thirty or forty feet into the air before fading into the night.

The stolen book, Creighton's notes—they weren't mystical madness. Something cataclysmic was happening here, something that defied all the laws of nature—if indeed those laws had any real meaning. Whether this was one of the nexus points he had described, a fleeting rent in the reality that surrounded us, only Creighton could say for sure right now.

For I could see someone in the bald spot. I couldn't make out his features from where I was, but I knew it was Jonathan Creighton.

I dashed forward until I reached the edge but slowed to

a halt in the sand before actually crossing into the glow. Creighton was there, on his knees, his hands and feet buried in the sand. He was staring about him, his expression an uneasy mix of fear and wonder. I shouted his name but he didn't hear me above the roar of the wind. Twice he looked directly at me but despite my frantic shouting and waving, did not see me.

I saw no other choice. I had to step onto the bald spot . . . the nexus point. It wasn't easy. Every instinct I possessed screamed at me to run in the other direction, but I couldn't leave him there like that. He looked helpless, trapped like an insect on flypaper. I had to help him.

Taking a deep breath, I closed my eyes and stepped across—

—and began to stumble forward. Up and down seemed to have a slightly different orientation here. I opened my eyes and dropped to my knees, nearly landing on Creighton. I looked around and froze.

The Pine Barrens were gone. *Night* was gone. It seemed to be pre-dawn or dusk here, but the wind still howled about us and the pine lights flashed around us, appearing and disappearing above as though passing through invisible walls. We were someplace . . . *else:* on a huge misty plain that seemed to stretch on forever, interrupted only by clumps of vegetation and huge fog banks, one of which was nearby on my left and seemed to go on and up forever. Off in the immeasurable distance, mountains the size of the moon reached up and disappeared into the haze of the purple sky. The horizon—or what I imagined to be the horizon—didn't curve as it should. This place seemed so much *bigger* than the world—our world—that waited just a few feet away.

"My God, Jon, where are we!"

He started and turned his head. His hands and feet remained buried in the sand. His eyes went wide with shock at the sight of me.

"No! You shouldn't be here!"

His voice was thicker and more distorted than yesterday. Oddly enough, his pale skin looked almost healthy in the mauve light.

"Neither should you!"

I heard something then. Above the shriek of the wind came another sound. A rumble like an avalanche. It came from somewhere within the fog bank to our left. There was something massive, something immense moving about in there, and the fog seemed to be drifting this way.

"We've got to get out of here, Jon!"

"No! I'm staying!"

"No way! Come on!"

He was wracked with infection and obviously deranged. I didn't care what he said, I wasn't going to let him risk his life in this place. I'd pull him out of here and let him think about it for six months. *Then* if he still wanted to try this, it would be his choice. But he wasn't competent now.

I looped my arms around his chest and tried to pull him to his feet.

"Mac, please! Don't!"

His hands remained fixed in the sand. He must have been holding onto something. I grabbed his right elbow and yanked. He screamed as his hand pulled free of the sand. Then I screamed, too, and let him go and threw myself back on the sand away from him.

Because his hand wasn't a hand anymore.

It was big and white and had these long, ropey, tapered, root-like projections, something like an eye on a potato when it sprouts after being left under the sink too long, only these things were moving, twisting and writhing like a handful of albino snakes.

"Go, Mac!" he said in that distorted voice, and I could tell from his face and eyes that he hadn't wanted me to see him like this. "You don't belong here!"

"And you do?"

"*Now* I do!"

I couldn't bring myself to touch his hand, so I reached forward and grabbed some of his shirt. I pulled.

"We can find doctors! They can fix you! You can—"

"*NO!*"

It was a shout and it was something else. Something long and white and hard as flexed muscle, much like the things protruding from his shirt sleeve, darted out of his mouth and slammed against my chest, bruising my breasts as it thrust me away. Then it whipped back into his mouth.

I snapped then. I scrambled to my feet and blindly lurched away in the direction I'd come. Suddenly I was back in the Pine Barrens, in the cool night with the lights swirling madly above my head. I stumbled for the bushes, away from the nexus point, away from Jonathan Creighton.

At the edge of the clearing, I forced myself to stop and look back. I saw Creighton. His awful transformed hand was raised. I knew he couldn't see me, but it was almost as if he was waving good-bye. Then he lowered his hand and worked the tendrils back into the sand.

The last thing I remember of that night is vomiting.

10. Aftermath

I awoke among the Razorback folk who'd found me the next morning and watched over me until I was conscious and lucid again. They offered me food but I couldn't eat. I walked back up to the clearing, to the bald spot.

It looked exactly as it had when Creighton and I had first seen it in August. No lights, no wind, no purple glow. Just bare sand.

And no Jonathan Creighton.

I could have convinced myself that last night had never happened if not for the swollen, tender, violet bruise on my chest. Would that I had. But as much as my mind shrank from it, I could not deny the truth. I'd seen the other side of the veil and my life would never be the same.

I looked around and knew that everything I saw was a sham, an elaborate illusion. Why? Why was the veil there? To protect us from harm? Or to shield us from madness? The truth had brought me no peace. Who could find comfort in the knowledge that huge, immeasurable forces beyond our comprehension were out there, moving about us, beyond the reach of our senses?

I wanted to run . . . but where?

I ran home. I've been home for months now. House-bound. Moving beyond my door only for groceries. My accounting clients have all left me. I'm living on my savings, learning Latin, translating Jon's stolen book. Was what I saw the true reality of our existence, or another dimension, or what? I don't know. Creighton was right: knowing that you don't know is maddening. It consumes you.

So I'm waiting for spring. Waiting for the vernal equinox. Maybe I'll leave the house before then and hunt up some pine lights—or *lumens,* as the book calls them. Maybe I'll touch one, maybe I won't. Maybe when the equinox comes, I'll return to Razorback Hill, to the bald spot. Maybe I'll look for Jon. He may be there, he may not. I may cross into the bald spot, I may not. And if I do, I may not come back. Or I may.

I don't know what I'll do. I don't know anything anymore. I've come to the point now where I'm sure of only one thing: Nothing is sure anymore.

At least on this side of the veil.

Afterword

Donald A. Wollheim is to blame. He started me on Love-craft. It was 1959. I was just a kid, a mere thirteen years old when he slipped me my first fix. I was a good kid up till then, reading Ace Doubles and clean, wholesome science fiction stories by the likes of Heinlein, E. E. Smith, Poul Anderson, Fred Pohl, and the rest. But he brought me down with one anthology. He knew what he was doing. He called it *The Macabre Reader* and slapped this lurid neato cool Ed Emshwiller cover on it. I couldn't resist. I bought it. I read it. And that was it. The beginning of my end.

The Macabre Reader is an excellent collection—Bloch, Wandrei, Smith, Bishop, Howard. Good stories—dark, eerie, intense, the emotions jumping right off the page—like nothing I'd ever read before. But the one that

grabbed me by the throat was "The Thing on the Doorstep" by somebody named H. P. Lovecraft. I was dragged
into the story by the opening line ("It is true I have sent
six bullets through the head of my best friend, and yet I
hope to show by this statement that I am not his mur-
derer"), captivated by the setting (". . . witch-cursed, leg-
end-haunted Arkham, whose huddled, sagging gambrel
roofs and crumbling Georgian balustrades brood out the
centuries beside the darkly muttering Miskatonic"),
blown away by the dense prose that tossed off words like
eldritch and foetor and Cyclopean and nacreous, that
spoke of poets who die screaming in madhouses, that casually mentioned strange, forbidden books and towns like
Innsmouth (where even Arkhamites fear to go) as if I
should be familiar with them.

But it was the heart of the tale that lingered in my mind
long after I'd finished it—the concept of another reality
impinging on ours, knowledge of which could drive you
stark raving mad: a dimension of perverse logic and bizarre geometry, full of godlike creatures with unpronounceable names, aloof and yet decidedly inimical.

My thirteen-year-old world did not seem quite so safe
and sane, my reality seemed a tad less real.

"The Thing on the Doorstep" delivered on the up-close,
breath-clogging horror that *The Macabre Reader*'s cover
had promised, but it also served as my Cthulhu Mythos
primer, my introduction to what would come to be
known as Cosmic Horror.

After that first fix, I started mainlining Lovecraft. The
local pushers—excuse me, *book dealers*—introduced me
to Arkham House books and I nearly died of an overdose.
Eventually I went cold turkey and kicked the habit. (Well,
not completely. Occasionally I'll reread a favorite story. I
can handle it now. Really.) But the Cosmic Horror concept still fascinates me. I used it in *The Keep* and I've used
it here in "The Barrens." I'll no doubt use it again.

So here's my official tribute to H. P. Lovecraft. I pur-
posely avoided rereading any of his fiction before writing
"The Barrens." I wasn't out to do a slavish pastiche; I

wanted to capture the Lovecraft gestalt as I remembered it. The Jersey Pine Barrens, by the way, are real, a truly Lovecraftian setting; all the Piney history and lore in the story is true, every locale except Razorback Hill is real. The style is mine, but the Cosmic Horror is Lovecraft's.

I'm happy with "The Barrens," but it's nothing like "The Thing on the Doorstep." That's the real thing. Read it (or reread it) when you get a chance.